PRINCE OF SHADOWS

BOOK ONE OF THE BLESSED

M.A. GUGLIELMO

MERIT PTAH PRESS

Copyright 2025 by M.A. Guglielmo

Published by Merit Ptah Press West Warwick, RI USA

contactmaguglielmo@gmail.com

All rights reserved.

Proofreading by Andi Marlowe

Copyediting by Janet Jones Bann

Developmental Edits by Jeni Chapelle

Cover design by Glass Slipper Webdesigns

CONTENT WARNINGS

Prince of Shadows has strong language, violence, the death of animals, and explicit sex scenes.

For my daughters, Chiara and Sabrina

1

MERI

Meritamun—the Lioness of Abdju to her fans and many enemies, and simply Meri to her friends—had a parasitic necromancer in her spine and only weeks to live.

That didn't mean she would tolerate laziness and lolling about by her crew.

She had a reputation to maintain, even this close to the end.

"If the lot of you don't saddle your mounts and put your asses on top of them, I'm leaving you all here." Meri's horse Nada, a pretty Kushian mare bred for speed and the desert as much as her rider, gave a snort of approval as Meri continued her lecture to the three men sprawled out in the shadow of a Witch Stone. The ancient arch had been visible for the past few miles of their journey through the bucolic pastures and farmland of the Soissons countryside. At times the structure had a blue-green tinge that suggested a type of metal, and from other angles it appeared to be polished stone. It smelled wrong, as did everything that had to do with witches.

"We've been on the road for weeks, the capital's less than an hour's ride away, and I'd prefer not to lounge around near something constructed by demons." Meri wrinkled her nose at the arch, its scent reminding her of clinging fog and pine resin. She was in desperate need of a bath and a good tumble, and wouldn't have wanted to dawdle this close to their final destination even if the cursed thing wasn't there.

"It's only a weather Artifact." Gallmau flashed Meri his usual warm smile as he looked up from the letter. Despite having read it aloud to her a dozen times, he had pulled it out again, as if he could wring more information from the words inked on expensive parchment. "The Noviodunam witches use arches like this one to increase rainfall for crops, that sort of thing. There's an Artifact down the road that's supposed to be haunted, though, if you want to check it out."

The council of sorcerers in Soissons known as the Noviodunam might say they were Artifacts, but Meri knew them as Witch Stones and that's what she would call them.

She also knew Gallmau was stalling. He had his reasons, and she sympathized to a point. But this whole damn trip had been his idea, and they needed to get moving.

"We have to finish our game." Tharin, a Kushian like herself, narrowed his eyes at his cards and glanced over at his twin brother, Karabil, who was waiting for him to show his hand. He might as well be looking into a mirror. "I'm about to take all of Karabil's money."

"I recall something about the Three Prophets calling gambling a sin." Meri didn't have the same sympathy for the brothers' reluctance to get going. "Aren't the two of you in a hurry to cheat some gullible Soissons soldiers while ogling the local women?"

"We'll get around to it." Karabil laid his cards out on the ground to a groan of disappointment from Tharin. Karabil might be the quieter twin, but he was also the sneakiest.

"Fine." Meri turned her attention back to Gallmau, who had dropped his eyes down to the paper again and was avoiding her gaze. "I'll ride up to the next Witch Stone, and you'd best be ready when I return if you want me to meet this witch friend of yours."

"The *Sorcier du Roi* of the Kingdom of Soissons has sent a formal letter asking for my assistance." Gallmau waved the parchment at her. He showed far more respect to witches with fancy government positions than she did. "Try to be diplomatic when I introduce you to him. We help him, he helps us. Honestly, Meri, he's one of the Queen's top advisors, not a Bone Lord."

Meri knew the royal sorcerer she had reluctantly agreed to meet wasn't a necromancer. Still, the thought of asking any witch for help made her skin crawl. A necromancer—a Bone Lord, in the common parlance—had cursed Meri as he lay dying by her hands and now lurked inside her. Gallmau's sorcerer might be her last chance to exorcise the undead spirit who would be freed by her death, but that didn't mean she trusted the bastard.

Unlike Gallmau, she saw no reason to delay doing something that had to be done. "I don't care if your Sorcier du Roi *is* a Bone Lord, as long as I get to sleep in a real bed tonight, preferably with a man next to me who snores less than you do."

Gallmau grinned, probably about the man in her bed, whom he would most likely try to lure over to his sleeping pallet. She knew he wasn't amused about the Bone Lord part. Meri had made some unwise choices in lovers in the past, but she had never tumbled a necromancer.

"We're on the main highway to Lutecia." Gallmau waved at the road to the capital city of the kingdom, paved and in excellent condition. "It's patrolled by the Gardes Soissons, and getting into the city after dusk will mean I'll attract less attention."

Given that Gallmau had the face of an angel, the physique of a bear, and a head of red hair, he would attract attention in any town they visited. Since he was also the bastard son of the former King of Soissons, his presence in the capital would cause even more of a stir, no matter what time they arrived. Her friend might have an invitation to return from the Sorcier du Roi, but that was no guarantee his presence would be welcomed by the reigning Queen of Soissons and the only legitimate heir, his younger half-sister. He had more reason to be worried about his reception than she did.

So Meri checked her always too-sharp tongue. Gallmau had returned home to ask the Court's head witch to cure Meri's curse in exchange for helping him deal with whatever crisis had prompted the letter. The least she could do was allow her friend a little procrastination while she checked out the road ahead.

She swung up into Nada's saddle, gave the mare an encouraging pat, and set off. Rumors of ghosts and hauntings always drew her interest, as Gallmau knew only too well. She couldn't pass up any opportunity to learn more about the death magic that had cursed her, if there was even the smallest possibility she could rid herself of the undead enemy buried inside her.

The next Witch Stone was only a few minutes' ride away.

This one was in the shape of an oversized grave marker, and it gleamed white in the late-afternoon sun like the gigantic tooth of a long-dead monster.

The wind shifted, and with it came the scent of magic too new and foul to be from the ancient structure. Except for witches, few people could sense spellcraft like she could, much less by sniffing it out. The Gift of speed the Prophets had blessed her with didn't often come with this odd talent. It had saved her life many times before, and this was no exception.

She focused on her heart pulsing in her chest, on the interval between the beats, and the world slowed as she sped up. As the stench filled her nose, damp and rank, like the wet fur of a dog, she swung off Nada and jumped to the ground. The horse continued at a brisk pace, unable to process yet that her rider was no longer on her back. Meri blew into the warning whistle around her neck and unsheathed the dual curved swords that had been the best gift from a night of passion she had ever received.

Her horse at full gallop could outrace any Continental steed with ease, but with her Gift Meri could run faster than the animal for short distances. With Nada at a steady trot, she moved several paces in front of the horse and had her weapons ready as the monster jumped out.

The assault would have stunned her with its speed and fury if her nose had not given her enough warning to sink into her powers. Instead, she tracked the unnatural creature's flight through the air and moved into position with a blade in each hand. She braced herself to strike her opponent, a large dog with pale fur and eyes that glowed with an unnatural yellow light.

A Death Hound. Where was its master?

She opened up great slashes in the Hound's belly with a

series of strikes as the animal soared toward Nada, jaws open. Most of her fellow speed fighters would have stayed in the space between heartbeats, wanting to remain secure in their speed until the kill was confirmed.

Then again, many of her fellow speed competitors in the arena hadn't seen how easily one of their kind died when exhaustion kicked in.

Meri pulled herself out, and the world roared back into its regular timeline. Her horse neighed in panic, shying away from the spray of blood from the Death Hound's wounds and galloping off down the road. The monster lay on the paving stones, viscera sliding out of the cuts in its abdomen as its jaws continued to snap and snarl. She sucked in a sharp breath at the sight, then regained her focus.

Her blows should have killed it three times over, but a Death Hound had its own necromantic magic, and even her water-enchanted blades weren't enough to end the damn thing. She would have to take its head, like she would take its master's if she could. Touched animals like this were rare, and the beast must be under the control of a nearby Bone Lord.

Gritting her teeth, she circled the beast, waiting for a good opening to strike at its neck. Diving back into her speed would be the easiest method, but if there was a necromancer nearby, she didn't want to use up her limited endurance finishing off an animal that was no longer a threat. Her warning whistle should rouse Gallmau and the twins to come and cover her back—Meri didn't call for help often.

The white Death Hound's infuriated throes grew weaker, and Meri raised a single curved blade to decapitate the monster. The same fetid smell reached her nose, and she flattened herself to the ground.

She whispered a quick prayer of thanks to the Prophets. A second Death Hound had approached with unbelievable silence to take her off-guard, but her regular reflexes were quick enough that the creature soared over her. That gave her a precious blink in time to sink into her speed again.

It didn't work.

A spasm ripped through her upper back, worse than a knife, and Meri knew what being stabbed in the back felt like, since it had happened more than once. A gasp of agony escaped her lips.

It was the necromancer inside her, lashing out and crippling her with pain. Her curse had never struck during combat, but this was the end of the three years' grace she had been granted.

Meri forced herself to jerk her right hand up, her blade catching the leg of the second Death Hound as it pounced on her. This one had fur of midnight black, eyes like glowing coals, and breath that reeked of rotten meat. It fought furiously to get its jaws around her neck, but she slashed at its cheek and used her remaining strength to send the creature sprawling.

She rose to her feet, bent over in agony as the pain in her back refused to let up.

Leave me alone, you bastard.

The infuriatingly relentless Death Hound advanced toward her on three legs. The other creature she had failed to behead, its pale fur now pink with blood, staggered upright. Both monsters stalked her, one drooling saliva from the cut on its jowls, and the other trailing loops of intestines onto the road.

Fuck. What did it take to kill these things?

The crippling wrenching in her spine eased, and Meri fought to drop back into her speed. She could feel herself beginning to slip into the familiar reality that allowed her to move faster than human eyes could track.

One of the hounds lunged, and she fell backward, stunned, her sword tumbling out of her hand. For an agonizing second, she could do nothing but watch its jaws open over her throat, yellow teeth specked with chunks of flesh. Her speed finally flooded through her, and she reached up to claw at its eyes, twisting the head away from her. Pinned to the ground, though, her lightning reflexes couldn't help her much more. Her depleted strength wasn't enough to throw the creature off, and the second hound was advancing toward her, paws padding in slow motion across the stones.

Panic constricted her chest. Her friends wouldn't make it in time. The undead necromancer inside of her would be unleashed upon the world. All her Gift could offer now was the opportunity to watch her death unfold at a leisurely pace.

2

MERI

Meri's strength gave out first, then her speed, and time came rushing back. The words of the final prayer formed in her mind, and she waited for the searing pain of the monster's teeth as they sank into her flesh.

But she never felt the bite.

Instead, the white Death Hound flew off her, knocked fully across the road by a flash of metal and wood. Gallmau stood over her, holding the shield he had used to pummel the beast. His massive round piece of armor, emblazoned with the royal crest of Soissons, had its own smell of magic —damp moss and aged oak. Prophets bless him, he had come in time. She opened her mouth to scream instructions at him, but he had paid attention to her teachings over the past few years. He slung his shield on his back and unsheathed his sword. With a few long steps, he reached the limping dark Hound and took off its head in one blow.

Her cursed spine had relaxed, perhaps with the anticipation of her death, and she reached for her speed again, scooping up one of her fallen blades and darting across the road toward the white Hound. Its ribcage had been caved in by the force of Gallmau's blow, but the monster was still beginning to rise to its feet for another attack when she brought the edge of her blade against its neck as hard as she could, hacking until the furred head dropped to the ground.

Once again she stepped out of her speed, arms and legs shaking. She had more endurance than most people who shared her Gift—much as Gallmau was far quicker than the average strength fighter—but this battle had pushed her beyond her limits. Of course, had her curse not struck at the worst possible moment, she might have been able to end all of this without Gallmau's help.

"What the fuck were those things?" her red-haired friend asked before turning back to the road as hoofbeats pounded up toward them. Gallmau had ridden the short distance from their afternoon camp bareback, with only his short sword and shield. Not the wisest choice when entering into a dangerous and unknown situation, but he had saved her life, so she supposed she couldn't scold him about it.

The twins pulled their horses to a stop and dismounted with their black powder pistols drawn—useless against death magic, but unlike Gallmau, they ignored her lectures —and stared around them in a mix of confusion and awe.

"Death Hounds." Meri's breaths came in gasps, and Karabil rushed over to hand her a canteen of water. He was thoughtful enough to pull out some dried fruit to go with it. She always craved sweets when she pushed herself this far, although the rush of relief they gave her faded quickly. "Animals with death magic. Some Bone Lords keep them as pets."

"We're less than an hour away from the capital." Gallmau kicked at the remnants of the dark-furred Hound. "What necromancer would dare to send things like this out to kill travelers with the Noviodunam so close?"

Meri chewed away at her fruit leather and took another long gulp of water. The Noviodunam was to the Kingdom of Soissons what the University of Abdju was to her home country, the Sultanate of Kush. Both were centers of magical scholarship and learning known throughout the world, and both were crawling with every sort of sorcerer—except necromancers. Other witches hated Bone Lords as much as she did. This was an unusual attack, and the sensible thing was to make haste to the capital and let the sorcerer soldiers of the Noviodunam track down the Bone Lord responsible.

A woman screamed, followed by a loud crash of breaking wood.

Gallmau whirled toward the sound, and Meri jerked her attention to the Witch Stone, as if more monsters might jump out from behind it. To the left of the bone-pale structure were carriage-wheel tracks leading into the trees, a detail she had missed until now. Her friend took off in that direction, incapable as ever of ignoring a damsel in distress.

"Leave the horses. We'll go on foot." Meri added in a few curses under her breath as she ordered the twins to follow Gallmau. She wasn't about to ignore a cry for help, but she would have preferred her friend put practicality before gallantry and let her assess the situation with her speed before he charged in. Still, her Gift had its limits, and if the Death Hounds' master was in the grove, she and her companions were trained to work as a team to take down the Bone Lord responsible for the monstrous dogs.

The four of them followed the carriage tracks to the wooded area, and no further cries broke the grim silence around them. The sun had dipped lower in the sky, filtering light through the dying leaves, a riot of colors ranging from yellow to dark burgundy. As they drew closer, Meri could make out broken trees and upturned earth and a glint of metal amidst the tangled growth.

The four of them entered the copse of trees with their hands on their weapons. Gallmau took the lead, as he usually did. His size either frightened their opponents or encouraged them to direct their attacks against him. This allowed Meri to circle behind their enemies and strike while they were occupied with trying Gallmau's strength and endurance, not to mention the magically enhanced protection of his shield. The twins fanned out on either side, in their customary role of searching for ambushes or loot, depending on their mood.

The smell hit her as soon as they advanced a few paces into the wooded area, the same dank odor of magic the Hounds had carried with them. As they moved closer, she picked up another scent. Clean and bracing, it came with a sense of cold that gave her a brief shiver. It was at once both foreign and tantalizingly familiar, and it teased the edge of her memories, drawing her back into a recollection she couldn't quite place.

The tracks ended as they pushed through more broken foliage, and the fragmented scene in front of them resolved into horrible clarity. Metal glinted from the wheels of a large carriage, lying upside down in the midst of a slaughter. Dead horses lay on beds of crushed branches and brush, their throats ripped out, with splotches of congealed blood staining the fall leaves around them.

Meri counted five human bodies who joined the animals

in the tableau of violent death. She drew in a breath of horror at the sight, even as used to bloody carnage as she was. All were younger men, dressed in light armor with muskets and swords. A small guard party, perhaps. Wealthy travelers often hired escorts for long journeys, and the dead were dressed the part. The amount of damage done to them was extreme—two were decapitated, and the others had hacked-off limbs and wounds so grave it was as if killing them once hadn't been enough.

Wisps of shadow floated through the air, landing softly on the ground. Their gentle descent jogged Meri's memory. She knew what the clean smell that overwhelmed the stench of blood and torn viscera was, not that it made any sense.

It was the scent of snow about to fall. Cold, bracing, and deadly if you weren't prepared for it.

Meri shook herself out of her reverie and blinked. The drifting fragments of black had vanished, if they ever had been there at all. This might be her curse again, the evil inside her choosing to cloud her mind rather than cripple her body with pain.

Gallmau came to a stop, holding up a hand, and unsheathed his short sword. He used his two-hander when fighting off a group, and the smaller blade and his massive shield with single battles.

And there was only one living person in the clearing.

A man crouched near the overturned carriage, his hand clutching something on the ground. As they approached, he rose to his feet. It was a slow movement, perhaps intended to signal he had no intention of starting a fight.

He was tall, at least by her standards, although Gallmau towered over him, as he did most men. Shoulder-length black hair framed the stranger's pale face. Meri often teased

Gallmau about his fair skin and freckles, which turned boiling red in the hot sun, as opposed to her dark brown coloring, but this shade of white was unnatural. It was as if he lived in a cave and never saw sunlight. His eyes, though, were a brown so much darker than her own they seemed black, along with his eyebrows and striking, long lashes. He was a beautiful young man, clean-shaven and well-dressed. Even covered with dust and blood, his fine wool clothing and elegant leather boots spoke to considerable wealth.

"What happened here?" Gallmau asked. He used the Soissons dialect spoken in the kingdom's capital and taught in many places in the world, including the harem school Meri had attended when she joined the Sultana's household as a child.

"We were attacked." The man spoke to Gallmau, his own command of the Soissons tongue flawless to Meri's ears, but he fixed his gaze upon her, not on the hulking man with a sword and shield asking him a question.

Both that and his stance were odd. Gallmau's size and weaponry should have the survivor's undivided attention. Meri was the most dangerous of the group, but the handsome stranger couldn't know that. Even odder, he stood with his arms by his sides, palms facing her. It might have been to show he had no weapons—although Meri had already spotted the empty scabbard at his waist and the sword that lay at his feet—but it felt like a challenge.

"My guards fought bravely"—his voice hitched for a moment, a fleeting hint of emotion—"but they stood no chance against her."

"Her?" Gallmau relaxed his stance, which irritated Meri. Running off at the sound of a woman screaming had been foolhardy enough on his part. Granted, she and the twins had followed him, but this was no time to let down their guard. She had expected to run into a necromancer, and instead they had found an attractive man who shouldn't be alive and traces of magic she didn't understand.

The survivor didn't respond to Gallmau. Instead, he stared back at her, his dark eyes glinting in the shafts of sunlight streaking through the trees.

"You're the owner of the carriage, then?" Meri stalked closer to him, her pulse quickening. Gallmau and the twins remained behind to guard her back, and her curved blades remained sheathed at her waist. She rarely took them out before she dropped into her speed. The man's long coat and trousers, dark and severely cut, could be those of a merchant dressed for discretion rather than opulence. Not typical attire for a necromancer, certainly. Many of them barely wore clothes. "Is there anyone else who lived, someone who could tell us more?"

The man glanced down at the overturned carriage, and Meri noticed a hand and forearm protruding from under the smashed vehicle.

Gallmau spotted it as well.

"Who is that?" Gallmau rushed over, disregarding every bit of advice and admonishment Meri had provided him about dealing with monsters, human or not.

The man's gaze flickered to Gallmau's face for the first time. "My mother."

Meri bit back a groan. Much as she loved Gallmau, he was terribly flawed as her partner in the business of monster hunting. He couldn't lie to save his life, bargained like a drunk sailor in a brothel after a year at sea, and insisted on risking his money, energy, and even his safety rescuing anything or anyone he thought might need his protection.

"I need a fighter, not a knight from the old tales," Meri

had told him the first three times she had turned down his offer to join her small group of monster killers for hire. She had given in because he was impossible to say no to and because he was quite useful when he did fight. But there was no charitable act, no matter how mundane or ill-advised, he could resist.

And Gallmau, having lost his own at a young age, held mothers in very high regard indeed. Even if they were buried under a carriage and most certainly dead.

"We'll get her out." Gallmau dropped his shield—losing the protection the object gave him—and sheathing his sword, bent down toward the thin arm limp on the ground. "Get ready, Meri."

The last thing she wanted to do was dive into her speed again so soon, and for a fruitless purpose that would only use up her strength for combat. But there was no stopping Gallmau when he got like this.

"No." The man's tone grew sharper, although he was still scarcely animated. Meri couldn't tell if he was so over-whelmed by the death around him he had shut away his emotions, or if he was trying to cover up his involvement in this mess. "You can't lift it, in any event."

The dark-haired stranger was in for a surprise. Gallmau's strength was as unearthly powerful as Meri's speed was. She found the space between her heartbeats, and the world slowed again. Gallmau reached down to grasp the carriage and forced the entire thing up into the air. Meri ran toward him, timing her movements so she arrived just as enough of the framework of the vehicle had elevated for her to get under it.

An elderly woman, so thin she appeared half-starved, lay underneath. Beside her, another body lay motionless.

Two corpses, and Meri wouldn't have time to pull them

both out. She scooped the old woman into her arms, pausing for the barest fraction of time as she realized the second body had disappeared. Only a patch of darkness on the dirt remained, more like a shadow than something real.

Damn her curse and the mind tricks it played to the hottest level of Hell.

She dashed out, laying the old woman gently on the ground as Gallmau released his hold and the remains of the carriage began a slow fall to the ground.

She broke out of her speed as the crash of wood and metal filled the air around them. She focused on the handsome stranger first, making sure he hadn't taken advantage of Gallmau's damned heroics to attack them. He had stepped back, with his head cocked to one side as if that might help him figure out what the hell they were doing.

Meri sympathized. She had no idea why they had risked themselves to drag a corpse out into the open when whatever killer had loosed the Death Hounds could attack them at any moment.

The dead woman in front of Meri drew in a deep breath and rose to her knees, her hands clasped in prayer. "Blessed be the Lady of Shadows, who has delivered us from death only so we can enjoy her cold embrace on another day."

3

MERI

Meri stood for a few seconds with her mouth open. The stranger's mother staggered upright, and Meri recovered enough to reach out to steady her. The old woman's headscarf had been torn from her head, revealing a bald scalp. Her skin, dry and creased with wrinkles, clung so tightly to her face she resembled a bony skull covered in paper.

The eyes regarding Meri, however, were dark and very much alive.

She reached out and squeezed both of Meri's cheeks, hard. "Such a beauty is my deliverer! What's your name, child?"

"Meri, honored aunt." The words of courtesy in Kushian spilled out of her mouth before she could help herself from speaking in her native tongue.

"Ah, you are from Kush, yes?" The elderly woman

switched easily to Meri's language. "A follower of the Three Prophets, then. Blessed be their names and deeds."

She tottered away from Meri, pulling her veil back over her head, and made a beeline for Gallmau, enveloping him into a hug before her friend could react. "My other rescuer, so handsome and tall! What do they call you, sweet boy?"

"Gallmau, madame." He tried to give the old woman a formal bow, but given she was squeezing his arms and remarking how muscular he was, he settled for a bob of his head. "We feared the worst when we saw you under the wreckage. Perhaps you should rest and have your son help you."

Gallmau gave the man in question a beseeching glance as he tried to extricate himself from the woman's grip, which only caused her to cling tighter and plant several kisses on his hands.

The woman's son had not moved from his position to rush to his mother's side, and his impassive expression held no sign of shock at her miraculous recovery. He raised one eyebrow in her direction and continued his silent observation of all of them.

Once again, Meri tried to judge whether his lack of reaction stemmed from the slaughter around them, or was something more ominous.

"The rest of our company are Tharin and Karabil, also from Kush." Gallmau managed to wave at the twins, interrupting their assiduous search of the bodies for money or other valuables. They both straightened, tucked a few choice finds into their pockets, and gave the woman deep and respectful bows. "What may we call you and your son?"

"Saints forgive me, I've not even told you who we are!" The woman raised her hands in supplication to the heavens, and Gallmau wiggled free of her embrace. "I am Naghwe—

Mother Naghwe, they call me—you need not bother with fancy titles for a humble old woman such as myself. This is my son Sinan—he's so handsome, isn't he? We're from Iotape, in the east. His merchant travels take him west frequently, of course, but I came with him this time. My hope was to pray at the shrine of the Lady of Shadows in Lutecia, but oh, such a calamity has befallen us!"

She gestured at the death around them with more enthusiasm than seemed appropriate for the circumstances.

Gallmau, who had flushed pink when Naghwe had talked about how good-looking her son was, tried to take her arm and push her gently in Sinan's direction. "It's not a sight fit for a lady, I'm afraid."

"Fit or not, it's what we found." Meri had recovered from her surprise that Naghwe was alive and decided the talkative old woman might as well chat about something useful. "Who attacked you, and why? Your son told us it was a woman."

"A she-devil from the bowels of Hell itself." Naghwe snarled out the words with particular venom. "She had two great beasts at her side, with glowing eyes and slavering jaws. Only the divine intercession of the Lady herself saved us."

Meri had gathered by now that Naghwe was a follower of Gallmau's religion, the Church of Saints, and this Lady of Shadows was a revered figure in her faith. "Why would a necromancer with two Death Hounds come after a trader and a pilgrim?" She couldn't make the pieces of this fit together, and her sense of unease was growing. "The Hounds came after me when I rode along the road, and Gallmau and I had a hell of a time putting them down. Yet they somehow left your son alive, and now this Bone Lord you speak of is nowhere to be found."

"An impressive feat, killing both of those beasts." Sinan reacted, finally, to her last statement. "I believe the woman who directed them was from the Order of Katil."

Meri licked her lips, her mouth suddenly dry. The Order was more of a bogeyman than a reality to the common people, but the fear with which the elites viewed them was something she had seen with her own eyes. Even her Sultana's royal vizier had spoken of them in hushed tones.

"You can identify a necromantic assassin on sight, yet you have no guesses why you were targeted?" Meri took a few steps closer to Sinan, her tone turning sharp. "They go after kings, viziers, maybe even the high and mighty witches of the Noviodunam. Not merchants. And it's expensive to purchase their services."

"Perhaps your group of Tomb Fighters were her true targets." Sinan held his ground. Perhaps he had simply guessed their profession, or maybe he had recognized her and the others from the fanciful stories that ran in the Continental papers.

Either way, the term irked Meri, although she had used it herself in casual conversation when she had been the highest-ranked speed fighter on the Continent. Her fellow elite fighters of the arena circuit, handsomely paid to put on choreographed battles for the enjoyment of large and well-paying audiences, tended to look down upon the messy business of killing monsters for money. Meri didn't care. Riches had been thrown at her before, and she had left those offers behind to fight creatures that attacked innocents with dark magic—be they beasts or men.

"You're quite familiar with Bone Lords and those who hunt them, for a trader." Meri placed a hand on her hip, her tone challenging but not overtly hostile. She wanted him to talk more, so she could judge if he was lying to them.

"Merchants need to be able to assess risk and weigh it against the chance of benefit." Sinan surveyed the bodies around him, and his mouth tightened. "My mother and I are in your debt for our rescue, and I didn't intend to offend you. I need to attend to funeral arrangements for those I hired for my protection and escort my mother to Lutecia before nightfall. Allow me to compensate you for your service. I have a fair sum of gold on hand. Please take it and go with our thanks."

"We couldn't possibly accept your money." Only Gallmau could deliver such an outlandish statement with such conviction.

Both of the twins tried to smother laughs with little success. Meri, who knew her friend well enough to understand he meant every word he said, didn't argue.

Something wasn't right about the handsome merchant and his pious mother. Maybe it was nothing more than a valid fear that a group of unsavory Tomb Fighters would choose to leave two more dead bodies in the woods and take off with whatever they could carry.

Maybe it was something else.

"Absolutely." Meri could hear the twins' snickers fade into sullen silence. "Take what coin and goods you can carry from the carriage and travel with us to Lutecia. We'll see you safely to the capital and report this disturbing incident to the authorities."

Gallmau gave her a grateful but surprised smile, while Sinan did little more than nod. Meri didn't need to turn around to guess at the twins' reaction to her refusing an offer of easy money.

The merchant's mother, on the other hand, was thrilled.

"The Saints bless you all." Naghwe spread her bony arms wide and beamed in Meri's direction. She had good teeth for an old woman, white and solid, with canines a little sharper than they should be. "I'll light candles for you all at the shrine of the Lady of Shadows and leave an offering at the House of the Three Prophets as well."

Sinan circled behind the carriage and bent over to retrieve something from the wreckage of the vehicle. Naghwe, for her part, took it upon herself to shower the twins with embraces and reverent declarations, all of which interrupted their attempts to pick up more valuables from the dead.

Gallmau came over to Meri and leaned in close. "You don't look happy."

"This all stinks of death magic." Meri shook her head, angry at herself for not being on top of this situation. "None of this makes any sense, unless Sinan is the necromancer."

"He can't be a Bone Lord." Gallmau eyed Sinan as the man pulled a traveling sack and a strongbox from the pile of shattered wood and glass. "Necromancers are all twisted and formed the wrong way from their curse, and he's—got quite a nice shape to him, don't you think?"

Gallmau and his dark-eyed boys. Meri shook her head. "He's gorgeous, and his mother's quoting of your scripture is hardly what I'd expect from necromancers. But why would an assassin from the Order of Katil with two Death Hounds be out here on the road to Lutecia, if Sinan is who he says he is? The Order doesn't send anyone out without a good amount of coin changing hands."

He grimaced. "I don't know, but it's another reason I need to talk to the Sorcier du Roi as soon as we arrive."

She had to concede that the royal sorcerer of Soissons, with the entire Noviodunam behind him, would know more about dealing with necromantic assassin guilds than she did. "Fine. I'll walk with Sinan and try to get more out of him. You should chat up the old lady. She seemed to like running her hands over your body."

Gallmau laughed. "Maybe that's why she was traveling to the shrine of the Lady of Shadows in the capital. It's an odd choice for a religious woman, that's for sure."

Meri had only a passing knowledge of Gallmau's religion, and knew a little about the Sacred Seven and not much more. "Is the Lady of Shadows a folk saint, then?"

"She's the patron of prostitutes and the, uh— female climax." Gallmau, despite his solid performance in convincing most handsome men who caught his eye to join him in bed, could be charmingly uncomfortable talking about the act itself. "Her shrine is in the worst part of Lutecia, and the city's bishop tried to have it burned down several years ago. Then he keeled over from apoplexy and died two weeks later. No one in the Church has had the balls to say a bad word about the Lady of Shadows since then."

"If it takes Mother Naghwe feeling you up to get to the bottom of this, then let her do it." Meri crouched down to pick up Sinan's sword from the ground and examined it closely. It was plain and utilitarian, but the balance was fantastic, and she recognized the wavy pattern on the blade. Only one place in the world made steel like this, and weapons from there cost a small fortune. An odd choice for a merchant who could pay others to do his fighting for him. However, a trader was more likely to have access to formal sword-fighting training than a Bone Lord. It proved nothing, other than Sinan had excellent taste in weapons.

Gallmau stole another look at Sinan and sighed. Meri couldn't blame him. Her friend had excellent taste in beautiful men.

"You're getting the best part of this deal, Meri." Gallmau whispered before straightening as Sinan came over to them carrying the lockbox and wearing the travel satchel on his back.

His mother scurried to his side and clutched his arm in her skeletal fingers. "You should offer our rescuers a toast, my dear. It's the least we can do."

Sinan gave her a brief nod. Placing the small chest on the ground, he used a key to unlock it and retrieved a ceramic jug from inside. He left the lid open, revealing bulging coin sacks and glittering jewelry.

Meri caught the glint of avarice in Tharin's eyes and was about to make a comment for him to keep his hands to himself, but Gallmau had already bent down to secure the lid and tuck the box under one muscular arm before Karabil had taken more than a few discreet steps in its direction.

"You must accept a small gift from us for all you've done." Sinan removed the wax seal from the spout, and an acrid smell of alcohol mixed with the scent of ripe pears wafted out, blending in with the odor of blood and death in the grove. "This is a bottle of eau de vie known as the Deathless Spirit. I brought it along for a wealthy client, but I'd like you to have it."

Gallmau nodded along with Sinan's description—of course he knew about some extravagant brandy worth a fortune—and he reached out to take a swig before Meri could protest.

"It's the real thing." He passed along the bottle to an eager Tharin and Karabil, who each gulped some of the liquor. "Not easy to get a hold of. You could get an invitation to Court with this bottle alone."

Sinan inclined his head toward Gallmau and gave him a hint of a smile. "I suppose you would know."

Gallmau's face turned pink again. So much for being a

secret royal, who had been—not banished, exactly—but strongly encouraged to leave the Court of Soissons.

Sinan retrieved the bottle from the twins and held it out to Meri. Her expression alone would have told him she wasn't going to take a drink, but Naghwe clucked her tongue in disapproval, and he pulled it away.

"For shame, offering strong spirits to a devout follower of the Prophets." Mother Naghwe wagged her finger at her son. "I can tell Meri avoids those vices forbidden by her faith."

"Some of them, at least." Meri gave Sinan her best flirtatious smile, and his eyes widened in a brief flicker of interest before he lowered his gaze. There was more than one way to get information out of a man, and Meri intended to use all of her skills to find out if Sinan knew more about the Death Hounds and the assassin who let them loose.

She gestured toward the path they had followed into the grove and gave the twins a quick hand signal to drop back and take the rear position as they departed. "We have three horses waiting near the Witch Stone. Your mother can ride on Gallmau's, and Karabil and Tharin will keep watch at the back on their mounts as we make our way to the city."

"There's a guard station only a half hour's walk from here." Gallmau tucked Mother Naghwe's arm into his own, to her evident delight, as they left the stench and sights of violent death behind them. "You'll be safe and can rest easy soon, madame."

Meri breathed in normal scents as they left the scene of the massacre, fresh smells of pine needles and earth. She allowed Gallmau to get a few paces in front of them and turned Sinan's sword over in her hand, wondering if returning it might be the best strategy to allay the merchant's suspicion of their motives. "This is a quality weapon. The workmanship marks it as being from the City of Jasmine, if I'm not mistaken."

"It was indeed forged there." Sinan's eyes watched her handle his blade, but he didn't hold out his hand for the weapon. "A gift from a generous host. I fear its craftsmanship is wasted on a merchant like myself."

Sinan did like to emphasize his supposed occupation. It certainly couldn't be much further from a death witch. There should be some ways to test that story in casual conversation.

Meri took out a small cloth from her pockets and cleaned off the stains on the blade. Then she made her decision and handed the weapon to Sinan. "There's someone else's blood on your sword, and you're still standing. I'd call that a fair showing in a fight."

"I would thank the Saints first and my limited talents second." Sinan accepted the sword and placed it back in its scabbard with a hint of awkwardness.

Standing this close, she was able to get a better look at him. In addition to his striking good looks, he was well-proportioned and walked with a lithe, easy gait. A travel pack made from a pale, silky material was slung over his shoulder, and he had taken the time to retrieve a peaked cap to cover the loose black locks of his hair.

Nothing about his appearance suggested a typical Bone Lord. All of the ones Meri had seen had been hairless, with a skeletal frame and bearing some disfiguring or bizarre mark—a curse earned from the death magic they used.

There could be much hidden by his clothing, of course.

Meri had to remind herself not to dwell on what Sinan might look like naked. At this rate, she was getting as bad as Gallmau.

"You said you were attacked by a necromancer from the

Order of Katil." Meri began the conversation with the one bit of useful information Sinan had provided. "Have you had much experience with magical assassins?"

That phrasing might have been too confrontational, too soon, but Sinan replied in calm, easy tones. "Blessed be Saint Kreztina, I'd not encountered one in the flesh before."

The devotional phrases common to followers of the Church of the Seven Saints rolled easily off Sinan's tongue. Most of those who belonged to Gallmau's religion held to the belief that Bone Lords could not speak the names of the Sacred Seven. Some who followed Meri's faith preached that reading out loud from the words of the Prophets would drive necromancers away. As for Meri, she preferred to back up her prayers with her blades.

"I've talked with several people who've witnessed their killings and read about their organization." Sinan walked beside her and matched her pace, neither rushed nor deliberately slowed. "Her face and arms had sigils carved into her flesh, and although the descriptions I heard did not do them justice, the Death Hounds by her side left little doubt who she was."

They started on the dirt path that led to the grand highway, as the sun dropped lower in the sky. The temperature was still comfortable, even for the desert-born Meri, and there was plenty of light left. Still, the talk of the Hounds and their near-fatal attack gave her a chill. They could not get to the horses and be on their way to Lutecia fast enough.

"Your mother mentioned you were from Iotape." Meri had fought at the arena there once and liked the eastern port town also known as the Free City. Even with its new veneer of respectable mercantile activity, the heart of Iotape was still the pirate enclave that had resisted efforts by various empires to crush or absorb it for centuries. But

Iotape was not far from Karakoncolos—the city of monsters, as the necromancer city-state was known—and she had heard Bone Lords walked the streets of Iotape openly after their success in the Witches' War. "But this is hardly a common route for a merchant from the Free City."

"Yes, goods traded between Iotape and the Kingdom of Soissons came in mostly by sea before the Witches' War. Now, of course, there's hardly much trade at all." Sinan sounded far less concerned by this than she would have expected from a man who made his money from the exchange of goods. "I brought along a few specialized items for old customers along the way, but the main purpose of this trip was for my mother to perform a pilgrimage at the shrine of the Lady of Shadows."

Meri thought about bringing up the oddity of a pious woman from a wealthy mercantile family worshipping at the altars of the patron saint of whores but held herself in check. She knew even less about Continental religions than she did commerce, and it was a sin to criticize the piety of others.

Especially when she was a sinner herself.

"Speaking of specialized goods, I have an interesting item I won in a bet." Meri reached into an inner pocket for a small leather bag. This gambit was a long shot, but something wasn't quite right with the handsome trader, and she wanted to try one more time to trip him up. "I've always wanted to ask someone knowledgeable about magical goods about it."

"I don't trade in those sort of wares." Sinan's voice grew a touch colder.

Out of suspicion she suspected he dabbled in necromancy, or did he consider the items beneath him? The merchant families of Iotape were wealthier than many of the Continent's aristocracy and could afford to be picky. It was impossible for her to get a good read on Sinan, and Meri didn't usually have a problem figuring out men.

"It's—not a business I care to engage in."

"That's unusual for a merchant." Meri was growing frustrated, and her next comment had more bite than she intended. "Traders aren't known for their moral scruples when it comes to business."

Sinan stiffened, a flicker of anger crossing his face for the first time. Then he relaxed and continued matching her pace along the packed earth path. The wide expanse of the main road to the capital city of Lutecia stretched out in front of them, and Karabil and Tharin sped up, moving past them toward the horses loosely tethered to pines near the white expanse of the Witch Stone.

"How did you come across this item, if I may ask?" Sinan's voice was cool and detached, holding nothing but polite interest.

"I did well in a game of cards with a ship captain once." Meri had also done quite well with that particular captain in bed, but this wasn't the time to share that story. "Cleaned him out, in fact. He put this on the table to try one last time to get his money back. He lost." She stopped and held out the pouch to him. "Supposedly it's a type of mineral that drains all of the magic out of Bone Lords. Do you think it's valuable?"

Sinan came to a halt as well and swung around to face her. Their gazes met, and for a moment, she expected him to confront her. Instead, he took the pouch in one hand, careful to not so much as brush against her skin, opened it, and poured the contents into his other palm. Blue crystals spilled out, and he picked one up with his slender, tapered fingers. "Amor Vitriol."

"Yes, that was the name." Meri tried to keep her tone light, as if she wasn't hanging on every word.

"These are obvious fakes." Sinan dropped the crystals into the pouch and handed it back to her, his lips pressed into a thin line. He knew she had been testing him. "Amor Vitriol is unstable in either fire or water. It must be kept in an arid environment but not exposed to as much as a spark. I'm told some of the Artifex guilds can create glass spheres to transport and store it."

Meri had talked to far too many local fortune tellers and renegade clergy over the past three years about protections against death magic, hoping to find some way to rid herself of her curse. Sinan had told her more about Amor Vitriol than she had learned in all that time.

"You know a good deal about goods you don't trade in." Meri took back the pouch of useless stones and put it in her pocket.

"What I do know"—Sinan picked up his pace as they drew closer to the main road—"is that most of the magical relics on the market are body parts of supposed necromancers."

Gallmau and Mother Naghwe were now several feet ahead, moving toward the Witch Stone and Meri's two countrymen, who were likely trying to stash the best of what they had looted from the bodies in their saddlebags.

"As long as they're dead, I don't care if Bone Lords get cut up and sold to the highest bidder." Meri had left the bodies of witches she had killed, necromancers or not, to lie where they had fallen. She didn't take trophies from the dead; it was one of her religion's proscriptions that she did obey. If other people wanted to, though, she wouldn't stop them.

"Children, mostly." Sinan's voice was cool and distant. "Often infants killed at birth. That's where most of the relics come from. Perhaps a few had some affinity for necromantic magic, but most were simply unfortunate enough to have a mark or deformity. In many cases, I've heard, it was the mothers doing the selling."

He stopped again and turned to her, his black eyes glittering dangerously. Ribbons of shadow began to swirl around him, and she breathed in the cold, bracing scent of his magic. "I don't suppose that bothers the Lioness of Abdju, of course. Tomb Fighters aren't known for moral scruples where *their* business is concerned."

4

MERI

Sinan was a Bone Lord, after all.

The necromancer had known exactly who Meri was and had strolled beside her without any visible concern, chatting casually with her until the last minute. That sort of calm confidence frightened her more than any snarling threat could ever do.

She kept her hands on her blades, watching as dark ribbons of cursed enchantment swirled around the handsome Bone Lord—a shield of some sort. She wanted him to make the first move before she sank back into her speed yet again, but Sinan didn't follow up on his verbal challenge with an attack.

Then another smell hit her, damp and sour.

She slowed the world around her, but she had been focusing on the wrong threat. Panic flooded through her as she spun around, the scent of danger directing her away from Sinan and toward her companions. One of the Kushian geldings had its throat cut, blood beginning to spray out from the wound.

A woman stood next to the horse, a short blade in her hands. She had it buried in Tharin's chest before Meri could even take off running. Her mind stuttered in shock, unable to process what had just happened to her fellow fighter.

Unlike Sinan, Tharin's killer made no effort to hide what she was. Her bald head and lower arms were covered in knotted sigil scars glowing a dull red in the dying light of the day. She wore utilitarian clothing, with loose trousers tucked into boots and a leather tunic. No armor and only a few knives at her belt to go with her main weapon.

Meri wasn't the only speed fighter here. The assassin from the Order of Katil was one as well.

She had fought her own kind before, both in ceremonial bouts and for real stakes, and she had fought Bone Lords before. But how could she kill someone who was both of those things?

Her body outraced her fear-muddled mind, and she was at Gallmau's side as the assassin finished off Karabil and turned her attention to the young royal. His eyes had begun to register fear and alarm, but he was only starting to lift his shield as she approached.

Meri switched from her two slashing curved swords to one, gripping the dagger at her waist as she threw herself in the woman's path. No, not Gallmau, not if Meri had a breath left in her body. The woman pulled up short as Meri charged, as if surprised to be facing a foe so similar to herself.

The assassin mumbled a few strange words, and Meri's feet gave out from beneath her. The woman strode toward

Gallmau with an unhurried pace in the sped-up reality she shared with Meri, her sword leveled at his neck.

Frantic, Meri kicked out with her legs. Nothing tangible bound them, only an insubstantial arc of shadow that slanted across her lower body. She reached for her other sword and swung both blades down on either side of her. The water magic of her swords worked again, in a way she didn't understand. The sorcerer who had crafted her favorite weapons had used his innate affinity to manipulate water and combined it with his knowledge of centuries of magical study to enhance the blades' power against death witches and their magic.

What had been only an absence of light became a tangible thing that could be cut, and her bonds fell away. Black shreds of whatever cursed force the woman had used against her fluttered up into the air like drifting ash, and Meri was free.

She jumped to her feet, her focus narrowing to only one goal—saving her friend's life. Gallmau's fingers gripped his shield, but the agonizing slowness of his movement meant the assassin would cut his throat before he could swing it into a position to defend himself.

Meri caught up and dealt two slashing blows to the woman's back before the assassin reached Gallmau. The blades deflected off a barrier around the woman, sending wisps of black into the air.

Switching tactics, Meri lashed out with her foot at the back of the assassin's knee, sending her sprawling.

It was not a good time to come out of her speed, but the woman did so anyway as she rose to her feet, and Meri followed suit, mindful of how limited her stamina was after the number of times she had used her Gift today.

The world caught up with them. The dead horses fell to

the ground along with the bodies of Karabil and Tharin, landing in a spreading pool of blood. Argant whinnied in alarm and bolted, and Gallmau swung his shield into the woman's face. Now the prince was in the fight as well, giving Meri a glimmer of hope. The assassin from the Order of Katil could mold shadow into armor, even change it into rope-like bindings, but both her reserves of magical power and speed were limited.

Back on the ground again after the blow from the shield, the assassin glared at them, her eyes wide with surprise and her mouth twisted into a snarl. Those eyes—they were far more disturbing than even the scars carved into her flesh, each as white as milk, with an oval slash of red in the center, like a bloody teardrop in place of a pupil.

Gallmau and Meri adopted defensive stances, with their usual positions reversed: Meri in front, facing the woman who had killed two of her closest friends, and Gallmau behind her.

Sinan walked past the Witch Stone to stand across from the assassin from the Order of Katil, and the woman whirled to face him. He stepped into a professional sword-fighting stance, and the scent of a deadly winter hung in the air.

Meri's instincts had been right, only she had failed to account for two necromancers, not one. That mistake had cost Tharin and Karabil their lives and might doom her and Gallmau as well.

Mother Naghwe popped out of thin air next, standing equidistant from the assassin. Was the old woman also a witch? This journey to Lutecia had turned into a nightmare.

For a long pause, none of them moved.

Meri forced herself to assess the situation strategically. Both Bone Lords couldn't be fighting together—she and

Gallmau would be long dead. Maybe they had blundered into a grudge match between the two, and Meri's original guess that the target had been Sinan was correct.

The assassin broke the silence first. "Do you keep company with Tomb Fighters these days, Sinan? They were kind to free me from your stunt with the carriage. Strong and not very bright. Perhaps that's where your tastes in flesh lie."

Meri thought back to the second body under the carriage she had seen—and then hadn't. Perhaps the woman could shadow-walk—slip from one location into the dark and then step out somewhere else. Meri had only seen it once—and had promptly beat a hasty retreat. She and Gallmau were in trouble, and they needed to exploit the divisions between these witches to get out of this alive.

"Who sent you, Cliona?" Sinan kept his guard up, and his attention focused on the assassin. The two death witches were on a first name basis. "The last I heard, the Order was not interested in making war against Karakoncolos."

Sinan must be from the necromancer city near Iotape. Cliona and the Order of Katil were not, and any enmity between two groups of necromancers could only work in her and Gallmau's favor.

"The only law of the Order is that a contract is a contract." Cliona gave him a wide smile, her teeth smeared with blood. Gallmau's hit had been hard enough do some-thing to the woman, despite the magical protections surrounding her. "You're every bit as pretty as they say. I'm going to enjoy digging those beautiful eyes of yours out of their sockets after I kill you."

Sinan didn't rise to the bait, but Mother Naghwe clucked her tongue in disapproval. "Such talk from one of our own.

Mark my words, Cliona, the Order will regret this day, no matter what the outcome."

Cliona ignored the old woman and whipped her head back to Meri and Gallmau. "Take some advice from a fellow paid killer—leave. This fight is between the two of us. Your handsome new friend has more murdered ghosts following him than even I have—including many of your precious Noviodunam sorcerers."

Something was off.

For a fearsome assassin from the Order of Katil, this woman was awfully chatty. She had struck hard and fast, going after everyone but Sinan. Now she was stalling, and there had to be a reason. This type of talk before fighting didn't serve any purpose, unless Cliona didn't think she could take on all three of them.

"She murdered Karabil and Tharin." Gallmau dropped his voice to an angry whisper, grief and anger choking the words out of him. "We can't walk away from this."

Meri raised her hand in a silent gesture for Gallmau to keep quiet. Part of her burned for vengeance, but she knew how to lock that rage away and focus on getting herself and Gallmau out of this situation. There would be time to think about payback later.

She spoke up. "The only good witch is a dead one. I don't care if you all kill each other off. The three of you will burn in Hell, and I hope it's sooner rather than later."

Cliona's mouth curved into a sneer, but her body posture relaxed a fraction. She had been worried they would jump in to help Sinan.

Good.

Meri had another plan, but it was a risky one. She focused on taking in as much detail about the two Bone Lords as she could.

Sinan had talked about the assassin having sigils carved into her flesh, and that hadn't been a lie. Information about magic was hard to come by, and much of what Meri had been told over the years had proven to be useless superstition or outright falsehoods.

Still, she had learned a sigil, whether it was a raised scar or fancy gold embroidery, could be a focus of a particular type of magic. None of the Bone Lords she had dispatched had possessed even one of the symbols, but Cliona's skin had at least five of the marks. Terrifying, but as she scanned the woman's body, she saw only two still burned dull red. Not only had the assassin depleted the energy that would allow her to sink into her speed, some of her death magic had weakened as well. She and Gallmau could do this. They could take her down.

"Without light, there is no shadow." Sinan gave as much reverence to the words as he had when invoking the saints of Gallmau's religion. He wore a hooded cape now. Calling it a cloak would have been generous—it was nothing more than a crude white cloth hanging from his shoulders, identical to a burial shroud. Meri counted no less than ten sigils, glowing a deep purple, on the fabric.

Holy shit, what had she gotten herself into?

"Without shadow, there is no light." Cliona responded as if by rote and then attacked.

It took every iota of discipline for Meri not to sink into her speed. She had done too much, in too short of time, and she had limited reserves left. If she had read the situation wrong and Cliona chose to attack her and Gallmau first, they would die.

Meri focused on her heartbeats, getting a sense of how long Cliona stayed in an accelerated state.

It wasn't long. From Meri's normal perspective of time,

the assassin vanished from her current position as a curtain of darkness fell over Sinan's form. Cliona reappeared, gasping and on her knees, near one of the dead horses.

Sinan sank into a classic attack form with his sword raised. There wasn't a mark on him. His stance struck Meri as odd at first, since his opponent was far out of his reach. Then a line of shadow extended out from his blade, slicing through the body of the horse and cleaving it in two.

Meri flinched, and behind her Gallmau gasped.

Well, that was another Bone Lord trick neither of them had seen before.

The blow missed Cliona, who dove into her speed again, and she reappeared next to Sinan. Her next attack was at normal speed, and Meri had an opportunity to see how much Sinan had lied about his sword-fighting skills.

He was well-trained by any standards, but his form was even more surprising considering he was a necromancer. Few of the ones Meri had encountered could put up any sort of physical resistance once their magic had been depleted. That was her main strategy—wear their powers down, then get in close and kill them. That wouldn't be easy to do with Sinan. She pushed that fear from her mind and tried to focus on one opponent at a time.

Cliona was a strong and savage fighter, with less finesse than Sinan, but possessing a brutal efficiency to her movements. Neither necromancer was playing around with their shadow powers, and Meri thought she knew why. The two opponents were all but on top of each other, striking and parrying with neither one getting in a definitive blow. They both must be inside whatever protection their magical armor gave them, and that meant Meri needed to get close to do damage.

Sinan landed a hit on Cliona's leg, opening up a wide

slice, and the assassin dropped to one knee, a grunt of pain slipping from her lips. He pulled back to reset for another blow, but Cliona took advantage of the momentary opening to strike.

The necromancer staggered back, the hilt of a knife protruding from his ribs. One of the purple sigils on his cloak flickered and dimmed.

Both Bone Lords were injured, and this was their chance. Meri focused all of her fury into striking back. Hard.

"Now," Meri told Gallmau and fell into her speed.

She closed the distance between herself and Cliona, and struck low at the woman's injured leg. The shadow protection the woman gathered around her acted as a shield for her upper body only, and Meri was able to land a solid cut with her curved blade.

Cliona sank again into her speed and was up and clashing against Meri's second strike in time to block it. Against a fellow speed fighter, Meri focused on using one of her curved swords while fending off the assassin's blows with a knife in her other hand. Their flurry of hits and misses on each other would have been a blur of motion to an observer, ending when Cliona again dropped out of her speed first, allowing Meri to smash the assassin in the face with the hilt of her sword.

Cliona was on her back, blood streaming from her nose as she spat out a curse.

Meri gripped her sword and moved in for the kill, but Gallmau's shout of warning gave her time to dodge a sword thrust to her head. It did not, however, help her avoid the smash of a fist to her abdomen. Her belly blossomed with pain, and she sank to her knees.

Karabil stood above her, his throat gashed and his eyes open and staring. His sword was raised over her, jerking down and back up again as if he was a puppet having his strings pulled by two different masters. She choked back a rush of nausea.

Sinan and Cliona. They were using their necromancy to battle through Karabil's corpse. Both Bone Lords were on their feet, hands at their sides with their palms facing outward.

It wasn't—possible.

Meri's mind flashed back to her first encounter with Sinan and how this same odd posture had struck her as threatening. Cliona stood on her injured leg, which she shouldn't be able to do, and no blood welled from her wounds. Sinan had pulled the knife in his abdomen out, and the son of a bitch didn't even look winded.

The horror of watching Karabil's lifeless body being used to attack her rooted Meri to the spot. She only shook off her paralysis after another shout from Gallmau. Her friend stood, his shield spattered with blood and gore, over a mess of blood and broken bone that was all that remained of Tharin.

Sheer, unadulterated rage filled Meri. People died in battle, yes, but this desecration of two young men who had come out of the poorest slums in her home city and become her trusted comrades was too much. She summoned up the last of her strength and lunged forward.

Focused on her magical battle with Sinan, Cliona wasn't expecting to be tackled around the knees. Instead of her curved swords, now lying on the ground, Meri had one of the several stilettos she kept on her at all times. She drove it up and into Cliona's chest, slipping it past the ribs on the left. The assassin's body convulsed underneath her.

It was a good strike, right into the woman's heart.

Cliona's body didn't go limp, however. It continued to

jerk, even as the red of her pupils widened to spreading pools of scarlet and her lips turned a grayish blue. A twisting mass of shadow formed over the assassin's chest, stretching and pulling into a shape reminiscent of the open jaws of a dog.

"Take her head." Sinan's voice floated over her, but Meri had already scrambled backward to find her blades.

The necromancer stood back and watched her. Karabil was at his side, his body now rigid but upright, with the sword still in his hand. She was sure Sinan didn't think she could use her Gift of speed again, or that she and Gallmau could overcome both his death magic and the undead Karabil. This was the time to finish both of them.

She limped back to Cliona's body, glancing up to see Gallmau standing by Mother Naghwe, his sword out. Meri had no idea who or what the woman was—necromancers were sterile, so she doubted the old woman could be yet another Bone Lord if she had given birth to Sinan.

Still, Meri didn't want to discount any further possible threat.

Kneeling on the assassin from the Order of Katil, Meri used one of the curved blades to carve through Cliona's neck. It was far from a clean job, and she was both exhausted and repulsed by the task. Under her, the writhing shadows on the woman's chest snarled and growled, and she knew all too well what it was—Cliona's cursed soul, trying to free itself from dead flesh and enter one of the living.

Too bad for Cliona Meri already had one unwelcome Bone Lord guest in her body.

She could feel her curse twist and squirm in her spine, uneasy with the nearness of another one of his kind. At least there was no crippling pain. Maybe the dead necromancer inside her didn't want any company.

Cliona's head finally rolled free, and the snarls from the shadow dog died away, but Meri didn't stop to savor the moment. She reached one more time for her speed, knowing the effort would cost her, and sprang up. She hit Sinan low and hard, as she had hit Cliona, and the maneuver worked.

Karabil started to crumple, the weapon in his hand dropping toward the earth. It felt like she had killed him herself, a second time.

Meri slipped back into normal time, straddling Sinan with both of her swords pressed against the sides of his neck. Drops of water glittered on the blades, their polished surfaces wavy and rippled like a disturbed pond. The magic in her weapons was responding to Sinan's power, and it wanted her to end his life like she had ended Cliona's.

"Gallmau, watch the old woman." Meri's back was to her friend, so she reminded him not to let his fanciful ideas of chivalry outweigh his common sense. "Listen to me, death witch. I've cleansed this earth of one Bone Lord, and I'm happy to make it two in a day. Tell me what happened here and why."

5
_____

MERI

S inan gazed into Meri's eyes, his face once again not betraying any hint of emotion. She had her knees on both of his arms and her full weight on his torso. He could throw her body weight off him—she wasn't Gallmau, after all—but she could end him with a quick press of her blades.

"I was attacked by Cliona of the White Isles." Sinan answered in calm, neutral tones, as if they were again discussing trading opportunities in Soissons. "She was an assassin from the Order of Katil. I haven't lied to you, Meri."

She didn't like hearing him say her name. It was too personal, too intimate, as if he wanted her to see him as a fellow human being, not a terrifying Bone Lord. Her fingers tightened, and the moisture on her blades turned pink as she drew blood from Sinan's pale skin. "You sure as hell didn't tell us the truth. Why did Cliona want to kill you, and why are you traveling to Lutecia? Are you planning an attack?"

Gallmau made a noise behind her, perhaps at the mention of danger to the court. The royal family of Soissons had always been a fervent supporter of the Noviodunam and their campaign against necromancers, although less vociferously now that the King was dead and his Qingian wife had her hands full running a kingdom foreign to her.

Meri mistrusted the aristocracy in general and the royal family of Soissons specifically for their treatment of Gallmau. Still, her friend would die to protect the queen and his half-sister, the princess. That meant Meri would battle at his side, no matter what she thought of pompous witches and spoiled aristocrats.

Sinan remained stone still. "I'm here as a representative from the Councils of the Living and the Dead to represent the interests of Karakoncolos."

Meri had to laugh, even as she became more determined to get the truth out of Sinan if she had to chop off pieces of him until she got it. "You're a monster—a Bone Lord—from an entire city of monsters, and you're telling me you're visiting as a diplomatic envoy to the royal court of Soissons."

"Yes," Sinan replied. "I'd assumed you and the prince of Soissons were here for the same reason I am. Or has no one told you yet?"

"Told me what?" Meri snarled out the words, her frustration mounting. "If I don't get a straight answer out of you, I'm going to tell Gallmau to snap your mother's neck like a rotten branch."

Gallmau let out a strangled sound. He could at least pretend he might hurt the old woman, although Meri knew he would have trouble doing it even if Naghwe was pointing a crossbow at his face.

A body thumped to the ground behind her. She twisted, fear rising in her gut as she tried to keep her hold on Sinan and see what had happened.

Gallmau lay on his side, his eyes half-open as he struggled to push himself up before collapsing. There was no sign of bleeding or injury, but something had to be very wrong.

Naghwe stood next to him, smiling, her incisors gleaming in the fading light.

"What did you do to him?" Meri couldn't keep the fear out of her voice. "Tell me or I'll kill your son."

"I poisoned him, my dear." Naghwe extended her arms, as if she wanted to draw Meri into an embrace. "With the brandy Sinan offered all of you, but you refused. Eau de vie, they call it here. Or in this case, eau de mort. The last part doesn't have to be true, though." She showed Meri a vial pinched between her bony fingers, a metal and glass cylinder smaller than Meri's little finger. "Poison in one half, the antidote in the other. It's the only thing that can save him now. I'll offer you a trade—my son's life for Gallmau's."

Naghwe was lying, she had to be. Meri gritted her teeth. She couldn't trust a death witch.

If she lifted her blades off Sinan's neck she was as good as dead, and her friend would die anyway.

Gallmau let out another gasp, and his face darkened. He gave one spasmodic jerk, then another, his eyes now open and wild with fear.

"Deal." Meri rushed out the word, unable to watch more of Gallmau's torment. If there was even a chance to save him, she couldn't live with herself if she didn't try. "Give me the vial, then I'll release Sinan."

Meri let one of her swords drop to the ground and held out a hand, keeping the other blade pressed to Sinan's neck.

Her position was awkward, her body half-twisted to keep an eye on Naghwe and Gallmau. If the old woman was desperate to save her son, maybe she would come close enough for Meri to get the vial and kill Sinan before he could react. She had to have some reserve of speed left in her, even if only for a fleeting moment.

Naghwe tossed the vial at Meri.

It was a wild throw, nowhere near Meri's outstretched arm, and without thinking Meri fell into the last of her speed and flung herself out as the metal and glass cylinder tumbled slowly in the air down to the paving stones of the highway.

She landed hard on the ground, pulled out of her speed by utter exhaustion, the promised antidote gripped tightly in her hand. Blood dripped between her clenched fingers before the pain in them registered. In her reddened palm rested a vial with a row of tiny spikes on the metal cap on one side accompanied by a skull in bas relief. The cap on the other end featured a branching tree.

Death versus Life. Chaos versus Order.

There was a divider between the two sides, and a yellow liquid filled the end near the tree. Only a drop of a brown substance remained under the skull emblem.

"The poison is on the spikes." Mother Naghwe's voice took on the tone of a teacher lecturing her students. "It works much faster in the blood than in drink, of course. Anyway, you're such a little thing, compared to your big strong man here. It will take you fast, child."

A cold ache crept up Meri's arm, and her tongue felt heavy and strange in her mouth. With her other hand, she flailed for her blades, only to see Sinan on his feet, holding both of her swords as he scrutinized the lapis lazuli set into the hilts. Her heart pounded inside her chest, panic and terror driving out any coherent thoughts.

"Now we come to the interesting part." Naghwe came closer, and Meri struggled to turn her attention back to Sinan's mother. The witch's dark eyes were bright with anticipation. "The other half does hold the antidote. I'm afraid there's only enough for one of you, though."

Fury burned inside, giving her strength to move. No, she refused to die this way, tricked and poisoned by a mad old witch and her Bone Lord son, as gorgeous as he was danger-ous. She crawled forward toward Naghwe on her hands and knees, holding the vial in her bloodied grip.

"Still a fighter, I see." Naghwe retreated behind Gallmau as Meri continued her slow advance.

Sinan strolled over toward his mother, his shroud-like cloak glowing with purple markings.

"You have a choice, my dear," Naghwe continued, crouching behind Gallmau.

So close, that awful poisoner was so close. Meri only had to go a little farther to get to her.

"On the one hand, there is the mind, which will tell you to use your remaining strength to drink the antidote. You'll be too weak after that to bother us, and I promise we'll let you live. It's the sensible, practical thing to do. Look out for yourself first."

The cold in Meri's arm spread throughout her body, and her mouth tasted like hot metal. It didn't matter. She had to do this, had to use whatever remained of her strength to save him. The distance between her and Naghwe stretched out, with Gallmau's spasming body a mountain in her path. At least the curse in her spine had stopped. For the first time in ages she felt no pain there at all.

"On the other, there's the heart." Naghwe sounded

downright cheerful. Beside her, Sinan stood with his sword at his waist and his hands out facing her. Shadows wove around him, like lithe dancers dressed in black, vying for his attention. "It tells you not to let this virile young man, so full of vibrant life, grow cold and still in the clutches of death. What is he to you, dear? A lover, passionate and demanding? Or maybe he's more like a younger brother, sweet yet frustrating. Which will it be, Meritamun of Abdju? You must choose—your heart or your mind."

Meri had made it to Gallmau, and Naghwe was behind him, her face lit up with anticipation. If only Meri could get close enough to smash her fist into the old witch's face—but she was too far away.

Meri reached her arm behind her, her fingers scratching at her left boot until the throwing knife hidden there slipped into her hand. She flung the blade toward Naghwe, her aim true despite the poison wracking her limbs. She watched as the knife struck the woman's throat—and then passed through her as if the death witch had been made of smoke.

Naghwe laughed and reformed, and the truth hit Meri.

Sinan's mother was a dead necromancer, like the one who currently lurked in Meri's spine. She couldn't be killed —she was already dead. Shocked, Meri froze, uncertain if she could even keep going. Then she turned back to her friend and knew what her choice would be.

Tears coated Gallmau's lashes as he opened his mouth to try and talk.

"Take it for yourself." He coughed the words out. "Please, Meri."

Meri glared at Naghwe and spat out the worst obscenities in Kushian her mind could come up with. She fumbled with her stiff fingers to open the vial, unsealing the portion with the yellow liquid under the sign of the tree. She raised the tiny container up and grabbed at Gallmau's face to open his mouth. His body was wracked by another violent spasm, and the antidote spilled uselessly down the side of his face, running off like a stream of tears.

Meri collapsed on top of Gallmau.

As Meri's vision blurred, Naghwe gave a deep sigh. "The world is a hard and cruel place. Even more so for those who listen to their hearts."

6
———

GALLMAU

Gallmau supposed he should recite prayers of thanks to Saint Attilio that he wasn't dead, rather than taking the Saint's name in vain every time he moved his head, but the after-effects of Mother Naghwe's spiked brandy were on par with the worst hangover he had ever had.

For Meri, the poison in the vial's spikes had hit much harder.

His hand brushed against her forehead as she shivered and cried out. The head wrap she usually wore had come loose, tight black curls spilling out.

He remembered when they had first met. Meri had shaved her head down to her scalp and wore gold earrings, looking like a Kushian goddess of old, fierce and uncompromising. Saints, she had seemed so tall and intimidating then.

Now she was like a sleeping child in his arms, crying out in a nightmare she couldn't wake from. He shifted his position on the hard wooden planks of the wagon the Gardes Soissons had commandeered from the passing wine distributor who had discovered Meri and Gallmau in the wreckage left after the battle between Sinan and Cliona. The merchant had sent a rider ahead to alert the soldiers, and Gallmau reminded himself to make sure the man received compensation for his good deed.

A few expensive electromantic lanterns had been hung on the sides to provide light as they waited for sunrise, and the wine barrels had been rolled off to accommodate those who couldn't make it back to the city on horseback. He and Meri fell into that category, along with the three bodies that lay still and cold on the bed of the wagon.

"Wake up." He lifted a piece of cloth soaked in the honey solution Meri drank after her forays into speed and pressed it to her lips. This time she swallowed a little. "Please."

"I won't go to Paradise." She twisted in his grip, eyes still squeezed shut, her words slurred. "The Bone Lords will keep me as an undead slave. The Prophets won't save me."

"Shush." Gallmau desperately wanted Meri to become more alert and have something to eat. Speed fighters, despite their invariably thin physiques, needed even more food than strength fighters such as himself. Without nourishment after forays into their Gift, they could slip into insensibility and die. Meri had done far more with her speed than Gallmau had ever seen. "It's all right. I'm here."

A creak and thump on the wooden boards announced the return of Tumas. His former commanding officer during his stint in the army was now a captain in the Gardes Soissons, and the sight of his familiar face leaning over Gallmau's poison-wracked body had been the one bright spot in the longest night of Gallmau's life.

"How is she, Your Highness?" Captain Tumas was a few years older than he was, broad of shoulders and with the stance and bearing of a man born to wear a military uniform. "We're close to moving out."

Gallmau sighed. He hadn't hoped to return to Lutecia without the Court knowing, of course, but arriving with the Gardes Soissons after a dramatic Bone Lord attack near the capital was hardly the discreet entrance he had planned. Being referred to by a royal title he didn't have any legitimate claim to made it worse. "You shouldn't call me that."

"If it's Monsieur le Roi you prefer, I'm happy to use it." Tumas gave him a bright smile as he uttered words of sheer treason.

The captain was a good man, and a better friend, but Gallmau had left the country in part to avoid the constant speculation that as the dead King's only son—illegitimate or not—he could take the throne away from the foreign-born queen and her daughter.

Well, that and the Sorcier du Roi telling him to get out of town.

"You know you shouldn't be saying that." Gallmau returned his attention to Meri, who was stirring in his arms. He pressed the wet cloth to her lips again. "Any sign of the two necromancers?"

"I think they left a while ago." Tumas jerked his head in the direction of the grove where Meri and Gallmau had first encountered Sinan. "We didn't find any of the bodies you mentioned, but there's a path of broken brush and trees leading out onto the fields. Maybe they dragged them away?"

Gallmau thought back to the horror of facing his friends

Karabil and Tharin as undead puppets controlled by a Bone Lord. It still made him want to vomit. "They made them walk out."

Tumas held up seven fingers—the Sign of the Saints—and bowed his head. "These are dark times, my friend."

They would be less dark if Gallmau had Meri by his side again. She knew more about fighting death magic than any of the arrogant sorcerers at the Noviodunam. He shifted her gently into more of an upright position.

She moaned faintly, and her eyelids fluttered.

"I wish she would wake up." Gallmau murmured the words, mostly to himself, but Tumas heard them.

"You were quite weak when we found you, and now you're back to your usual complaining self." Tumas came closer and leaned over Meri. "If the death witches used the same poison on her as you, it would take longer for someone her size to recover. Besides, from what I've heard of the Lioness of Abdju, she'll be up and fighting soon enough."

"I hope you're right." Gallmau stretched out his legs. He felt sore and stiff, his head throbbed, and he had nowhere near his usual strength. Sinan and his poisoner of a mother could rot in Hell as far as he was concerned. Of course, since they were both Bone Lords, they were damned no matter what. "Has the runner returned?"

"He'll be back soon enough. He's the fastest messenger in the Gardes." Tumas straightened. "The Secrétaire will know about it now, and we'll have both an Army surgeon and a Noviodunam *medicus* waiting for us when we arrive."

"I don't want to make a spectacle of myself." Gallmau was used to blundering into court etiquette disasters, but this Bone Lord catastrophe was on a whole new level of awful.

"Maybe it's best if the common people know you're back." Tumas laid his hand on Gallmau's arm. "If anything happens to you in the palace, get word out to me. There are many in the Gardes and the streets who will rally to you."

Gallmau had hoped the treasonous rubbish he had overheard in the towns they stayed in during their journey wasn't widespread in the capital as well, but apparently even soldiers in the army agreed with some of it. "The Queen is the closest thing I have to a mother. I won't hear any talk against her. You've been spending too much time drinking with those university radicals who want to overthrow the monarchy."

"You've been spending too little time learning about the politics of Soissons." Tumas shook his head, then turned to respond to a call from outside the wagon. He gave Gallmau's arm a squeeze and jumped off to talk to one of his men.

Gallmau clapped himself on the head in frustration, and the jolt finally woke Meri.

She tried to pull away from him, her eyes now open and wild.

"Everything's fine." Gallmau held her in one arm while fumbling for the bottle of fortified water. "We're alive, and we're safe. Drink this."

She drained the contents, then took in a breath. "What happened?"

"That antidote vial was Mother Naghwe's idea of a hilarious prank." Gallmau helped Meri into a sitting position against the side of the wagon, regretting the loss of her warm skin against his. He didn't bed women—at least not often—but holding someone close he cared about had felt powerful and comforting after the awful events of the night. "I was able to see and hear what was going on after she poisoned us, but I couldn't get my arms and legs to move for hours."

"Maybe they thought we were dead." Meri took the bag of army rations Gallmau handed to her and began devouring the contents with wild abandon. She didn't even stop to ask if the food met her religious standards.

"No, they knew we were alive." Gallmau hesitated, overcome by the guilt and shame of how badly he had failed to protect his companions. All of his strength and training had done nothing to save Karabil and Tharin, and he had been helpless while Meri tried to fight both Sinan and Naghwe. "I kept trying to get my body going again, and you slid off me. My arm was over your face and then..." He had to stop for a moment, his voice choking with the memory. "I was crushing you, stopping your breathing. Saints, it was horrible. I managed to make some kind of noise, and Sinan came over and moved you so you could breathe. Then the cheeky son of a bitch told me to stop wiggling around so much."

"Why would he do that?" Meri stuffed another piece of bread in her mouth.

Her hands were shaking as she reached out and tried to lift the bottle of water to her lips. Gallmau had to help hold it up before the bottle dropped from her weakened fingers. She was as powerless as he had been hours ago, but if he had recovered, she should too.

"Sinan knew who I was, and he knew you were King Syagrius's son." Meri sounded incredulous, like she was outraged Sinan and his mother had spared their lives. "He was arguing with me about Tomb Fighters killing baby necromancers for relics right before Cliona attacked."

"A Bone Lord lecturing us about morality." Gallmau rolled his eyes. "He and his mother were doing the same things to the bodies while we were lying there."

Meri stopped trying to drink, her lower lip trembling, as Gallmau cursed himself for letting that slip. She struggled to her feet, pushing off his attempts to stop her. He gave up and held her by the waist.

"When I saw Karabil and Tharin, I wasn't sure what to think, and Tumas didn't know either." Gallmau prayed he had done the right thing. Meri didn't need more trauma tonight.

"What did that bastard do to them?" Meri couldn't walk yet, but that didn't stop her from trying to fling herself across the bed of the wagon.

Gallmau tucked her under one arm and held up a lantern to illuminate the bodies.

Karabil and Tharin lay on their backs, arms crossed on their chests and tied with strips of cloth. As battered and bloodied as their bodies were—Gallmau felt sick as he recalled bashing Tharin's undead form over and over again with his shield—they had both been posed in a manner which suggested solemnity and peace. Three coins had been laid on their faces. Silver on one eye, and gold on the other. A copper marker had been placed on their lips.

"I wasn't sure if this was some sort of death magic or not." Gallmau wished the religious tutors who had tried to beat every story about the Saints into his skull had told him anything useful about other religions. Meri at least knew the basics of his faith. He knew next to nothing about hers. "We lifted the bodies onto the wagon and left them as they were. Tumas has sent for a Religious from the House of the Prophets in Lutecia."

"A copper coin for the third Prophet, so the deceased may tell the Divine of his good deeds during life." Meri's voice was hoarse with grief, but it grew stronger as she continued. "A silver one for the second Prophet, so the deceased may see back to the sins he has committed and repent. Lastly, a gold coin for the first Prophet, so the deceased may see Paradise itself."

"This is how your people bury their dead?" Gallmau had suspected that, but why two Bone Lords would spend all that time and effort preparing corpses for a religious burial was beyond him. All faiths preached that Bone Lords had powers from Hell itself. At least he thought they did.

"How were they positioned?" Meri's weight sagged against him, and Gallmau put down the lantern to help her sit next to the bodies. "When you found them, did their heads face South?"

"Yes." Gallmau, who had spent every summer of his childhood on the fishing boat his mother's family depended on for their livelihood, had a flawless sense of direction on land or sea. "Also, Sinan and Naghwe talked in a language I've never heard most of the time. But at one point I heard them chanting in Kushian. I couldn't make out most of it, but you've taught me the word for Paradise, and they used it."

"I don't understand how they knew to prepare the bodies." Meri didn't protest when Gallmau pulled her close and gave her a hug. Her eyes were wet, but no tears ran down her cheeks. "Or why Sinan and Naghwe could chant the Prayer for the Dead. They're not supposed to be able to say holy names or enter sacred places."

"Well, Bone Lords do worship death, after all." Gallmau felt all of this conversation about religion had gone way beyond his rather vague conviction that saying prayers to Saint Attilio, his patron saint, was the right thing to do, but making an offering or two to the Sea Spirits off the coast wouldn't hurt, either. "Stands to reason they'd know all about funerals."

"This is Cliona." Meri turned her attention to the third body. The assassin had been wrapped in the same shroud-like material Sinan had used as a cape, and her severed head had been carefully bound to her chest with cloth strips. Both of her eyes had been removed, and black thread used to sew the eyelids shut. "She threatened to dig Sinan's eyes out of their sockets, and I guess he did the same to her when he won."

Gallmau shivered. He didn't like monsters, the human or the animal kind.

Maybe it was that fear which had driven him to join Meri and her two countrymen from Kush after his experiences in the Witches' War. The four of them had taken out some dangerous creatures, but the death magic they had seen today dwarfed anything they had encountered before.

The floorboards creaked again as Tumas came back onto the bed of the wagon. His face broke into a grin when he saw Meri awake. "Good to see the two of you ready to fight." The captain bowed, scooped up Meri's hand, and gave it a kiss. "Mademoiselle, Tumas de Concarneau, Officieur de Fortune in the Gardes Soissons, at your service."

Something approaching a smile crossed Meri's lips. "Good evening to you, monsieur. Don't pledge your service to me so easily; I just might accept that offer."

"Stop flirting and tell me if the runner's back." Gallmau was glad for the distraction Tumas had provided, but he was anxious to learn how the news of his return had been received.

"The runner notified the Secrétaire that the King's son was back with the most beautiful arena fighter in the world and the two of them had a tussle with a few Bone Lords. That got the old man's attention."

Gallmau could only hope the runner hadn't used those

exact words to describe him to the officer in charge of security for the entire royal household. "Well, I suppose it would be hard to keep this quiet."

He thought of the Queen receiving the news and winced. Best if he found Zhang Jue, the Sorcier du Roi, and told him everything before facing her. After all, it was before dawn, and the news shouldn't have spread too far. He still had a chance of making it back into the palace his way, rather than causing a scene that might upset the Queen even more than his return.

"Will the Gardes Soissons be waiting for us when we arrive in the capital?" Gallmau hoped it would be a small contingent, no more than a dozen or so.

Tumas's smile broadened. "Not only us, Your Highness. There was already a mob on the streets waiting for your arrival as the runner rode back. By the time we arrive, half the city will be there."

7

GALLMAU

Gallmau mumbled obscenities under his breath as they entered Lutecia over the main bridge connecting to the island that held the city proper. The massive stone thoroughfare, constructed of connected short arches and wide enough to accommodate both multiple carriages and pedestrian walkways on either side, had been completed early in King Syagrius's reign, long before Gallmau's birth. On a typical day, it provided a dramatic view of the river running through Lutecia, with multistory government buildings lining the shores and the great dome in the center of the Noviodunam gleaming in the distance. Also typical would be the brisk traffic of horse-drawn carts and vendors on foot selling everything from firewood to coffee.

But there was nothing typical about today.

Tumas had been right—half the population had come

out to gawk at the procession. Throngs of people clogged the bridge, preventing any forward motion and forcing the Gardes Soissons to shout and push the packed bodies out of their way.

He slumped against the side of the wagon, wishing as he often did that he wasn't as difficult to hide as a large red bear.

This was a disaster. Not only had he returned to Lutecia against the Queen's wishes and without any warning, he had arrived with a cohort of soldiers who kept expressing more loyalty to him than the crown. Worse yet, most of the city was watching him do it. He'd be lucky if Xiaolian didn't have him thrown in the dungeons.

"What are you doing?" Meri had regained some of her strength and all of her bad temper as they traveled toward the capital. She had been only a little mollified to learn Sinan had left her curved swords and Gallmau's treasured shield by their unconscious bodies. At least the news that both her beloved Nada and Gallmau's steed Argant survived the slaughter had cheered her up. "Get up and wave at them, you dumb ox."

"You're always grumpy when we've been beaten like a rug." Gallmau did his best to glare at her, but Meri could all but castrate a man with her eyes. He dropped his gaze back to the floor of the wagon.

"I don't lose often, but when it happens I don't mope. I get back into the fight." Meri bit off another chunk of the cheese her now numerous admirers in the Gardes Soissons had given her, along with a few offers of marriage. She had alternated between eating and describing increasingly violent scenarios of revenge against Sinan during the whole trip. "Stand up beside me. I'll get their attention for you."

Meri, unlike Gallmau, was both accustomed to and

happy with being the center of attention. She continued, jabbing a finger in his direction. "Rumors will be flying around, including that you're injured or dead. Maybe someone will ask who would want to send an assassin from the Order of Katil after you. Perhaps the royal family will come up. This could get ugly fast."

"Then I should keep my head down." Gallmau didn't want to snap at her like that, so soon after he'd been afraid she wouldn't wake up, but Meri didn't understand the politics of the royal household.

Neither did he, but that wasn't the point.

"You're returning to Lutecia as a hero." Meri was impossible to argue with under normal circumstances, much less now that she was this riled up. "A healthy hero entering the palace with plenty of supporters in the streets who want to see him stay that way. I don't care to mysteriously succumb to my injuries after meeting the Queen. Do you?"

Gallmau started to say there was no possibility of that happening, but the warnings the Sorcier du Roi, Zhang Jue, had given him before he had left Lutecia were an unpleasant voice in his head, reminding him that the threat of losing of the crown had provoked worse actions. With a sigh, he rose to his feet, then helped her stand up beside him.

There was a sudden silence in the crowd pushing and shoving to get a better look. Then the cheering started.

The roar was so loud and overwhelming Gallmau might have shrunk back into the limited privacy of the wagon walls, if Meri hadn't grabbed his arm and lifted it into the air. Unlike other speed fighters Gallmau had met, Meri spent hours training to increase both her skills and stamina, and she used what strength she had left to shove his hand to the sky in triumph as she shouted, "Long live the prince!"

The mob screamed that phrase back, and then it was nothing short of bedlam, with people trying to climb onto the wagon to get close to him. Tumas and his troops were forced to beat back members of the crowd, but a few made it past them, including a number of women throwing both kisses and articles of intimate clothing in his direction.

Gallmau kept telling himself it would all be over soon— one way or the other—but the ride to the palace stretched out as their procession advanced at a snail's pace. The inhabitants of Lutecia, from pickpockets to the grand dames who ruled the upper ranks of polite society, were usually united in an air of jaded indifference toward events that riled the rest of the country.

He had never seen the city so frantic and frenzied.

They pulled through the outer gates of the palace complex, with the Maison Militaire du Roi—the royal palace guards—slamming the gates behind them. Gallmau jumped off the wagon to help Meri down, just as the Secrétaire and his private bodyguards came toward them.

The Secrétaire was long past his prime, having been from a noble family close to Gallmau's grandfather. His family's stature, which far outstripped its wealth, had led to him being left in the role of supervising the royal household when King Syagrius the 13th, Gallmau's father, had ascended to the throne. Everyone thought the old son of a bitch would die off and be replaced by someone more politically palatable to the new regime. The years trudged on, and so had the Secrétaire. King Syagrius was dead, his controversial Qing wife was queen, and his bastard son had just arrived with a mob of supporters at his back, but here the old man stood, bent over and wearing both the robes of his office and his usual dour expression.

The Secrétaire bowed toward Gallmau, or at least

bobbed forward a little more than his usual hunch. "Welcome, Monsieur de Rohan."

Gallmau had been neither recognized as a legitimate son nor denounced by the Church as an illegitimate child of indiscretion and thus had existed in a confused state of being too royal to enjoy a normal life and not royal enough to warrant much of a title. In the Court, there had been talk of making him some sort of duke and marrying him off to the daughter of a family deficient in either courtly influence, money, or both. No consensus on a suitable candidate had ever been reached. As Gallmau had little interest in a wife, the lack of agreement about his marital prospects had been a relief.

"Good morning, Monsieur le Secrétaire." Gallmau was sure the old man had a real name but had frankly never bothered to learn it, having hoped the old coot would die by now. "Allow me to introduce my companion, Meritamun of Abdju."

"Mademoiselle Meritamun." The Secrétaire clicked his heels together and bowed deeply in Meri's direction, coming dangerously close to toppling over. "It is my honor to make the lady's acquaintance."

"We had a bit of trouble on the road." Gallmau did his best to sound dismissive about his close brush with death. The details of their harrowing escape were best left to a discreet conversation with Zhang Jue. "Of a magical sort. I was hoping to have a word with the Sorcier du Roi about it."

"The honorable Zhang Jue is, unfortunately, otherwise occupied." The Secrétaire pursed his lips. "And Madame is expecting you."

"Oh." Gallmau shifted his feet. In upper society, everyone was a monsieur or madame of something. When the term was used alone it referred to only one person—the

Queen of Soissons. "I'm honored Madame wishes me to attend upon her. However, given the circumstances of my arrival, I should seek the counsel of Magus Zhang Jue first, so that my report to Madame might be more—complete."

"She is expecting you *now*." The Secrétaire's tone grew icy, and his wrinkled face turned more sour. His guards, younger by decades than the Secrétaire and still decrepit, did their best to glower at Gallmau.

By Saint Attilio, Gallmau could have toppled over the lot of them with a good shout, but power in the Maison du Roi had little to do with physical strength and everything to do with tradition.

"I'll present myself to Madame immediately, then." Gallmau bowed to the Secrétaire and his guards and offered his arm to a perplexed Meri. The two of them walked away toward the garden maze, as Gallmau kept his pace as slow and stately as he could manage.

"So, we're going to see the Queen?" Meri asked. "Or was that a load of horseshit for the old fool's entertainment?"

"I have to talk to Zhang Jue first." Gallmau dropped his voice to a whisper, even though he doubted the Secrétaire and his doddering company could hear them if he was shouting. "He sent me that letter asking me to come back. I'd much rather face Queen Xiaolian with him beside me."

"Aren't we walking toward her right now?" Meri glanced back at the Secrétaire and his guards. "They're not following."

"That's because they don't know about the window." Gallmau, having grown up at the palace, was intimately familiar with its grounds, especially the maze. An over-the-top botanical monstrosity of tall hedges, fountains with water spilling from the mouths of fanciful beasts, and gates leading to nowhere, the garden had been both a fascinating place to play when he was a child and a convenient location to have a tryst or two when he was older. "At the far end, there's an exit to the Queen's zoological garden with two of her personal guards stationed there. That's where the Secrétaire thinks I'm headed."

Meri glanced at the imposing walls of green around them. "I'm not sure if pretending to get lost in here will save from us from an expected appointment with Queen Xiaolian."

"It might provide a cover story when we show up late—with Zhang Jue." Gallmau weaved his way through the paths of the maze at a rapid pace.

While Meri kept up, she was breathing heavily. That damn poison had drained her. She should be resting, but Gallmau wanted more than the Sorcier du Roi's support when he faced the queen. Zhang Jue had to help them put an end to Meri's curse. Time was running out, and he'd have to deal with the consequences of his actions later.

A few minutes of twists and turns later, he led Meri into a cul-de-sac of greenery. It was one of the many dead ends in the maze, most of which held a whimsical statue or a mirrored orb as consolation. This one contained only a design marked out on the ground in different colored gravel —an open hand on the right, and two fingers spread into a V-shape on the left—the Sign of the Saints. Gallmau walked over to one of the four foliage walls and brushed aside branches to reveal a locked gate about half his height. He lifted up a large rock next to the gate and was happy to spot the keys resting exactly where the gardening staff always put them. After unlocking the gate, he ducked under the low opening and walked through, motioning Meri to join him.

Inside was a small clearing dominated by a multi-tiered fountain spraying water into the air. Great detail had been given to its central statue, an ominous hooded figure brandishing a book as one might hold a weapon. Arrayed around the base like an attacking force were beasts that represented the first four saints—a lion for Saint Elesbaan, a stag for Saint Attilio, a falcon for Saint Kreztina, and an owl for Saint Thaschus, patron saint of witches.

The Fountain of the Malandanti—whose official title included a fancy word for Bone Lords—was better known as the Fountain of Letha. The last necromancer to sit on the Noviodunam Synod, Letha had been burnt alive by her fellow witches and her seat in their meeting room destroyed. She was said to have cursed quite a few things on her way out, including the fountain.

That reputation kept most people out of this section of the maze, which was why Gallmau liked it.

He pointed to some thinning plants up against the walls of the palace. "There's a pantry off the kitchen in this spot, with a window that's easy to open from the outside."

Meri laughed for the first time since their run-in with the necromancers. "Something tells me you needed to sneak back into the palace often during the wild days of your youth."

Gallmau grinned back at her as he went over to brush the foliage away to expose the stone and plaster side of the building. The window was high up on the wall, but he could reach the latch on the outside by standing on his toes. After opening it, he bent down and extended his hand. Meri stepped on it, and he lifted her with one arm up to the window. Sometimes his strength was an advantage even when he wasn't fighting. Despite her fatigue, she clambered into the building with little difficulty, and he followed suit by pulling himself over the windowsill so he could crawl in.

Gallmau's strength made getting up to the sill and over

the top easy, but his size made going through the opening awkward. That, and the length of time since he had used this unusual entrance to the palace, caused his entry to be slow and far from graceful.

Too slow, in fact, to realize someone had been waiting for his arrival and was pointing a large kitchen ladle in Meri's direction. She was short and slender, with chestnut hair falling in ringlets that framed her heart-shaped face. Her day dress was practical and far too modest for typical Court attire, yet somehow exuded more style than the cleavage-baring fashions favored by women courtiers.

Saints, Valentina should not be here.

"What are you doing?" Gallmau reached to grab the woman's arm, thankful Meri hadn't sliced and diced his sister's best friend before he had come in. Threatening Meri without a damn good back-up plan—like Naghwe's poison and Sinan's shadow magic—was near suicidal. An oversized spoon wasn't going to cut it.

Valentina tried to shake her right hand free, then used her left hand to slap him across the face. "Waiting for you, you oaf. Let go of me."

Meri stood facing the two of them, her arms crossed over her chest and murder in her eyes. "If you don't like Gallmau's hand around that pretty little wrist of yours, I promise you'll like my hands around your neck even less."

"This is the Royal Palace of Soissons, not a dirty arena full of unwashed rabble who grovel at your feet." Valentina yanked her hand away as Gallmau confiscated the ladle, then squared her shoulders and glared back at Meri. Apparently, she knew exactly who the Lioness was and already didn't like her.

"What's wrong with you?" Gallmau had always been on good terms with Valentina, even if she made him feel like a particularly dim-witted student who hadn't finished his lessons. "I've been away for two years, and this is the welcome I get—a slap across the wrong cheeks."

"You shouldn't have returned like this." Valentina was too upset to even scold Gallmau for his suggestive comment, which was unlike her. "Coming back without warning, with a mage-killer by your side, and then sneaking into the palace is beyond foolish. Madame is *waiting* for you."

Gallmau often forgot Valentina was a witch—a medica —as well as a physician. The medici taught and studied at the Noviodunam and used magic when treating their patients, but no one thought of them in the same way as *incensori*, for example. Speaking of fire witches, Gallmau would be willing to bet a round of cider that Jacques Collin de Plancy was the one to blame for Valentina's hostile reaction to Meri. The aristocratic incensor had been engaged to the medica before breaking it off so he could court Gallmau's sister Rixende.

Yet another reason why he hated Jacques. Besides, they didn't need a witch in the family, even one from the de Plancy line.

"I have to talk to the Sorcier du Roi first." Gallmau gave up trying to charm his way out of the situation and resorted to the truth out of desperation. "Help me find Zhang Jue, and I'll present myself to Madame."

"He isn't here." Valentina snapped the words back, but her lower lip trembled, as if what she was telling him frightened her. "As usual, you have no idea what you've blundered into. Please. Go to Madame. I knew you would try to sneak through this window, like you always do when you don't want to get caught. I came here to stop you from making even more of a mess than you've already done."

"Let me talk to Rixende, then." Gallmau didn't want to

face the Queen by himself, and he needed to ask Zhang Jue if he could help Meri. "She could get me in to see the Sorcier du Roi."

Valentina pulled back from him, and the anger faded from her eyes, replaced by tears. "Your sister isn't in the palace either. You need to talk to the Queen. Now."

8

GALLMAU

G allmau hated how quickly the three of them walked the path through the kitchen and servant halls to a side entrance into the Queen's garden. Despite the argument with Valentina, Gallmau arrived not much later than the guards had expected, since they stood ramrod straight, staring into the maze with their hands on their swords—totally missing his entrance behind them.

In fact, Queen Xiaolian spotted them first, her beautifully arched eyebrows rising as Valentina led Gallmau and Meri around the lotus pond to the pavilion where Xiaolian sat with a book upon her lap. Courtiers, poets, and artists had fallen over themselves exalting the beauty of the Qingian bride the late king had brought to Soissons over his advisors' objections, and even more than two decades later she could pass for Rixende's older sister. Only a few wrinkles around her eyes and an air of weariness hinted at her age. As always, she wore an elegant gown that combined the silks and colors of her home country with the cut and styling of Soissons fashion.

The zoological garden was reserved for the reigning monarch of Soissons, and even members of the royal family had to request permission to visit it. It had driven his sister mad with jealousy that she couldn't play in it anytime she wished.

In addition to unusual plants and trees, the grounds were home to a host of Touched beasts—animals with magic. Peacocks crackling with electricity wandered over the grass, and the cat curled up in the sun near the pavilion had a sphere of water hovering above it. The larger creatures were kept in elaborate structures, like giant birdcages. There was a new addition since Gallmau had left, an Azhdarchid. The giant bird-like creatures were said to be Archaics—beasts who had been walking the earth since the dark time before the coming of the Saints. The monster opened its toothed beak wide and screeched fire as they approached.

"Your Most Saintly Majesty." Valentina sank into a deep curtsey and pitched her voice a tad higher than it needed to be. The guards started, whirling around in surprise, and Meri didn't bother to suppress a snicker. "May I present Monsieur Gallmau de Rohan and his companion Mademoiselle Meritamun d'Abdju, as you requested."

"Thank you, Dottoressa de Almania." Queen Xiaolian never failed to address Valentina with her family name and formal title as a physician, even though most witches were addressed by their first name, with Magus as the honorific. The medica straightened out of her curtsey and left the garden with perfect poise, even while throwing Gallmau a glance that indicated she would whack his hand with the soup ladle if he screwed this conversation up.

"Leave us." Xiaolian directed this first at the guards, who bowed and left, albeit with dark glances in Gallmau's direction.

When she turned her gaze on Meri, though, Gallmau knew he had to say something. He didn't want to face the Queen by himself, and Meri wasn't going to leave him without a fight that would get them both in trouble.

"Madame la Reine." Gallmau gave a deep bow, the way he had been taught—the right way—then stood up. "I know much has happened since we last spoke. Mademoiselle Meri has important information to add to our conversation, and I would ask you allow her to remain."

"Such a courtier's manner, Gallmau." Xiaolian sounded more resigned than infuriated. "And here I was expecting you to sneak into the palace through some window to avoid speaking to me."

The heat rose in his face at that.

With a sigh, the Queen gestured to the chairs facing her own seat. "Very well, then, please invite your infamous companion to join us."

Gallmau nudged Meri toward the pavilion. She gave him a sideways glance but held her tongue and allowed him to pull out one of the rosewood chairs for her to sit on. He didn't take his own seat, but instead knelt in front of the Queen and lifted the teapot sitting in front of her to fill first her cup, then the one in front of Meri, and lastly his own before sitting down. He always felt like an overgrown pet animal in front of his stepmother—large and ungainly—the exact opposite of the woman who radiated a delicate fragility as much as she did an iron will and uncompromising resolve.

Xiaolian said nothing at first, only accepting the teacup he offered her and taking a small sip. After giving Meri a subtle nudge with his foot to drink the tea, Gallmau followed suit. The hot liquid smelled of jasmine, and he resisted the urge to swig it down like brandy and get this whole confrontation over with.

"I was concerned by the reports you and Mademoiselle Meritamun had been attacked outside the capital." Xiaolian rested her cup on the table. "Perhaps if you had sent word to me that you would be returning to Lutecia, a proper escort could have been arranged."

"With all due respect, Your Majesty, that would only have increased the number of dead." Meri kept her language diplomatic, at least by her standards. "Regular troops aren't of much help against Bone Lords. The more the bodies pile up, the greater power the necromancers have."

The Queen watched Meri's face closely, but when she spoke she directed her words to Gallmau. "You didn't ask my permission to leave the palace in the first place."

"I left because you wanted me to, Madame." The words spilled out of Gallmau before he could stop them. It wasn't as if he didn't understand why Xiaolian might resent her husband keeping his bastard son in the palace even after she finally gave birth to the legitimate child the country had been waiting for. But if the threat she thought he presented to Rixende's inheritance of the throne was that concerning, why hadn't she told him herself? "The honorable Zhang Jue told me those were your wishes, and I wouldn't have come back if he hadn't written to me. Please, ask the Sorcier du Roi to join us in this discussion. He'll confirm I'm telling you the truth."

"The honorable Zhang Jue is dead." The Queen's voice

was level and emotionless, but her hand shook as she placed her book on the table. "Killed by the necromancer who abducted my daughter."

Gallmau could do nothing more than stare at the Queen, unable to believe what he was hearing. The death of Zhang Jue was a blow in and of itself. He had been clinging to the hope the Sorcier du Roi would be able to help Meri with her curse, even if his witch-hating friend was far from comfortable with the idea. But the thought that his only sister might be in the hands of a Bone Lord was more than he could handle. "Rixende has been taken—from the palace?"

The Queen didn't answer his question. Instead, she held out her hand, her fingers appearing too slender for the jewel-encrusted rings that encircled them. "This letter from the Sorcier du Roi. Show it to me."

"You think *we* had a hand in this?" Meri had kept her mouth shut for more of the conversation than Gallmau had expected, but she reached her breaking point at the worst possible time. "I think you should look closer to home. The heir to the throne of Soissons abducted, the royal sorcerer murdered—all under the noses of the witches of the Noviodunam? Your Majesty, I have a hard time believing that. So should you."

Xiaolian drew back, her posture stiffening. "You presume too much, mademoiselle."

"I presume only that I have greater experience killing necromancers than most." Meri pointed to Gallmau's chest, and he stared down stupidly before he remembered the letter was hidden in a pocket sewn into the fabric of his shirt. Meri had insisted upon it.

Getting it out involved partially disrobing and using his belt knife to cut the cloth to speed up the process. He did so, cringing at the offense to court etiquette. Granted, no one expected much from him at court, but he usually succeeded in keeping his clothes on in front of the Queen.

"Most Bone Lords care about their territory, dead things, and little else." Meri kept her eyes level with Xiaolian's. "There are two exceptions. The Order of Katil, who kill for money, and the death cultists in Karakoncolos. The attacks you describe don't sound like the work of a feral necromancer hiding out with a heap of bones in a cave somewhere."

"That's Monsieur de Plancy's opinion as well." Queen Xiaolian also didn't address the incensor by his witch title, but instead used the aristocratic family name of Jacques's mother. There was less stigma about having a child who became a sorcerer than there had been years ago, but titles and surnames didn't pass down to witches, even in Soissons. The de Plancy family had petitioned for Jacques to keep his name and title through the maternal line, and King Syagrius had granted the request. "He's sure Karakoncolos is involved, and that his father's banishment and the disbanding of the *benandanti* allowed this all to happen."

Jacques's father, Odart of Dol, was the architect of the Witches' War, which had been touted as an end to the scourge of necromancers upon the earth. That conflict had ended in abysmal defeat, and the benandanti— the Noviodunam's Bone Lord hunters—had paid a price for that failure, as had Odart himself.

Good thing, too. Odart was a real son of a bitch.

Gallmau clutched the letter in his hand as the meaning of the Queen's last statement struck him. "The officers of the Gardes Soissons knew nothing about this, but Jacques is in your confidence?" That damned overbred fire witch shouldn't know more than loyal soldiers. Then he thought about Tumas's near-treasonous statements and the unrest among citizens in the countryside. He had to admit the Queen might have good reason to keep the current crisis secret.

How long it could be kept quiet was another matter.

Meri snatched the letter from him and gave it to Xiaolian. "Here it is. Your sorcerer asked Gallmau for his assistance in a matter of grave import to both himself and the kingdom. Long on flowery language, short on details."

The Queen studied the parchment. "It has the Sorcier du Roi's seal, like the other invitations."

"What other letters are out there?" Gallmau couldn't take much more of this. "Rixende's in danger. You have to believe I'd do anything to rescue her. I swear upon Saint Attilio I'll fight an army of Bone Lords to get her back."

"You might have to do that." Xiaolian rested the paper beside her. "I have sent a message to Karakoncolos that we hold them responsible for the princess's abduction and threatened war if they don't return her."

Gallmau shot a glance toward Meri. The Witches' War, as most people called it, had ended six years ago in a total rout. The Synod of the Noviodunam attempted a direct attack on Karakoncolos, deep in the heart of the wild country of Zyx in the East, and Soissons provided both monetary support and troops for the effort. The Noviodunam's best sorcerer fighters, able to rain fire or bring bolts of lightning down on their enemies, came close to their goal of wiping the Bone Lord city off the map—until a single necromancer who became known as the Prince of Shadows rallied the remaining death witches and turned the tide of the battle. Most of the regular soldiers, including Gallmau, arrived too late to take part in the fighting, and hundreds of mages were killed or committed suicide rather than face unimaginable tortures at the hands of the necromancers. A few hadn't succeeded in choosing death over captivity—Jacques had been taken alive, then returned in a controversial hostage exchange.

At the time, Gallmau and his fellow soldiers shared the common opinion that fewer witches in the world was a good thing. The necromancers disappeared back into their mysterious city of monsters, which was described as similar to Hell, only with fewer amenities, and the Soissons army returned home.

Gallmau, sixteen at the time, had missed the larger implications of the defeat. Odart of Dol had strung up some merchants in Iotape on the way out, dealing a major blow to trade relations between the eastern port city and Soissons. Worse yet, the governor and ruling council had expelled any Noviodunam-trained mages in their territory and recognized Karakoncolos as a sovereign city-state.

King Syagrius had made a serious error in taking the side of the Noviodunam in that conflict, and the Queen might be about to make the same mistake.

"The death witch who left us on the road told me he was from Karakoncolos." Meri leaned forward, her expression of suppressed fury at the Queen's accusations against Gallmau changing to the intense interest of the hunt. "Sinan said he was coming to your court to represent their interests."

Xiaolian paled. "One of the Bone Lords who attacked you threatened to come to the Noviodunam tonight?"

"Please, tell me what's happening." Gallmau felt like punching someone. Sinan, preferably, but he might take out his frustration on a wall or two if he wasn't told the truth. "I've made a most solemn pledge to you, and Meri will stand by my side, but we must know how to help."

Queen Xiaolian closed her eyes for a moment. When

she opened them, her words were clear and firm. "After Rixende was taken, Zhang Jue left to investigate a location where she might be held, after sending out letters to those he thought best suited to rescue her if he failed. I have pledged Rixende's hand in marriage to the sorcerer who brings her back to me."

9

MERI

Meri walked through the great doors of the Noviodunam compound on Gallmau's arm. Her friend cleaned up rather nicely, as it turned out. He wore an emerald-green brocade vest under a black silk jacket with a high collar, and she caught more than a few admiring glances thrown in his direction. If she hadn't been so on edge about entering a compound full of witches, she might have found the pining looks amusing.

Meri also liked her own outfit, made in the Continental style of a corseted waist over a wide skirt, as opposed to the tunic and loose trousers favored in the harem. She did have a pair of those pants underneath, in case she ran into a serious fight. The satin fabric of the dress fell in stiff folds that looked like molten gold, and the wide sleeves flared at her elbows. She was thin enough—despite her boundless appetite, her speed ability meant she would never have a lush figure—that the laced-up bodice wasn't confining. Best of all were the special pockets sewn into the back of the dress, which concealed her two sword blades while their elaborate pommels served as a dramatic feature of the dress itself. The queen had sent a small army of maids and seamstresses to Meri's spacious guest rooms to help her dress for the event, and the women had worked wonders in a short period of time.

As the Noviodunam had official status as a separate state, only two royal guards had accompanied Queen Xiaolian when she entered through the massive scarlet gates ahead of them. Sorcerers dressed in robes with the colors corresponding to their magical affinity lined each side of the pathway leading from the gates toward the Palais de Feu. Meri had learned the domed building housed the Synod meeting chamber, along with various other offices, and even a ballroom, where the party to honor those who had come to help Soissons during this crisis was being held.

The pathway was well lit, both with electromantic lanterns—orbs of crackling white, like lightning imprisoned in small spheres—and incensori torches featuring flowing molten fire. She had seen such melding of engineering and magic before, but never in such extravagant quantities. The Noviodunam itself made this display easy to put on. Like all the centers of magical education and administration throughout the world, it had been built around a Witch Stone, like the one Karabil and Tharin had died next to. The Noviodunam's Witch Stone—Meri refused to call it an Artifact—particularly enhanced fire magic, much as the one in the university for witches in her home city of Abdju amplified the water magic of aquamancy.

The scent of magic was everywhere. Meri had to try and block it out—the clean, sharp smell of electricity from *fulgari* sorcerers wearing amber and silver, and whiffs of sulfur from their red-and-black fire mage colleagues. This much witchcraft, so close and powerful, sent a rush of panic through her strong enough to make her light-headed. She waited for her curse to strike, for the agony in her back to start up again, but she felt only a crawling sensation between her shoulder blades from the undead necromancer who lurked there.

Afraid of your enemies' magic?

If her dead foe could understand her mocking thoughts, he gave no sign.

Meri knew her show of bravado was meaningless. Zhang Jue, the Sorcier du Roi she had reluctantly agreed to see about the Bone Lord who possessed her, had been murdered before she and Gallmau could even ask for his help. Her curse had struck in the middle of her fight with the Death Hounds and only Gallmau's quick intervention had saved her. And the three years of life she had been told she had left were coming to an end.

But this wasn't the time to let a choking sense of dread overcome her. Even if the chances of ridding herself of the curse were now slim, she had work to do. She had promised the Queen, and more importantly, Gallmau, that she would do everything in her power to save Rixende. Her confident appearance at the Noviodunam was the first step.

She breathed in and out, forcing herself to keep her head high and an enigmatic smile on her face as she and Gallmau came closer to the Palais de Feu. As they approached the stone steps leading up to the columned exterior of the building, a man dressed much like Gallmau, but in colors of scarlet and charcoal, approached them. A silk scarf outlined with gold sigils hung over his courtier's outfit, but the aroma of wood smoke around him already told Meri the man was an incensor.

"Good evening, Monsieur de Rohan." The fire witch was tall, with dark blonde hair and pale eyes. His accent and mannerisms marked him as an aristocrat who happened to be born with magical talents, and Meri had already guessed his name without Gallmau confirming it. "I'm sorry you were out when I called upon you earlier this evening."

"You're awfully formal tonight, Jacques." Gallmau gave Meri a 'this is the asshole I was telling you about' look. "Since we're all pretending to be polite, allow me to introduce Mademoiselle Meritamun d'Abdju."

"The lady's reputation precedes her." Jacques Collin de Plancy added cold derision to his words, as if he didn't expect Meri to even understand Soissons, much less grasp the insult.

"As does yours, monsieur, or magus, if you prefer." Meri's command of the Soissons language was near flawless, thanks to years of instruction in the Sultana's harem, and she enjoyed watching Jacques stiffen at her retort. She had little patience for spoiled nobles in general, and for snooty witches in particular.

"I've heard you've already accosted Magus Valentina in the palace." Jacques studied her for a moment, biting down on his lower lip. "I trust you're aware you accept a magical contract to behave nonviolently while you're inside the Noviodunam."

"I'm usually quite peaceable, monsieur." Meri didn't stop smiling, even if she felt like shoving one of her stilettos between his ribs. "Except when witches such as yourself don't act the same toward me. Alas, that has already been the case since I've entered your fair country."

"You were attacked by necromancers near a maladanti

Artifact." The outrage in Jacques's voice indicated how touchy he was about being compared to those who practiced the wrong kind of magic. He gave up on the verbal battle with Meri and turned to Gallmau. "I need to know what happened. The Queen is not willing to divulge anything, and I have little to go on but the gossip of soldiers. You'd be doing yourself a favor by giving me information that could keep us all safe."

"I'll be doing myself a favor by having a cider and not talking to you at all." Gallmau steered Meri away from the incensor and up the stairs.

"It was Sinan of Karakoncolos, wasn't it?" Jacques shouted the question at their backs. Gallmau kept going, but Meri turned her head to see the fire mage shaking, his facade of diplomacy slipping away. "The Prince of Shadows is in Soissons."

They both fell silent for the rest of their walk into the Palais de Feu as the implications of Jacques's words sunk in. Sinan wasn't only a powerful necromancer who had fought off an assassin from the Order of Katil, then left them disarmed and helpless. He was the Prince of Shadows, the Bone Lord whose mere name evoked panic from regular people and witches alike.

Gallmau spoke first, breaking the tension as he leaned down to whisper in her ear. "That was the best put-down of Jacques I've seen since Valentina threw a glass of wine in his face when he broke off their engagement."

Jokes about her verbal sparring with the incensor were all well and good, but Meri needed to know more about Sinan and why he was here. The necromancer's words—"*I'd assumed you and the prince of Soissons were here for the same crisis that prompted my visit*"—came back to her.

"Even the Prince of Shadows can't take on the entire

Noviodunam." She turned over the events of the violent confrontation on the road to Lutecia in her mind, trying to understand why the most notorious Bone Lord in the world had let her and Gallmau live, then joined his undead necromancer mother in funeral rites for Tharin and Karabil. "Why would Sinan risk coming to Soissons, if the city of monsters is behind the abduction?"

"I suppose he's the best death witch they have in Karakoncolos, so they picked him." Gallmau frowned, as if a thought had occurred to him. "Is Sinan really a necromancer prince, do you think?"

Her friend, sweet though he was, was as hopelessly focused on royal lineage as the other Continentals Meri had encountered. For her part, she didn't think much of kings or queens, or for that matter, even sultans or sultanas. Being born into money and power wasn't particularly difficult. Holding on to it, on the other hand, was an impressive skill. That was one reason Meri did respect her Sultana.

They stepped through a smaller set of doors into the ballroom, and Meri stopped wondering if Bone Lords had their own royalty or favored the anarchy espoused by radicals and freethinkers.

It was quite the display.

Gallmau had told her the Noviodunam had its own vetted servants—maids, chefs, gardeners—and the famed Shields of Thaschus, the Noviodunam's private army. Several of those elite soldiers, dressed in elegant uniforms of dark gray coats buttoned over black trousers, stood at attention around the hall. Most were men, but some identically dressed women were among them. All were either huge or lean and muscular, with no body types in between. Strength and speed—the Shields recruited exclusively from candidates with those Gifts. Waitstaff bustled around tables piled with food and drink, while a group of musicians played in the corner. In the center, an enchanted fountain lit up the room with gold flames that sprayed out from the top and flowed into its wide basin, like the fire had been turned to liquid.

Meri's apprehension gave way to a grudging sense of awe.

"The Lioness of Abdju." A booming voice, at once familiar and—she had to admit—quite welcome, came from across the room.

A minute later, a tall and regal man came up to them, wearing the official robes of a Kushian sorcerer, embroidered silks in teals, aqua, and glistening white—the colors of water. His turban, which framed an older and distinguished face with the same coloring as Meri's own, featured a star sapphire set in the center.

A genuine smile came to her lips. Yes, it was him, and her old lover lived up to his name, in both bearing and in dress, not to mention his magical skills.

"Allow me to introduce the Grand Vizier of Abdju, Abarsam the Magnificent." Meri crossed her two arms into an X on her chest and bowed. The full salute, which she had often performed in the arena to the delight of her Continental fans, incorporated her famed curved swords. Best to keep those hidden, though. She liked Abarsam very much, but here he was a witch amongst witches, and she was in enemy territory. "Grand Vizier, may I present Monsieur Gallmau de Rohan."

"A pleasure, Your Highness." Abarsam bowed even more deeply in Gallmau's direction, and Meri could see her friend squirm.

"It's a pleasure to meet you as well, but I have no title of note, much less the one you're trying to give me."

Gallmau gave Meri a sideways glance of half-alarm, half-shock. He clearly hadn't been expecting her to recognize any of the sorcerers at this event, much less be on good terms with one. "I'm surprised you and Meri—know each other."

"Forgive an old man an understandable mistake." Abarsam had a twinkle in his eye as he replied to Gallmau's discomfort with the royal salutation. Oh, but the famous water mage was always the charmer, wasn't he? "In Kush, the son of a king is—the son of a king. Your fame precedes you, Monsieur de Rohan, if that's what you wish to be called. As do the tales of your adventures with my dear Lioness here."

"How did you get here so quickly after the princess's abduction?" Meri knew that for all of Abarsam's powers, he couldn't have traveled from Kush to Soissons in the few weeks since the kidnapping.

Seeing him sparked a flicker of hope she tried to repress without success. She'd be lying to herself if she hadn't thought about asking Abarsam for his help with her curse. But she had been at once fearful the Grand Vizier wouldn't be able to expel the dead necromancer and worried about what he would expect in return if he succeeded. Better to be dead and free, than alive and imprisoned, even in a cage studded with diamonds. Now here was Abarsam, representing a potential lifeline—and the fear of losing her freedom.

"I was in the south of Soissons and came as soon as I received word of this dreadful affair." Abarsam raised his eyes heavenward. The Grand Vizier was a consummate diplomat and could navigate the complexities of both Kushian and foreign politics with ease, but his religious devotion was not a convenient front. He was truly pious. "I give thanks to the Prophets my son and I were close enough to offer our services."

Abarsam turned and gestured to a group several paces away. It was comprised of a gaggle of court women, all with plunging necklines and cascades of jewelry, gathered around one young man. Strikingly handsome, he bore an unmistakable resemblance to Abarsam. His broad shoulders were set off well by a long jacket in dark blue, covered in silver sigils. She drew in a breath and concentrated. The man—or his coat—smelled like the silt-laden waters of her home. Armor enchanted with magic, and all disguised as courtly clothing.

"Nice outfit." Meri grinned at the Grand Vizier. "Your magic always smells the same to me."

"My son Baahir." Abarsam beamed at the young man, then turned back to Meri. "I see your unusual talent is as strong as ever. His coat has my magic in it, as do your blades. Quite clever of you to make them part of your dress for this evening."

Meri wasn't surprised Abarsam knew she had her swords on her—after all, he was the one who had given her the enchanted weapons—but she had hoped they wouldn't be as easy to spot.

"Well, you've caught me." She added a purr to her words, hoping flirtation might get her out of this situation. "Are you going to confiscate them? Your colleague, Magus Jacques, has already warned me of dire consequences if I misbehave tonight."

"There's no issue with you bringing weapons inside this space." Abarsam indicated their opulent surroundings with a wave of his hand. "Using them, however, would be—inadvisable. I handled the arrangements myself. Employing any magical talent or object, including your swords, to harm anyone here would unleash a fatal curse."

"That sounds like something we'd like to avoid." Gallmau reached out to a passing server, who deposited a glass of wine into his hand. After a moment's reflection, he took a gulp. "I take it you and your son plan to join the rescue party?"

"Indeed, Your Highness." Abarsam blithely ignored Gallmau's earlier admonition about titles and gave him a warm clap on the shoulder. "I'm here to support the Court of Soissons during this trying time. To think a beautiful virgin princess could be spirited away by a necromancer from the royal palace—it's like a dark tale spun by a story-teller in the *souk*. Yet here we are. I'll do all within my power to bring your sister back to the loving arms of her family."

The Grand Vizier left out the part about the Queen's promise to marry Rixende off to one of her rescuers, but Meri knew him well enough to be sure he had considered the political advantages of his offer of assistance. Abarsam could cement ties between Kush and Soissons and make his son the consort of the next Queen in one fell swoop.

Gallmau had been gazing at Baahir, perhaps assessing his potential as a husband for his sister, or maybe as a tumble for himself, but he snapped his attention back to the Grand Vizier. "Meri and I will also be going."

Abarsam frowned. "Princess Rixende's abductor is a necromancer of frightening power. Even your and the Lioness's strength of arms would not be sufficient to over-come such a fiend."

"We have a letter from Zhang Jue." Gallmau swigged at his wine again, a grumpy expression on his face. "He asked me to return and help him, and when I did I found out my sister had been taken."

Abarsam stared back at him, and Meri could all but see the Grand Vizier's mind analyzing the new information. "Magus Zhang Jue must have wanted you and the Lioness to accompany him. Two protectors are allowed with each invited sorcerer. You are brave indeed, and I of all people know how tenacious Lady Meri is in battling monsters of all kinds. But you can't hope to overcome this level of death magic without a sorcerer by your side. Nor will the Synod allow it."

"We'll see," Meri answered before Gallmau could start a fight with one of the strongest aquamagi in the world. Her friend's face had darkened with anger, and this was not the time to argue. "The Queen requested our presence, and she has a right to attend the Synod's meetings."

The Grand Vizier opened his mouth to speak, then closed it into a tight smile. "Magus Jacques is the current moderator of the Synod since Magus Odart's...retirement. I must defer such questions to him. In the meantime, may I suggest trying the artistry of Qing cuisine. The chefs here have produced a special menu for my party, with meat approved by the head of the House of Prophets in the city. As for you, dear prince." Abarsam turned back to Gallmau. "I hope you have an opportunity to talk with my son. I think you'll find the two of you have much in common."

Meri saluted the Grand Vizier again, even as Gallmau gave him a half-scowl, and Abarsam slipped away into the crowd.

"Since when are you so fond of witches?" Gallmau rounded on Meri even as he shook the glass in his hand at a passing waiter to ask for another drink. "Any cider here?"

A young woman wearing brown witch robes whisked away his glass and ran off. Hopefully she'd find something that would cheer her friend up.

"Abarsam and I have a history." Meri hesitated. She wasn't concerned about sharing the salacious details of her past romances with Gallmau—they teased each other about their conquests all the time. Her relationship with Abarsam, though, was more complicated than the one night of lovemaking they had shared. She found him difficult to talk about. Besides, Gallmau had taken a risk returning to Lutecia to try and save Meri from her curse, only to find the one witch he trusted dead and his sister in the hands of a Bone Lord. He wanted to be everyone's protector. She needed to solve problems her way—and now the two of them had crises that couldn't be overcome without the help of witches like Abarsam, even if they both hated the thought.

Best to stick with simple facts and leave her feelings out of it. "I've turned down his offers of marriage twice. Technically I did agree to a temporary marriage when I bedded him a few years ago, but it was only for the night."

Meri scanned the room for the Qingian cuisine prepared for the Grand Vizier while Gallmau digested that information. In the time it took for the Noviodunam server to dash back and deposit a large glass of cider into Gallmau's hand, she had walked the two of them over to the display and Gallmau's attention had been diverted to what Continental men considered the exotic marital arrangements of her homeland.

"You can get married for one night?" Gallmau knocked back some cider while Meri accepted a plate of steaming dumplings garnished with a delicate lotus flower. "Even though the men can have multiple wives?"

"Rich men have as many lovers as they want everywhere." Meri felt a flash of irritation but restrained herself from a snippy retort by taking a bite of a tender and fluffy dumpling. It was delicious, and Gallmau didn't mean any harm. But seriously, his own birth proved her point. "I thought the sovereign of Soissons could take a legal consort."

Gallmau stopped mid-drink, then copied her own stalling tactic by stuffing half a plate of Qingian food in his mouth. He chewed for a while before answering. "There's a Royal Mistress position, but my father didn't appoint anyone to it while he was alive."

Meri bit her lip, wishing she could take back her earlier comment. Gallmau's mother had come from the wrong family background and the wrong part of Soissons to be granted such formal status, even if she had given the King his only son. She tried to think of a way to walk her words back, but Gallmau, who hated this kind of conflict, changed the subject on his own.

"Standing around to eat is awfully odd, but I suppose witches have to be contrary about everything." Gallmau held out his hand for another plate of food and handed it to her. Instead of a formal banquet, the Noviodunam had arranged tables of food and drink in between the groups of guests, so people could walk around and sample the offerings. "Go on, tell me how Abarsam was between the sheets."

"He has several wives, and they've clearly taught him a thing or two." Meri took the dish of noodles, now guilty enough to give Gallmau more details. "Abarsam had asked the Sultana for my hand in marriage before I left the harem, and I succeeded in getting out of that. Then he tracked me down on the Continent at one of my arena fights. We female fighters weren't as available as the men— they had a long line of rich women they were expected to entertain—but certain customers couldn't be refused. So I bedded Abarsam, and I enjoyed it. He proposed a second time, and even when I refused he gave me my blades as a gift."

Jacques, who had been engaged in a whispered conversation with Queen Xiaolian in a far corner of the room, stepped forward and clapped his hands. The sound echoed far too loudly in the room to be natural, and the golden flames from the fountain dimmed to a more somber color of dark blue.

"Mesdames et messieurs, welcome to the Noviodunam." Jacques cast one more glance back at the queen, who stood erect and grim-faced between her two royal guards. "I'm honored to have so many members of the court and illustrious citizens of Lutecia visit us tonight. I regret to announce, however, that I will not be accepting the position of Councillor de la Sorcellerie this evening."

This provoked gasps and a brief flurry of chatter from many of the courtiers in attendance, although none of the robed mages around them showed any surprise.

"He was supposed to become Zhang Jue's assistant tonight." Gallmau drank down more of his cider and grimaced at the fire witch. "There's some sort of magical ceremony attached to it where he swears his fealty to the royal family and what not."

"Is it similar to the Kushian loyalty curse?" Meri, having made short work of the noodles, sipped from a cup of fragrant tea. She couldn't fault the witches of Soissons for their hospitality. "Abarsam told me mages aren't allowed to advise the Sultana unless they submit to it. The curse prevents them from harming the Sultana or any of her relatives, but it's not simple to undergo. He told me it took him weeks to recover from the effects when he was younger— bragged about how draining it was, essentially."

"Yes, it's like that." Gallmau stared over Meri's shoulder

for a moment, as if he had caught sight of someone interesting, then turned his attention back to her. "Jacques's father, Odart of Dol, took the oath as well, back when he was the Councillor de la Sorcellerie. Knowing that asshole, they probably had to force him to do it."

Meri knew the name, and judging by the savage twist of pain in her back, her undead necromancer remembered Odart as well. The Noviodunam Bone Lord hunter had protected and shielded her old enemy, absolving the wealthy and well-connected man of charges of necromancy and allowing him to continue his torture and murder of innocents. The tea turned bitter in her mouth, and she had to stop herself from spitting out her disdain for the hypocrisy of the witches around her onto their gleaming marble floor.

Standing before the fountain, Jacques continued his speech. "I've deferred my acceptance of the great honor of service to the Queen because I have a more urgent task—tracking down the Honorable Zhang Jue's murderer and rescuing the Dauphine, Mademoiselle de la Reine, Rixende of Lutecia."

There was more than muttering at that. Shouts rang out, along with sobs and a babble of questions. Jacques attempted to speak again but could not make his voice heard above the roar.

Queen Xiaolian rose from her chair and stepped forward. The noise from the crowd faded away to a tense silence, and every eye in the room turned toward her.

"It is with great sorrow that I confirm this terrible news." Xiaolian's tone was as even as ever, but her eyes appeared haunted, and she carried herself with an air of exhausted grief. "My daughter Rixende has been abducted by a necromancer. My devoted servant Zhang Jue lost his life trying to free her, after sending letters asking for the assistance of other great sorcerers. I have come here to honor those who have offered to rescue the heir to the throne and put an end to the foul death witch who took her."

A stunned silence followed her words.

The Queen continued, "For this service to the Royal Court of Soissons, I pledge my daughter's hand in marriage, along with the title and lands granted to the royal consort of the Dauphine. I will now receive the brave sorcerers who will journey tomorrow to confront this fiend and grant them my approval and the blessings of the Saints."

10

GALLMAU

Gallmau had already cracked his glass of cider, his hand clenching into a fist as the Queen spoke. Despite knowing what she would say, hearing the proclamation announced in public had hurt. His sister was proud and independent to a fault. She would marry to advance the interests of her country and not for love, but the political intrigue surrounding the match would thrill her.

Now, when Rixende was helpless and imprisoned—if she was alive at all—she was to be nothing more than a prize in a battle between witches.

Jacques presented himself to the Queen first, kneeling before her and promising to burn Rixende's Bone Lord abductor alive. Abarsam followed next, presenting his handsome son and launching into a carefully phrased speech.

"Abarsam's son isn't all that bad." Gallmau made that grudging allowance as he watched Baahir answer a few questions from the Queen in slightly inflected Soissons with quiet deference and a wide, attractive smile flashing white against his rich brown skin.

"I'd imagine Rixende wouldn't be too disappointed coming home to him in her bed every night." Meri gave Gallmau a lascivious wink, and Gallmau relaxed.

He was afraid he had insulted her by prying into her relationship with the Grand Vizier and his abrupt response to her question about the Office of the Royal Mistress. Maybe if his mother had lived through his birth, the King would have granted her the title. Or maybe she wouldn't even have wanted it.

"Perhaps you could try him out in the sack yourself before deciding he's good enough for your sister."

"You have a low opinion of my morality." Gallmau did his best to sound offended, although the thought of spending a night with Baahir was far from unpleasant. Once again, Meri had shaken him out of his feelings of worthlessness, and he needed to start acting like he belonged here. The Queen had requested he and Meri present themselves as the final rescuer team and welcomed him back to the Court. He didn't want to think about the likely reason she had forgiven him so easily—her fear Rixende wouldn't return at all.

He could start by looking presentable. The liquid in his cracked glass had begun to leak out over his hand and the cuff of his suit, so he waved down another of the Noviodunam novices who were acting as waiters. A young man with a pale freckled face and mop of curly dark hair came over, wearing a gold and white *simar*—a sort of magic scarf the witches of the Noviodunam favored—hanging down in vertical bands over his brown novitiate robes. "I'd like a fresh cider, please. My cup's sprung a leak."

The novice gave him a mischievous grin and tapped the side of the goblet. The glass grew warm in Gallmau's hand and reformed back into its original shape, without any visible defect.

"There, I fixed it for you." The young man ran his eyes over Gallmau without trying to hide his interest and added, "If I can do anything else for you this evening, Monsieur de Rohan, all you have to do is ask."

"Obviously, my low opinion of your morals is more than justified." Meri leaned over to sniff Gallmau's magically repaired glass as the Artifex Guild novice left to attend other guests. "His spell smells like hot sand and burning metal, and he was shamelessly trying to get you into bed."

Gallmau wanted to point out that being propositioned by a good-looking witch wasn't his fault, but once again caught a glimpse of the slender man dressed in black who had attracted his attention earlier. He wore a powdered wig of the type favored by rich bankers from Diutisc in the north and had his back to Gallmau as he watched the proceedings with rapt attention. Gallmau craned his neck, trying to get a better glimpse of him. Handsome enough, at least from a rear view.

"Your doctor witch friend is also joining the rescue." Meri's comment jerked Gallmau back to the presentation of sorcerers. "Is she planning to take out the Bone Lord with more kitchen implements, or will she at least pack a scalpel?"

Valentina came forward and dropped into a curtsey in front of the queen. Like her ex-fiancé Jacques, she had struck a balance between her status as a close confidant of the heir to the throne and a Noviodunam-trained mage when choosing her clothing. She was dressed in a fashionable but conservative gown of sky blue and gold—medicus colors—and a simar embroidered with healing sigils.

"That's the thing, she can't fight." Gallmau respected Valentina's loyalty to Rixende, but a battle with a Bone Lord strong enough to kill Zhang Jue would be incredibly dangerous. Even Jacques, an incensor with battlefield experience, was taking two Shields with him, and Abarsam had his son and a bodyguard twice Gallmau's size. "The medici can't even serve as military surgeons, much less use their Gift to harm others."

"Her magic smells different than most." Meri's nose could sniff out spells and curses anywhere, a skill that had come in handy in their adventures over the years. "Powerful and astringent. Like witch hazel."

"Makes sense for a medica, I suppose." Gallmau could see Jacques scowl as Valentina rose to address the queen. Clearly Valentina hadn't told the incensor she was planning to join the quest. That served the bastard right, but Gallmau could understand his concern. "She was the youngest professor of medicine ever at the University of Amor, as well as teaching at the Noviodunam before she resigned over that hostage exchange scandal that got Odart kicked out."

Meri glowered at the name. Gallmau didn't remember telling her about the former head of the benandanti, but she probably knew him by reputation. Everyone hated Odart, even his son Jacques. The man didn't even have his own magic. Odart was a mirror mage and needed to drain the abilities of other witches to do anything magical.

When he turned back to the Queen, she was accepting the Sword of Soissons from a velvet pillow. She touched a kneeling Valentina's shoulder with the blade, as she had with the others. Then she arranged Jacques, Abarsam, and Valentina into a line so the crowd could again cheer the heroes who planned to take on the necromancer who had kidnapped his baby sister.

He muttered a quick prayer to Saint Attilio that Rixende was alive and unharmed. It didn't matter what it took; he had to save her.

Scanning the room, he realized the well-dressed man who had caught his eye was nowhere in sight, despite his earlier fascination with the spectacle. Come to think about it, Gallmau could have sworn he had seen him before.

"Which one would you take to your bed?" Any of Meri's remaining irritation about her earlier tiff with Valentina had faded away. "The son of a Kushian aquamage, an aristocrat incensor, or a medica with a temper and a thing for ladles?"

"Sinan." Gallmau realized too late why he had found the man so familiar, not to mention so attractive.

"I think that pretty Bone Lord put something in your poison I didn't get with my dose." Meri put her hands on her hips as she faced him. "Like a lust potion. You can't be serious about wanting to fuck Sinan."

The Prince of Shadows was here, somewhere, and they needed to stop him.

"I call upon any others here who have been asked by the Sorcier du Roi to join in this noble quest." Queen Xiaolian's voice rang out over the crowd, and Meri darted forward.

"That's us." She glanced over her shoulder at him. "Let's go and show these witches a thing or two."

"Sinan's here." Gallmau, despite his long stride, had to hurry to catch up to Meri and whisper in her ear. "I saw him earlier, but he was in disguise..."

Meri shook her head. "You think Sinan put on fancy clothes and strolled right into the Noviodunam, filled with sorcerers who want to burn him alive? If I didn't know how much you can drink, I'd swear you've had too much cider."

They pushed their way through the throng of people cheering the Queen and the champions, and Xiaolian spotted Gallmau. She gave him a firm nod to encourage him to come forward, but he still looked around, dread growing in his chest, even as Meri plucked at his sleeve to pull him toward the Queen.

"I'm here as a representative from the Councils of the Living and the Dead to represent the interests of Karakoncolos." It was Sinan's voice, and the same words the Bone Lord had told Meri when she held him down with two swords at his throat.

The buzz of conversation in the hall ended in a collective gasp of shock.

Sinan stepped out of the crowd to face Queen Xiaolian, and he didn't look like a merchant tonight. His shroud cloak hung from his shoulders, cursed sigils glowing purple over the dead white of the fabric. Underneath his hood, his eyes were marked out in black and red face powder, giving him the appearance of a talking skull. "You sent a message to the Blessed threatening us with war. Here is our answer."

Most people in the room stood frozen with shock, but Gallmau whirled and ran for the Queen. Meri, bless her soul, was already in front of Xiaolian, her blades out and ready. She had sunk into her speed as soon as Sinan started talking. Gallmau joined her and hissed a command at the two Garde Royale members who stood staring at the Bone Lord.

"Stand behind the Queen, now." Gallmau made sure the useless soldiers scrambled to protect their rear flank and turned to watch Sinan walk up to them. His movements were unhurried, even as Jacques summoned a swirling circle of fire that spun at his chest level, and every Shield in the room rushed forward.

Abarsam grabbed the incensor's arm. "Call off the Shields. He's under the same curse we are and is protected by it."

"I understand the Grand Vizier personally attended to tonight's security arrangements." Sinan gave Abarsam a mocking half-bow. "An enchantment to transform the water inside anyone who attacks another with magic into heated vapor, boiling them alive from the inside out." The young necromancer surveyed the array of swords, muskets, and a few bayonets aimed in his direction with unperturbed calm. "A fascinating death. I'd be most intrigued to see it."

"Stand down." Jacques snapped the words out, and the Shields of Saint Thaschus lowered their weapons, although they remained arrayed in a circle around Sinan. Guests jostled behind them for a better look at the necromancer, and the surprised silence gave way to an excited babble of voices. "Why are you here?"

"I believe I've already answered that question." Sinan walked closer to Meri and Gallmau, his black eyes moving from their faces to the Queen's. He pressed his fingertips together in a gesture that mimicked a prayerful stance, although it looked more like a predatory insect about to pounce. "The Councils of the Living and the Dead in Karakoncolos deny any knowledge of the abduction of the Dauphine of Soissons, Rixende Grimoard, or the assassination of Zhang Jue of the benandanti."

"You've come far to merely claim you had no involvement." Queen Xiaolian spoke in measured tones, but Gallmau was close enough to feel the faint tremble in her slight frame. "I confess I'm not sure how to address you, having never met a necromancer before. Would you prefer Monsieur Kaya, perhaps? I understand your father is a member of that family in Iotape."

The necromancer's cover story of being a merchant from the Eastern city wasn't entirely a lie, then. Sinan's eyes narrowed. He had taken the Queen's mention of his family name as a threat, and it was quite possible Xiaolian meant it as one. Odart of Dol had hanged several prominent citizens in Iotape after his loss in the Witches' War, but he had exchanged one living hostage for the safe return of Jacques from Karakoncolos, along with three Noviodunam students accused of necromancy. Gallmau had always wondered why the Bone Lords would trade a prisoner of war for a merchant. Now it made sense. Odart had abducted Sinan's father.

"I could care less what you call me." Sinan came to a halt a few feet from Meri and Gallmau. "We have no titles in Karakoncolos, no kings or queens, and as for family, all of the Blessed are as one."

Well, that settled the question of how the Bone Lords ruled themselves. They were short on pomp and fancy titles, and long on radical thinking and scary face paint.

"You state your people had no part in this diabolical plot yet claim kinship with whoever did it," Queen Xiaolian continued, her voice icy. "I didn't threaten war against your city-state without forethought to the consequences. If you came here to issue threats to me in person, you may do so and take your leave."

It was a stinging rebuke, and Sinan paused for a moment before responding. "I also came here to offer my assistance. If one of the Blessed took unprovoked action against your family and the Kingdom of Soissons, then they have gone against the current interests of Karakoncolos."

Gallmau's mouth dropped open, and Jacques broke into sarcastic laughter. "You're offering to come along with the rescue parties, then. I suppose you also plan on being joined in holy matrimony with the princess if you return her after your people orchestrated her abduction?"

"Allow me to clarify." Sinan let out an exasperated breath at Jacques and turned his attention back to Xiaolian. "Drop your threat to attack my country, and I'll find whoever kidnapped your daughter and take her back by any means necessary."

"The Kingdom of Soissons will do what is necessary to protect our citizens and the Grimoard line of succession." Queen Xiaolian sounded a little less certain now, perhaps as surprised by Sinan's offer as Gallmau was. "I have only your word Karakoncolos wasn't involved, and I must do what's best for my country."

"Was it in your country's best interest to support the Witches' War?" Sinan waved at the crowd around him, now more curious than hostile. The necromancer was taking a different direction now, and perhaps a more dangerous one. "You put troops and money behind the Noviodunam and their obsession with hunting down and killing every one of us. They failed miserably and took their frustration out on the innocent citizenry of Iotape. Now you have no diplomatic relations with a port city that accounted for forty percent of your exports and imports. Your economy is in shambles, many of your people have been reduced to begging on the streets, and there's talk in the taverns and gazettes about overthrowing the foreign-born queen who sits on the throne."

Gallmau winced. Sinan might be a Bone Lord, but he was telling some uncomfortable truths, and people were listening to him.

"You've said enough." Jacques moved toward Sinan, but Abarsam put a hand onto his chest with a sizzle, like water quenching fire.

Saints, this was turning into a mini Witches' War of its own.

The necromancer kept talking, his words now more for his fascinated audience than the queen. "Your heir to the throne, who will rule for no other reason than an accident of birth, has been taken, and what do you and the great Noviodunam do about it?" He pointed around him, at the fountain that once again flowed with golden fire, the array of feast items and drinks, and the well-dressed guests who were hanging on his every word. "You throw an enormous party and talk about marrying off the young woman if you get her back alive."

Gallmau hated to admit it, but Sinan had a point about that as well. He took in a deep breath and resolved to jump into this fiasco and face the consequences later.

"Magus Abarsam." Gallmau often tried to make his all-too-loud voice softer in court, to avoid unwanted attention, but this time he let it ring out loud and clear. "I think it's time to continue this conversation in private. Maybe we shouldn't ignore any offers of assistance"—Gallmau gestured toward Sinan—"even ones from an unlikely source."

Jacques opened his mouth, probably to tell Gallmau to shut the hell up, but Abarsam seized upon the suggestion with obvious relief. "A wise proposal, indeed. Madame la Reine, may we continue the conversation with our unexpected guest in the Synod meeting room?"

"I think that would be best." The Queen placed a hand on Gallmau's arm, and he turned in surprise to see approval in her eyes.

Jacques stood fuming for a moment, then motioned to the Shields. They moved to clear a path through the crowd and stood at attention in two lines leading toward a pair of gold doors at the far side of the room. As Abarsam muttered quick instructions to his son and bodyguard, Gallmau and Meri walked ahead of Queen Xiaolian toward the doors, with her Royal Guard trailing behind her.

Gallmau glanced back and saw a wary Sinan nod as Abarsam made a sweeping gesture for the necromancer to follow him. Jacques extended his arm out to Valentina, but the physician ignored it and walked on her own through the phalanx of guards.

They all ended up in front of the gleaming entrance to the Synod meeting room.

"Madame la Reine, I regret to say that even the sovereign of Soissons is only permitted two guards within the Synod chambers." Jacques gave both Gallmau and Meri a look of intense irritation. Gallmau's suggestion had not sat well with the incensor. "Although Monsieur de Rohan and Mademoiselle Meritamun came most ably to your defense, there's no safer place within the Kingdom than behind these doors, even with a necromancer among us."

"Of course, Magus Jacques." Xiaolian gave the incensor a frosty smile, pointedly not using his family name for once, and gestured to her Garde Royale soldiers. "You're both dismissed. Send a message to the National Assembly about tonight's events at once."

The two guards bowed and left.

The Queen held out her arm. "I'm most intrigued to see this famous chamber."

Gallmau hooked his elbow into hers, feeling like an oversized bear asked to transport a delicate porcelain vase.

Jacques chewed his lower lip, then turned to Sinan. "The last necromancer to enter this room was Letha the Witch, two hundred years ago, right before she was dragged out and burnt at the stake." He raised his arms, and the doors burst into flames. "After you."

Sinan studied the fire that roared over the gold doors yet somehow consumed nothing and gave off little heat. He closed his eyes, as if to concentrate, then opened them as shadows rippled along the floor toward the entrance.

The flames sputtered and died.

The entire wall in front of them bucked wildly for a second, and then both doors flew open as if there had been an explosion behind them.

Gallmau felt Xiaolian flinch. Beside him, Meri muttered several curse words in Kushian. Sinan strolled into the chamber without even glancing back at the incensor, and Gallmau gritted his teeth and followed, the Queen on his arm.

11

SINAN

After slipping into the Noviodunam in disguise, announcing his presence to the most dangerous mages in the world, and blowing the doors of the Synod meeting room open, Sinan's first thought as he entered the infamous sanctuary was how anticlimactic it all felt. The space smelled like wood smoke and dust and was far less awe-inspiring than he had expected—a little stuffy, in fact.

There were no windows, which was hardly surprising considering the need for security when the ruling body of the Noviodunam met. The wall panels painted with arcane sigils and stylized animals representing the various magical guilds—except for his own, of course—contributed to the space's enclosed, suffocating atmosphere. Lighting came from torches on the wall that fused incensor flame magic with artifex design, producing the type of showy display

Sinan had mocked in the overdone fountain in the ballroom outside.

The ceiling was painted as a living night sky, with stars that twinkled and planets that glowed, and the heavens rotated around a circular panel representing the Zodiac. A rectangular table dominated the room, surrounded by ornate chairs with high backs and decorations matching the guild panels on the wall.

For Sinan, the only seat that mattered was the one that wasn't there.

At the far end of the table, opposite the incensor throne, an empty spot threw off the symmetry of the arrangement and made the entire room awkward and unsettled. The torches near it burned lower, and the other chairs were spaced further away from it, as if trying to avoid proximity with the spot where the Throne of Letha had once stood.

He paused for a moment and offered up a prayer to the Lady of Shadows, thanking her for allowing him to gaze upon the location where Saint Letha had been condemned to her martyrdom.

Then he turned to watch his enemies trail into the room after him.

Gallmau strode in first, his shock of reddish-blond hair tamed into a queue with a velvet tie that matched his ornate waistcoat. He looked like the hero prince in a storyteller's tale tonight, handsome and regal, as he walked in escorting Queen Xiaolian. Sinan reminded himself to focus on him as an opponent and stop thinking about how attractive he was.

Meri came in next, her water-cursed blades now openly secured at the waist of her dress, the golden material contrasting with her smooth, dark skin. Her eyes never left him as she entered, beautiful and calculating. He remembered all too well the sting of her two swords pressed against his neck as she had pinned him to the ground, and the sensation of her body on top of his—terror mixed with desire.

Aside from Abarsam, she would be the most dangerous person in the room.

Valentina came in next, her cheeks flushed and her steps uncertain. She made sure to keep her distance from him, even to the point of drawing close to Meri as the Lioness joined Gallmau in standing on either side of Queen Xiaolian. Apparently even a Tomb Fighter was a more welcome companion than he was. Then again, Sinan's last meeting with the medica hadn't been under the best of circumstances.

The half-shattered doors opened one last time for the two remaining people joining them. Sinan's stunt with the warded entrance to the meeting room had been an unnecessary flaunting of his power, not to mention a drain on his reserves when he needed it most. Still, shaking up the Noviodunam mages had given him a deep sense of satisfaction. How shaken up was evident by the late entry of Abarsam and Jacques. The former had been delivering a tongue-lashing to Jacques, judging by the incensor's furious but sullen expression as Abarsam curtly told him to attempt basic repairs to the wards. For his part, the Kushian aquamage was all grace and diplomacy as he guided Queen Xiaolian to an elevated seat a few paces away from the table.

Sinan worried most about Abarsam where a magical fight was concerned. He understood the basics of the truce curse that had been placed on everyone who had entered the Noviodunam hall tonight—it was a water spell of incomparable complexity and power.

Whether it truly applied to Abarsam as well as everyone else was something only the Grand Vizier knew for sure.

He turned his attention back to the emptiness at the end of the table, reaching out with his senses for any hint of the power that had once rested there. Letha was one of the central martyrs in his mother's new religion, and he had heard the effects of her death pyre curse still lingered in the Noviodunam. Did he dare find out if more than that remained?

Naghwe had been eager for him to use this opportunity to restore Letha's Throne—another impossible task added to his already full list.

He had to focus on his top priority: getting Xiaolian to hold off on attacking his city. The Council of the Living had plans if he failed—they had plans if he didn't survive tonight—but his offer to help locate and rescue Rixende was his main bargaining chip to buy more time for Karakoncolos to prepare for another invasion.

"The full body of the Synod will meet later tonight." Abarsam made sure Xiaolian was comfortably seated in what had to be the chair designated for the sovereign of Soissons and left Gallmau and Meri to stand on either side of her, playing the role of her Garde Royale.

Before sitting in the Aquamage Throne, decorated with a silver fish leaping over stylized waves, Abarsam gestured to the Medicus Throne, marked by a serpent wrapped around a tree trunk. "Magus Valentina, as you are the highest-ranking medicus mage in the chamber, please do us the honor of sitting in the chair for your guild."

"Thank you, Grand Vizier." Valentina cast an anxious glance at Sinan before she sat. Her chair was closer to the empty end of the table where he stood than Abarsam's. "I should point out, however, that I have resigned from my academic post at the Noviodunam."

Jacques stalked back from the doors, which he had fixed

enough that they at least swung shut. Sinan sincerely hoped the full repair would take an excessive amount of time and labor on the fire mage's part.

"Your refusal to accept the protection of the Noviodunam almost cost you your life in Iotape, Valentina." Jacques threw himself onto the incensor chair, which featured a bird with wings of fire as a symbol of his guild. "This plan of yours to join the fight against the necromancer who took Rixende is even more foolhardy."

The medica's eyes flashed, and Sinan wondered if the incensor was set on infuriating everyone in attendance tonight. "Apparently, Magus Zhang Jue did not share your low opinion of me, since he requested my assistance with the same invitation you received."

Jacques let out a long, angry breath of frustration and turned his attention to Sinan, who had elected to remain standing, still trying to sense any presence of Letha in the darkened end of the conference room. "Go ahead and crouch in the dust of what used to be the death witch chair. Whatever charred bits of Letha the Witch remain are supposedly buried underneath the floor."

Sinan, initially furious at the insult, tried to process what he had heard. Could the Noviodunam mages who had martyred Saint Letha have been foolish enough to inter her remains in the Synod meeting room?

Letha's undead spirit, if he could raise her, might give him the answer.

Ghost magic wasn't his strong suit, of course. But bones —well, other than shadow work, osteomancy was one of his greatest talents.

He steadied himself with a few deep breaths and reached out with his Gift. In the empty space where the throne had been there was a floor of clay tiles, and underneath that, packed earth. Sinan could detect thaumaturgic power in the earth, tiny life forms living and dying, and when he stretched his senses, bits of bone. Human in origin and half-decayed, they were scattered into the soil. Concentrating harder, he sensed pieces of a femur and part of a broad shoulder blade—remnants of a body which had been consumed by fire but not entirely disintegrated into ash.

He felt the empty framework of what had once been living osseous tissue and pushed his powers to call to it. He had extended himself far too much this evening—Naghwe would chide him for this, assuming he lived long enough to face his mother's criticism—but the temptation to connect to one of his religion's greatest martyrs was too strong.

Something stirred in the earth. It was a dead, empty thing, a mere scrap of mineral matrix that would appear to the human eye as little more than a pale pebble.

Sinan could tell it was much more than that.

The room quieted as a sense of unease spread to the other living inhabitants. They might not be as attuned to necromantic forces as he was, but the sense of expanding power, of chaos itself, would be evident to even those without a trace of magical awareness—and the mages in the room must know now he was planning to do something major.

The clay tiles of the floor exploded in a spray of dust.

A grinding noise filled the air—a disturbing sound, like steel scraping against rock—and the first part of the skeleton broke through. Finger bones emerged from the disrupted earth like pale fungi, followed by the carpal bones of the hand, and finally an entire arm reached up to grasp the conference table.

Valentina gasped, and Jacques let out a curse that wasn't in keeping with court etiquette.

The magic accelerated after that, and Sinan no longer needed to expend his limited reserves of energy into what followed. Saint Letha had been awakened, and she no longer needed Sinan to return to where she had spent so many hours in the company of those who would eventually condemn her to death and gloat as she died screaming in the flames.

Revenge was always a potent incentive for a spirit to return, and Letha had good reason to hate the Synod.

Another bony arm grasped the table, and a headless skeleton faced the horrified faces of Sinan's enemies. More bones boiled up from the disrupted earth and began to form the base of a seat. The skeleton sank into a sitting position, leg bones morphing into the bottom of the chair. The additional skeletal material became more varied, with rows of incomplete small skulls from young infants mounted on the throne's arms, and ribs of different sizes splaying out to form the shape of wings on the seat's back. The intricate bones of an adult skull, from large curved plates to the delicate pieces that fit into the empty nasal cavity, flew together. One of the skeletal hands held the newly recreated skull up, as a bony fist on the other arm opened to reveal a gold sphere. That hand popped the object into the left eye socket, then reached up to rest the skull on the crest of the throne.

Sinan blew out a stream of air and shadow at the throne. Dust and grime flew up into a dark mass in the air, and a face took shape—a woman with hawk-like features who had one eye open and glaring and the other gleaming a dull gold.

Letha opened her dust-cloud mouth and screamed.

Gallmau and Meri jumped, but other than moving to shield the queen with their bodies, wisely made no move to attack Saint Letha. Jacques lost the last of his self-control and sent a fireball at her that lit up the room and sent out a searing blast of heat. An arc of water struck the flames as Abarsam moved to counter the incensor's attack, leaving only a mist of vapor.

Letha hung in the air a moment longer, her features contorting into a sneer of dismissal, until her dust dispersed into the air in the room.

"Enough, Jacques!" Abarsam bellowed the command at the younger mage, all pretense of diplomatic poise dropped. "You have no concept of the risk you're taking."

Sinan's knees shook, the toll of his expenditure of power hitting him hard. His reserves were far too low—Valentina alone could take him in a fight—and his only recourse was to bluff his way out of this.

He walked over to the new Throne of Letha, sat down, and leaned back.

"Thank you." Sinan draped an arm over the fused bones of the throne and addressed Jacques. "This seat will do nicely."

The incensor flushed, both hands gripped into fists, as Sinan waited to see if Jacques would incinerate him with a surge of fire. He couldn't even muster up a shadow shield at this point, so if Abarsam hadn't been truthful about the truce curse applying to everyone, Sinan would die on a chair fashioned from the remains of Saint Letha the Ever Despairing.

Even his mother would approve of a death like that.

A snort of laughter broke through the tension, and Gallmau touched two fingers to his head and gave a mocking salute. "You walked right into that one, Jacques."

"If it's not too much trouble"—Valentina had recovered enough to put a sarcastic bite in her words to the incensor—"perhaps you could avoid provoking our necromancer guest into summoning vengeful spirits into the conference room until after I've left it."

Abarsam cleared his throat. His outward calm had returned, even as his words held an undercurrent of anger. "I believe it's best to wait to address what has occurred until the full Synod meeting later tonight. Our current discussion is about the rescue of the Dauphine of Soissons, and that is all."

"There's nothing to talk about." Jacques reached into his suit jacket—Sinan watched closely to see if he would pull out a magical weapon—but the incensor threw a rolled sheet of parchment tied with a red silk tie onto the table. "Magus Zhang Jue sent out letters for assistance prior to his death, along with strict instructions regarding the composition of each rescue party—a group of no more than three, comprised of a mage capable of slaying a necromancer and two companions of his choice. The Grand Vizier and I, accompanied by our chosen guards, will be the only ones involved in the rescue."

"I have the same letter." Valentina also produced a rolled parchment. "We don't know what abuses or injuries the princess may have suffered during her captivity, and it's crucial she have access to medical care as soon as possible. I've hired two guards with military experience. They will suffice."

Gallmau spoke next, his amusement over Jacques's discomfort gone, replaced by irritation. "I've got a letter too, and Meri and I know something about killing Bone Lords."

More than merely something. The Lioness and her prince partner were infamous killers of the Blessed, but they had taken down other mages as well.

"You don't have a sorcerer, dear Prince." Abarsam gestured to the chair across from him, featuring a stylized catfish underneath a cloud divided in half by a jagged line. The throne of the fulgari guild, which the recently murdered Sorcier du Roi had belonged to, sat empty. Zhang Jue had been more than a mere electromage, though. His command of weather magic and knowledge of Artifacts was legendary, as was his ruthless cruelty toward any of the Blessed unfortunate enough to fall into his clutches. "I have no doubt my dear friend Zhang Jue reached out to you and Lady Meri hoping for the two of you to stand by his side. You both have bravery and honor in abundance, but without a skilled practitioner of the magical arts you won't be able to assist in this battle."

It was odd Zhang Jue would ask the king's exiled son and his notorious Tomb Fighter partner to serve as his bodyguards, when he had his choice of blindly loyal Shields to choose from. Then again, everything about the abduction of the princess of Soissons been bizarre from the start.

Gallmau glared at the Grand Vizier, but Meri wasn't paying attention to his speech. She had crouched down to whisper into the Queen's ear.

"The death witch doesn't have an invitation." Jacques substituted an insult for Sinan's name, since there wasn't much else he could do with the truce curse in place. "His false protestations that Karakoncolos had nothing to do with this crime aside, the Sorcier du Roi chose only a select few for this mission, and we represent those able to travel by tomorrow."

"Why is this so convoluted?" Sinan had no way to refute the incensor's point that he didn't have a letter from a member of the benandanti asking the Prince of Shadows for help, but he had to point out the absurdity of this entire affair. "Both the government of Soissons and the Noviodunam are willing to start a war with my people over this incident, yet the matter isn't important enough to send more than one incensor and an aquamage. The princess was abducted weeks ago, but you waited until a formal dress ball to announce she had been taken. If Zhang Jue asked for help from Kush, he must have asked for the same from his own country. Why would you wait for a feast but not for the best sorcerers Qing has to offer?"

"I can't believe I'm defending Sinan of Karakoncolos, but he makes a valid point." Valentina was an unusual source of support, but the two mages' refusal to allow her to help had made him and the medica unlikely allies. Gallmau and Meri had grown oddly quiet, and Sinan couldn't guess what the Tomb Fighters were thinking.

Queen Xiaolian, who had leaned over to listen to another whispered comment from Meri, turned her head to look at Abarsam after Valentina spoke.

The Grand Vizier avoided her gaze and folded his hands in front of him. "I'm not at liberty to discuss the reasons behind our strict timeline in the present company and neither is Magus Jacques. Both Magus Valentina and Monsieur de Rohan have the Synod's eternal gratitude for their offers of assistance, but we cannot accept them. As for you, Magus Sinan," Abarsam used the standard honorific, albeit grudgingly, "you came to the Noviodunam to be heard, and we have provided you with both the privacy and safety to do so. We will do no more."

"In gratitude for this unprecedented courtesy, you unleashed an undead spirit into the conference room and restored that monstrosity you're sitting on." Jacques jabbed a finger at Sinan. "Technically you didn't attack us with magic directly, but unleashing Letha is worse. Our recommendation to the Queen is that Karakoncolos is too great a threat to her kingdom and the world to remain standing, and you have only proved that tonight."

This exchange with Jacques was pointless, and Abarsam wasn't about to divulge any more information. Fine. Sinan needed to speak to the only person in the room who could compel information from the Synod.

"Maybe the members of the Noviodunam in attendance aren't at liberty to discuss the details of your daughter's abduction because they're the ones that took her." Sinan focused on the Queen and no one else. "A new declaration of war against their enemies, public sympathy for their fight against my people and maybe"—Sinan extended his hand in Gallmau's direction—"a new heir to the throne who doesn't share your reluctance to get involved in the affairs of witches."

Gallmau looked ready to say something, most likely ill-advised and threatening, but Meri hissed a warning, and he kept quiet. Jacques, of course, managed to outdo anyone else in the room when it came to losing his temper.

"How dare you accuse me of being involved with the princess's abduction." Jacques was out of his chair now, and he cupped two fireballs in each hand, as his voice choked with anger. "Zhang Jue was like a father to me, and I would die for Rixende."

"Enough." Abarsam slammed his fist against the table, and the flames in Jacques's hands fizzled into vapor. "The invitation, a magus of sufficient ability, and the ability to travel between dawn and dusk tomorrow. These are the absolute requirements, and the full Synod will vote to agree with us tonight. This discussion has ended."

"No." Meri drew both of her weapons, and the rasp of her blades sliding out silenced the room. "It's only just begun."

12

SINAN

Sinan tried to call up his shadow armor as the Lioness of Abdju started walking beside the conference table toward him—and failed. To make matters worse, while Meri strolled along, flipping the blades in her hands as if she was entertaining an arena crowd, Gallmau began to move parallel to her along the other side of the table.

He wasn't the only one alarmed by the actions of the Tomb Fighters.

Jacques stood up with an expression of offended outrage, but the prince didn't as much hit him as merely flex his biceps as he passed, and the fire mage ended up sprawled on top of the table.

Valentina, possessing a good deal more sense, stayed in her seat and kept her hands folded on her lap as the King's son walked past her. On the other side, Meri passed

Abarsam, who lifted his palm and conjured a small sphere of water to float above his hand. A silent warning about the truce curse, no doubt.

Meri's weapons, if she used them against Sinan, would invoke the curse.

Any relief that might have given him vanished when he realized it was the young prince he needed to worry about. While Meri was making a beautiful and deadly spectacle of herself, Gallmau was walking up to him without any weapons or powers that would trigger a gruesome death if he attacked Sinan. Without his shadow armor and without the ability to magically retaliate without bringing the curse down on him, Sinan would be no match for the prince's strength. Gallmau could tear him limb from limb, if he felt like it.

The pair moved closer, neither in any hurry, and it took all of Sinan's self-control to maintain his casual posture on the throne chair. This would be an excellent time for Letha to make another appearance.

No undead saints rushed in to help, and Sinan tensed as Meri came within striking range.

The Lioness swung around to stand next to him and crossed both swords against her chest in an arena salute. Sinan had barely begun to process she wasn't trying to kill him when Gallmau clapped a huge hand on his shoulder and tossed a rolled sheet of parchment onto the table.

"We're going with Bone Boy." Gallmau grinned down at Sinan after that insult, ignoring the glare Sinan gave him in response. "We have an invitation, our schedule is wide open tomorrow, and I think our spooky friend here has proven he can fight his own kind."

"He even has a fancy new chair." Meri eyed the infant skulls lined up on the throne, symbolic of the murders of

Blessed infants slain before they were old enough to protect themselves, and gave a pretend shudder. "Not my decorating taste, but I think it suits him."

Sinan glanced from one Tomb Fighter to the other, still in shock at the stunt they had pulled off, but doing his best not to show it.

"Are you both mad?" Jacques had recovered from being thrown onto the table, and now he sounded more incredulous than furious. "The two of you make a living killing his kind, and now you plan to join forces with him."

"The Lioness of Abdju thinks we're all witches." Valentina didn't appear as surprised as Jacques and Abarsam, or for that matter, Sinan himself. He had not seen this coming. "You told them they needed a mage who could fight a necromancer. They decided to get one who *is* a necromancer."

"The full Synod will not approve this." Abarsam shook his head. "Nor should they."

"The Synod should not refuse to abide by the rules they have set up for my daughter's rescue." Queen Xiaolian spoke up at last, and her words had a hard edge, despite her serene expression. "You have outlined what is required of anyone wishing to return my daughter. My husband's son has met all of the Synod's requirements, and he will go with my blessing."

"With all due respect, Your Majesty, this is not a decision the Queen of Soissons can make." Jacques turned to Xiaolian. "This affair has taken the life of a Synod member, and as an independent sovereign state, the Noviodunam has the final say in the matter."

Queen Xiaolian rose to her feet. She was not a tall woman or physically imposing in any way. Still, Sinan held his breath as she approached the incensor.

"The Noviodunam is an independent state, yes." Xiaolian placed both of her hands on the table and locked eyes with Jacques. "A tiny enclave, inside the great city of Lutecia, and the much larger country of Soissons. I cannot overrule the decisions of the Synod of the Noviodunam, but I can make decisions for my country. And if those decisions require making it difficult for anyone or anything to go in or out of your compound, I think you'll find the Noviodunam to be quite small indeed."

The threat hung in the air as Jacques sat, stunned. Sinan would have enjoyed the moment, if he hadn't still been wondering if Gallmau and Meri were going to kill him.

Abarsam finally spoke. "Your Majesty, you have my sincerest apologies. I consider myself a mere guest in your country. If, in your wise opinion, you wish Monsieur de Rohan to join our company with his chosen companions, I will support this at tonight's meeting."

Jacques opened his mouth to speak, then shut it again, which was the smartest thing he had done all night.

"I doubt my opinion will be deemed important by the Synod, Madame la Reine." Valentina inclined her head toward Xiaolian. "But if the malandanti have formed themselves into a government and agree to hold others of their kind accountable for their crimes, I think this should be encouraged. I would ask, if you would allow me the honor, to have your blessing to join the quest as well."

"Of course, Dottoressa de Almania." Xiaolian took her hands off the table and looked straight at Sinan. "Do you agree to this arrangement?"

"So." Meri leaned over to whisper in his ear, her breath soft and warm on his cheek. She was far too close to him, even if she wasn't touching his skin. He felt an aching want that was all but unbearable. "Are you in?"

Sinan snapped his fingers, finding he needed a physical movement to perform even the simplest magic, and shut off the sound around them before he spoke. "I don't want or need your help."

The first part of that statement was true, but the second was a lie. Sinan could either agree to join two Tomb Fighters with a grudge against him or admit defeat. The Synod would only let him help if Xiaolian gave them no other choice.

"We don't need or want a Bone Lord, but this is the only way we can save Rixende." Gallmau put his hand on Sinan's shoulder again, and this time his fingers brushed against Sinan's ear. The touch sent a familiar jolt of lust and revulsion through him. He had enough reserves left to lash out with a remnant of his shadow wards, and the prince yelped and removed his hand.

"Touch me again," Sinan put as much threat and malice into his words as he could, "and I'll shrivel the skin off your fingers and leave you nothing but uncovered bones for a hand."

"We'll take that as a yes." Meri pointed to the expectant faces of Xiaolian and Abarsam. Valentina had leaned over to argue with Jacques. "Let the Queen hear your answer. And your conditions, which I'm sure you have."

Sinan tried to steady his breathing and block out the closeness of the two Tomb Fighters. Being near them threw off his ability to think. Taking on an unknown and powerful adversary while trying to avoid being killed by Meri and Gallmau would be insanely risky. Not agreeing to it would be admitting defeat.

If there was one thing Sinan hated more than Noviodunam mages and Tomb Fighters, it was personal failure.

He snapped his fingers again, and the sound enchantment vanished. Queen Xiaolian stood waiting for his reply, and Valentina cut short her heated exchange with Jacques to hear his response. "I'm not joining a rescue party for your daughter, Your Majesty, if you're planning to invade my home at any moment."

"I'm satisfied with your response to my letter," Xiaolian said. "You may send word to your Councils, if they are the proper authority in Karakoncolos, that I will not authorize any military actions against your city-state or support those from other parties while you are aiding this effort."

Sinan wasn't naive enough to think Xiaolian couldn't change her mind, but given it was in her interest not to get involved in another foreign war, this was the best he could hope for.

"As for yourself, Monsieur Kaya, I would be happy to extend the protection of the government of Soissons to you tonight and for as long as you are involved with the rescue." Xiaolian pinned Jacques with her gaze again. "I'm sure the Synod will as well. I ask only that you not harm any of my subjects with your magical talents."

"He can't walk out of here and onto the streets without causing a riot." Jacques spoke for the first time since the Queen had threatened both him and the Noviodunam. "If anyone attacks him—and I can't even guarantee the Shields will follow orders when it comes to the Prince of Shadows— his version of self-defense will leave a large body count."

"Allow us to help you leave the Palais de Feu." Abarsam turned to Sinan, his voice now resigned. "I understand you wouldn't want to go with the Shields, but I can offer you an escort by my son Baahir."

No, Sinan would not let himself be walked out like a stray cur on a leash. The trouble was, he didn't have a better way of leaving the compound safely. He tugged at the shadows around him with his mind, but without much effect. The entire Noviodunam was warded against shadow-walking.

Sinan gave up trying and glanced at Meri. "The three of us need to speak tonight in private about this partnership."

"We're not interested in joining you at whatever gravesite you're haunting while in town." Meri turned to Gallmau. "Where are we carousing this evening?"

"La Pissotte." Gallmau gave Sinan another grin. "Best cider in Lutecia. It's right behind the east wall of the palace. Look for some drunks getting tossed out onto the street and you'll find it without any trouble."

Not only was Sinan stuck with these two, they were both quite smug about trapping him in this arrangement. To make it worse, he'd need to expose himself to the general public to even meet with them.

He pulled at the shadows again, and this time added in a silent prayer to Saint Letha, asking for her assistance as the humble worshipper who had brought back her throne. Shadows slid up the sides of the chair, responding to his command. The Throne of Letha was restored, and he could use its power to escape the Noviodunam.

"La Pissotte it is, then." Sinan stood up and without further comment stepped off into the shadows.

13

_____

SINAN

Fatigue hit Sinan hard when he came out of the shadows. His control had weakened to the point that he had only moved himself several hundred paces from the Synod meeting room. At least he was outside the Noviodunam walls, but he was exhausted, dizzy, and an obvious target. He didn't even have his sword, since he could have hardly shown up armed to a formal ball while disguised as a merchant from Diustic.

He leaned against the stuccoed wall of a two-story house and blinked to clear his vision. The corner he stood in was dark, but the nearby street was lit by gaslights, and there was a fair amount of foot traffic going by. A shout went out behind him, and he whirled around to see an infuriated barmaid shoving an inebriated man into a puddle of water on the cobblestone streets. She added several colorful insults and an admonition to keep his hands to himself before re-entering a decrepit building and slamming the door shut behind her.

Sinan squinted at a battered wooden sign swaying from a post on the building. He had come out within spitting distance of La Pissotte, the tavern the two Tomb Fighters had insisted on as a meeting spot. Its dirty windows blazed with light, and he could hear shouts and off-key drunken singing even at this distance.

Lovely. He would provoke a bar brawl merely by walking inside, even if he made an attempt to disguise his appearance. He needed at least an hour to regain his strength before their meeting.

Focusing on the map of the city he had memorized, he began to move in the direction of the City of the Dead, the vast urban cemetery which held a reserve of necromantic power deep enough to refresh him and allow him to summon his mother as a corporeal spirit for her advice. It would be a long walk, but it was the safest place nearby. Xiaolian's promise of protection might not be enough to restrain those of her subjects who hated and feared the Blessed—and that category included everyone in the city.

As he trudged along, hood pulled down to cover his face, he took stock of all that had happened, obsessing over his mistakes and errors in judgment, rather than celebrating his successes. He had survived the evening and stopped the imminent threat of war with Soissons, but at a cost. Gallmau and Meri had neatly manipulated him into flaunting the Synod's restrictions on the rescue parties, putting himself in the absurd position of working with two dangerous enemies while trying to kill a third.

The fog of self-doubt and internal criticism only stopped when he realized he was being followed. His fatigue had weakened his senses but not eliminated them. Careful not to give any sign he had noticed his pursuer, he bowed his head further, as if in exhaustion, and reached out to find death.

A block went by before a flash of necromantic energy attracted his attention. It wasn't much—a small animal, perhaps. He spotted a carriage rumbling away and heard faint squeaks. As he drew closer he could make out the flailing shape of a large rat lying in the street, its forelegs struggling as its lower body remained paralyzed. Next to it was another rodent, this one fully crushed by the passing wheel and the source of the death energy.

He reached down to pick up the wounded rat and silenced its cries of agony by breaking its neck. The direct involvement in the shift from the order of life to the expanding chaos of death gave him a rush of power. He was nowhere near his full strength, but he should be able to work some ghost magic. Phasmancy didn't take anywhere near the power that shadow work did.

Too bad he was terrible at it.

Sinan's powers to manipulate shadow were the most powerful of any of the Blessed in centuries. That wasn't a mere boast—Sinan had been told this by members of the Council of the Dead who had died hundreds of years ago and had a basis for comparison. Ghost magic, on the other hand, had never come easy to him, when it had come at all.

He used a spoken spell to bind the animal's soul before it could escape into the Holy Void of Chaos. A novice at ghost magic would have done it better, but when he rested the furry body on the ground and rubbed his hands clean on his trousers, the rat stirred. The rodent rose to its feet, its movements jerky. An unnatural blue light emanated from the animal's tiny eyes, illuminating the filthy cobblestones under Sinan's feet.

Excellent. Sinan had a good idea of who was following him, and a Noviodunam-trained mage—especially one with access to the secrets of the benandanti—would be tracking death magic, not trying to keep visual contact with him.

"Go." Sinan pointed along the street. It wasn't typical to use verbal commands with an undead animal, especially such a small one. A *corpus animatum* should be easily controlled by the mind alone, according to his instructors in Karakoncolos. But his teachers weren't here to pick apart his spellwork, and Sinan wanted to confront the pursuer on his own terms. "You are bound to my commands and must obey."

The rat rose unsteadily onto his hind legs. Its body was now powered by magic, and it had none of the reflexes or speed of a living animal. It was little more than a meat puppet. Still, all he needed the creature to do was stagger down the road and act as a decoy.

The rat sniffed the air, and its eyes brightened, the blue light increasing in intensity.

Sinan frowned. Granted, he hadn't used this spell before, but as far as he could remember, the undead animal shouldn't be acting this way.

With a waddling motion totally unlike a normal rodent, the rat staggered closer to Sinan, then jerked forward. Sinan jumped back, a curse escaping his lips. The rat, for its part, ignored him as it bit into a moldy baguette lying on the ground.

"You couldn't possibly eat something that big." Sinan grabbed the end of the bread, but the animal hung on, its eyes blazing as it was lifted into the air. "Even if you were alive, which you're not. You're dead. Start acting like it."

The rat released the baguette, which was covered in a green mold and stank like an open sewer. Sinan resorted to pointing and tried another command spell. After twitching a few times, the rat gave him a wounded look and began to stomp away.

Sinan tossed the bread on the ground and drew shadow around himself. He stood, blending in with the night, until a cloaked figure passed his hiding spot. The traveler moved with caution, not speed, and Sinan could sense the magic around him.

After a moment's hesitation as he reached Sinan's position, the man took off again. The rat made a more consistent target, since a corpus animatum was as obvious as death magic could get, and within a few minutes Sinan was trailing after the man stalking him. He waited until the street traffic thinned before mentally directing the rat to take a quick turn, and the animal cooperated this time. A temple to the Three Prophets loomed on one side of the street, a handy landmark on the maps Sinan had pored over, and he was confident his decoy was leading the mage into a blind cul-de-sac.

His pursuer paused at the entrance to the alley, scanned the street around him, then strode toward the undead rat. Sinan walked out of his enveloping cloak of shadows after him.

The man summoned a ball of fire and sent it floating up into the air. The narrow space between the two buildings ended in a high wall, as the maps had predicted it would, and nothing more than a pile of refuse was illuminated by the light.

In a rattle and clank of debris, the rat backed out of the mass of garbage, dragging half a croissant with its teeth. The undead animal dropped the bread as the unnatural light of fire magic filled the space and turned to snarl at the mage, its glowing eyes still visible.

Sinan chose that moment to send streamers of his power through the space, and the incensor whirled around, finally understanding the trap he had walked into.

"There is no shadow without light, and no light without shadow." Sinan stepped into view, his hands at his sides in preparation for battle. In truth, he was in no shape for a fight, but if he was going to bluff he wanted it to be convincing. "I'd have thought you wouldn't be interested in another duel with me, Jacques, considering how our last one turned out."

Jacques Collins de Plancy slapped his hands together into the pose of non-violence with alacrity. He shook his head, and his hood fell back, revealing his face. "I didn't come to fight you."

"You've been stalking me through the streets with a benandanti spell." Sinan pushed back his hood as well and gave his old enemy a grim smile. "I'd hardly consider that non-threatening behavior."

"I wanted to speak to you privately." Jacques broke off as the rat dragged the croissant past him, the animal pausing long enough to growl at him, even with its mouth full. "By the Saints, what is that thing?"

"A corpus animatum." Sinan was tired, irritated, and in no mood to explain the basics of death magic to Jacques. "Did Odart of Dol not teach you about them in your lessons?"

"I didn't accede to my father's request to join the benandanti, and I don't regret the decision." Jacques took a deep breath. "Look, I had no choice but to follow you. The Shields are in an absolute frenzy, and they would never let me talk to you alone."

"Are your guards still despondent they didn't slit your throat when they were supposed to?" Sinan was all too familiar with the Shields of Quartus, who were commonly thought of as the personal guards of fighting mages in the Noviodunam. In truth, their main purpose was to ensure mages weren't captured alive by the Blessed. Jacques's own guards had failed him in that, and he had been Karakoncolos's prisoner before Odart had used Sinan's father as a hostage to get his son back. "If you have something to say to me, go ahead."

"Why are you working with the King's bastard and the Lioness of Abdju?" Jacques blurted out the words with his usual lack of restraint. "They hate your kind."

"I seem to recall you were the first to reject my offer to assist in the recovery of the princess." Sinan snapped the words out, but inwardly wondered if Jacques might be telling the truth. The incensor was taking a huge risk in leaving the safety of the Noviodunam, and if he wanted to try and kill Sinan, he wouldn't have attempted it alone. "An alliance with the two of them was hardly my first choice."

"If Rixende dies, Gallmau becomes the Dauphin." Jacques ran his fingers through his hair, forgetting his pose of submission. Sinan watched him closely but said nothing. Physical gestures, spoken spells—no mage of sufficient power needed those aids, and Jacques could probably set things on fire when he was asleep. "That's if she's even alive."

"You expect me to believe the entire Noviodunam can't discern if the heir to the throne of Soissons has passed beyond the veil?" This conversation was wasting Sinan's time. "Please stop pretending you don't know the benandanti can perform simple necromantic spells."

"The benandanti have been disbanded." Jacques sounded at once bitter and relieved. "My father is in forced retirement, and Zhang Jue only kept his position in the court out of deference to the loyalty oath he submitted to as Sorcier du Roi. There's no one left who will admit to knowing how to do that type of magic. But you must know."

"I'm not giving away valuable secrets to an enemy for no reason." Sinan made a gesture to the rat, which had been gnawing at the croissant with great enthusiasm but to little effect. The animal hobbled closer to him. He would need to release its soul soon, as it was unkind to leave a simple beast as a corpus animatum for any longer than necessary. On the other hand, Jacques would make a perfectly satisfactory undead servant, and Sinan regretted that both his agreement with the Queen and Karakoncolos law prevented him from turning the fire mage into one. "Leave me alone, and I'll try to restrain myself from killing you."

Sinan pulled on the shadows and was gratified to see that some of them responded. With his fatigue, he was only capable of moving a block or two away, but Jacques didn't know that.

"Rixende was taken to an area in the south guarded by a modified weather Artifact." Jacques got the words out in a rush. "Terra Amata. The entire area is now walled off by a mist, and the only entrance is through the Artifact itself. It adapts to the mage's affinity. I'll need a fire spell to unlock it when the time comes, and Abarsam will need his water magic. Nothing we've tried has had any effect on it, and believe me, half of the Noviodunam worked on it."

Sinan stilled. Artifacts were trouble he did not need. He knew little enough about Artifacts related to death magic, like the one Karakoncolos was built on top of and the smaller one near where Meri and Gallmau had been attacked.

"Please." Jacques's unexpected use of the word jerked

Sinan's attention back to the conversation. "Tell me if Rixende's alive."

"She's among the living, yes." Like it or not, Sinan needed information from Jacques, and it sounded like the fire mage was willing to give it to him. "My mother reached out beyond the veil to confirm it. She'll tell me if she dies."

"Did Naghwe say anything else about Rixende?" Jacques knew his mother was a corporeal spirit, of course. After all, his father had been the one who had killed her.

"No." Sinan didn't want to give Jacques any more details than he had to. "You're telling me that whoever did this was able to manipulate an Artifact to wall off a chunk of the countryside?"

"And sent back Zhang Jue's headless body with a shadow letter daring me to go after him." Jacques's voice was grim. "I already had the Sorcier du Roi's instructions of what to do if he was killed, but the shadow letter gave a specific date and time when the Artifact would open. Tomorrow, between dawn and dusk."

The Synod's strange behavior now made sense. They had waited as long as possible to make the news public, but they couldn't wait long enough for help to arrive from Qing or their other allies. Most of the Noviodunam mages would think a shadow letter could only be sent by one of the Blessed, proving the culprit was a necromancer. That wasn't true, but given the stiff penalties for even reading about death magic, it did rule out most of the mages in the city.

Except for benandanti like Jacques's father, Odart of Dol.

"I know only a handful of the Blessed who know anything about Artifacts, and none of them would have any interest in using one to keep the princess of Soissons hostage." That was true for Karakoncolos, but Sinan couldn't exclude the possibility that the Order of Katil was involved. They had sent Cliona out to kill him, and they guarded their secrets well—by killing anyone who might expose them. He still thought this mess could be a Synod plot to blame Karakoncolos, but he didn't think Jacques would have risked his life to speak to Sinan if he was part of it.

But there was another powerful mage involved in all of this—Abarsam the Magnificent.

"Perhaps you should investigate the Sultana of Kush. The University in Abdju has an entire department devoted to the study of Artifacts."

"That's why Abarsam's here," Jacques said. "I knew he was in the country, and I contacted him as fast as I could after Zhang Jue's death."

"So did Zhang Jue send Abarsam one of these invitations the two of you were going on about, or did you just give him a fake one?" Sinan knew the answer even before Jacques gave a reluctant nod.

"When Gallmau showed up with an invitation, Abarsam and I decided it would be best to set limits on who could attempt to get past the Artifact. Maybe Zhang Jue did reach out to the King's bastard for help, or maybe Gallmau and the Lioness forged theirs and convinced the Queen it was real. Then there's Valentina, who also received one. She showed it to me, and it has the Sorcier du Roi's seal. None of it makes much sense."

The only thing that did make sense was that this was an ambush, possibly for Sinan, or maybe even Jacques. In any event, whoever joined this quest would become a target if they weren't one already.

Sinan paused, knowing he shouldn't ask his next question—or at least shouldn't care about the answer. "Are you going to let Valentina go into this obvious trap with hired guards?"

"No, I got her to agree to go with me instead of a second Shield." Jacques threw up his hands. "Aren't you more worried about who you're taking with you? Gallmau will be the next King if Rixende dies, and even if he isn't that ambitious, the Lioness of Abdju might want to switch her title to the Queen of Soissons. Letting Rixende be killed and blaming you for it—that's their plan."

Sinan thought back to the two Tomb Fighters on the road to Lutecia and Meri crawling over to Gallmau, willing to sacrifice her life for his. Hardly the actions of a calculating schemer who was using the young prince for her own ends. "I'm not sure if I agree with you about their motivations. Either way, it doesn't matter. I intend to kill whoever put Karakoncolos at risk of war and anyone else who gets in my way. Including you. I'll see you in Terra Amata."

14

———

SINAN

Half an hour later, Sinan returned to the spot across the street from La Pissotte, annoyed with himself, Jacques, and the undead rat. The rodent had shadow-walked away from Sinan when he had tried to release its soul, which shouldn't be something a simple corpus animatum could do. Enough time had now passed that the Lioness and Prince Gallmau must be inside the tavern, and he felt as irritated about meeting the two of them in public as he did with his failed exorcism of his uncooperative death construct.

He crossed the street and pushed the front door of La Pissotte open. Stepping inside, he encountered a rush of warm air that brought odors of roasted meat and packed-in human bodies. He had considered and discarded the idea of trying to disguise himself for the meeting. Sitting down with the two Tomb Fighters would tell everyone who he was.

Meri and Gallmau weren't difficult to find. They were seated at a center table heaped to overflowing with pitchers of beverages and food. A bookish-looking young man dressed in court silks held a wine glass in one hand and massaged the prince's arm with the other. Another courtier with tousled black hair, a broad chest, and tight-fitting pants was chatting with Meri. He did not look like he spent much time with books.

Conversations stilled as Sinan walked to the table, and chairs began to scrape as more of the room's inhabitants realized a Bone Lord had entered the tavern and turned to stare at him.

This could get ugly fast.

Sinan had excellent spells to defend himself, but most of them involved killing as many of his attackers as possible in a short period of time. He didn't want to wipe out a building full of the Queen's subjects before even starting this quest. In another few moments, though, the only table in the place whose occupants weren't staring and pointing at him was the one with the two Tomb Fighters and their admirers.

Sinan came to a stop in front of the table. He had put his hood up and still had his sacred face paint in place. Gallmau's courtier, who had been going on about poetry, gave a gasp of alarm. He and the other man scrambled away without Sinan needing to say a word, which Sinan found quite gratifying.

"Look, Meri." Gallmau stretched back in his chair. He had changed into less formal clothing, and the white shirt he was wearing clung to his sculptured chest and arms. "Bone Boy decided to join us."

Meri nibbled at the piece of cake. She had thrown Gallmau's formal jacket over her arms for her visit to the tavern and looked as gorgeous and predatory as she had during the ball. "He also scared away my plans for the evening."

"You insisted I come to this disreputable location to discuss the partnership you forced upon me." Sinan did his best to look menacing, which usually didn't require this much effort on his part. "I'm here."

A chair hit Sinan in his legs. Gallmau gestured to the seat he had kicked out at him from under the table. "Sit down, then. I'm drinking cider, but they should have brandy around here. Real brandy, I promise, not the cursed kind you gave to me."

"You can't poison me, and I can't get drunk." Sinan sat down, mostly to make himself less conspicuous. The tavern grew tense and quiet, never a good sign. "You two do get paid to kill my people. I'd have assumed you'd be spending the evening getting ready for the quest tomorrow."

"We're celebrating in advance." Meri took a bite out of a large butter pastry and gave him a malicious smile. Right. The Lioness knew how uncomfortable Sinan was and had every intention of drawing this meeting out.

Celebrating seemed to involve alcohol for Gallmau and tasty food for Meri. As for the rest of the entertainment, both of them obviously liked handsome men. Sinan's mind, unbidden, began to wander into thoughts of what the two of them might be doing in their beds later tonight, and with whom. He jerked his attention back to the present.

"Why can't he get drunk?" Gallmau asked Meri. He pushed a bottle of cider toward Sinan. Speaking of food and drink, both would be welcome after an exhausting day when there had been little time to have either. But breaking bread with his two enemies wasn't something Sinan was willing to do. He pushed the bottle away.

"He has a protection sigil against poisons." Meri pointed

to the correct symbol on Sinan's cloak, which was—concerning. "Bone Lords are resistant to that sort of thing. Now fire, that's another story."

"Do you even know or care where we're going tomorrow, and what we might face?" Sinan now had solid information about the events surrounding Rixende's abduction, and if he was concerned about what they were walking into, both the Lioness and the prince should be even more worried. "My notion of planning for an upcoming battle is quite different than yours."

"If you did prepare like us, who might you like?" Gallmau indicated the people in the tavern with a wave of his hand. Even the prince was joining in with this game, trying to get a rise out of him.

Sinan had already sized up the crowd for potential threats, dismissing the table the two courtiers had retreated to as he eyed men with practical clothing and hard faces. Even more concerning, a massive man leaning against the far wall with a mug in his hand had to be a Shield of Thaschus, even if he was no longer wearing his uniform.

He hated being exposed to so many enemies at once. His heart was pounding, and a prickle of sweat threatened to smudge his sacred face paint. Dozens of eyes were upon him, filled with a mixture of fear and fascination. Sinan couldn't wait to get out of here.

Gallmau took back the bottle of cider Sinan had refused. "Since you're not going to eat or drink, but go straight for a tumble, tell us who you like. We might be able to introduce you to someone fun."

The only two people in the room Sinan would care to share a bed with if he could were sitting across from him.

Saints, he hated himself for that.

He stood up. "This is a waste of my time. Drink yourself into a stupor and fuck whomever you choose. I'm leaving."

"Sit back down." Meri shook her head in irritation. "By the Prophets, you're a prickly bastard. Do that sound trick of yours. We don't chat about business with a whole room eavesdropping in." She cocked her head in the direction of the Shield leaning against the wall.

Perhaps there was more to their mocking banter than simple spite.

Sinan took his seat and created a bubble of quiet around them. Meri still lowered her voice as she leaned forward. "Abarsam told me there's a Witch Stone involved, and we're traveling to Terra Amata before sunrise. Do you know anything useful?"

"Jacques gave me the same information." Sinan was impressed Meri had succeeded in prying the truth out of the Kushian aquamage.

"How did you and Jacques talk without trying to kill one another?" Gallmau poured himself the cider he had offered Sinan. "By the way, it's not easy to get me drunk."

"He wanted to ask me if Rixende was dead. There's a type of phasmancy—ghost magic—that can reveal if someone has passed beyond the veil."

Gallmau stilled. "Is my sister still alive?"

"Yes, she is." Sinan felt an odd flutter in his chest as relief flooded over Gallmau's handsome face.

"What else did the fire witch say?" Meri demanded.

"Jacques thinks Gallmau wants to ensure Rixende dies, so he becomes the Dauphin and you become the future Queen of Soissons." Sinan saw Meri's mouth harden at the accusation, but her face otherwise remained impassive. "Is that true?"

Gallmau didn't handle the question as calmly. He half-stood up, perhaps to shout at Sinan or take a swing at him, but Meri grabbed his shoulder to stop him. After a moment, Gallmau spat out, "That's a filthy lie, and the next time I see that overheated fire boy I'm going to give him a good smack. Now it's your turn to answer me. If we get my sister back safe, what are your plans? I don't want a Bone Lord as my brother-in-law."

"I can't believe we're discussing this." Sinan held up his hand and began counting off reasons on his fingers. "I have no interest in marrying anyone, much less one of my enemies. I don't want to act as breeding stock for the Grimoard dynasty, and as one of the Blessed, I'd be unlikely to succeed in that capacity. Finally, I find it repellant your sister is being used as the prize in this farce of a quest. The whole affair is like a tawdry coffeehouse tale."

"That's how the best stories go, though." Gallmau settled back in his chair, not as skilled as Meri at putting on an air of nonchalance but trying anyway. "Fight the undead army, kill the necromancer, rescue the princess—the court poet's working on a new poem along those lines right now."

"Does your story include outright lies by the heroes? Abarsam doesn't even *have* an invitation from Zhang Jue." Sinan stopped mid-rant and flinched. His shadow shields, which reacted faster than his mind, were swirling around him, and Meri's blades were less than a foot from his face.

"What is that?" Her voice dropped to a low growl, and the expression of hatred on her face was so intense Sinan kept up his protections even when Gallmau grabbed at her arm. Even the prince looked startled by her sudden hostility. She must have used her Gift to get her weapons into position.

By the Lady, she was fast, even for a speed fighter.

He felt a tug on his sleeve and looked down to see his

undead rodent servant perched on his arm, eyes glowing blue and whiskers twitching in interest.

"It's a rat." Gallmau had a talent for stating the obvious. "With funny eyes. Put your blades away, Meri. You've been awfully stabby lately."

"It smells like death magic." Meri jabbed one of her blades at the animal, but Sinan expanded his shadow armor, and the tip of her sword stopped as if hitting a stone wall.

Sinan didn't want to start a full-blown battle with the Lioness, but he wasn't afraid to demonstrate his ability to defend himself. Abarsam's water swords had impressive power, but they couldn't get past his shadow shields as long as he had the strength to maintain them. "It should. It's a corpus animatum I created. If you react like that every time I use my Gift, this is going to be a difficult partnership."

"How many other undead slaves do you have?" Meri kept her swords gripped tight in her hands. "Victims you murdered, then stole their souls so they'd be cursed for eternity—I want to know."

"Only this one." Sinan hadn't expected a Tomb Fighter to accept either him or his abilities, but Meri's reaction to the small animal was excessive. "He'd been run over and was dying anyway. Besides, Karakoncolos law forbids turning a human into a corpus animatum."

"Your city is protected by drowned men who crawl out of the water to tear the flesh off their victims."

Meri knew about the *hortdan*, Karakoncolos's aquatic army that defended the underground waterways leading to his city. Her hatred of his people aside, she was oddly focused on corpse spells.

"The hortdan are ancient soldiers cursed centuries ago for razing a city and slaughtering everyone in it." Sinan tried a muttered spell to force the rat to leave before the Lioness became more violent. It had no discernable effect on the animal. "They've been haunting the rivers of Zyx long before Karakoncolos was founded."

A good thing, too, since they guarded the water routes crucial to delivering food and other goods to his underground home. Although they did make travel by boat more exciting than it needed to be.

Gallmau held his hands out for calm, and Meri jammed her blades back into their scabbards. The prince leaned forward to regard the undead rodent. "Nice pet you have there. Maybe he wants some cheese."

"It can't eat food. It's dead." Sinan gave up arguing with Meri and focused on stopping Gallmau from hand-feeding the disobedient death construct his limited grasp of ghost spells had created.

The prince held out a piece of cheese from the plate in front of him anyway, and the rat scrambled off Sinan's arm and hopped onto the tabletop.

Meri's hands flew to her sword hilts again.

Why hadn't he spent longer trying to release the animal's soul? His creation might need a full exorcism, and he didn't have the skills or time to do that. He might have to ask for his mother's help, which would be humiliating.

The rat stood up on its hind legs and waddled over to the prince, sniffing the air and ignoring Sinan entirely.

Unlike Meri, Gallmau appeared amused by the corpus animatum. "You don't like obeying your Bone Lord master, do you?" The prince pointed to the platter in front of him and addressed the rodent in soft, sweet tones, as if the creature were a small child. "And you're polite enough to accept my friendly offer of dinner, unlike him. So here you are— three of the finest cheeses in Soissons."

The animal's whiskers quivered at the piece in Gallmau's huge hands. Then it sprang forward with a snarl, landing on top of the food. The prince pulled back, startled, and the rat and the entire platter of cheese vanished into shadow.

"That was creepy as fuck." Gallmau grabbed his mug of cider as if it might disappear as well. "Can't fault your pet for its taste, though."

Three men walked up to the table, and Sinan dismissed the barrier that kept sound from escaping or entering their space. He knew how this would go, and the time for talking was over.

Two of the trio were visibly intoxicated, with the anger and overconfidence that comes to some men with strong drink. Those he could deal with, possibly by injuring them severely but not fatally. The third was the Shield.

"Fucking death witch, burn in Hell." One of the drunks led with that, which wasn't promising. Sinan sent more shadows swirling around him and began to rise to his feet. He had only promised not to harm any of the Queen's subjects unless attacked. This was a set-up by the Shields, and he wasn't about to risk his own life by trying to avoid killing people who wanted him dead.

Gallmau sighed and wiped his mouth on his sleeve. "I'll take the two drunks. You get the big guy."

"Fine." Meri put on a flirtatious smile, which was highly inappropriate for the situation. "Sinan, shadow-walk out of here. We've got this."

"I said, burn in Hell!" The man who had spoken first tried to grab the back of Sinan's neck and began to punch at the shadow shield.

Sinan could use the bands of power to slice the man's hands off, but the fool would bleed to death in short order. His powers were all—or nothing but death.

"I don't need the two of you to defend me." Sinan sent a jolt of power through his shields, and the man cried out in pain. That was about it for nonlethal force, and the next time the man tried to touch him, it would be the last thing he ever did. There were shouts from people in the tavern and chairs started to turn over as a crowd gathered around them.

Not good, not good at all.

"You need us to stop a massacre." Meri stood up and whipped off the coat she had draped over her dress for the ball. Under her breath, she snarled, "Now, I said."

Sinan raised his hands and faded into shadow. He hated to leave like a coward and allow two people who despised his kind to fight for him. Holding himself inside the darkness, he murmured a prayer to the Lady to give him strength and prepared to step out again. Like it or not, he had joined forces with the bastard prince and the Lioness of Abdju, and their enemies were his, at least for now.

Meri was suddenly on the table, her long skirt gone, posing like a Kushian court dancer with a tight gold top, uncovered arms, and flowing silk trousers that must have been underneath her Continental-style dress. She waved a pair of large men's pants in the air as if they were a battle flag.

"Not the first man who's lost his britches after one look at me, and he won't be the last." Meri pointed to the Shield, who was on the floor, red-faced and naked with his shirt knotted around his legs.

Laughter and shouts of "Lioness! Lioness!" rang out from the crowd.

Gallmau grabbed both of the drunks who had been staring open-mouthed at the Shield by their shirts and hoisted them over his head as if they weighed no more than tankards of ale.

"I know most of you think these two are pretty deep in their cups to pick a fight with the Lioness of Abdju and me." His voice boomed out over the room, and the crowd pointed and roared in mirth as the men clawed at the air helplessly. "But I say, they're not drunk enough." He lowered the men down, then dropped them the final foot in a heap on the floor. "Free drinks for the whole pub—on me!"

The crowd roared and surged forward, slapping Gall-mau's back as Meri blew kisses and brandished her swords in a coquettish pose.

"That's our true king!" shouted someone to general applause, and Sinan allowed himself to slip away, the heat and noise of the merriment fading away into the cool silence of shadow.

15

MERI

By noon of the following day, Meri found herself in the unusual situation of hoping a Bone Lord would show up to join her.

She stood with her arms folded, regarding the Witch Stone in Terra Amata. It was similar to the one on the road to Lutecia where Tharin and Karabil had played their last game of cards. Also arched-shaped, it was taller and wider than the one near the capital. Dense fog obscured the landscape beyond the arch, blotting out an area close to a full day's march in length and a similar distance in width. The mist had an unnatural movement to it, a writhing motion like something inside wanted desperately to get out.

When they first arrived, Meri refused to accept Jacques's insistence that every attempt to pass through the fog had failed. She dragged Gallmau with her, and they walked into it with weapons drawn—and then walked out right back to their original starting point.

From then on, the day had played out like most quests Meri had participated in—hours of boredom waiting for minutes of sheer terror.

Gallmau ambled up to her, handing her a canteen of sweetened water, even though she hadn't needed to drop into her speed. The only danger they had faced so far was falling asleep after lunch.

"Any sign of him?" she asked as she took a sip, knowing the answer.

Along with the other two teams of rescuers, they had begun their journey to Terra Amata in the predawn hours, accompanied by twenty Shields of Thaschus and a similar number of the Gardes Soissons. It had hardly been a surprise that Sinan hadn't shown up to spend quality time on horseback with those kinds of enemies, but they had arrived hours ago and the Prince of Shadows had not deigned to appear.

"Nothing yet." Gallmau joined her in watching the activity in front of the Artifact, where Abarsam was making his attempt to open the arch. Jacques had taken most of the morning to get his group in, which consisted of himself, Captain Caron—the same Shield who had tried to start a bar fight with Sinan last evening—and Valentina. Despite Jacques's history with the pretty medica, or perhaps because of it, he had taken her in place of his second Shield bodyguard.

The hot-tempered fire witch might still be at it, had Abarsam not insisted he try the pattern of magic Valentina had suggested, over and over again, as she scribbled notes on his failed attempts.

Large brass bowls filled with water were placed in a

circle around the Grand Vizier, as he stood quiet and still in front of the arch. Even Meri, who had experience watching Abarsam do magic, was initially perplexed by his inaction. Then she noticed the wisps of vapor from the bowls, the liquid inside of them evaporating at a rapid rate. One of the symbols on the Witch Stone's surface began to pulse, emitting a flickering blue light. Abarsam gave a nod of satisfaction, then left both his guard and son behind at the portal and walked toward them.

"The Artifact should open again soon." Abarsam waved at the Witch Stone, and another sigil glowed blue.

Jacques, Valentina, and Captain Caron had been able to walk through when the incensor's red glowing marks spanned the entire arch. It looked like Abarsam was well on his way to reopening it.

"With the learned Magus Valentina's suggestions and my observations of Magus Jacques's initial attempts, I was able to solve the puzzle with my water affinity. A slower method than the incensor technique, but I'm confident it will save time in the long run."

Meri handed the canteen to the Grand Vizier. Aquamages risked dehydration when using their magic for long periods of time. "You didn't want to throw a tantrum and hurl fire at the thing until it opened? It certainly took Jacques long enough with that approach."

The Kushian aquamage smiled and accepted the flask, taking several long swallows before answering. "My colleague has the typical temperament of an incensor, I agree. I apologize for that, as well as for doubting your resolve to join this quest. Partnering with the Prince of Shadows is a bold move—and a risky one."

"He's not even here, so we're not in much danger." Gallmau sounded glum. Both he and Meri had reluctantly concluded Abarsam had been telling the truth—they needed a witch to get inside and rescue Rixende. "So, why does everyone call Sinan a prince? He made it sound like Karakoncolos is a paradise for radicals."

"Sinan's blood is as common as it comes." Abarsam, the son of poor water sellers, nevertheless was a firm believer in monarchy. "Necromancers have no concept of the Divine-given right of rule that belongs only to those of royal blood. They live together as animals do, bickering and arguing unless they need to band together against their enemies. Sinan's mother, the *venefica* Naghwe, used her sex magic to seduce one of the Iotape merchants who made his fortune trading with necromancers. Her son earned his sobriquet during the final battle of the Witches' War—by killing more than a hundred of the Noviodunam's best with his shadow powers."

Meri felt a brief stab of pain in her back, where her own undead necromancer lurked and waited to cause her death. He had been a veneficus—a male version of Naghwe.

"If Sinan does show up, do you think he really wants to rescue my sister?" Gallmau blurted out the question that must have been more at the forefront of his mind than the necromancer's nickname.

"It would, oddly enough, be in Karakoncolos's interest to drive a wedge between the Noviodunam and the royal family of Soissons by killing one of their own to return the princess." Abarsam turned back to watch the progress on the arch, where two more of his blue water sigils now glowed. "It would also be in Sinan's nature to kill both of you after you helped him reach that goal. He sees himself as the protector of the malandanti, if not a true prince."

"That's comforting," Gallmau said, then added more diplomatically, "Good luck out there, Grand Vizier. Of the available alternatives, your son Baahir would be my first choice as a brother-in-law."

Abarsam inclined his head toward Gallmau and turned to Meri. "I'll pray for your safety and success in this venture. You know this already, my dear Lioness, but cold and fatigue are a necromancer's best weaknesses to exploit. They feed off the deaths of any who confront them directly, and exhaustion will do more good than a fireball—no matter what Jacques thinks."

A short time later, Meri watched as Abarsam, Baahir, and their giant guard walked through the arch as the fog beyond it thinned, showing a rocky trail leading up into a grove of trees. Inside the arch were overcast skies and a light sprinkling of rain. She blinked. Jacques, Valentina, and Captain Caron had walked out into a sunny meadow.

"That time it opened up onto a different location," Gallmau confirmed. In addition to his usual excellent sense of direction, the prince had frequently visited this location in Terra Amata with the royal household. He had even retrieved a hunting map of the region and taken it with them.

Within seconds, the thick white fog rolled back over the half-circle opening, and Abarsam's party disappeared.

"Are you sure you want to walk through that thing?" Gallmau's old friend Tumas's voice caused them both to turn. "This whole affair stinks of the devil."

The Gardes Soissons captain had come over with some ale, which Gallmau accepted with a pleased expression.

Gallmau took a gulp from the bottle and gave Tumas a grim smile. "If I have to go talk to the devil to get my sister back, then that's where I'm going."

"You've already been talking to him." Tumas scanned the area around them, apparently looking for Sinan.

"Where's your pet death witch, anyway? The Shields talk of little else but revenge and fear where he's concerned."

Meri, consumed with worry Sinan wouldn't show up and anxiety that he would, was about to snap at the captain to mind his own business when she breathed in the scent of falling snow.

"He's here." Meri didn't know where, exactly.

The next moment, a spasm wracked her spine, and it was all she could do to remain standing. Maybe Abarsam had been right about Sinan wanting to kill them, only wrong about the timing. If Sinan knew about her curse, he could work with the undead necromancer to kill her, then finish off Gallmau. Panic and pain hit her hard, and she reacted by pulling her blades.

"What are you talking about?" Gallmau shoved his bottle at Tumas for safekeeping and spun around in confusion. "I don't see anything."

"She can smell magic." Sinan's voice came from the ground, which made no sense at all until Meri spotted her own shadow acting strangely. The patch of darkness on the grass underneath them lengthened, and Sinan walked out to stand next to them.

Tumas mumbled a few curses, then switched to a prayer and made the Sign of the Saints. Another shape went from shadow to solid form—Mother Naghwe, all smiles and sharp teeth.

Meri sent up a silent prayer herself and gripped her blades as she faced the two necromancers.

"*Divinatio nidore.*" Mother Naghwe stepped closer to Meri and her swords with quick, bird-like steps. "Such an unusual talent. What do you smell from me, my dear?"

"Grave dust." Meri snarled the words out, her swords only a foot away from the old woman's neck. Could she kill a ghost with her water blades? She was about to find out. "And figs, for some damn reason."

"If you intend to attack me rather than work together, get it over with." Sinan had washed the gruesome face paint off but had kept on his burial shroud of a cloak over a close-fitting tunic and trousers. As before, he looked too damn beautiful to be a Bone Lord. The necromancer's sword was at his waist, and he had a travel pack in one hand.

"Glad you finally showed up, Sinan." Gallmau put his arm over Meri's shoulders and succeeded in getting her to sheathe her weapons with a few soothing whispers. He indicated Tumas. "Allow me to introduce Captain Tumas of the Gardes Soissons." He pointed to the circle of Shields who had gathered around to stare at the two Bone Lords. "You've probably tried to kill most of this lot already, so I'll pass on the formalities."

Sinan gave Tumas an unfriendly glare, which he then extended to everyone else. The Shields bunched together in a defensive formation, and a few of Tumas's troops who had wandered over took several steps back. The captain held his position by Gallmau's side, his face tight.

Sinan didn't bother with social niceties. "I'm here at the Artifact. I can kill you both, then go in, or you can join me as we discussed. It's up to you."

"You're quite confident how that fight would end, aren't you?" Meri struggled not to let her pain show on her face. If Sinan was already manipulating her curse, she didn't stand a chance. If he didn't know about it, she didn't want him to find out.

"Based on how the last one went, yes." Sinan ignored Meri and turned to Naghwe, which pissed her off even more.

His undead mother rubbed her hands together and reached out to hug him. "One last gift, then."

Over a dozen sigils on Sinan's cloak glowed bright purple, and Meri swore under her breath. She had never seen anything like it, and based on the startled gasps from the group of Shields, she guessed they hadn't, either.

Naghwe disappeared back into a pool of shadow on the ground, and Sinan walked to the Witch Stone without another word to either Meri or Gallmau.

The two of them had little choice but to grab their own packs and weapons and follow, after Gallmau gave Tumas a pat on the shoulder and a promise he'd be back to drink ale with him.

"This is a terrible idea." Meri couldn't walk without a limp, and Gallmau reached out for her hand, his face filled with concern.

"I think Sinan's enhancing my curse." Meri hesitated for a second, since there was so much she hadn't shared with Gallmau. "If he knows and can control me through it, we're both dead. He already has too many advantages, and he doesn't need us once we're away from the Gardes and the Shields. We should try to kill him after we go through the portal."

"I'm not even going to consider that." Gallmau lowered his voice as they drew closer to the arch, where Sinan now stood with his back to them. "We're going to need all the help we can get to save Rixende, not to mention that stabbing a fellow soldier in the back is dishonorable."

"Your honor's going to get you killed one day." Meri dragged herself forward, biting her lip as the spasms wracked her spine again. The undead Bone Lord inside her had barely made his presence known since the Death Hound attack. Sinan had to be helping him.

"Dottoressa de Almania said opening the Artifact was different for every mage that tries it." Gallmau tried that out as a conversation starter with Sinan. The necromancer hadn't bothered to acknowledge that they had followed him. "Something about affinities that matched—I didn't understand most of what she said."

"I don't need advice from Valentina about my magic." Sinan didn't so much as turn his head in Gallmau's direction.

"Well, that's what Jacques thought, and he had us waiting half a day to get the damn thing working. Abarsam listened to her and solved it in an hour."

Gallmau's comparison of Sinan to the incensor finally got the necromancer's attention.

He swung around. "I know how to get past it. What I don't know is if you're planning to pick a fight with me first." Sinan directed that part of his tirade at Meri, who stood with her arms crossed and her mouth set in a scowl.

"Go ahead." Meri steadied her voice, but she held herself as if she was in pain, and anyone trained in combat would recognize it as a weakness. "Just don't expect us to help you kill someone to do it."

Gallmau started to say something, but didn't get a chance. Sinan swung back to face the arch, his hands at his sides in a position Meri now recognized as an attack stance. Dark bands wove around the Witch Stone, and it cracked with a sound like the earth was about to split open under their feet. Then it shattered, chunks of its apex crashing into the dirt, leaving only two tilted pillars.

Meri stood, stunned. She had seen Sinan fight Cliona, but this demonstration of his power was breathtaking. He wasn't known as the Prince of Shadows for nothing.

"Fuck. Me." Gallmau, for his part, couldn't come up with anything more eloquent than that.

Sinan shot him an impenetrable look. Meri doubted the necromancer was concerned about Gallmau's foul language, and he couldn't possibly have misunderstood the cursing as a salacious invitation.

Hopefully Gallmau hadn't meant it that way, either.

Beyond the ruins of what had been an arch, the mists again began to clear, opening up to reveal a dirt road passing by the ruins of a church and cemetery, all under gray, sullen skies.

"Are the two of you coming?" Sinan turned to them with evident impatience. "We need to walk in at the same time."

Gallmau glanced at Meri, who pushed down the pit of fear in her stomach and walked to stand by the necromancer's side. The three of them approached the space between the broken pillars, which could have fit three Meri-sized people easily. Gallmau, on the other hand, took up far too much room and was forced to brush against the odd material of the Witch Stone and rub shoulders with Sinan at the same time.

That didn't go over well. As they stepped past what remained of the arch and onto the rough road, the necro-mancer quickened his pace, brushing off his arm and leg as if Gallmau had been a muddy dog who dirtied his clothing.

"As I said before, don't touch me." Sinan motioned them along with an angry wave of his hand. The mist began to creep forward, and both Gallmau and Meri sped up to avoid it. Within another few seconds, there was nothing behind them but thick fog. Getting out was going to be as hard as getting in.

"We get it, you don't like to cuddle." Meri walked with a smoother stride, now that the stabbing pain in her back had eased. "Why is the fog back? I thought you broke that cursed thing."

"I can't destroy an Artifact, especially one that enhances the powers of a weather mage." Sinan slowed his pace as they reached the graveyard. "I took a short cut in opening it. Also, I don't need to kill something every time I use my Gift."

"You still feed off death." Meri wasn't about to let this go. Maybe she wanted to goad Sinan into attacking them, so Gallmau would go along with her plan. Maybe she was so frustrated and angry about her curse that the Prince of Shadows was an easy target. "All of your kind do."

Sinan huffed in exasperation. "Consider this graveyard." The necromancer bent down to run his gloved hand over a flat grave marker, half covered by grass. "There's thaumaturgic residual—even though there were only about fifty souls buried here, over the years. I don't need any power from it right now, with what my mother gave me—but yes, the dead help my magic. They also help the grass to grow and worms to live. I don't know why I'm bothering to explain all of this to you, since you hate my kind so much you're probably not even listening. I need to find out where we are in Terra Amata. The portal would have placed the mages in three different locations."

"I was right when I thought each time the Artifact opened the view had changed," Gallmau said. "There were landmarks I recognized from the map that were nowhere near each other. Even the weather was different each time."

"You have a map?" Sinan straightened and turned to Gallmau, his posture less hostile. "Good. Show me where the others are."

"So you can murder them?" Meri asked. "We agreed to work with you to find Rixende and kill the necromancer who abducted her. I didn't sign up to help you get revenge on your enemies in the Noviodunam—or on us for that matter."

"Jacques's group entered the portal from the eastern boundary of the mist." Gallmau ignored Meri's glare of outrage as he answered Sinan's question in precise detail. "When Abarsam opened it, he came from the western side. This old church is in the southern part of the area enclosed by the mist, near a small lake that should be north of us."

"That's helpful information from one of you, for once." The wind whipped at Sinan's shroud cloak, and his black hair fluttered like a raven preening its feathers. Maybe Meri felt a chill because she was standing next to a necromancer in a graveyard. Or perhaps the temperature had dropped since they crossed through the fog. "I'd assume the Artifact would set all three groups as far away from where Rixende is being held as possible, and nowhere near each other in the unlikely event Jacques or Abarsam would want to work with me. That makes heading north the logical choice."

"You haven't answered my question." Meri stepped closer to Sinan, and the young necromancer let his hands fall to his sides.

"You haven't answered mine," Sinan responded. "Are you challenging me to a duel?"

"Hold on a minute." Gallmau stepped in between Meri and Sinan, which given his bulk, was quite effective. "Meri's angry because she thinks you've already attacked her with your magic."

Meri bit back an oath. Why was Gallmau so damn honest all the time?

Sinan tilted his head to one side again, as if both Gallmau and Meri baffled him. "I wouldn't do that."

"Because you're such an honorable monster, I'm sure."

Meri drawled the words out, sarcasm dripping from each one.

"I don't attack first unless there's no possible chance I could lose." Sinan said this with flat certainty. "Other than the Order of Katil, few of my people would, except the untrained ferals the two of you hunt for money. There are risks inherent in starting a fight with one of the Blessed—and death isn't the worst of them."

Meri drew in a shaky breath. Maybe Gallmau was right, and this wasn't the time to antagonize the necromancer. The awful pain and spasm in her spine had stopped, and if Sinan was working with the necromancer who had cursed her she should be screaming in agony now.

Sinan relaxed his hands more as Meri took a step back. "What do you think I did to you?"

Meri gave Gallmau their hand signal for silence. Thank the Prophets she had taught him that one first. "Other than poison the two of us, you mean?" She tried to change the subject and not answer the question.

"That was my mother's doing." Sinan rounded on Meri, his posture threatening again. "As was her decision to let both of you live. I offered you a small fortune to leave me alone to finish the fight with Cliona, and you didn't take it. That was after the two of you let the assassin out from under the carriage I had dropped on top of her. Then you threatened to take my head off with Abarsam's blades."

Gallmau stepped between them again. He reached into his bag and pulled out the map. "Here. Let's stop arguing and focus on getting my sister back."

Sinan came close enough to Gallmau to take the map, keeping a suspicious eye on Meri. "What's the building on the other side of the lake?"

"A royal hunting lodge." Gallmau motioned for Sinan to

keep the map, and Meri didn't protest. The small gesture of goodwill would help defuse the situation she had created, and Gallmau had memorized every detail on it anyway.

"I came here often with my father—the King, I mean, Saints rest his soul—when I was younger. We even brought Zhang Jue with us a few times, but he spent the trip reading, not hunting."

"Could it be the place the necromancer is holding Rixende?" Meri came over to stare at the map as well, pretending the distraction worked as well on her as it had on Sinan.

"It's close to where we came in." Sinan pored over the map, his eyes, framed by a fringe of long lashes, scanning the document. Why was he so damn attractive, and why couldn't Meri stop thinking about that and focus on not being killed by him? "So easy to get to. It would be a good place to ambush us."

"Not if I scout it out first while the two of you provide some distraction." Meri pointed to the hill in front of them. "That's north, let's go. Save the dueling for the next time you and Jacques go after each other."

16

SINAN

Sinan was none too pleased with either the weather or his companions. The wind had picked up, and flakes of snow swirled around them. The change from the warm fall temperatures outside the mist was striking, and it had to be from the Artifact. Weather control was a rare and dangerous talent, and his shadow magic wouldn't help him overcome it. The dead Sorcier du Roi, Zhang Jue, had been known for that skill, but Sinan had never heard of a necromancer with similar talents.

Of course, he was more likely to face danger from the Tomb Fighters than the cold. Meri had taken a small lead, and Gallmau was behind him, so Sinan was boxed in by the two of them. He had no idea why the Lioness was so furious with him. It could be she was regretting her choice to work with one of the Blessed, or maybe seeing Naghwe again had caused the outburst. His mother had that effect on people.

He considered shadow-walking away from the two of them and traveling to the hunting lodge his way. That had its risks, though. Whoever controlled the Artifact had used it to set up powerful shadow wards around Terra Amata, which had made entry through the arch with Gallmau and Meri his only option. There could be additional shadow wards around the chateau. Plus, if the lodge wasn't where Rixende was being held, he would be searching for her alone, without the assistance the Tomb Fighters could provide.

The prince had given him the map—touching Sinan's wrist in the process, damn him—but the piece of paper was nothing next to the knowledge the prince had of this area and his sister. Sinan was glad he had put on his gloves, and not only because of the decreasing temperatures. Gallmau didn't appear capable of interacting with him without physical contact. The brush of the prince's fingers against Sinan's ear in the Synod meeting room was still burned into Sinan's memory—both the pain and the sexual arousal it had brought with it.

Another blast of wind hit him, this one as fierce as daggers, and he drew more power from his heat sigil to keep his body warm.

"There's the lake." Meri had taken out a hooded woolen tunic from her pack, and she pulled it over her head as they reached the top of the rise. The body of water was sizable and surrounded by trees. On the far ridge, a roof was visible in the greenery. They would need to walk around the body of water, then climb up another steep elevation to get to the building. Lots of exposure, and plenty of time for anyone inside the lodge to spot them.

"This weather is strange." Gallmau blinked away a few snowflakes that clung to his lashes and rubbed his beard.

Everything about the prince was a reddish blonde. The color reminded Sinan of berries and honey, and he was furious with himself for focusing far too much on Gallmau's good looks. "It's never cold here this early."

"It's from the Artifact." Sinan thought the two of them had guessed this by now, but when they exchanged worried glances, he concluded they hadn't. Meri had an unsettling amount of knowledge about magic, but few people outside of formally trained mages understood much about Artifacts —or Witch Stones, as Meri insisted on calling them. Sinan certainly wished he knew more. "I'm confident whoever took Rixende knows we're here."

"I'll need to be closer to the other side before I can drop into my speed." Meri surveyed the lakeshore with a frown. The winds had picked up, whipping the surface of the water into waves crested by foam. "We could try to go through the trees to be less exposed."

"The underbrush is too thick. We have to walk along the lake's edge." Gallmau had come close to Sinan again, and awareness of the warm solidity of his body wasn't helping Sinan's concentration any. "There's a switchback trail leading up to the lodge on the other side. Once we get to it, Sinan and I'll create a fuss, and you can scout for us."

They started down the rocky slope, the trees getting closer together as they descended. Gallmau went ahead this time, his unerring sense of direction leading him to a rough trail.

"The other necromancers I've fought would have passed out by now." Meri gave Sinan an appraising glance as they picked their way around tree roots and brush. "You don't look half-starved, either."

"Speed fighters need more nourishment than those without necromantic Gifts as well." Sinan was already winded trying to keep up with the two of them, but he wasn't going to admit it.

"The Prophets gave me my Gift." Meri snatched back a tree branch that was about to hit Sinan in the face without obvious effort. She moved like a cat through the woods, all grace and no wasted movements. "You have a curse, and the Divine has forsaken you. I'm not anything like you."

"You said you hate all witches." Sinan tried to keep his footing on the uneven path without taking his eyes off Meri. Gallmau was a hulking shape a few feet ahead. Shadow armor or not, he hated being this close to enemies this strong. "Do you think the Prophets have forsaken Abarsam as well?"

"Leave the Grand Vizier out of this." Meri ducked beneath another branch, increasing her pace enough that Sinan had to scramble to keep up. She was already trying to tire him out, and they hadn't even reached the lake yet. "He's loyal to the Sultana and to Kush. Unlike the Noviodunam witches, who have their own agenda."

"Excellent, we finally agree on something." Sinan was relieved when Meri stopped, since he needed to catch his breath.

That relief faded when Gallmau held his hand up for them to stop and be quiet.

Meri crept forward, her movements so deft she didn't make a sound coming up beside the prince. Sinan wasn't able to imitate her silent progress, but he did his best not to loudly break any branches as he approached them. They were standing several paces from the shore, still in the relative cover of the trees.

"I saw something in the water." Gallmau shook his head, speaking in a low whisper. "Something big—it doesn't make any sense. I've fished here before; there's nothing that size in there."

Sinan closed his eyes and concentrated on the lake. Compared to the vigorous cycle of life and death in the greenery around him, the lake had less thaumaturgic activity, which would be expected from a body of water. He couldn't detect any major necromantic power inside it, like the undead hortdan who patrolled the underground rivers and canals of Karakoncolos. "I don't sense anything unnatural in the water. Let me go first. My armor should stop anything."

Sinan stepped out onto the shoreline of the lake. If anyone in the lodge had missed them at the top of the ridge, they would spot him now. He walked forward several paces, his shadows swirling around him. They took a fair amount of power to maintain for long periods of time, and the increasing cold meant he needed to draw on his heat sigil, which took far more energy. Not only was it not related to his strongest affinities, it wasn't even death magic. He had dressed in practical wool garments but not for conditions more commonly encountered on mountaintops in the winter.

Gallmau and Meri came out of the woods, catching up to him quickly.

"Nothing wants a bite of you, I guess." Gallmau's breath hung in the air, a puff of white vapor, as he spoke. "Not that you don't look tasty. Wait, that's not what I meant to say."

Sinan had no idea if the remark was meant as an insult or a terrible attempt at flirtation. He gathered his cloak around him tighter and circled around a boulder to put some distance between him and the prince.

All that did was earn him a wet slosh as he stepped into a water-filled dip in the ground.

A sharp pain struck him in the hand, under his shields, and Sinan cried out and scrambled up the bank away from Meri and Gallmau. The two Tomb Fighters stood staring at him as he held up his wrist, a single puncture mark oozing blood.

"You're awfully jumpy." Meri stood with her back to the lake, as did Gallmau. Had she done something to him with her speed? She had been able to get under his shields when he fought Cliona, but why she would settle for a tiny wound on his hand was a mystery. She already knew he was immune to poisons—and he doubted she would use a weapon like that.

Then the damn undead rat popped out of a patch of shadow and hissed at him.

Sinan took a step backward, cursing, and Meri and Gallmau started laughing. The Lady of Shadows must be punishing him for his pride. If he had only asked his mother for help, the rodent would have been exorcised by now and in the peaceful Void of Chaos. Instead, the animal had tracked him all the way here for the sole purpose of biting him.

Then a gray-brown gelatinous mass emerged from the lake in a spray of water, and Gallmau was gone.

Sinan took a few seconds to understand what he was seeing. Gallmau was thrashing in the water, fighting some sort of giant fish. Meri must have used her speed to swim out to him, as she was out there as well, swords flashing as she stabbed at the thing. From his glimpses of the beast, it must be close to twice Gallmau's height in length, with finger-like projections around its wide mouth. A catfish the size of a carriage?

His talents weren't well suited for the situation. Meri or Gallmau could be injured or killed if he tried to throw knife-like bands of shadow at the thing. The only option was to go into the water and direct a strike at the fish's head.

Sinan could swim well, but the water would be cold, and he wouldn't be able to maintain his body temperature for long. He drew more power from his sigil and ran forward.

The rat attacked again, this time biting at his face, and Sinan stopped long enough to rip the animal off him and throw it to the ground.

"Begone and haunt this spot no more!" Sinan tried a half-remembered exorcism spell, which only made the rat chatter its teeth in rage as it stood in his path.

A series of sharp cracks filled the air, and the surface of the lake turned white, ice spreading at a fantastic rate. Gallmau screamed out Meri's name, and other than his struggling shape, the water's now frozen surface was pale and featureless, with no sign of the beautiful speed fighter.

Sinan ran forward, slipping and sliding on the ice. He had enough power to demolish half the valley, but that wouldn't do any good. Meri was trapped underneath, about to drown if she hadn't already, and he was good at death, not water rescues.

Gallmau screamed his name, and Sinan twisted to see the prince frantically pointing to his right. The rat was on the ice, sniffing and digging furiously.

Half-running, half-falling, Sinan reached the spot.

Meri's water-cursed blades lay next to a mound of ice as clear as a window pane. Inside was a small pocket of air and a face pressed up against the surface.

Sinan motioned for Meri to dive, and she sank into the dark water. He sent as little shadow power into the ice as he could. The surface exploded into fragments, leaving a dark pool of open water. He flung himself down on his stomach and crawled forward as the weakened ice underneath him cracked and groaned. The water began to solidify again, clumps of bobbing ice coalescing into an even thicker sheet.

This wasn't a natural phenomenon. Whoever controlled the Artifact was assaulting them with its weather powers, making Sinan's abilities useless in the face of crippling cold and wet.

Meri burst out of the water and flung her upper body out onto the frozen surface. Sinan grabbed her arms and pulled as more ice formed around her lower body, clinging to her and trying to drag her back under. She shook herself into a blur of movement, sending water and snow flying as she climbed to her feet, her blades already back in her hands.

"Get Gallmau out, you son of a bitch." Meri shoved her blades into her scabbards and tried to fight off his hands as Sinan dragged her away to a more solid patch of ice.

At least she hadn't stabbed him. His gloves slid along her arms, and he had to remind himself that layers of leather and fabric protected him from touching her soft skin. He could do this, could hold on to her long enough to get her across the lake to the shore. Then he'd help Gallmau.

They stumbled across the frozen surface, the wind howling and snow flying everywhere. They were out past the center of the lake, and the far shore was closer than the side they had started on. Sinan tried to keep them going in a straight line toward it.

"I'll go back for him, I promise." The cold gnawed at him, siphoning off more and more of his strength. The wind had shifted direction, blowing directly against them. "Get to land and find the trail. We have to get up to the lodge, no matter what's waiting for us inside."

The ice began to fracture again as they approached the pebble-strewn sand of the lakeshore. The water's surface wasn't frozen solid enough yet and barely held his and Meri's weight.

Meri stumbled onto the shore and slumped down, sodden and gasping. The wet and cold would kill her as effectively as drowning would have. Sinan pulled off his shroud cloak, activating the warmth sigil with more power than he should have, and put it over her shoulders and head.

"It's heat magic, that's all." Sinan was afraid she would rip it off, given her fear of the Blessed and their powers, but she only looked up at him, tears freezing on her lashes.

"Don't leave him out there." Meri's fury and pride were gone, replaced by the desperation Sinan had seen when she thought Gallmau was dying from Naghwe's poison.

"I'll get him." Sinan turned around, his feet numb with cold, and focused on shadow, and shadow alone.

His magic crept forward, a path of darkness in an expanse of white. He stepped onto it, the surface now solid and secure, and trudged forward. His shields went out around him, blocking the worst of the wind.

He couldn't keep up this expenditure of energy for long. His cloak allowed him to both store and focus different affinities, but his shadow powers didn't need any additional support. They weren't infinite, though, and he needed to find Gallmau and break him out of the ice, if the prince was even still alive.

The winds screamed, and the snow intensified into a white-out. His shadow path was as open as ever, but he had no means to find Gallmau.

A pair of pinpoint blue lights shone in front of him, and Sinan mumbled a prayer to the Lady to apologize for his stupidity in rejecting the help she had repeatedly provided.

"Cheese." He focused on the tiny eyes of the undead rat,

blazing through the snow. "Remember the food Gallmau gave you? He has more. Find him, and he'll give it to you."

The lights blinked once then began to move forward, and Sinan followed them. The snow was thick enough that he was all but on top of Gallmau before he realized it.

The prince was punching the ice in front of him, pulverizing it into pieces and trying to pull himself further out of the icy prison he had been trapped in. He stared up at Sinan in surprise, the icicles coating his hair and beard so thick he appeared one with the storm.

Sinan spread his hands and exploded the surface of the lake in front of him. It was more destructive than the maneuver he had used with Meri, and Gallmau wasn't able to shield himself under the water.

Gallmau floated face down at the end of it, and Sinan lunged forward to grasp the prince's shoulders. He groaned and clutched at Sinan, dragging him toward the water. Frantic, Sinan sent out eight legs of shadow from his back to stab into the ice, turning himself into a parody of a spider to hold himself in place as Gallmau pulled himself out of the water and to his feet.

A pair of glowing blue lights scurried up the prince's arm, and the rat materialized on his shoulders, sniffing the air for potential cheese rewards and looking rather pleased with itself.

"Follow the path." Sinan pulled back his shadow appendages and stood up on unsteady legs. He gestured to a now narrow stretch of black that stretched out over the ice. "Your weight will break through otherwise."

He would have fallen, but Gallmau reached out an arm to steady him.

"Don't touch me." Sinan mumbled the familiar warning and staggered forward.

He needed to focus every last bit of his will to keep the path open. He gestured for Gallmau to go first, allowing the heavier man to trudge along on the more solid segment of shadow as the surface underneath his own feet grew more tenuous, more like the absence of light it truly was.

His shields weakened, step by step, and the snow screamed around him, ripping away the last shreds of heat. He no longer had any sense of direction, and the best he could do was extend his shadow path for Gallmau, hoping the young royal knew where he was going.

After an eternity of shivering cold, Gallmau stopped, and Sinan realized the prince was standing on the shore, holding out his hand to him.

Sinan stared down at his feet at the thin ice cracking under his weight. The water rushed up to suck him under, the cold extinguishing the last of his shadow bridge, and with it, any chance of survival.

17

GALLMAU

Gallmau no sooner made it off the ice than the Saints-damned fish that had gone after him pulled Sinan underwater.

Meri was nowhere in sight, and with the blinding snow all Gallmau could see was a hole in the ice and Sinan's head slipping under the surface. The magical shadow bridge Sinan had created to get him off the lake was gone, so Gallmau's only choice was to crunch through the ice up to his waist and grab one flailing arm. He succeeded next in getting his hands around Sinan's shoulders and yanking him above the surface. The catfish had one of Sinan's legs in its mouth, and it thrashed back and forth, trying to fight off Gallmau and drag its prey to the bottom of the lake.

Gallmau had the advantage of his strength and the water being shallow enough that he could plant his feet and haul both Sinan and the catfish out of the water and onto dry land. Meri popped into view, straddling the fish and stabbing both her blades into the monster's head.

"Why won't this thing die?" Meri had Sinan's cloak hanging off her back, and between that and the fish blood spraying over everyone, including Gallmau, she looked more terrifying than a pack of Bone Lords.

Sinan's leg came loose from the fish's mouth, and Gallmau lifted him up and placed him on the snow-swept sand. The necromancer's lips were blue and his eyes closed. Gallmau knelt next to him and pressed his lips against his, blowing in a breath to get him to start breathing. He had a fleeting moment of hesitation, recalling warnings about Bone Lords using the bodily fluids of their victims to enslave them. If that was going to happen, he'd prefer his eternal downfall to come from something more exciting than spit.

He pressed on Sinan's chest, hoping to expel any water without cracking the young man's ribs, then bent down and gave him another breath. Maybe, if Sinan survived, he wouldn't be ungrateful enough to turn Gallmau into an undead slave.

Meri gave a shout of triumph, and Gallmau twisted his head to see the catfish sprawled dead in a pool of dark red.

Beneath him, Sinan jerked and sat up.

Gallmau tried to hold on to him, but Sinan twisted out of his grip and scrambled away, coughing lake water out of his lungs.

"Leave me alone." Sinan sent a warning arc of shadow slicing into the ground between them, then wiped off his lips with his hand. "You put your mouth on me."

Apparently, he was going to be an ungrateful wretch. Gallmau should have expected that. "I wasn't making a pass at you, I was trying to get you to breathe." Gallmau went over to see how Meri was doing, since Sinan was clearly not in the mood for further rescuing. She had sheathed her blades and was kicking at the side of the fish.

"What is this thing?" Meri directed the comment at Sinan, who was still retching. One of the strange symbols on the cloak she was wearing glowed a faint purple. Sinan had said he didn't need something to die every time he used his powers, but the death of the catfish had revived him and his magic.

"It's a big fish." Sinan succeeded in standing up, but he looked unsteady.

Meri came over to him and took off the cloak, holding it out to him. "I know it's a big fucking fish. I want to know if it's magic."

"It was Touched, yes." Sinan took his cloak back from Meri and wrapped it around him. The purple symbol dimmed. He must have drawn down its power right away. "Animals can have Gifts as well as humans. What's more important is that someone was controlling it."

"Forget about the catfish from Hell." Gallmau was cold and shivering and that meant Meri had to be in much worse shape. Sinan had his fancy magic sheet, but he was still drenched. Low temperatures and wet clothing would be a death sentence for all three of them if they didn't get to shelter soon. "We have to go to the chateau."

"I didn't see a sign of anyone there." Meri hugged her chest for warmth, although her clothing wasn't as wet as it should have been. Sinan had given her his own cloak to warm her up, so maybe he wasn't a total ungrateful bastard, as long as there was no touching involved. "It's a steep trail. I can't go back into my speed anytime soon."

The time for speed was over. Stamina alone would get them through this, and Gallmau had plenty of that. His two companions were another story.

"I'll carry both of you if I have to." He reached out to extend a hand to Sinan and wasn't surprised when the necromancer jerked away.

Gallmau found the trail and let Meri go first, with Sinan in the middle. He didn't think the necromancer was going to make it up the mountain path, dead fish or no dead fish. Cold and exhaustion—those were the weakness Abarsam had told them to exploit—and Sinan was half-drowned and chilled to the bone. They had to fix that, and soon. There would be dry clothes and bedding to spare in the lodge. The royal family had servants and guides who maintained all of the far-flung properties of the throne.

The storm intensified, as if enraged that the three of them were still alive. Gallmau could make out Sinan in front of him, but the snow was too thick to see Meri. They were on the right trail, but with the current conditions, it would be easy to step off and fall into the logs and snow-covered rocks below.

"Can you see her?" He had to shout over the roar of the storm. Sinan paused, as if considering the question, then fell backward.

It was abrupt enough that Gallmau barely had time to catch him. The necromancer struggled for a moment, before giving up the futile effort of trying to undo the grip Gallmau had on him.

Gallmau turned Sinan to face him. The necromancer's eyes looked glassy, and his mumbled threats were barely audible. Gallmau placed one foot between Sinan's legs and lifted the Prince of Shadows up and over his shoulders. He still had his shield and his travel pack on his back, but he could handle Sinan's added weight with ease.

What he couldn't do was stop Sinan from using magic on him for daring to carry him to safety.

"Don't even think about hexing me, understand?" Gallmau held on to Sinan's legs with one hand and marched forward.

He came upon Meri a few strides later. She had kept to the path, but her breathing was labored and her legs shaking. He held out his free arm, and she leaned in with a grateful sigh.

"I can pick you up too," Gallmau offered, but Meri shook her head.

"I think we're close enough I can make it." She clung tighter to him, and the wind howled through the trees. "If there's anyone I missed up there, you're going to need your sword arm."

That wasn't a pleasant thought. Gallmau tried to pick up the pace without exhausting Meri. Sinan wasn't struggling. Maybe he had finally realized he wasn't going to get up the mountain on his own two feet, or maybe he had passed out.

A rush of relief went through him as they came out of the trees to the spot Gallmau remembered as a wide clearing in front of the three-story stone structure.

Then his heart dropped.

The blizzard winds swept through with such ferocity he couldn't see a handsbreadth in front of his face. Meri sagged beside him, and he hoisted her up into the crook of his arm and kept going.

He knew where the front door should be, on the side of the structure, below arrow-slit windows set in massive stone walls. The building had originally been an ancient fort. Compared to the extravagant chateaus his father and many of the nobles had built closer to villages and roads, this hunting lodge was positively rustic.

The snow around him had turned into shards of ice, stinging his exposed face and forcing him to bend forward to advance against the shrieking gales. It was hard not to think there was something intelligent and malicious behind the storm. He knew there was no more than several paces between him and the protection the building offered, but he couldn't tell what direction to take.

Gallmau focused in on his memories of the lodge and fixed the location in his mind. The first time he had come here with his father he had been thirteen, hoping to get closer to a man who had always been remote and unyielding. The king had little time and even fewer words for him during that stay—until he promised his son the Shield of Soissons if he succeeded in taking down the magnificent stag they were tracking. Gallmau felled the animal with a single arrow and was rewarded with a few words of rare praise and the spelled shield.

After the hunt, Gallmau felt as if he could walk on clouds—until they returned to the chateau with the trophy and a host of courtiers. One of them made a crude joke about Gallmau's conception, and the king laughed and agreed with the sentiment.

Even at that age Gallmau knew his mother had been a courtesan before she died giving birth to him, but he had always fantasized his father loved her. With a few brief words of banter, the King had revealed he thought little more of Gallmau's mother than he would a hunting bitch who produced a promising pup. Everything about that day was seared into his memory—the embarrassment, the crushing disappointment, all in front of the stone walls of the lodge and the vivid green backdrop of the ancient forest around it.

Gallmau didn't need to see where he was going. He had walked the path to this lodge with his shame and anger hundreds of times in his mind.

Trudging forward with Meri under his arm and Sinan on his back, he retraced every miserable step he had taken that day and came upon the bolted wooden door a few minutes later. After fumbling with the latch, he gave up and kicked it in. If anyone inside wanted to attack them, he had told them he was here.

There was immediate relief once he was inside the thick walls. The wind snarled and smashed the door open and shut behind him, but he had already made it past the mudroom and up the stairs to enter the house proper.

Meri squirmed out of his grasp and together they laid Sinan down on the floor of the trophy room, which featured a huge fireplace on a wall bristling with antlers and horns from both common forest prey and rare Archaic beasts. Somewhere in that display of trophies might be the remains of the stag Gallmau had shot for his father, another gift the man had been given and never appreciated.

Sinan groaned, his eyes fluttering open for a brief second. He had stopped shivering, even as Meri's and Gallmau's teeth chattered, and his black hair glistened with icicles and frost. On his cloak, most of the sigils were no longer visible, having faded away into the white of the shroud. The violet symbol remained, now dim and flickering as if its energy had been drained away.

Sinan would die of the cold soon, even if they were out of the wind.

"Get those wet clothes off him." Gallmau hoisted his shield in one hand and his short sword in the other. "I need to make sure there aren't any nasty surprises in the house and find some blankets."

Meri gave an exhausted nod and sank down next to the necromancer.

Gallmau didn't have time to search through the whole

chateau, but a quick survey of the rooms on the first and second floors revealed no evidence of either threats or recent visitors.

He ended up using his shield as a tray to carry down whatever bedding he could find, along with clothes left in the servants' quarters. His walk downstairs became a run when he heard an unfamiliar scream. Bounding into the room, he brought himself up short as he saw Meri wrestling with Sinan.

She grabbed at the necromancer's arm, yanking off one of his gloves as the man thrashed, then gave Gallmau an exasperated look. "He's not making sense, and I can't touch him without him yelling."

Gallmau seized some of the blankets and brought them over, but Meri shook her head. "Come over here and hold him down."

"Why?" Gallmau asked, afraid of the answer. Meri had unsheathed one of her water blades and was holding it over the necromancer.

No, Gallmau could not let Meri do this. "He risked dying to get us out of the lake. You can't murder him."

"I'm trying to save his life." Meri fixed him with a glare fierce enough to melt the blizzard that still roared outside into warm spring puddles, and Gallmau gave in and pinned Sinan down.

His fingers gripped Sinan's bare, cold arms, and the necromancer screamed again. Undressing him in any dignified way proved impossible, and Meri resorted to using her blade to slice Sinan's sodden clothing into ribbons so they could peel the fabric off him.

It was truly awful. Sinan cried out like they were torturing him, eyes wild and unfocused. He cursed them, mumbled words in a foreign tongue that sounded like a prayer, and at one point begged them to stop.

They finally managed to strip him naked, and Gallmau couldn't look away from Sinan's pale, beautiful body, as Meri scrambled to get the blankets and bedding. Other than on his head and face, Sinan had none of the body hair of a grown man, but everything about him, from his defined chest, narrow hips, and proportioned limbs, was flawless and perfect, like a toppled marble statue of a young god.

"There." She wrapped several wool blankets around Sinan, as Gallmau lifted his hand from Sinan's arms and chest, horrified at the red imprints of his fingers on the necromancer's skin. Meri had Sinan cocooned in the dry bedding in short order, then leaned on his chest and cupped her hands around the thick cloth she had put over his wet hair. "We're not trying to hurt you. We only want to get you warm."

Sinan's eyes flickered open, and for a moment he sounded lucid. "The two of you don't even understand what you're doing."

He gave a half-laugh, half-sob, and his eyes rolled back, head lolling to one side.

Meri pressed her fingers to his neck, then to his wrist.

"He passed out, thank the Prophets, but his pulse is weak." Meri yanked at her wool tunic and motioned for Gallmau to help her. "Come on, you can take a woman's clothes off, too, even if you're not that excited about what's underneath. I'm going to strip and crawl under the blankets with him. Then you're going to do the same thing."

"I don't think that's a good idea." Gallmau was quite sure about that, even if Meri's suggestion did make practical sense. He pulled off her tunic and shirt and helped her out of the men's trousers she had put on for their quest. He let her slip out of her smallclothes herself.

"You need to change anyway, and you'll give off more heat than I will." Meri was shivering and nude now as well, and she slipped quickly under the mass of bedding next to Sinan. She gave him a tired smile. "I'll get to brag I bedded two princes in one night."

Gallmau started to laugh then stopped, his conscience getting the better of him. "He thought we were trying to—I don't know, rape or torture him. Waking up next to me isn't going to make him happy."

"He should be happy to wake up at all, after what happened." Meri brushed a lock of Sinan's black hair away from his face and regarded him with interest. "All Bone Lords have a curse. Why isn't there anything wrong with him? He's—too perfect."

"Maybe he's broken on the inside." Gallmau took Meri's advice when it came to taking off his wet clothes, but he stayed upright and found a large enough thick coat to wrap around himself. He carefully dried off Meri's blades and scabbards and laid them down next to her. She didn't go to sleep with them more than an arm's length away. "I'll join the two of you after I get the fire going and get us some water, but I'm not getting naked."

It was far from the heroic start to his sister's rescue he had hoped for. He and Meri had come close to being eaten by a cursed fish, and the Bone Lord they had partnered with was half-frozen and unconscious. If the unnatural storm outside had spread throughout Terra Amata, was Rixende protected against the weather, or was she cold and shivering in some crude cell?

Worrying about his younger sister wasn't going to help him save her. Making sure his companions recovered enough to help him free her would. He set to work. By the time Gallmau lit the heating stove inside the fireplace, pumped some well water, and spread all of their clothes and gear out to dry, exhaustion won out over his guilt. He took off the coat and crawled into bed with Sinan and Meri.

Sinan lay oddly still, moaning when Gallmau tried and failed to get under the bedding without touching the necromancer who had made it abundantly clear he didn't like physical contact. Sinan's skin wasn't clammy, at least, and his breathing was deep and steady.

Meri, usually the lightest of sleepers, only fluttered her eyelashes open for a second at Gallmau then rolled over to rest her head on Sinan's chest.

It wasn't easy to lie there and not think about how handsome and naked Sinan was, all while trying not to press up against the man. What Gallmau should do was banish filthy thoughts from his mind and get the rest his body needed.

Several inappropriate dreams later, he jerked awake at the rasp of a sword being pulled out of its scabbard.

18

GALLMAU

"If I carried you here just so you could try to stab us in our sleep, I'm going to be downright pissed." Gallmau sat up and had no trouble locating the weapon he had heard drawn and the person who held it. Sinan knelt on the floor near his travel pack, which Gallmau had carefully placed near the stove to dry, not wanting to know what might be inside. The necromancer must have quickly thrown on the servant clothes Gallmau had brought to the room, since he now wore a pair of trousers and an unbuttoned shirt under his shroud cloak.

"What did the two of you do to me?" Sinan kept his grip tight on the hilt of his sword, but he didn't rise to his feet.

Gallmau recalled what the necromancer had said about never starting a fight he had any chance of losing. Sinan couldn't be fully recovered from last night, and he had a reason to be suspicious. Meri *had* cut his clothes off while Gallmau held him down.

Still, the necromancer was more fun to be around when he was unconscious.

"Let me see." Gallmau decided not to go for his sword and instead try talking to Sinan. He stood up from the tangle of blankets and walked over to his clothes. The storm still howled for their deaths outside the lodge, but the room was now comfortably warm, even though Gallmau was nude. "First, I pulled you out of the mouth of a demon catfish while Meri stabbed it to death. Then I carried you up the damn mountain to the only shelter available. After that, we saved you from freezing to death. Feel free to thank us for any one of those actions."

Sinan's eyes had traveled up and down Gallmau's body when he had first gotten up, but he averted his gaze now—a little too quickly. Maybe the necromancer did like men, or maybe it was all wishful thinking on Gallmau's part.

"Don't even think about it." Meri popped up in front of Sinan, the necromancer's sword now in her hands.

He jerked back in surprise, not as accustomed as Gallmau was to speed fighter tricks.

Meri was naked as well, and although Gallmau tried to respect her privacy during their adventures together, he had seen her before with little or no clothing on and knew what a stunning body she had.

Now, though—she was a vision of beauty and anger, her skin glowing in the red light streaming out of the stove and her uncovered hair shining like a halo above her head. The room was dim otherwise, as the high windows on the wall were dark. It was either too late at night or too early in the morning to be awoken by someone pulling a weapon on them, and Meri looked like Saint Kreztina herself, ready to smite demons with her speed and sword.

Sinan rose to his feet empty-handed, his eyes wide as he stared at Meri. "Are you one of us?"

"I would not recommend accusing Meri of being a Bone Lord when she has your sword in her hand." Gallmau wriggled into his pants and came over to see if he could stop Meri from doing something rash.

"Are you a venefica?" Sinan was not letting go of this line of questioning, which wasn't good for his health.

Meri laughed, which might be a sign she wasn't going to kill Sinan, or might be because she wanted to mock him before she skewered him with his own sword.

"I'm awfully good under the sheets, but I'm not a demoness who drains the life from the men she fucks." She handed Gallmau Sinan's sword, which was quite a relief, and went to grab her clothes. "I think you breathed in too much water when that fish tried to eat you."

"You drained power from me for hours." Sinan sounded deadly serious—although he tended to sound deadly even in casual conversation. "First from my cloak, although you shouldn't have been able to activate any of my sigils. It should have warmed you, nothing more. Then I was next to both of you for hours, and you sapped most of the thaumaturgic power I'd stored up. A speed fighter couldn't do that, but a venefica could."

Meri didn't respond to Sinan. Instead, she pulled on her pants and ignored him.

"The only Bone Lord parts of you that weren't drowned froze when I got you out of the water." Gallmau had a growing sense of unease about both what Sinan was saying and Meri's strange reaction to it. She wasn't one to back down from a confrontation. He still felt obligated to take her side. "You're lucky to be alive, but you're wondering why you're tired and out of sorts with your death magic."

"The cold would have killed me, yes." Sinan answered Gallmau without taking his eyes off Meri, even though she had her back to him. "But it couldn't feed off the sigils in my cloak. I should have woken up hours ago, even after what you did, and I shouldn't be this weak."

Meri stiffened, and Gallmau worried she would turn around and shut up Sinan permanently.

Instead she collapsed.

Gallmau dropped Sinan's sword and rushed to her side, panic rising in his chest. She arched, the spasms so severe only her head and feet touched the floor. When her body finally loosened, she tried to twist and rise then fell face down. For a moment, Gallmau thought the dim light in the room was playing tricks with his eyes. The bare skin on her back had begun to ripple, as if a rock had been tossed into a pond of flesh.

He reached out his hand to her, unsure of what to do. Part of him knew Meri would never want to reveal her secret to Sinan. The other, terrified part wanted to get on his knees and beg the necromancer for help.

"Don't touch her back." Sinan came over and crouched down next to the two of them, his eyes alight with curiosity. A few wisps of shadow swirled around him, nothing like the bands of dark Gallmau had seen previously.

A face took shape in between Meri's shoulder blades, pressing up through the skin to form jutting eyebrows, a nose, and a wide, voracious mouth. Gallmau swallowed down a rush of nausea, not wanting to see this horror but unable to look away.

"Well." Sinan let out a sigh. "This explains a lot."

"You know magic. Do something to help her." Gallmau turned to Sinan, fury mixing with mounting fear. None of her previous attacks had been this bad, and he had never seen the dead Bone Lord who had cursed Meri. Why was this happening now?"

"Gallmau." Meri's voice cracked with agony, but there was no panic there, only resignation and resolve. At least she was still able to speak. "Get my blades and tell that son of a bitch necromancer to stay out of this."

Sinan cocked his head, that odd movement he made when non-Bone Lords did things that confused him. "I think you should do what she says."

Gallmau rushed back to their makeshift sleeping pile and grabbed both curved swords, pulling the blades free. He crossed back to find the mouth on Meri's back forming soundless words as Sinan watched intently.

"I don't know what you plan to do with these, but I don't think you're even strong enough to lift them." Gallmau didn't want to get any closer to the snarling visage on her back, but he was desperate to help her any way he could. He held out the hilts to Meri, who pushed herself up on her arms and took both swords before collapsing back on her stomach.

She breathed in and out for a few seconds, then raised her arms behind her and slashed at her back, letting out a choked sob.

"Meri, no." All Gallmau could see was blood and flayed skin, and for the first time in his life he felt light-headed at the sight of violence. He had seen men die—and women, too—but the damage Meri had inflicted on herself affected him more than any of the battles he had been in.

"*Assecula daemonium.*" Sinan rose to his feet and went over to his pack, rummaging through it and taking out a wrapped parcel before crossing over to the stove and lifting the kettle on top of it. "I've read about it, of course, but I've never seen one inside a living person. Fascinating."

"What the fuck are you even saying?" Gallmau grabbed the shirt he had been about to put on and balled it up on Meri's back, pressing as blood oozed and turned the white linen fabric red. "Stop with that Bone Lord babble, and do something useful."

"I'm making tea." Sinan didn't sound upset by what had happened in the slightest, which made Gallmau wish they had left him to be eaten by the catfish. "It would have been helpful to know in advance one of my Blessed-hating companions on this trip was possessed by an undead veneficus."

"Help me sit up." Meri interrupted Gallmau from walking over to Sinan and throttling him. He carefully lifted her, alarmed by how much blood was seeping into his shirt.

"How often do you use Abarsam's blades on your assecula?" Sinan poured steaming water into a bowl and came over to rest it on the floor, along with his parcel. He unwrapped the package. Inside was a white, waxy square, a pile of sweet-smelling dried leaves and flowers, and strips of cloth with sigils on them.

"Once a month if I'm lucky." Meri used one arm to hold the shirt on her back and the other to push Gallmau away from her. She regarded Sinan and his supplies with suspicion. "More often if I'm not. In any event, you're not using any of your death magic on me."

Sinan shook his head, put the sigil-marked strips into his pocket, and picked up the white square. "This is olive oil soap." He gave it to Gallmau along with a soft rag and motioned to the bowl of warm water. "Take that dirty shirt of yours off of her and wash the cuts with this. I can't touch her, and she wouldn't want me to anyway."

That was an odd choice of words, but Meri certainly would prefer Gallmau tend to her wounds than a necromancer. He followed Sinan's instructions, washing and drying the bloody slashes, then applying a poultice of herbs the necromancer handed to him before binding Meri's chest and back with strips of cloth. He could see a framework of older, healed scars as he worked.

Meri had never told him how bad her curse had become. She should have trusted him. She should have told him everything. What if this was when the undead necromancer inside her finally killed her? He didn't know what he would do if he lost both Meri and Rixende on this cursed trip.

While Gallmau finished up the bandaging, fear and anxiety spiking through him, Sinan brought over three steaming cups. As he had promised, they contained fragrant tea that wouldn't have been out of place in one of Queen Xiaolian's formal parties. He sat down cross-legged and took a sip. "I need to know how an assecula daemonium ended up in a Tomb Fighter's back."

"Is that what Meri's dead Bone Lord is called?" Gallmau had had enough of strange words and events he couldn't understand.

"Some of the Blessed can maintain their souls after their bodies die." Sinan pushed a cup of tea toward Gallmau, pulling his hand back so he didn't brush fingers with him. "Often through a binding to part of their remains. I was able to raise Letha because the Noviodunam was foolish enough to bury her burnt bones in their meeting room. But the soul can also be inserted into a different body and live on as a sort of parasite."

Sinan offered the third cup to Meri, who made no move to take it.

Gallmau reached out to touch her shoulder. "Maybe he can help. At least tell him how it happened."

"I didn't cut a Bone Lord's head off fast enough." Meri picked up the cup, drained it, and lifted her chin as she replied to Sinan. "I didn't make the same mistake with Cliona, and your mother stopped me before I could get yours off."

"It must have happened recently," Sinan ventured and drew back in surprise when Gallmau shook his head.

"It's been three years." Meri put down the cup. "I was on the arena circuit in Diutisc when a mother broke into our quarters to beg me to save her only child. He'd been taken by a Bone Lord, and the local authorities wouldn't do anything about it. So I did."

"That's not possible." Sinan shook his head. "The assecula daemonium curse kills its victims in days, maybe weeks at most. If it's done properly, the Blessed then becomes a corporeal spirit. I've heard of some using the corpse of the person they possessed as a vehicle for a little longer, but not years."

Meri kept talking, her gaze far away. "Everyone knew he was a necromancer, of course, and everyone knew he preyed on little kids. Even when the Noviodunam sent their top death witch hunter to Diustic to investigate, nothing was done about him. So Rerek kept killing children—until I showed up."

"Rerek of Diustic was absolved of all charges of necromancy by Odart of Dol himself." Sinan said the name with more icy hatred than Gallmau had ever heard—and he had listened to plenty of people curse out the former head of the benandanti. "Rerek was—well, still is—a powerful venefi-cus. His primary affinity is poison."

"I didn't know any of that." Meri folded her arms against her chest, wincing as she did so. "I couldn't save the woman's son or the other child we found there. It was—the most horrible thing I had ever seen. The arena and the money it brought me weren't enough after that. I returned to Kush, and Rerek was waiting for me there."

"He attacked you when you returned?" Gallmau had never heard the whole story, only bits of it. Meri had made it clear it wasn't a subject she was willing to discuss.

"No." Meri stared down at the floor, her voice low. "He went after my younger sister. I had come back to Kush with a few arena fighters I was friends with. They helped me. I found him, and I killed him. But I was too late to save Sanura."

"Three murders you tried to stop." Sinan rubbed at the back of his neck, frowning. "Three years since you killed him."

"A witch told her that was how long she had left." Gallmau knew that part. "We had a contract to stop a poisoner in Amor, but Meri cut a deal with her—after we made her promise to stop putting things in people's wine that shouldn't be there. Like arsenic."

"You were going to let her go anyway," Meri replied. "She started crying about her ten children who would starve without her, and you folded immediately."

Gallmau wanted to interject that the woman had poisoned men who deserved it anyway, but he needed to focus on Sinan, now that the secret was out. Hope surged up inside him. "If you know all about this curse, can you help? I brought Meri to Soissons to see if Zhang Jue could do some-thing, but we found out he was dead when we arrived."

"Zhang Jue was a high-ranking member of the benan-danti, and Odart's closest ally." Sinan was certainly familiar with the Noviodunam's Bone Lord hunters. Then again, he had killed a good number of them in the Witches' War. "He would have ordered Meri's execution. Even Abarsam would have been obligated to report her to the Synod, and they would have agreed with the Sorcier du Roi. The Novio-dunam considers any physical contact with one of us a crim-inal act, much less a full assecula daemonium possession."

Saints, bringing Meri to Zhang Jue would have been a disaster. "But you're a necromancer. You know how the curse works, and that means you know how to get rid of it."

Sinan fell silent for a moment, then bit his lip. "The curse is advanced ghost magic, and that isn't my strong suit. There's also the issue that Rerek has been feeding off of me and the thaumaturgic power I stored in my sigils. He's more powerful now."

"You made your pet rat a ghost." Gallmau made a mental note to give the freaky little guy another piece of cheese if it showed up again. The rodent had certainly proved itself a boon companion on the frozen lake.

"That enchantment didn't go the way I wanted it to." Sinan looked uncomfortable, then continued. "What I could do is a summoning spell to call up my mother and other members of the Council of the Dead. The Artifact has created shadow wards around this entire area, but they can appear here in non-corporeal form."

"No." Meri's mouth was set in a firm line Gallmau knew all too well. "I'm not going to become an undead slave to Sinan or Mother Naghwe. I'd rather die."

"That's ridiculous." Gallmau pointed to Sinan. "We saved his life, and he owes us. Granted, he saved ours first, and we did let a sex demon feed off him by accident, but the point is he should help us, and he's willing to do it. You can't say no."

"Yes, she can." Sinan wrapped up the soap and remaining herbs and went over to his pack to store them. "She chooses death. That's her right, and I'll respect that."

Gallmau went over to Sinan, grabbed his shoulder and spun him around. Sinan gave a hiss of pain, even though Gallmau hadn't been as rough as he wanted to be. "Call your talking ghosts and ask them how to save Meri. Now."

This couldn't be happening. After all this time, they had finally found someone who might be able to rid Meri of her curse—and he wouldn't help her. Without Sinan's intervention, Meri might not be strong enough to leave the Chateau, much less help Gallmau rescue Rixende.

"What part of 'I worship death' do you not understand?" Sinan rubbed at his bare chest where Gallmau's hand had touched him, then began to button his shirt to cover up his skin. "It's a central tenet of our beliefs. I don't know if we could successfully expel Rerek from Meri without killing her, but it's her choice to refuse the attempt. Not yours."

"The two of you need to shut up." Meri had risen to her feet, and both swords were in her hands.

For a moment Gallmau wasn't sure if the blades were meant for him or Sinan. Then he followed her gaze to the wall of hunting trophies. One of the mounted antlers had begun to vibrate, plaster crumbling around its wooden base. Something was moving behind the wall.

Or someone.

Sinan dove for his sword, and Gallmau backed up to retrieve his own.

The wall shook violently, and one arm burst out, then another. Within a few moments a portion of it had collapsed, and a man with antlers on his head and the same gruesome mouth as the shape on Meri's back stepped out into the room.

"Rerek." Meri held her ground, but her hands holding the swords shook. "That's him."

Gallmau looked at Sinan. "Now can you do something?"

"Yes." Sinan lifted his blade, and his shadow ribbons began to swirl around him. "I'm going to try to not die. I suggest you do the same."

19

MERI

Meri had led all three of them to their deaths, and she could tell Rerek knew it. The undead veneficus stood in front of them, teeth bared in an eager smile.

Even in her bleakest thoughts she hadn't imagined she would be responsible for Gallmau and Sinan both dying along with her before even finding the Bone Lord who had kidnapped Rixende.

Rerek had used her to drain Sinan, the only person among the three of them who knew how to kill a necromancer who was already dead. Gallmau had fought his way out of a frozen lake and carried her and Sinan up a mountain, but his sword arm and shield were no match for death magic. Meri was no longer half-frozen, but she hadn't rested enough to restore her speed.

No, they didn't have much of a chance against Rerek, but

Meri had chopped the head off the death witch who had murdered her sister and countless other children once, and she'd be damned if she didn't die trying to do it a second time.

As Rerek stepped forward, his antlered head silhouetted against an entire wall of mounted horns, Sinan didn't hesitate. He sent several thrusts of shadow magic at Rerek as he wielded his blade in the air. The technique had worked well against the assassin Cliona, but the ribbon-like strikes had little effect on the veneficus. Every hit only sparked a green flash of protection around Rerek, outlining his unnatural form in an eerie light.

Rerek ignored Sinan's blows and advanced toward him, his eyes a pale white, devoid of any pupils, yet somehow gleaming in anticipation. Meri fought the urge to sink into her speed, knowing her stamina was limited. Her water blades might have more impact upon Rerek than Sinan's weakened shadow powers, and she wanted any strike she landed to count. She might only get one chance.

Gallmau, as she should have expected, mistook her discipline in not attacking as a sign she was too injured to fight. He charged in with his short sword, and Rerek turned in his direction, the twisted smile on the dead necromancer's face widening.

A noxious cloud of greenish smoke billowed toward the prince, and Gallmau ended up choking and gasping on his knees, as the undead Bone Lord strode forward to loom over him, a heavy bone club now in his hand.

Sinan rushed in to block the blow with his own body. Rerek slammed the club against his shadow shields, once, then a second time. Sinan's ribbons of protection grew fainter with each hit.

Meri dropped into her speed and moved. She pushed

Gallmau away from the hovering cloud of green, then stepped in and swung at Rerek's neck as he lifted his club against Sinan a third time. Both her speed and Rerek's distraction gave her a solid chance to land two quick blows with her blades.

It was a chance she missed.

Rerek avoided the two strikes, his toxic green barrier preventing her from striking his now-corporeal form. Meri was forced to retreat across the room before she dropped back into the normal stream of time, exhausted.

Gallmau and Sinan pulled back to a far corner, and the young necromancer talked in low, urgent tones as the prince nodded. The two sprang into action, with Gallmau picking up his shield and charging toward Rerek as Sinan circled around the two of them, sending shadow slashes through the air in movements as precise as a ritual dance.

Rerek came to a halt, light flashing around him as Gallmau started to bash his shield against the invisible barrier around the undead death witch.

This was their hope. Even weakened, Sinan had the skill and power to land repeated blows on Rerek's defenses, and Gallmau had more strength and stamina than any fighter she had ever seen. If she could help them, use her speed to slip inside Rerek's defenses and get her blades through his neck, they could end this.

Only she couldn't.

She tried again and again, but her body, weakened by the pain of Rerek's curse and the physical toll of escaping the storm, wouldn't listen to her. She could only stand, cursing herself, as the momentum of the fight changed.

Rerek swung his club at Gallmau, and an explosion of green light slammed into the prince. He was tossed across the room and against the wall of mounted antlers, his sword lying by his side and blood streaming from his head. A scream ripped out of her, so despairing and animalistic she hardly believed it had come from her own throat.

Sinan moved in to protect Gallmau, his sword flashing, but Rerek must have been waiting for him to get within range of his other, awful power.

The cloud of poison, bright green and writhing like a nest of snakes, enveloped Sinan. He gasped, his hands going to his throat, and dropped to his knees, trying to cough out the poison and failing.

That left only Meri and Rerek standing.

It had been fated to end this way. She would pay now for what she had done to Rerek, and there were no regrets in her mind, except for the three young lives she hadn't been able to save—and the life of the young Soissons princess who meant everything to Gallmau.

Meri waited until Rerek was only an arm's length away to move, pretending to stand trembling and awed by his monstrous shape before she lashed out with her blades. Her arms felt as heavy as stone, and the air she sucked in burned its way into her lungs. She fought on, slashing again and again, but every time Rerek's magical shield blocked her.

He waited, the smile on his face a grinning rictus of hatred, until her blows faltered, then grabbed her by the neck with both hands.

"Kill you." His voice was a raspy remnant of the melodious speech she had heard from him so many years ago.

His resurrection had left him less human and more bestial, but no less dangerous. Smooth and educated, he had bought off or blackmailed those in power, and his crimes had been covered up by the likes of Odart of Dol. Those who had chosen to look the other way as he preyed on children were as damned to the tortures of Hell as Rerek was.

"Slow. Yes. Very slow." He lifted her off her feet and slammed her into the wall, and pain shot from the back of her head down her spine. The fingers around her windpipe opened a fraction, allowing a trickle of air through. Her death would take a long time, and then he would finish off Gallmau and take whatever was left of Sinan—if the two of them were unlucky enough to live that long.

Her vision blurred with pain, she barely recognized the small shape that scurried toward Rerek's feet. The veneficus wore a long robe, and she realized now his feet had transformed into hooves.

A tiny tail swished, and Sinan's ghost rat reached out to bite the undead Bone Lord.

Dazed with pain and lack of breath, Meri was possessed by an insane desire to giggle. The little rodent grasped the edge of the fabric of Rerek's robe and tugged at it, eyes burning with blue light. The action was so hopeless, so pathetic, Rerek hadn't noticed. Instead he leaned closer, dragging a sticky tongue over the side of her face. She felt revulsion and desire at the same time and realized the veneficus was feeding off of her. On the floor, the ghost rat was backing up, dragging a strip of shadow from Rerek's form.

The dark blot on the floor stretched out, and then a boy stood there, his face solemn. He had light skin and tufts of straw-colored hair under a felt hat, and wore the odd suspenders and deerskin short trousers Meri had seen in her time in Diurstic.

Her mind must be slipping into madness, because as she watched the child reached into Rerek—inside him—and pulled.

A pale arm emerged, and a second boy joined the first. His clothes were similar, and his face—Meri knew that face. She had that visage burned into her mind and would never forget the ravaged little body she had carried out of Rerek's obscene mansion. His mother's screams still rang in her ears during her nightmares, as did the woman's prayerful thanks to Meri that she had at least a body to bury. The other child they had found there had been dead longer, his features distorted by death and decay.

Two of Rerek's victims stood behind the undead veneficus, and then another arm emerged from his hulking form.

A little brown arm, wrists jangling with copper bracelets.

Meri screamed, thrashing in Rerek's hold.

He tightened his grip on her, digging his nails into the skin of her neck, and Sanura stepped out onto the floor without the veneficus even noticing.

She was a head taller than the two young boys—she had been ten when she was murdered—and dressed in her play clothes, with a head wrap pulling back her long black curls and hoop earrings that had been her pride and joy.

Meri's dead little sister looked up at her and smiled.

She pulled out a knife and the two boys followed suit. The children encircled Rerek and began stabbing him, and Meri could only stare in shock, her mind reeling.

After the first strike, Rerek screamed in fear and rage, and his hold on Meri weakened. She sucked in a grateful gulp of air and fell to the floor. Her mind told her she needed to find her blades and join the fight, but her body was wracked with pain, and she could do nothing more than roll to her side and watch as the attack unfolded.

The blows came fast and sure, each delivered with a solemn expression by the three children. His flashing shield couldn't stop them, and his flailing arms and the cloud of green fog he spread around himself had no effect. There was no bleeding, only gaping holes of void in his body left behind by the knife cuts. Nothing he did—his howls of rage, curses in different tongues and accents, or towards the end, his weeping cries—stopped the relentless work of Sanura and the two boys.

Rerek fell back on the floor, sprawled out with his antlered head twisted to one side, like a slaughtered stag ready to be hung up and gutted. Sanura knelt beside him and began to saw through his chest with her knife. The two boys dropped their weapons and reached with their hands to pull both sides of the ribcage open. The undead veneficus's ribs were blackened and brittle, and they cracked into dust as the cavity was opened up. Inside, there was a mass of squirming tissue, greenish-black and viscous. Sanura reached inside with both arms and pulled a fourth child out of the dead Bone Lord.

He was emaciated and naked, with a hairless head that had two soft nubs on top, like a starving fawn in the forest, waiting for a predator to end his misery. As the new child stumbled to his feet, the three ghost children stood up to face him. The first boy came forward and engulfed him in a hug before his own body blurred and disappeared. The second boy, whose dead body Meri had brought back to his grieving mother, also embraced the fourth child. Within another moment, that young murder victim had faded away as well.

The boy pulled out of Rerek's chest faced Sanura, trembling. She reached out and took both of his shaking hands in hers.

"You can go now." Meri's sister sounded as bright and caring as when she was alive. The boy nodded, somehow understanding her Kushian dialect, and his form blew away like fog in the wind.

Sanura turned to Meri and walked up to her, her steps light and joyful. She knelt to stroke Meri's face, her small fingers cold as the ice swirling outside the chateau. "I did it, Meri. I saved you from him. You're safe now."

20

SINAN

S inan tried to vomit again, but his retching produced only some sour liquid in his mouth. He had nothing left in his stomach, and Rerek's poison had spread too far for his body to expel it. There was no power left in his antidote sigil, and even his health rune had faded away. His cloak was the immaculate white of a burial shroud—as it should be when death was this near.

His body disagreed that throwing up wasn't worth trying, and another wave of nausea wracked him. Death was the final mercy, and it would come soon.

He was lying in his own vomit on the cold floor of a *cabinet à l'anglaise* off the main floor of the chateau. The not-so-rustic hunting lodge of the King of Soissons had been outfitted with a water closet with running water, a marble floor, and stucco reliefs on the walls depicting stylized flowers and animals of the hunt. Candlelight from the sconces on the wall gave the illusion the beasts were frolicking in a white plaster garden.

It was a bizarre place to die.

Gallmau had carried him into the small room cradled in his arms like a child. It was worse than the humiliation of being carted up the mountain on the prince's back, but at least it gave Sinan some privacy in his last moments.

Heavy footsteps thudded outside the room, and Gallmau opened the door to peer in at him. "Are you feeling any better?"

Sinan wasn't, in fact, going to feel better until he lost consciousness and died. He refrained from sharing this with Gallmau. He hated to admit weakness in front of his enemies, even if it was obvious he was helpless.

"A little," Sinan lied.

He closed his eyes, hoping Gallmau would leave, but the prince came into the room and placed a large tray on the floor. Steam from a jug of hot water floated up into the chilly air of the water closet.

A moment later, Gallmau's powerful arms were around his shoulders, pushing him into a sitting position. Sinan tried to protest about being touched, but at this point his heart wasn't in it.

"I know you're a scary Bone Lord who doesn't like hugs." Gallmau took a washcloth and wiped Sinan's face before lifting a cup of warm tea to Sinan's lips. It tasted like honey and flowers, and Sinan's powers had weakened to the point where the prince's touch was close to tolerable. "But you need to try and hold something down. I'll make us all dinner once we figure out what to do with the ghost."

"Sanura's still corporeal?" Sinan guessed Meri wouldn't handle that well.

If he wasn't dying, he could give them advice about what

to do now that Meri's *assecula daemonium* had been destroyed by the spirits of the children Rerek had murdered. Even though Gallmau and Meri weren't badly hurt, the two of them would be in awful danger once they left the chateau. Rerek hadn't sent the ice storm or kidnapped Rixende, and whoever had done both of those things would be even more powerful than the undead *veneficus*. Sinan knew Meri and Gallmau well enough by now to be sure they wouldn't hesitate to go up against whoever had taken Gallmau's sister, even if they didn't have a mage fighting alongside them.

It was surprising how much it bothered him that the two Tomb Fighters might die without his help.

"Meri's worried her sister's soul can't go to Heaven—well, she calls it Paradise, but I'm pretty sure it's the same place." Gallmau put down the cup after Sinan shook his head, unable to drink any more of the tea. "I found this in the pantry when I went to look for food. Meri wants me to ask you if it's real."

He pulled a glass sphere out of his pocket. It looked as fragile as a soap bubble, and inside hundreds of small blue stones hung suspended as if time and gravity didn't apply to them.

Sinan thought for a moment he was hallucinating from the poison.

There was enough Amor Vitriol in that sphere to cripple hundreds of necromancers, perhaps as much as had been used in the final battle of the Witches' War.

Gallmau had mentioned Zhang Jue had accompanied the King on the visits to the chateau on occasion, but why would the Sorcier du Roi hide such a valuable weapon in the kitchen of a remote hunting lodge? Now Meri had her hands on it, which could give her an advantage over

Rixende's abductor—assuming he was one of the Blessed. It could also help her kill any of Sinan's people she faced in the future.

"Yes." Sinan told Gallmau enough of the truth to push the Tomb Fighters into the right decision. "It's real. If you use it, it will help you with the ghost."

It would destroy any trace of necromantic energy on the entire mountain. Sinan would die, but he would anyway from the poison, and it would be worth it to have less Amor Vitriol in the world.

"Good." Gallmau sounded relieved. He unfolded a blanket and wrapped it around Sinan's shoulders. "I brought that white soap you like, so you can wash up. I'll come back when Meri and I have fixed everything, and we'll have a nice hot meal."

Sinan leaned his head against the stucco wall, his movements sluggish, as if he was swimming in sand. Gallmau patted him on the back and walked back to the door like an amiable bear deciding not to eat the injured hunter he had found in the woods. How strange that someone like him, trained from birth to hate and fear the Blessed, could show Sinan kindness.

"Gallmau." Sinan found even speaking was an effort. "Thank you."

The prince's face broke into a wide smile, and it was as if the candlelit and foul-smelling room had been drenched in sunshine. He was the most beautiful man Sinan had ever met.

"You're welcome. Try to rest. I'll be back soon."

Then Gallmau was gone, and only the room's shadows were left to give Sinan what cold comfort they could. He tried to dredge up enough strength for the pre-burial ritual of the Church of Death.

He succeeded in pulling off his borrowed clothing, leaving only his cloak, after multiple pauses to regain his breath or to dry heave. Drained, he curled up on his side, and even the cold marble floor under his nude body wasn't enough to overcome his fatigue. Eventually he was able to at least scrub at his skin with the warm water and soap Gallmau had provided.

The poison had advanced through his body, and gray-green lines branched under his skin. Every breath was an agony now, and in the end he could barely wrap his cloak around himself and pull his hood over to cover his face.

He lay there wrapped in his shroud, reciting the funeral prayer to the Lady of Shadows, the ninth and final saint of the pantheon, and waited to die.

There was a knock on the door, and Gallmau's voice rang out. "Sinan, Meri has another question."

Sinan scrunched his eyes shut and tried to ignore the prince.

But Gallmau was kneeling by his side a moment later. "You don't look good. Your cloak is all white, too. Meri said that meant it was broken."

"My sacred garment is fulfilling its final function." Sinan wanted to prepare himself as well as he could for his entry into the Holy Void of Chaos, and Gallmau was not helping his focus. He had made it through about half of the opening lines of the funeral prayer, and if he could hold on for another quarter of an hour, he might complete the first cycle of the liturgy.

Gallmau pushed the hood off Sinan's face, his gaze concerned. "What function is that? You should be lying on the blanket. The floor is too cold."

"I'm dying." Sinan realized Gallmau was not going to grasp subtle hints. "Ask your question quickly."

"No, I'm not going to let that happen." Gallmau had already started to scoop him into his arms as he spoke.

Sinan tried to protest, but his head was full of fog, and Gallmau's body was much more comfortable than the icy floor. The shroud cloak protected his skin from the prince's touch, and his powers had waned so much his Blessing was barely active. Maybe he could tolerate a brief contact with the prince without fabric between them, if only to enjoy the touch of someone else's skin against his for the last time.

Gallmau moved quickly, and in a few seconds Sinan found himself back in the room where they had fought Rerek. Bits of plaster covered the floor, and wisps of necromantic energy floated in the air like flecks of ash. Sanura stood in one corner, stroking the fur of Sinan's ghost rat as the animal perched on her arm. She had a smile on her face, both sad and triumphant at the same time. Meri was on her knees in front of her sister's ghost, sobbing.

"Sinan says he's dying." Gallmau stood with Sinan in his arms as Meri climbed to her feet and whirled around.

"No, he's not." Meri made that sound like a command Sinan couldn't refuse. She still wore only trousers, with bare feet and the bandage Sinan had instructed Gallmau to put on her wounds wrapped around her breasts. She gripped the sphere of Amor Vitriol in one hand, and the sight of the Lioness of Abdju holding the most dangerous substance the Blessed had ever faced was absolutely terrifying. "You helped me destroy Rerek. There has to be a way to fix this."

Gallmau placed Sinan down at the piles of bedding the three of them had slept in. Meri yanked off part of the shroud cloak and stared in horror at the poison expanding across Sinan's body like cracks in a crumbling wall.

"Rerek's magic is still in this room. I can smell it." Meri thrust the Amor Vitriol in Sinan's face, and he tried not to jerk away. "Tell me how to get rid of it and convince Sanura to go to Paradise."

Sinan doubted he could influence a corporeal spirit as powerful as Meri's undead sister even if he wasn't half dead. The blue stones in the glass sphere would do it, though, and then the cursed substance would be gone, unable to be used against his people.

"Use the Amor Vitriol." Sinan managed to get those words out.

Meri looked at the sphere and back to Sinan, her voice frantic. "You said it was unstable in water and fire. What do I use?"

Sinan closed his eyes, thinking of the final battle of the Witches' War, when Odart of Dol had used Amor Vitriol against the defenders of Karakoncolos. So many of the Blessed had died then, burnt alive or hacked to death by the Shields. Smoke and fire were everywhere. His mother fell in combat against Odart—as he lay wounded and helpless watching.

It was the end of Karakoncolos, the end of his mother's dream—and then Sinan was granted the shadow powers he had been waiting for his entire life. He had enough strength to turn the tide and crush the Noviodunam forces who planned to destroy his city. The incensori, the fulgari, and most of all, the hated benandanti in their black and silver—he killed twice as many of the enemy as his people had lost in the battle. Then he rallied the surviving Blessed, and his city had been saved from destruction.

Sinan had become the Prince of Shadows in a hail of glowing embers and the stench of burning bodies, and he saw no reason not to end his life the same way.

"Fire," Sinan said, and not even a heartbeat later he

watched as Meri yanked open the door to the stove and hurled the sphere inside.

It glistened for a moment on top of the red coals, then exploded.

Blue light filled the room, scouring away every trace of death magic, and Sinan's consciousness with it.

21

SINAN

Lips, soft and plump, pressed against Sinan's mouth. Desire flared inside him, and he kissed back, the intimate contact warm and inviting. As his eyes fluttered open, his mind registered that this time it was Meri's mouth on his. He felt no pain, none of the mix of agony, repulsion, and lust that even brushing his skin against the living brought with it.

Also, he wasn't dead.

Sinan pushed himself up into a sitting position as Meri pulled away, smothering a laugh.

Gallmau hovered over the Lioness's shoulder, looking anxious. "Is he breathing now?"

"He stuck his tongue in my mouth, so I think he's on the mend." Meri beamed at Sinan, which was even more surprising than the fact he was still alive.

"What did you do to me this time?" Sinan touched his

lips, unsure why the contact with Meri hadn't triggered his Blessing. As pleasant as the sensation had been, the inability to touch another without pain had been the price for his Gift.

All around him, the room had been cleansed of necromancy. The wisps of Rerek's power had been wiped out, and Sanura and the ghost rat were gone. He tried to reach out, to sense death in the chateau or the earth around him, but felt nothing. It made him uneasy.

"You stopped breathing," Gallmau said. "Meri tried to breathe for you. Then you woke up."

"That's not what I meant." Sinan looked over at the heating stove.

The door gaped open, and a pile of smoldering embers glowed where the Amor Vitriol had been released. In his weakened state, he shouldn't have been able to survive contact with a small amount of the material, much less the full sphere.

Could he have lost his Blessing, and along with it, any shred of affinity for death magic? Fear rose up in him, but he smothered the emotion and tried to focus. Perhaps he had been able to tolerate Meri's touch because she had recently carried not one, but four undead spirits in her body. His Blessing allowed him contact with the dead.

Sinan reached out his hand to Gallmau. "Can I—touch you?"

The prince blushed, and Meri laughed. "Gallmau's been waiting for you to ask him that for a while."

Gallmau reached out his arm, and Sinan ran his fingers over the prince's forearms, stroking the smooth skin over hard muscle. He felt no pain or revulsion, only a pleasant sensual experience.

The prince was quite red now and avoided Sinan's gaze. "I thought you didn't like to get too close to us."

"It doesn't hurt." Sinan only realized he was voicing his thoughts when the words came out of his mouth. His Blessing wasn't something he wanted known outside of Karakoncolos.

"That's your curse?" Meri moved closer to him.

Sinan found that while his mind told him to pull away, his body was rooted to the spot. She was far more dangerous to him now than she had been before, but he was thinking more about kissing her than protecting himself.

"You can't touch other people. The death magic changed you on the inside, where we can't see it."

"It's not a curse; it's a Blessing." Sinan didn't know why he was arguing with Meri about semantics at a time like this. "It's different for every one of us. Sometimes the Blessing is an alteration of the physical body, and sometimes it involves the mental sphere."

"You could touch yourself, right?" Gallmau asked.

Sinan realized he was not only incapable of sensing death around him, he was naked other than his shroud cloak, which had been half torn off him in the explosion of the Amor Vitriol. He drew the fabric closer to cover his chest and lower body, and tried to summon his shadow shields.

Nothing happened.

He focused on thinking logically, not on his growing panic. He was still one of the Blessed, and all of this had to be nothing more than a temporary side effect.

"Because if you couldn't even pleasure yourself, that would be awful." Gallmau furrowed his brow, clearly following this line of thinking to its natural conclusion. "What about corpses?"

"Yes, I can touch the dead, and no, don't you dare accuse of me violating the deceased." Sinan gave up on the shields and glared at Gallmau. "It's a grave sin. Well, not with a corporeal spirit, but that's different. They can choose to have sex with the living."

"That explains why Naghwe enjoyed touching Gallmau so much." Meri ran her fingers up along Sinan's exposed arm, imitating how he had touched the prince. "Have you ever been with someone? Or did this so-called blessing of yours come when you were a baby?"

"I was nineteen when I received my Blessing." Sinan had flinched at Meri's first touch, but he found that he liked the light touch of Meri's fingertips against his skin, and there wasn't much point in trying to hide his secret any longer. "Before then I had no necromantic powers at all, even though my mother was one of the Blessed. Everything came to me at once, when we were under attack in the Witches' War. I haven't had a lover since then. It's hard enough to have someone brush against me."

"How old are you?" Gallmau continued with his questions even as he handed Sinan a pair of trousers and another blanket. "They say Bone Lords can live to be two hundred years old."

"I'm five and twenty." Sinan pulled on the pants and wrapped the wool cloth around him, aware of Meri watching him with bright, avaricious eyes. His modesty should be the least of his problems. He was cold, desperately hungry and thirsty, and couldn't perform death magic.

Sex should be the last thing on his mind.

Gallmau added wood to the stove and began fussing around with the kettle. The prince had promised to feed him, and the son of King Syagrius kept his promises.

"Six years without anyone in your bed." Meri pressed

against him and pulled part of his blanket over her shoulders. It was warmer like that, and her soft skin next to his felt so good. "That's a long time."

"The Lady grants us both a Blessing and our affinities." Sinan recited some of his faith's teachings in an effort to distract himself from his growing arousal. "Some Blessings are more challenging than others, but all are holy. I'm fortunate mine allows me to defend my people."

"Mother Naghwe did give birth to you, then." Gallmau came over to both of them with a kettle and cups and motioned for them to drink. "I thought Bone Lords couldn't have babies."

"Sometimes we can, especially the venefici." Sinan sucked down one cup of tea, then another. Telling the truth might not be the wisest decision, but he had to make them understand. "I can't help you free Rixende with my magic right now. It's gone, along with my Blessing. And I—don't know when it's coming back."

Meri didn't look as concerned as Sinan felt. "You said Amor Vitriol had been used in the Witches' War. Did the other necromancers exposed to it ever regain their death magic?"

"Most were slaughtered when they became helpless." Sinan had to push away the memories of that day, the people he knew and loved who had been killed because of the substance. "The few who survived didn't handle the loss of their Gift well. The chose the path of Chaos in the months following the battle."

"Suicide, you mean." Gallmau came back with a platter of pantry provisions—hard cheese, sliced smoked sausage, and pickled cornichons. "That's a sin."

"In the Church of Saints it is." Sinan placed a piece of sausage in his mouth, savoring the taste of spice and salt. He had always tried to preserve some of his former life's pleasures, like food and drink, but the more he used his necromantic powers, the further away he drifted from living human sensations. Now he could taste and feel everything, and he wanted more of it. He pressed closer to Meri, the fear of pain from contact with her fading. "In our Church of the Dead, it's a sacrament."

Meri gestured for Gallmau to join them. He had been occupied cleaning up the room and preparing more plates of food. He finally sat down, eyeing Sinan and Meri's close contact with unease, as if he wanted to join in but wasn't sure.

"Two of our people who survived the Amor Vitriol began to have some ability to do simple death magic, like sending a shadow letter, after a few months." Sinan tried to remember more details but couldn't. It had been such a turbulent time, and there had been so much grief, so much rebuilding. "That wasn't enough for them, and they didn't wish to go on. Many of us have our Blessings revealed when we're young, along with our affinities. Losing everything—it was too much for them to bear."

"But you were a normal person for nineteen years." Meri popped a sour and crunchy pickle into Sinan's mouth, her fingers lingering on his lips. "Other than having a sex demon for a mother, being raised in a death cult, and living in a city of monsters."

"You need a sorcerer for this fight, and I'm useless right now."

"Maybe you can't appear out of shadows or turn them into weapons anymore, but you know about necromancy and can handle a blade." Meri did like to focus on practicalities. "Gallmau and I weren't planning on help from witches anyway. Once day breaks, we'll head out to find Rixende.

Even without your powers, you're still fighting alongside us, and that's all I care about."

"I thought you'd want to kill me." Sinan wanted to hope Meri and Gallmau saw him as an ally and not an enemy, but he had too many reservations about Tomb Fighters and their hatred for the Blessed.

"I would never do anything like that." Gallmau's words wouldn't have rung true when they first met, but Sinan had lain dying and helpless on an icy floor as the prince tried to comfort him, and he believed him now. "You saved our lives on the lake, you fought against Rerek with us—we'll watch out for you. I'm sure that death magic thing you do will come back. You seemed awfully good at it."

"I was planning to kill you." Meri sounded every bit as sincere as the prince. "Especially since I thought you were helping Rerek torture me."

"I did help him, but not intentionally." Sinan needed to be honest with Meri and Gallmau and needed them to be honest with him in order to have chance to survive this quest, much less save Rixende. Not too much truth at once, though. "It would help if we could share information."

"We could share many things." Meri ran her fingers up Sinan's neck and began to play with his hair.

It was a deliberate seduction, and he wanted nothing more than to surrender to it. He glanced over at Gallmau, who was doing his best not to look at either of them. Sinan wondered if the two were lovers who also bedded other people or fighting companions who went off to find their own partners.

"I'd like to know about that death witch with the antlers." Gallmau rose to get more food and came back with a small box and a bottle tucked under one arm. "How did

Rerek wipe the floor with us, then get taken down by little kids?"

"Meri tried to save three lives." Sinan had to be careful about what he told the two of them. The Lioness, in particular, might not take the full truth about her sister Sanura well. "The dead children haunted Rerek, and were part of the assecula daemonium and fighting it at the same time. They each gave Meri one year of life, trying to protect her. When Rerek drained my powers he made sure to take away my poison protection sigil. His appearance was timed so he could make Meri watch as he killed the two of us, then torture her to death. Revenge against her meant everything to him, but he failed to account for the children also taking the power I had stored up. They used it to destroy him."

"Sanura wouldn't leave me." Meri's voice cracked as she said her sister's name. "She kept petting that ghost rat of yours and saying I was still in danger. Do you think"—she choked on the words, then regained control—"she's in Paradise now?"

"I don't know." Sinan chose his next words with care. "Sanura presented as a powerful corporeal spirit, and they often cross over the Veil to Chaos only when they choose to."

"Who was the fourth child?" Gallmau asked. "The little boy they pulled out of the death witch's body."

"That was Rerek." Sinan didn't know if Meri and Gallmau could accept that monsters weren't born, they were made. "As a young child, suffering through what he would later put others through, perhaps, or maybe as who he could have been. Sanura helped him and the other two victims cross over."

Meri drew her knees up and hugged her chest. "She

shouldn't have saved me. I failed her. I failed those two little boys."

"She loves you." Sinan watched as Gallmau came over to Meri's other side and slid his arm around her.

The simple act of offering someone comfort through physical touch had been impossible for Sinan so long that he hesitated before realizing he could rest his own hand on her other shoulder. "There are ways to tell if she's crossed over or to communicate with her if she hasn't. I know you don't like our magic, but we know a good deal about ghosts."

"We need to celebrate, Meri." Gallmau patted the bottle beside him. "We always do, after a fight. Even when we lose, and even when we lose someone close to us."

Meri gave a laugh and wiped her eyes. "Is that why you brought out that bottle?"

"Yes, for me and Sinan." Gallmau pulled away and uncorked it, and a familiar scent of alcohol and pears wafted out. "Some Deathless Spirit I found in my father's wine cellar here. Quite appropriate, I think. Will you drink with me?"

Sinan nodded and took the cup Gallmau offered him. This time he didn't try to avoid touching the prince's hand as he did so. There was no discomfort, only a pleasant tingle with the contact.

He knocked back the liquor, savoring the flavors. "What about Meri?"

"I found some sweets for her." Gallmau produced a small box lined in velvet—he must have been quite busy scouring the chateau for useful items while Sinan had been incapacitated by Rerek's poison. Inside were fanciful creations made from almond paste—a plump pig, plums and apples, and even what might have been a mouse or rat, complete with a square of confectionary cheese. "Maybe we can save the rodent one for Sinan's little ghost friend."

Meri reached up to touch Sinan's face. "I'd like a tumble rather than candy. You can get drunk now, and it's been years since you bedded someone. What do you say to that?"

Sinan had started to sip the second cup of the brandy Gallmau poured for him, and he coughed some of it out in surprise. Meri sounded giddy, as if relief that the veneficus who had killed her sister and possessed her was gone forever made her want to reach out for what she needed right now, and damn the consequences.

Even if what she needed was sex with a necromancer.

It was like Meri to be direct, and Sinan certainly wanted to be with her—and with Gallmau.

The prince squirmed. "I could leave the room."

"Why?" The brandy had already given Sinan a pleasant buzz—he wasn't used to being unprotected by his antidote sigil. He considered that agreeing to sleep with two Tomb Fighters who had been contemplating killing him a day or so ago might not be the wisest decision, then plowed ahead anyway. "I thought you'd be interested as well."

"I guess so." Gallmau gave Meri an outraged look when she giggled at his hesitation. "All right. Hell yes, I want to, but I didn't know if you preferred men or women."

The most important question should be if Sinan would consider sex with someone who wasn't one of the Blessed, but the customs of Soissons were so different than those in Karakoncolos. "I had men and women as lovers when I was younger. Many in Karakoncolos stay celibate, but it's not required. Not many would want to lie with an *inimicus*, but I —never minded."

"That means enemy, I thought," Gallmau said.

Meri took Sinan's convoluted response as a solid yes and

began to run her hand over his chest, then strayed lower. She stroked his hard length under his trousers, her fingers warm and soft.

"It does." Sinan took in a deep breath, his desire clouding his ability to even think. "We use the same word for people who aren't the Blessed."

"Both of you talk too much." Meri reached over to pull Gallmau closer to them, lifted off his shirt, and undid his trousers.

"You and I have never—done this." Despite his half-hearted protest Gallmau allowed himself to be undressed, and he was as erect as Sinan was, although not even tipsy. "Are you sure you're well enough for this, Meri?"

"Kiss him and shut him up," Meri told Sinan, which wasn't a difficult order to follow.

He pressed his lips against Gallmau's, the two of them sharing the sting of brandy on their tongues. Sinan shifted his weight onto Gallmau, which should have had as much of an effect as trying to topple a small mountain, but the prince let him push him onto his back.

The two of them broke off their kiss for a moment as Meri straddled Gallmau. She had already disposed of her clothing, and she ground against him with sinuous movements of her hips.

"Meri's hard to say no to." Gallmau gasped that out, then reached to pull Sinan down on top of him. "Kiss me again. Harder."

Sinan laughed, the absurdity of their situation striking him, and pushed his tongue into the prince's mouth. He ran his own hands down Gallmau's chest, admiring the hard angles of the prince's muscled torso, then traced a line of gold hair down the muscled expanse of his abdomen.

Gallmau somehow succeeded in removing Sinan's

trousers even with Meri thrusting on him. He ran his hands down the curve of Sinan's spine, hesitating a moment before descending lower to cup the swell of his buttocks in his powerful hands.

Meri rolled off Gallmau, panting, and turned her attention to Sinan. "I want you between us." The words rushed out of her in a gasp, and she had yanked him on top of her before he had a chance to tell her yes.

He kissed her, deep and slow, as she thrust her hips up toward him until she found the rhythm she wanted and let him slip inside her. Gallmau was on top of him now, the swell of his erection pushing at him from behind.

"Do you want me?" Gallmau whispered the words into Sinan's ear, his breath warm and panting. "Tell me if it's what you like."

"Yes." Sinan could barely get the word out, his own breaths coming fast, and the incredible sensation of being able to touch and touching back overwhelming him. "Don't stop."

Meri wrapped her legs around both of their thighs, and they ground together in a tangle of skin and sweat until all three of them were spent. Sinan lay there pressed between both of their bodies for a long moment, sweaty and gasping.

With a sigh of satisfaction, Meri rolled out from under them to curl up on top of the blankets, her eyes closing in exhaustion in seconds.

Gallmau pulled away from Sinan and found a soft shawl in the mess of fabric around them to drape over Meri. Her chest, still bound with the bandages over the slashes on her back, rose and fell in a steady rhythm as she slept. The two of them stared down at her, not saying anything.

"Well." Gallmau patted Meri's shoulders and looked up at Sinan with an amazed expression. "That just happened."

Sinan pulled Gallmau's head down for another kiss. "Find some oil and pour me more brandy, and it can happen again."

22

MERI

Meri awoke to the cool touch of Sinan's hand on her shoulder. It took her a few seconds to remember what that meant.

"Are you well?" The necromancer looked—more human, somehow. He had stubble around his chin, and his dark eyes had lost that dangerous glitter. "Gallmau and I have everything ready for us to head out, but I should change your bandage first."

Meri pushed herself into a sitting position and blinked into full awareness. "You can still touch me."

Sinan gave her a rueful smile. "And I'm still useless as a sorcerer."

Until last night, Meri wouldn't have believed necromancy could be cured, much less that she would hope Sinan's curse would return so he could help them with his death magic. Then again, before they had defeated Rerek she might not have tumbled a Bone Lord, either.

She waited until he had cleaned and redressed the wounds on her back before pulling on her now-dry garments and going to relieve herself. When she returned she noticed a breakfast laid out near the fire, including hot tea and a warm porridge. Gallmau hated to see anyone go hungry, and he always handled the cooking when they were traveling. It was unusual he wasn't around to urge her to eat more.

"Gallmau went out to scout our surroundings." Sinan stowed the supplies he had used on her wounds in his travel sack as he spoke. His pack, made from a pale silk fabric similar to his shroud, had kept his belongings protected even when he had been dragged underwater by the demon catfish. Her own pack was long gone, since she had thrown it aside to gain better speed when she had tried to rescue Gallmau from the same beast in the lake. "The storm's over, but whoever created it is still out there. If this was our welcome, Jacques and Abarsam were probably attacked as well."

"Or they could already have found Rixende." Meri wanted Gallmau's sister to be safe, but she also liked to win, and they had lost valuable time fighting the storm and Rerek.

"I can't sense if the princess is still among the living." Sinan pulled a small leather pouch from his pack and brought it over to Meri. "Even basic death magic is beyond me now, but I was hoping you might be able to use these relics."

Meri opened the pouch and pulled out two small objects. Both were spherical, their surfaces gleaming white except for a red mark, like a drop of blood. She turned them over and saw fine red lines on the opposite side and a short stalk, as if they had been stone buds lopped off a petrified plant. They had a hard, smooth surface, more like ivory than polished stone. It took several moments for Meri to figure out why they looked familiar.

"These look like Cliona's eyes." Meri wasn't often squeamish, but she did have her limits. "Please tell me they're not."

"I turned them into bone after I removed them." Sinan sounded detached and clinical about digging out the eyeballs of the necromancer assassin. "It's the first step in creating a talisman from someone with a shadow affinity. Others of the Blessed could do much more with such powerful relics. We have our own craftsmen, similar to the Artifex Guild in the Noviodunam."

"Let me guess." Meri kept Cliona's petrified eyes cupped in her hand, both fascinated and repulsed. "Your artifices make cursed jewelry and attractive vials to store poison in."

"Cursed or enchanted, poison or medicine—everything depends on how you use it." Sinan sighed. "Or can't use it, in my case. I've seen mages with no necromantic abilities use relics like these. Since you were recently possessed by an assecula daemonium, maybe they would work for you."

"I'm not trying necromancy." Meri slid the spheres into the bag and handed them to Sinan. "Please take your eyeballs back. You told me you considered relics to be gruesome trophies from murdered babies the first time we met, remember?"

"We don't take trophies. We take useful body parts from those we love and those we hate." Sinan tucked the bag into a pocket, perhaps hoping Gallmau would be more accepting of Cliona's eyeballs. "In a duel to the death, the loser surrenders their physical remains to the winner. In a natural death, many of the Blessed will pass on their bodies to those they cherished during life."

"I don't want chopped-up bits of dead people, whether I hated them or not." She could sense Sinan wanted to reach out to her, to continue the rapprochement they had started last night. That made her uneasy. It wasn't that she regretted the sex—it had been wonderful, and she had needed a catharsis—but there was such a gulf between the two of them she couldn't imagine how they could bridge it. Perhaps it was enough to know Sinan wanted their mission to succeed as much as she and Gallmau did. More than that was too much, and too scary.

Sinan watched her face, as if seeking clues that would help him understand her. "What if Cliona's relics could help you communicate with Sanura?"

The agony of seeing her murdered sister's body years ago flooded back, along with the fresh grief of knowing Sanura's soul had clung to this world only to save Meri. "I want my sister to be at peace. She suffered not only before her death but after it, because of me. I have my memories of her—she was in my dreams last night. I don't want the ability to call her up from the grave."

"She hasn't passed into the Holy Void of Chaos if she dream-walked into your sleep world last night." Sinan turned his attention back to organizing his travel pack and cleaning his sword, as Meri tried to absorb what he had said. She took a deep breath, reminding herself that Sinan, even without his necromancy, still thought and spoke like a Bone Lord. Last night couldn't change that.

"We should go now." Gallmau leaned in from the doorway. His posture was stiff, and he avoided looking at Meri, instead directing his comment at Sinan. "The sun's up, and the snow and ice from last night are melting."

Now, what had gotten into him? Gallmau sometimes expressed regret about his tendency to sin, but after a few prayers and some cider, he was back to bedding whichever handsome local man had caught his eye. Granted, tumbling a necromancer like Sinan might require a few extra offerings to his patron saint.

"I suppose I should take your advice and put this on." Sinan held up the breastplate for Gallmau's inspection. "Do you still think we should head North?"

"We'll stick to your plan." Gallmau turned to leave without a word to Meri, and Sinan tagged along after him, peppering him with questions about the layout of the terrain.

Now she was annoyed. Granted, she had never joined Gallmau in bed with a man before, but it wasn't like his preferences were a surprise to her. She couldn't figure out if he was jealous of her being alone with Sinan or embarrassed about last night. Either way, they didn't have the luxury of Gallmau sulking. They had barely escaped with their lives and still had no idea who or what they would face next.

Cursing men and their moods, Meri crammed the food into her mouth, strapped on her swords, and followed them. After securing the door of the chateau, the three of them made their way down a different trail off the mountain, through the monstrous trees of the ancient forest that surrounded the hunting lodge. They could have made faster headway on the sunny meadow that began as the elevation flattened, but Gallmau set a pace so slow Meri wanted to scream.

The prince kept ignoring her, even as he chatted with Sinan about their location and where to search for Rixende next. She decided to let her friend be, hoping he would get over whatever imagined insult he blamed her for on his own. Since the two men were absorbed in their conversation, she picked up the pace, determined to scout out the trail ahead by herself. Then she stumbled over a rise in the ground and almost fell. It was clumsy of her, but she hadn't fully recovered from yesterday. It was an entirely insignificant event, except that Gallmau lost his mind over it.

"You need to be more careful." Gallmau rushed over and began inspecting her for injuries as if she had run through a gauntlet of assassins from the Order of Katil. "Your back could start to bleed more, and you're still exhausted from last night."

"What are you raving on about?" Meri slapped away Gallmau's hands. "You've been a miserable grump since I woke up, and now you're acting like I'm a walking glass figurine. I slept more last night than you and Sinan did."

Meri had been too exhausted to be fully pulled from sleep by their carousing, but the two men's impressive stamina had half-woken her a few times. Too bad all that sex hadn't distracted Gallmau from his need to be too protective, too much of the time.

"Last night is what caused the problem." Gallmau shot a glance at Sinan, perhaps for support. The necromancer stood staring at them with his head tilted, clearly as baffled as Meri was by the prince's behavior. "My—member was inside your—well, you know what happened."

"You can say we fucked." Meri often found the prince's embarrassment when it came to talking about sex cute, but she wasn't in the mood for this nonsense. "None of the ferocious nuns who taught you making babies is a dirty terrible thing will pop out of the ground and whack your hand."

"You could be with child." Gallmau's face was flushed again, but it was from anger, not shame. "My child. It could be hurt by the fall or in the next fight we're in. You shouldn't be here. It's not safe."

Meri stared back at him, speechless for a moment. Then she exploded.

"We fucked once, and now you think you can tell me what to do." Meri stood with one hand on her hip, her fury so hot she wanted to spit. Getting too close to men was dangerous. You started to think of them as friends, and then they began to think with their cocks. "This is why I don't bed the men I fight with."

She had taught Gallmau all he knew about hunting monsters. He had no right to try and take over this particular quest and act like she was a helpless maiden who needed rescuing. She wasn't Rixende.

At least Sinan had dealt with the morning after their night of passion by giving her the romantic gift of petrified eyeballs. That had been far preferable to this nonsensical fight with Gallmau over a theoretical baby.

Sinan had turned his attention away from their argument to stare out at the horizon. The temperatures had climbed back up to a comfortable level, the sun shone in a bright blue sky, and nothing but soft grass and wildflowers stretched ahead of them except for a copse of trees in the distance. When the necromancer turned back toward them, though, his face was troubled. "Perhaps the two of you could have this conversation later, in a less exposed position. I can't"—he let out a breath, as if frustrated by himself—"give us any warning about an impending attack, much less help to stop one."

"No, we need to talk about this now." Gallmau wagged a finger in her face, and she had serious thoughts about dropping into her speed and slicing it off. "You didn't tell me any details about your curse until it was almost too late. For the

Saints' sake, you didn't even let me know Jacques's father lied and shielded a child-killing Bone Lord. Odart should be arrested and brought up on charges for that crime alone."

"What difference does it make now?" Meri reached up to grab Gallmau's shoulders. Rerek was dead, and she was free. Imaginary babes and corrupt necromancer-hunters were future problems she would deal with if she had to. All she wanted was to get to Rixende before the other two groups did.

Trying to shake some sense into Gallmau didn't work, of course. She had to go up on her toes to reach his upper arms, and he was about as movable as the chateau they had stayed in. It ended up becoming an awkward embrace, and Gallmau enveloped her in a hug.

The Prophets damn the man, he was too hard to stay mad at.

"Sanura came into my dreams last night and told me she saw two futures." He pulled her closer to him. "In one there were children, yours and mine. In another, you died."

The grief that came with hearing her sister's name overwhelmed her. No, Sinan couldn't be right. Sunara must have been released by the Amor Vitriol to journey to Paradise with the guidance of the Prophets. That's where she should be, in an eternal garden filled with lush, green grass and the music of running water, safe in the love and acceptance of the Divine. Her sister shouldn't have to fight on as a ghost, trying to warn them about possible futures.

"Get down. Now." Sinan's words had the deadly command he had used when he had his necromantic powers, and Meri slipped into her speed.

The Azhdarchid came down so quickly Meri had to move fast even while using her Gift. The beast was the largest of the Archaic birds she had seen yet, with a wing-

span of at least thirty feet, an enormous beaked mouth, and
shadows streaming off its coarse downy coat.

A Bone Lord Azhdarchid. Lovely.

The damn thing would have been a monster even if it
hadn't been cursed. It was headed straight for Gallmau, who
had yet to react to Sinan's warning. The necromancer was
taking the sensible route by throwing himself flat on the
ground.

Slashing at the creature's underbelly as it descended for
the kill would have been Meri's first choice, but assuming its
shadow armor worked as it did for human necromancers,
she wouldn't be able to do enough to stop it from snapping
Gallmau's head off.

That meant she had to get close and knock it off its
intended path.

As the winged beast swooped lower Meri launched
herself up in the air and caught its flat, splayed feet with
both hands. Enormous, but weighing less than she did, the
Azhdarchid lurched off course. Wings flapping, the creature
struggled to right itself before it arrived at the next logical
decision, which was to bend its long neck underneath its
body and drive its bill through her heart.

Meri kept in her speed and released her hold at the last
moment, landing hard on the ground. Time rushed back to
its normal pace, and the monster alighted near her, wings
now folded into another set of limbs. It advanced forward
with a stilt-like walk, using the three-clawed joints of its
wings like forelegs. Its eyes, bright and intelligent, glowed a
faint orange as it glared at her and screeched what she could
only assume was a challenge to fight to the death or
complaints about her hitching a free ride.

Meri backed up and drew her blades, trying to draw the
thing away from her two companions, but the Azhdarchid

lunged forward with its beak and tried to spear her like a wriggling fish.

She didn't dip into her speed, cautious about expending energy she didn't have, and that was a mistake. As ungainly as the creature appeared, it could manage a good pace on the ground. Her first dodge to one side worked well, although the slashing blow she tried to land failed. Then the animal swung its great crested head and sent her sprawling.

The Azhdarchid moved in for the kill, its beak gaping open.

Sinan was suddenly above her, close enough to the animal to get a hit inside its shadow armor with his sword. The blow cut a shallow slice into the creature's muscular neck, but once again the Azhdarchid used its crest, and it rammed a blow into Sinan's chest.

Meri recovered enough from her dazed state to sink into her speed and drag Sinan away from the beast. As drawn out as it felt, the battle with the winged predator had taken so little time Gallmau hadn't had a chance to join the fight.

Now he did, and the balance changed.

Gallmau used the same approach he had with Rerek, bashing at the shadow protection around the creature with his shield. The Azhdarchid screeched in fury and smashed its bony head against Gallmau's treasured family heirloom, but the prince had the advantage over the looming but light-weight creature. He pushed the monster back from both Sinan and Meri, not even trying to land a sword blow.

As the dark ripples of energy protecting the Azhdarchid began to dissipate, the creature apparently concluded the three of them weren't tasty enough to require this much effort. It took off with its odd gait, then spread its vast wings and soared upward.

Gallmau lowered his shield and wiped sweat off his brow. "Why the fuck does every monster known to humanity want to track us down in this Saints-forsaken place?"

"A beast master." Sinan gasped out the words, and Meri was alarmed to find the necromancer sagging against her for support. The breastplate Gallmau had found for him had a sizable dent, and Sinan's breathing was shallow. "That's what the necromancer we're facing is. The fish and now an Azhdarchid—they're both Touched."

"We have to find a place to let you lie down and rest." Meri slid her shoulder under Sinan's arm to prop him up and made shushing sounds to stop the necromancer from lecturing them about theories they could do nothing about. "The trees should provide cover to stop that flying monstrosity from attacking us again."

"No time." Gallmau's voice was grim.

Meri lifted her head in alarm and followed Gallmau's gaze.

Three riders were approaching, each on horses that looked comically small, like ponies. Only the mounts weren't undersized, it was their riders who were too large. Each man barreling toward them with dust kicking up from his horse's hooves was taller and broader than even Gallmau and dressed for battle.

"Shields of Thaschus." Sinan got the words out, then paused for breath. His chest was injured, and she'd bet some of his ribs were broken.

They could have used his sword arm in this fight—not to mention his Bone Lord powers—but he couldn't do much in his current situation. She and Gallmau would need to take out the three fighters and try to protect Sinan at the same time.

"They're not wearing those fancy Shield uniforms." Gallmau slung his shield on his back and pulled out his two-hander. "Whoever they are, I'll deal with it. Get behind me."

No, not this again.

"I'm going to do what I can before they get here." Meri prepared to slip into her speed, despite Gallmau's protests.

But Sinan was the one who gripped her arm. "Don't attack them directly. If they're Shields, they would've trained against speed fighters, and they'll have the best protection the Noviodunam artifex guild can provide. Focus on the horses."

Meri couldn't imagine Shields of Thaschus defecting and joining up with a Bone Lord, but whoever the men were, they looked ready to finish the job the Azhdarchid had started.

Time slowed around her as she ran, and she reached the three riders when they were still a good distance from Gallmau and Sinan. The riders were focused on the prince and the reach of his sword. Meri had to take away the advantage their mounts gave them.

Even with her speed, she couldn't kill or maim all three of them as they charged forward, and Sinan's warning had made her more cautious. The men were dressed in dark colors and nondescript light armor, but their bearing and weaponry indicated they were well trained and equipped. Still, they had to be nothing more than high-priced sell-swords, and Sinan's natural fear and hatred for the Shields must be clouding his analysis. The Noviodunam's private soldiers hated Bone Lords.

Meri used one of the small daggers she hid under her garments to slice through the girth attaching the saddle on the rider on her right, then moved to the rider on her left.

The man seated on the middle horse was harder for her to reach, and she knew she had little time left to stay in her speed.

Worse yet, if this trick didn't work, she wouldn't be of much help to Gallmau.

The middle horse pulled ahead of the others as time ticked slowly and the leather girths began to separate. Hopefully, the sudden twist of the saddles would send the men flying off their mounts. She caught up to the rider in the middle, knowing she would need to drop out of her speed soon, and tried to slip her knife through the leather band. Her hand brushed against the rider's leg and sparks filled her vision.

She dropped to the ground, falling out of her speed and losing any control of her limbs. Her fear barely had a chance to register before her head struck against something hard and unyielding. Darkness rushed up to engulf her, and she felt nothing at all.

23

GALLMAU

Gallmau knew Meri should have been back by his side in the blink of an eye, and when she wasn't, that meant trouble. Then she collapsed to the ground, and everything went red.

He planted his feet and waited with his sword over his right shoulder, trying to channel the fury he felt into killing the men who had hurt her. Gallmau had no idea how injured Meri was, or even if she was alive. Those thoughts had to wait. He had to survive himself before he could help her, and that was all he could focus on.

The first rider burst toward him, his arm gripping one of the curved blades the Shields favored for combat on horse-back, as his two companions followed on his heels. Gallmau had trained with fighters aspiring to join the Shields—hell, he had considered trying to join the order himself. He would need every scrap of knowledge he had learned about the famed guards of the Noviodunam to survive a fight with not one, but three fighters as blessed with size and strength by Saint Attilio as he was. He prayed Sinan was wrong and he wasn't facing actual Shields.

Two of the riders went sprawling off their horses as their saddles twisted. Meri had been able to sabotage their girths after all. Then the first rider's horse started, as a flash of white-blue light and a loud bang resounded through the air.

That was more luck than Gallmau had expected. He swung his sword at the momentarily distracted rider and landed a solid blow to the man's left arm, toppling him off the horse.

The man recovered faster than he had hoped, scrambling to his feet and blocking another hit from Gallmau's sword. The two of them traded blows for a few fast, furious seconds before Gallmau had the briefest opening—the other fighter had come in under his guard, with his face a handsbreadth away. Gallmau brought the pommel of his sword up and into the man's nose, hearing the sickening crack as bone shattered, the fragments driving backward and into the man's skull.

The man hadn't even hit the ground before another ear-shattering blast resounded, and a blaze of light blinded Gallmau.

He blinked spots out of his eyes to see another of the giant fighters on the ground, Sinan's sword through his throat. The third was limping toward Gallmau—hurt by the fall off his horse, perhaps. Sinan had something small and metallic in his hand, and he threw it at the approaching man.

This time Gallmau figured out Sinan's trick, and squeezed his eyes shut as the device detonated. The sound and blaze of light halted the man's advance and gave

Gallmau an opportunity to rush the fighter. The man knelt on the ground, a hand covering his eyes. Gallmau hesitated a moment, the surge of battle fever fading as the reality he was about to kill an injured and blinded man sunk in.

The pause cost him. The man drove a short blade up and into Gallmau's shoulder. It could have been a killing blow—but the man's strike went wide, as if on purpose, which didn't make any sense. Hot agony seared through Gallmau's arm, and he lashed out with his own weapon. The blow was off-balance and poorly directed, but the man was rising to his feet, his ruse over, and Gallmau's blade caught him beneath the edge of his helmet. He crumpled, blood spraying out from the severed vessels in his neck.

Sinan came up beside him, and the two of them watched as the man became still and lifeless on the blood-soaked grass.

"Who the hell were they?" Gallmau shook from exertion and revulsion, his ears ringing from whatever Sinan had used against their enemies. He knew the glory of war was nothing more than a charade, a lie told to make the horror of killing other people more palatable. This had been self-preservation, but the rush of satisfaction he felt over the death of three intimidating opponents sickened him. "If they were Shields, they should have been in uniform and helping us, for Saints' sake."

The necromancer beside him only said, "I don't sense anything. No power at all."

Gallmau snapped out of his post-battle fugue of guilt and reflection, and jogged over to the spot he had seen Meri fall. As he tried to quell a growing sense of panic, he mumbled prayers to anyone he could think of—his patron Saint Attilio, the sea gods his older relatives chanted to, even the Prophets of Meri's religion. Then he knelt beside her limp body.

Blood soaked Meri's dark curls, and her eyes were closed.

Gallmau pressed his fingers to her neck, willing a pulse to beat against his skin.

She groaned, and there was a weak flutter under his fingertips.

"Wake up, Meri, please." Gallmau patted her chest and abdomen, searching for injuries, and gently shook her. She didn't respond.

"She's alive?" Sinan caught up to him, but the necromancer was now gasping between words. He had saved Gallmau's life by joining in the fight, but it had cost him. "We need to get to the trees. I can't help you carry her, but I could take your pack, maybe."

Gallmau shook his head and lifted Meri over one shoulder. "I'm fine. Lean on me if you have to."

There was nothing quick about their pace. Even with Gallmau half-dragging Sinan as he carried Meri, the journey to the grove of trees took far too long. He kept scanning the skies overhead and swiveling his head to check the horizon, fearing a return either of the cursed Azhdarchid or more armed men bent on killing them.

Gallmau let out a sigh of relief as they passed by several tree trunks and into the shelter of canopy of leaves above them. Then he spotted a path of crushed vegetation to their right.

Someone or something as large as a man had come through here recently. To hide or maybe to hunt? Gallmau squeezed Sinan's shoulder and jerked his head toward the broken twigs and flattened ferns. Sinan nodded, and Gallmau lowered Meri to the ground at the necromancer's feet. Meri was unconscious, and Sinan looked like he was about to collapse, but Gallmau needed his hands free to face whatever might be waiting for them in the woods.

He stepped forward with caution, each foot placed to avoid excessive noise. This was a hunt, like any other he had been on, and surprise would be his best ally.

It took about ten paces before he came upon the body. The man lying on his back on a tangle of tree roots and moss looked oddly peaceful in death. His arms were crossed over his chest, as if he had been laid out in a casket for viewing. In both size and clothing, he was indistinguishable from the three fighters who had attacked them on horseback. Gallmau wasn't sure whether to be relieved or horrified.

He had his short sword out, ready to strike a killing blow if this was another trick, but the man's gray pallor and bluish lips weren't compatible with life. His armor was untouched, and there was no blood or other sign of violence. How had he died?

A shout from Sinan rang out, and Gallmau scrambled to get back to him. The necromancer stood over Meri protectively, his sword in one hand and another of his small explosive devices in the other.

"I'll give you one chance." Sinan sounded as menacing and ominous as ever, even as his knees wobbled and he struggled to remain standing. "Drop your weapons and surrender or I'll shred the flesh off your bones while you're still breathing."

A large bush with red berries shook, as if in terror at the necromancer's words, and a woman stumbled forward, her hands up and her voice frantic.

"No, please." Valentina's hair fell in a tangle around her

shoulders to her waist, and her arms and face were covered in scratches. "Sinan, don't hurt me."

Gallmau rushed toward Valentina as the necromancer sheathed his sword and leaned against a tree trunk for support.

Thank the Saints they found her.

"What happened?" Gallmau let the Amoran physician collapse against him, then lowered her into a sitting position and crouched beside her. "There's a body close by, dressed similar to the men who attacked us."

Valentina choked back a sob, her usual self-control and focus lost. "It all happened so fast, the lightning, the rain. Captain Caron went forward alone to scout out any danger and never came back. A group of attackers came after us on horseback after he left. Jacques told me to run, and he tried to fight them off—but they had weapons enhanced with aquamancy."

"Was Abarsam with them?" Sinan asked. He was panting now, his chest moving in an odd motion.

Gallmau hated to think the courteous Kushian aqua-mage Meri had been so fond of could have taken part in murdering his rivals, but Abarsam's easy countering of Jacques's fiery tirades in the Synod meeting room was still fresh in his mind.

Valentina shook her head. "They were fighters, all as big as Shields. One of them found me hiding here and attacked me. His hands were around my throat, and I panicked..." Her voice trailed off, and she stared off in the distance, her lower lip trembling.

Gallmau put a hand on her shoulder. They had found the only person in this Saints-forsaken place who could help Meri, but Valentina was in a state of nervous shock, traumatized by what she had seen—and what she had done.

"Did you disrupt his heart rhythm?" Sinan adopted an interested tone, as if unique magical ways to kill people were a fascinating topic for him. Of course, since he was a death witch, they probably were. The necromancer held out a water flask toward the medica, his face tightening from the effort.

Valentina drew back from Sinan and gave Gallmau a panicked look. He took the flask from the necromancer and put it into her hand, encouraging her to drink. She raised it to her mouth and took a few sips, then stopped as if the memories of what it had taken to survive were too much to bear.

"The medici are weakened by death, especially if they've used their magic to bring it about." Sinan glanced down at Meri's unconscious form, then continued, "As opposed to our *caromancers*, who gain power when they take a life. Otherwise, the two are quite similar."

"I am *nothing* like a flesh witch." The medica snapped the words back at Sinan, and suddenly, some of the old Valentina was back. "I'm a healer, not a killer. Using my Gift to harm another is against the oath I swore to Saint Thaschus."

"You had a right to defend yourself, and you used it." Gallmau had never been happier about Sinan's ability to offend and outrage other witches. "I know you're shaken up, but Meri was injured in the fight and she's—not waking up." Gallmau tried to steady his voice and failed. "If you have more water, do you think you could help her?"

Valentina dropped the flask on the ground and scrambled over to Meri, as if she had only now noticed her. "Gallmau, tell your necromancer to stop distracting me when I have a patient to attend to." She knelt next to Meri and began to examine her, muttering what were either healing prayers or more insults for Sinan, all in Amoran.

She lifted Meri's eyelids and examined them first. "Her pupils are equal and not too large." The medica used her knuckles to rub on Meri's breastbone, which Gallmau found rather harsh. Meri apparently agreed, despite her condition, because she reached up with both arms to try and stop the discomfort.

"Both sides moving well." Valentina nodded to herself, running her fingers over Meri's head and pressing on the back of her neck.

She continued to poke and prod, checking for pulses in the neck and wrists. She placed her ear on Meri's chest and listened. Then she closed her eyes and put both of her palms on Meri's forehead, her eyes closing in concentration.

Gallmau didn't have Meri's ability to sniff out different types of magic, but he could tell Valentina was using her healing Gift.

"It's a shock to the cerebrum, nothing more. No blood is pooling against the brain tissue, and her electrical patterns aren't severely disrupted."

"Is her skull fractured?" Sinan pulled off his strange traveling bag and opened it. He began to lay wrapped packages on the ground. "I have healing supplies, if you'd agree to use them."

"Not everything is about bones, and I suppose I don't have much choice." Valentina unwrapped one of Sinan's parcels with the caution she might use in opening a basket of vipers and drew back in surprise. She held up the strips of silk imprinted with sigils Meri hadn't allowed Sinan to use before. "Where did you get these? They've been prepared by a medicus."

"Or a caromancer who used to be a medica." Sinan and

Valentina locked eyes, and Gallmau remembered Valentina had resigned her position in the Noviodunam when three young students accused of necromancy—including a protégé of hers—had been given to Karakoncolos in the prisoner exchange that had freed Jacques.

Valentina dropped her gaze first, turning her attention to the other supplies in Sinan's pack. "I lost my travel sack and my simar when I ran, but these will help." She turned to Gallmau. "I'm going to bind her head and heal the wounds on her back as well. Your shoulder is next—a clean cut, but it needs treatment, and you also have a scalp laceration I can work on. Then you need to force Sinan to let me help him. He has several rib fractures and a contusion on one of his lungs—I can tell that even from this distance. He shouldn't be standing, much less threatening to flay me alive with shadow magic."

"No." It was Sinan's turn to recoil from Valentina. "No one from the Noviodunam is using their magic on me if I can help it."

"I don't have to touch your skin," Valentina assured him.

She knew about Sinan's Blessing, as the necromancer called it.

"You'll let her help you, or I'll sit on you until you agree." Gallmau needed his two companions back to fighting form. He had prayed to his Saint—and a few other deities as well—and they had sent Valentina to them. They needed her help, and she needed their protection. "You can touch him without hurting him now."

The medica's head snapped up. Maybe he shouldn't have shared the necromancer's personal information quite so readily. "You're not cursed anymore?"

"I wasn't cursed." Sinan put his head in his hands and slid down into a sitting position, his face grimacing in pain.

"My Blessing is gone for now, along with my Gift. There was Amor Vitriol in the hunting lodge we took refuge in, and Meri had to use it to save my life. I can't do any necromancy at all."

"Water magic, Amor Vitriol, and attackers who've been trained like Shields." Valentina bit her lip as she wrapped the fabric around Meri's head, activating the sigils with deft touches of her fingertips. "Whoever took Rixende knows our weaknesses and exactly how best to kill us."

24

SINAN

His cloak thrown over underbrush and tree roots didn't make for a comfortable hospital cot, but Sinan was more concerned about Valentina using her magic on him when his own Gift was gone, leaving him no way to defend himself.

"I don't think this is necessary." Sinan lay on his back with his shirt off. He would have been uneasy shaking gloved hands with a medica as powerful as Valentina, much less remaining still while she spread her spellwork over his vital organs. She had arranged sigil-marked bandages over the black and blue mess that was on the right side of his chest and was tapping her fingers over the symbols like a musician picking out a tune on an instrument. He couldn't even sense her magic, much less tell if she was doing something horrible to him. "I heal fast anyway."

"Stop squirming and let her do her job." Meri was awake and upright now, although in a terrible mood.

The medica had been able to restore the Lioness to consciousness with the sigils Sinan had carried from Karakoncolos, along with her medicus abilities to manipulate living tissue. Then she worked on Gallmau. Her success in healing the two of them had transformed Valentina. Her eyes were bright and focused, and the sigils on her recovered simar glowed with power. As she used her magic on Sinan, the scratches on her arms and face from her panicked flight into the woods faded away.

He hoped she wouldn't want to backslide by taking revenge on him when there wasn't a damn thing he could do to stop her.

Meri took another long drink of water and shoveled food she had taken out of Gallmau's pack into her mouth. She looked better than Sinan would have believed possible a mere hour ago, and he was grateful Valentina had helped her. The sight of her limp body on the ground had affected him more than he wanted to admit. He was less grateful Meri was enforcing Gallmau's orders that Sinan allow the medica to heal him.

Meri, for her part, was furious Gallmau had insisted the four of them stay under cover in the grove through the night, both for her to rest and to avoid them being spotted again by the Azhdarchid. Gallmau's harping on Meri's theoretical pregnancy wasn't helping matters, either.

She jabbed one of the remaining marzipan candies from the chateau in Gallmau's direction. "We're stuck here for hours, instead of heading out to hit them hard while they're recovering from losing four men."

Gallmau was busying himself setting up a rough camp for the four of them. He had ventured out to examine the site of the attack on Valentina and Jacques, retrieving Valentina's pack and her simar in the process, but had returned quickly when he had spotted the Azhdarchid flying overhead. "With your—delicate condition, you need to rest."

"Not the baby thing again." Meri rolled her eyes.

"I'm not going to be like my father, bedding whoever he wanted and tossing women away like a set of clothes he wore once." Gallmau arranged the firewood he had collected with more force than necessary. "Your baby will be in the line of succession for the throne of Soissons, and I don't want it to be a bastard like me. As soon as we save Rixende, we need to go back to Lutecia and get married."

Meri laughed. "I'm five and twenty and haven't been knocked up because I know what herbs to take if my courses don't come on time. Also, Valentina healed me, and she didn't say anything about a baby."

Valentina gave a polite cough and paused her work on Sinan. "If the two of you had intercourse only last night, I would have no medical or magical way of determining if Meri was with child."

"It was the three of us." Meri's words choked a surprised noise from Valentina. Sinan opened his eyes to see if the medica was yanking out part of his lungs or healing him. She frowned, her face scarlet. He went back to squeezing his eyes shut and trying to shut out the conversation the two Tomb Fighters were having.

"I don't want to marry you, Gallmau." Meri sounded even angrier, and Sinan didn't want to be pulled into this argument. "You don't like women. You like to fuck men. Pretty men, like Sinan. Who, by the way, I also fucked. So maybe this imaginary babe of yours will be his."

Sinan opened his eyes again, and this time he and

Valentina had matching expressions of dismay at the awkward turn the argument had taken.

"That Azhdarchid had a shadow affinity, like I have." Sinan tried to shift the conversation from the sex last night to strategy and tactics against their unknown enemies. "Like the catfish had. We have to be facing a beast master."

Gallmau ignored that gambit, his voice rising in concern. "It could be a little Bone Lord baby. All of those Noviodunam witches would try to kill it, and I'd have to fight them. That's even more reason for us to have the wedding right away."

"Tell him Sinan can't make babies, just to shut him up." Meri directed this comment at Valentina. Sinan would prefer the medica wasn't distracted while she was doing magical things to his organs, and besides, Valentina wasn't the necromancer expert here.

"I am the son of a venefica." Sinan realized after the words came out that this wasn't what Meri wanted to hear. "It's not impossible, only unlikely. Let's talk about the beast master instead."

"Sinan's mother is a sex demon." Gallmau sounded vindicated. "Which means he's half sex-demon and could be the father."

"You should know all about that, since you were fucking our new sex demon friend through most of the night."

Valentina broke in before Meri could escalate things further. "I'm close to finishing up my work. Sinan, tell us what you know about beast masters."

"They have an affinity for Touched animals and can use them against their enemies, even at a distance." Sinan thought back to the two attacks with grudging admiration for their unknown enemy's skills. "The one we're facing must be powerful, if he can control a catfish underwater and an Azhdarchid in the skies."

"Jacques and I were attacked with water-enhanced weapons, so that also tells us something." Valentina shifted to direct medicus healing as she talked, pressing her palm against Sinan's ribs, the warmth of her skin soaking into his chest. His breaths eased, the awful air hunger he had been enduring dissipating.

"What, exactly, does that tell us?" Meri's tone was sharp.

Valentina had hit upon a topic that shifted the focus of the conversation. They all knew there was an aquamage in Terra Amata, and a powerful one at that—Abarsam.

"Unlike beast magic, aquamancy is hardly a common affinity in necromancers." Valentina spoke like an authority on the subject, which was annoying, even though she was correct. "Not to mention that the men who attacked us looked like Shields of Thaschus. How does any of this make sense if we're dealing with a single necromancer?"

"It doesn't." Gallmau laid out a small feast of cheese, hard sausages, and more of the marzipan candies on top of his bedroll, making sure a lioness's share of the food was close to Meri. "We're facing a team of witches."

Valentina gave a satisfied nod at Sinan's chest and left to sit next to Gallmau and the food. Sinan propped himself up and took a gulp of air, waiting for the searing pain that no longer came. He accepted water and a sausage from Gallmau, finding himself to be both ravenous and thirsty.

"Do you think Abarsam is helping the necromancer who took Rixende?" Gallmau asked Sinan the question, but it was Meri who answered it, her eyes blazing in fury.

"The Grand Vizier would never work with a Bone Lord." Meri came to Abarsam's defense with a startling heat.

Sinan knew she had met the aquamage before, but he was surprised she felt so protective of any sorcerer, even one from her own country.

"*You're* working with one." After Sinan pointed this out, he slid away from Meri, since injured or not, she was frightening when she was this angry. "Abarsam handled Jacques's temper tantrums in the Synod meeting room easily enough."

"The Grand Vizier is loyal to the Sultana and to Kush." Meri was glaring daggers, but at Gallmau, not Sinan. "He'd have no reason to abduct a princess of Soissons, and attacking Jacques makes no sense. He wins no matter who finds Rixende. Xiaolian would have to reward any foreigner who risked his life and that of his son in her daughter's rescue."

"We could be up against a group of necromancers, or however unlikely, mages working with a Bone Lord." Valentina accepted some cheese from Gallmau, which made the prince flash one of his dazzling smiles in her direction. Sinan had no idea how Valentina could not all but melt at the sight, but she barely seemed to notice.

"Could it be the Order of Katil?" Gallmau asked. "Cliona was one of them."

"The Order could pull something like this off." Sinan wanted this mess to come from the Noviodunam, but the evidence was damning that they were fighting a beast master, and at least one of the Order's assassins had been involved in the plot. Cliona had accepted a contract on Sinan's life, and that couldn't be a coincidence. "They have the resources to hire sellswords who could look like Shields, and they have beast masters among them. But at a basic level they're independent contractors who compete against one another for money. They sometimes work in small groups on larger contracts, but they like to get in, kill someone, and get paid."

"The throne of Soissons has many enemies, domestic and abroad, who could have hired the Order." Valentina directed this at Gallmau, making the point that Kush was not among them. "I also wouldn't put it past some of the former benandanti to work with a necromancer if it fit their agenda."

"The ones that didn't take the loyalty oath, sure." Gallmau had started the fire, and he added on more wood to provide some light and heat during the night. "Zhang Jue and Jacques's father Odart are the only two witches in the Noviodunam who submitted to it."

"Odart is bound by a loyalty curse to the Grimoard line?" Sinan had heard of Soissons's version of the enchantment, which prevented the sorcerer from harming a member of the royal family. From what he knew, it applied only to the lineage of the old Grimoard kings. Queen Xiaolian wouldn't be protected by it, but her daughter Rixende and even Gallmau, who wasn't a legitimate heir, would be.

In other words, it was a blood spell. How like the royalty of Soissons to use necromantic magic when it suited their purposes.

"Odart is bound, yes." Gallmau used a knife to divide the hard sausage and cheese into smaller pieces for everyone to eat, avoiding any eye contact with Meri. "So is Abarsam— but to the Sultana of Kush, not to the Grimoard line."

Meri's eyes were murderous now, and Sinan remembered the number of knives she carried on her. Maybe moving over to sit by Valentina would be a good idea.

"Jacques was scheduled to take the loyalty oath right

before Rixende was abducted." Valentina's voice had a hitch in it now. "He couldn't afterward because he would have been weak for days or longer. He told me his father tried to convince him not to do it. Is there—any way Jacques could still be alive?"

"What did you find at the site of the attack?" Sinan was curious about what had happened to Odart's son. Granted, the incensor was likely dead, but this entire quest had made little sense since Karakoncolos had first received Queen Xiaolian's threatening letter about her daughter's abduction.

"Lots of burn marks and soaked grass," Gallmau responded. "If Jacques took anyone out before they got him, his attackers took their dead with them."

Sinan had all too clear a memory of the damage Jacques had inflicted upon his people and doubted the fire mage had been overwhelmed before killing some of his attackers. The incensor had taken them all on to give Valentina a chance to live. This shouldn't matter to him, since the medica was technically as much his enemy as Jacques was, but somehow it did. She deserved to know what had happened to Jacques, and if he had his Gift back, he could at least give her that comfort.

"Did you see an area with large bloodstains?" There was an uncomfortable silence, and Sinan reminded himself his companions might not be as comfortable discussing death as he was. "That would tell us if they harvested his relic there or took him away to do it later."

Gallmau looked puzzled, even as Meri's eyes hardened and Valentina paled. "Relics are—old bones of Saints and stuff like that. What are you talking about?"

Meri swung into an explosion of movement. She grabbed Sinan's pack, rummaged through it, and threw a small bag at Gallmau.

The prince caught it out of the air, opened it, and examined the contents without any indication he understood what they were. "Are these marbles? Because you can't roll them with that weird bump on them."

"Sinan cut Cliona's eyes out of her sockets and turned them into bone." Meri was also comfortable talking about death and explaining hard truths to Gallmau. "He's asking you if there was evidence they did that to Jacques before dragging his body off."

"Actually." Sinan hesitated, because Valentina had put her hand to her mouth as if she was about to retch. "It wouldn't be his eyes."

"His heart." Valentina choked the words out. Clearly, even though Jacques had broken their engagement to woo Rixende, she still had some fondness for the man. After a deep breath, she continued in a more clinical tone. "With a captured incensor a necromancer would want the heart. That would mean cracking open the chest, perhaps by sawing through the sternum. There would be significant evidence left behind."

"I didn't see that amount of blood." Gallmau shook his head. "My guess is they left with Jacques as soon as they could, leaving one man behind to take out Valentina, because they didn't think she'd be much of a threat."

"That would make sense." Sinan had been thinking along the same lines. "Harvesting the relic is best done right after death for optimal power, or better yet—starting the removal while the captive is still alive."

There was another uncomfortable stretch of quiet before Gallmau stared at the white orbs in his hand with the blood-drop pupils and asked, "If these are magic, could Valentina use them to call for help from Naghwe? Not that

I'm looking forward to seeing Sinan's undead sex demon mother again."

"No," Valentina answered before Sinan could explain further. "I've already broken enough rules of my guild. I'm not experimenting with necromancy."

Meri turned toward Gallmau. "Valentina and I aren't willing to use Cliona's eyeballs, but since you're accusing Abarsam of treachery, maybe a member of royalty such as yourself should volunteer to try Sinan's death magic."

The prince paused as he was about to take a bite out of a chunk of cheese. He shook the relics in his hand, as if about to roll dice. "You want me to try to cast a spell with these?"

"I don't think you're the most likely choice to use a necromantic charm." Sinan didn't want to insult him, but the prince was in every way the opposite of the Blessed.

Gallmau considered the cheese in one hand and the eyeballs in the other. He furrowed his brow. "I could give it a try, I guess. It's probably a mortal sin, but that's what confession's for. Maybe I could call up your little rat friend."

"Ghost magic is especially difficult." Sinan was about to continue, but Gallmau was already holding up the food and making kissing noises to call the undead animal to him. It was patently the worst first attempt at a necromantic spell Sinan had ever seen.

And yet, the damn ghost rat showed up seconds later, popping out of a shaded spot on the ground and ambling over to snatch the cheese out of Gallmau's fingers as its blue eyes glowed in delight. Sinan couldn't use Cliona's relics to even send a shadow letter, but the prince had somehow summoned a corpus animatum that should have been destroyed by the Amor Vitriol. The rodent, perhaps to humiliate Sinan further, cast another stretch of shadow with no apparent effort and vanished again.

Gallmau sighed and put Cliona's relics back into the pouch. "You asked me to try death magic, and I did. Maybe the little guy will go for help after he finishes the cheese."

"What was that?" Valentina pointed at the spot where the ghost rat had vanished, then let her hand fall. "Never mind. I don't want to know."

25

MERI

Meri held out one of the swords Abarsam had given her, watching as the tip of the blade vibrated. In her other hand, she held one of Sinan's ghost lanterns, glowing enough to illuminate several feet around her.

She had never tried anything like this. Her curved swords were infused with the Grand Vizier's aquamancy—she knew that much. They had proved to be potent weapons against monsters and death magic. Now, here she was, using a necromancer's ghostly lamp to help her cast her own water spell.

As the exhausting day had slid into twilight, Sinan had shown her and Valentina everything he had brought with him in his pack, an obvious ploy to defuse the tensions between her and Gallmau. She knew about the medical supplies, but not about the nature of the waterproof silk of his pack, which was woven from the webs of a horrifying Archaic spider-like monster that lurked around Karakonco-los. He had also brought food rations known as corpse meat —and was puzzled by the women's lack of interest in trying the necromantically preserved beef.

Two other items caught her attention—and fascinated Valentina, who deluged Sinan with technical questions. Meri cared only for their usefulness. The first was a metal sphere, created by an Artifex that somehow both he and Valentina knew, which emitted an ear-splitting bang and a flash of blinding light. It required no magic, death or other-wise, to use. He had only one left, having used the others when he and Gallmau were fending off their attackers. Since Meri had little interest in non-lethal weapons, she insisted Valentina take the device, and the medica agreed, after some hesitation.

The second were ghost lamps, miniature versions of the beautiful hammered-bronze lanterns of Western Kush, with star shapes cut out of the metal to create a delicate cage for the light within. They were more elegant and strange than the electromantic lanterns she was familiar with and required some magic to activate. Sinan couldn't turn them on, and Valentina wouldn't, even though the necromancer argued that even if they relied on necromantic power, there weren't any actual ghosts inside, so why should it be a problem?

Meri had touched her blades to the ghost lamps and was surprised when the two of them emitted a fractionated glow of green light. She grabbed one, announced she was taking first watch and looking for drinking water, and had left the camp before Gallmau could stop her.

Meri turned to the right, and the blade stopped vibrat-ing. Turning left brought out a faint tremble in the steel.

Progress. It had occurred to her that if her blades could activate a magical device from Karakoncolos, perhaps the ghost
lamp could allow her to use her weapons as water-divining
rods. Perhaps it was sacrilegious, but if the Prophets truly
disapproved of her trying witchcraft, why would they allow
her to succeed? After all, the man who had created the
magic in the blades was himself a pious follower of the
Three Prophets. Devout, but ambitious. Could Abarsam be
ruthless enough to help kill off his competitors? She didn't
want to think of it as a possibility, but in the back of her
mind she thought of the coincidence that Abarsam had
been in the South of Soissons, close enough to arrive in
Lutecia in time to lend his assistance to Jacques. He had
even convinced the incensor to pretend that Zhang Jue had
sent an invitation to him.

After another quarter of an hour of painstaking focus,
she heard a faint burbling of water in front of her. Her
blades had led her to a small stream—one more gift from
Abarsam the Magnificent. She knelt beside the rushing
blackness of the water and said a quick prayer of thanks to
the Prophets before filling the water pouches she had
brought with them. Little things could get you killed as
easily as large ones, and all of them needed to keep up their
strength if they were to have any hope of finding Rixende
and getting out of this forsaken trap alive.

Then she added another prayer, that she wouldn't have
to fight her old lover.

She rose to her feet, then froze as she spotted a faint
glow of light in the looming shadows of the monstrous trees.

The desire to fall into the comfort of speed was overwhelming, but she pushed it aside. Valentina had been
adamant that if Meri used her Gift again before she fully
recovered, the searing head pain she had experienced

would progress to unconsciousness or even death. When it came to healing, the medica had proven she knew what she was talking about.

Instead, she used one of her blades to extinguish the light in her hand and moved with careful silent steps. She recognized the odd greenish glow as the other ghost lantern before she could make out Sinan's graceful silhouette.

The necromancer paused, as if he realized coming up on her too quickly might be hazardous to his health. In the darkness, the light he dangled from his hand cast a pattern of stars over his ethereal features and ink-black hair. Sinan could have been one of those desert demons from the tales of Kushian storytellers—unnaturally beautiful strangers who approached travelers at night, some intent on murder, others on seduction.

She held up her own lamp and used her sword to let it blaze light before walking up to him.

He had a smile on his face as she approached. "You've mastered your ghost lamp quickly, for someone who didn't want anything to do with the magic of the Blessed."

"You're a bad influence on me." Meri came closer to him, then reached out to stroke the side of his face.

His eyes gleamed with interest, but he didn't reach out to touch her back. Instead, he asked permission. "I'd like to kiss you again."

"Such a polite death witch." Meri reached up and pulled his face down to hers.

He opened his mouth a fraction, his tongue darting in and sending a shiver of desire through her. They pressed closer, and as he ran his hand down the concavity of her spine to the small of her back, she ground her hips against his, enjoying the low moan that escaped from him.

Meri pulled away from Sinan, laughing. "If we go much

farther, I'm not going to be of much use as a guard. Did Gallmau send you out here to check on me?"

Sinan didn't try to pull her back into an embrace but didn't move farther away, either. "He wanted to go himself, but I convinced him Valentina would be nervous if she woke up and found me watching over her."

"Thank you." Meri decided Sinan saving her from a fight with Gallmau deserved another kiss, and their mouths moved together for a long moment, leaving both of them breathing fast and hard. "I think Valentina makes you nervous—or is it aroused?"

"More of the first than the second," Sinan admitted.

"And me?" she asked, pressing her chest against his and tracing patterns on his neck with her fingers.

Sinan let out a small sigh. "More of the second than the first."

"Good." Meri liked the sound of that. Not that she was jealous of Valentina, but she was already sharing Sinan with Gallmau, and that was quite enough.

Speaking of her favorite bastard prince, Meri needed a plan to give her time to get over her anger at him for accusing Abarsam of the unthinkable—even as she allowed there was a chance Gallmau was right. That wasn't something she wanted to admit to him.

She pressed her lips near Sinan's ear. "Gallmau needs rest, and I need him to stop talking about babies and marriage so I can focus on getting us out of this alive."

"I could try to distract him." Sinan said this in all seriousness, as if seducing Gallmau would be a challenge. "He gave Valentina his sleeping roll, so maybe he'll want to come over to mine."

"He'll want to, trust me." Meri gestured to the water pouches slung over her shoulder. "Bring these back for me and get Gallmau off so he's sleeping when I finish first watch."

Sinan laughed—a lovely sound, nothing like what she would have expected from a Bone Lord—and then his face took on a more somber expression. "I could sense when an owl killed a rabbit near the camp. Some of my Gift is coming back, but not much and not fast enough, especially since we're facing more than one sorcerer."

One of the sorcerers could be Abarsam. No, Meri wasn't going to believe that. "We don't even know where our enemies are located, much less who they are."

"I think they'll send out the Azhdarchid in the morning to see why their men didn't return." Sinan thought about battle the way she did—logically trying to guess his opponent's next move, then planning how to counter it. In many ways, the two of them weren't so different. "If we can spot it in flight, we might be able to trace its path backward toward whoever is controlling it. It's likely the beast master would keep Rixende close to him."

"It's a good idea." Meri slipped off the straps of the water bottles and dropped them to the ground. "I have a bad one, if you're interested." She let her hand run down the front of his chest, then lifted up the smooth fabric of his shirt to stroke the hard curves of his abdomen. Making love again to someone who should be her worst enemy wasn't the wisest decision, but she didn't care. Her hand moved lower, and she undid the drawstring on his trousers.

Sinan pulled her toward him and began moving over the skin of her neck and chest with his mouth, arousing her with a series of gentle nibbles. Heat flushed through her body, flaring between her thighs.

Getting close to death did this to her—made her treasure the pleasures of life even more.

"I like your bad idea." Sinan worked his way back up to her ear, pulling on the lobe with his teeth. "Maybe I can distract you and Gallmau tonight."

Sex in a forest at night had its challenges. By the time Meri undid the rest of Sinan's clothing and he helped her take off her pants, they were both laughing at the clumsiness of it all.

There was nothing clumsy about how Sinan pressed her up against a tree trunk, lifting her off the ground with surprising strength. The two of them moved together with a steady rocking motion, the friction sending waves of pleasure through her. She climaxed first, biting him hard in his shoulder to stop herself from crying out. He came inside of her a moment later, gasping for air as if she had drained his breath away with her passion.

The two of them spent a few frantic moments scrambling to rearrange their clothing and pick up the ghost lanterns they had left on the forest floor, as Meri scanned their surroundings for any hint of danger.

"Sorry about your arm." She touched his shoulder, but Sinan shook his head and lifted his shirt as he brought his ghost lantern closer to him. Meri could see her bite marks in Sinan's pale skin, but as she watched, the flesh smoothed over, gleaming white like polished bone in the green glow. Meri repressed a shiver. The afterglow from their lovemaking still warmed her body, but the unnatural healing reminded her Sinan was still alien and unknowable.

"I'm glad I won't need Valentina to cure me again, but I'd be happier if I could even adjust this lamp." Sinan cupped the lantern in one hand, and the dim light remained unchanged.

She had thought she had hidden her revulsion well, but his gaze slid away from her as he spoke. She leaned forward to kiss him, unsure why she felt guilty. Whatever happened, this attraction she and Gallmau had for Sinan couldn't continue outside the confines of their current situation.

"Gallmau. Don't forget." She pulled on Sinan's shirt to straighten it. "I'll come and get you for second watch. Make sure he's too exhausted to wake up."

He grinned at that, then bent to pick up the water pouches. He took a few steps into the darkness and turned back. The ghost lantern's patterned light played over his features, and once again he changed from an attractive young man to something eerily beautiful and not quite human. "Thank you for not killing me when I came out to find you—and when we first met."

With that bittersweet reminder of their history, he slipped away into the shadows.

Meri passed the rest of her watch uneventfully after her tryst with Sinan and returned to the camp to find the necromancer wrapped in a sleeping Gallmau's muscular arms. Sinan woke with her light touch on his face and wriggled out of the prince's embrace without waking him. Meri pressed her lips to Sinan's for a brief moment, then crawled into the warm space next to Gallmau.

She regretted her choice of sleeping arrangements when they all awoke in the pre-dawn darkness. Gallmau was talking to Meri about the Royal nursery and wedding arrangements before she could even untangle herself from the bedroll. She responded with a string of obscenities in every language she could swear in, which was a long enough list to eventually shut him up.

The food Gallmau had brought had run out, so they broke down and ate a hurried breakfast of Sinan's corpse meat, which fortunately tasted like ordinary dried beef. She mumbled a prayer of apology over it, hoping that made it less impure before they all headed out.

The sky started to lighten as they passed through a stretch of cleared and abandoned farmland and into the cover of another grove of trees. The Azhdarchid should be out and about soon. Gallmau laid out a rough map of their surroundings with a collection of twigs and detritus from the forest, which mercifully distracted him from bringing up Abarsam or harassing her about how she felt.

Sinan hunted around for a suitable tree for climbing, as Valentina recited an impressive litany of facts about the Azhdarchid. She had written something called a mono-graph about the monster, and among its other not-so-charming attributes, the giant Archaic creature enjoyed feasting on corpses and flew only during the day. They had left a tasty trail of dead bodies for the flying beast to find, but they had no way of knowing how many more foot soldiers their enemies had at their disposal.

Sinan scrambled up one of the largest trees Meri had ever laid eyes on with enviable ease. She could have made it to the top faster, of course, but a firm shake of Valentina's head and Gallmau's stricken look when Meri suggested it ruled out that possibility. Sinan vanished into the vast canopy above them as the hum of morning birdsong burst into a crescendo.

When he came climbing down a short time later, sunshine had begun to stream through the green leaves above. Dropping the last several feet to the ground, he made his way over to Gallmau's rocks and twigs outline. A sheen of sweat made his skin gleam in the dappled light, and he smelled like crushed green leaves.

"There." Sinan pointed to a spot on the crude map north of their current location, where Gallmau had built a small pile of pebbles. "The Azhdarchid flew from that direction. You said there were caves in the bluffs there."

"They're not as comfortable as the lodge, but we camped in them a few times while hunting." Gallmau used a branch to draw a line from their current location to the rocks. "The caves could be used as a shelter, but I'm not sure why Rixende's abductors would have selected them as a base over the chateau."

"North is where I thought they might be holding her." Sinan pointed to a series of light-colored leaves Gallmau had laid out. "Is that the river that empties into the lake?"

"It passes close to the caves, and there should be some cover along its banks." Gallmau glanced over at Valentina, then Meri. "Maybe the two of you should stay here. It would be safer."

Meri was close to pulling out one of her knives at this point, but Sinan broke in before she could show Gallmau exactly what she thought of his suggestion. "Splitting up now would be unwise. It's possible our enemies are using a blood trail to track the rescue parties. Meri and I are the least likely people to have left any residue for that spell, but everyone else on this quest is well-known at Court. Even if the Order is doing most of the work, I'm sure someone from Lutecia is part of this."

"No one sucked any blood from me in Court that I remember." Gallmau rubbed at his chin, mercifully distracted from his idiotic plan to take on their enemies without her help.

"It could be a different bodily fluid." Sinan raised an eyebrow at the prince. Gallmau turned pink and gave the necromancer an embarrassed grin back.

"If that's true then they'd be able to locate Abarsam and his party." Valentina eyed the leaf river on the map and left unsaid the possibility the Grand Vizier was among the sorcerers doing the tracking. They were all thinking it, anyway, even Meri. "He would have stayed close to water if at all possible. Aquamages are incredibly powerful near their element."

Sinan suggested Gallmau take the lead as they made their way toward the river, which mollified the prince and prevented Meri from coming to actual blows with Gallmau. As they marched over the unprotected expanse of a meadow, their feet crunching over dried fall grasses, she and Sinan took the rear position, much as Tharin and Karabil had in their old crew. They kept Valentina in the more protected spot in the center of their group.

At least this was the most exposed they would be until they approached the caves. Gallmau had estimated they had about an hour's walk at a brisk pace until they reached the river, which they could follow up in elevation to the caves. Hopefully the damn flying monster their enemies were using to hunt for them would be too busy with the carnage they had left behind for at least that long.

A breeze picked up, cool and pleasant against Meri's face. The scent it brought was anything but. She blew a short note on her whistle to get Gallmau and Valentina to stop. "Fire magic. I can smell it, and something else—"

Sinan finished the sentence for her. "Death."

Meri pushed past the others, an aching weight in her chest—grief and despair mixed with hope she was wrong.

She wasn't.

The first body would have been too burnt to identify, if the giant bodyguard hadn't been wearing a curved sword with a hilt studded with turquoise—the color of water. Another weapon enchanted with aquamancy, another gift from the most powerful water mage in Kush to someone he had treasured.

Baahir lay dead several feet away, curled on his side as if to protect himself. The enchanted blue kaftan his father had given him was untouched and untouchable by fire, but his face was scorched and blackened, and there was a musket hole in his forehead. A beautiful, brilliant boy with his entire life in front of him, cut down far too soon.

Bile rising in her throat, Meri stumbled forward until she sank to her knees beside the last victim. Abarsam the Magnificent lay on his back, his arms outstretched, as if to embrace the heavens above him. A fire-blackened hole was all that remained of the center of his chest, and both of his eyes had been cut out.

Rage blocked out her vision, and anger constricted her chest until she thought she wouldn't be able to take another breath. She would find who had done this and kill him, if it was the last thing she ever did.

A hand, large and warm, rested on her shoulder. "I'm so sorry." Gallmau squeezed her arm, his voice choked with sadness. "I don't know what to say."

"I do." Sinan crouched down across from Meri, scanning the body. "This doesn't make sense."

Meri exploded. "What about this doesn't make sense to you? One of your kind murdered Abarsam, then mutilated his corpse. He's in Paradise now, and I swear by all Three Prophets I'll send his killer to Hell."

"Whoever did this isn't one of the Blessed." Sinan wasn't backing down. "That I know."

"He's right." Valentina had been bent over examining Baahir's body, but she straightened and walked over to them.

"You're taking the word of a death witch now." Meri had

to lash out at someone, and Valentina was an easy target. "Abarsam was hacked up the same way Sinan used to create those bone eyeballs you pretended to be so horrified by."

Valentina said nothing in response, only biting her lower lip and hugging her chest with her arms. There were dark circles under her eyes that hadn't been there this morning. Too much death for anyone who wasn't a necromancer.

"That's the point." Sinan's voice was flat, without emotion. If Meri snarling the insult she had used as a seductive nickname last night affected him in any way, he wasn't showing it. "It's exactly what I did to Cliona. That's why it wasn't one of my people."

"Arguing about this here isn't helping," Gallmau broke in. "Let's get to the water and out of sight, then we can talk—and try to get the story straight."

"That's your problem." Sinan directed this comment at Gallmau, the other person he had fucked last night, to make everything a little worse. "You keep thinking this is your story—a heroic poem about wise sorcerers, evil necromancers, and princesses who need saving. That's not what's happening here."

"What's happening is that I'm going to kill the Bone Lord who did this, and if you get in my way I'll take you out as well." Meri snarled the words at Sinan, and Valentina broke her silence.

"Meri, you need to listen." Valentina gestured around her at the expanse of death and charred grass. "This has been staged to make it seem like Abarsam and the others were attacked by a fire mage and then mutilated by a necromancer. It's the exact inverse of what happened to me and Jacques. If I hadn't killed my attacker, I'm willing to bet my body would be in a pool of water, with my eyes cut out. A good story for an aquamage joining forces with a Bone Lord.

Only I'm a medica, and a necromancer like Sinan wouldn't want my eyeballs."

"I'd want your hands." Sinan added this without a hint of remorse, and Valentina clasped herself tighter and shuddered.

Meri stared down at Abarsam's body, some of her blood-red anger dissipating into confusion. "What should your kind have chopped out of him?"

"His kidneys." Sinan pulled at the burnt remains of the Grand Vizier's clothing, and he and Valentina spent a few minutes examining the body as Meri sat back and tried not to get sick. "There's no incision on either side of the flank, and they didn't go through the abdomen, either."

"You're back to blaming the Noviodunam for everything." Meri had trouble admitting when she was wrong, granted, but the condition of Abarsam's body didn't prove anything. "You think there's no necromancer involved at all."

"There's a beast master here, no doubt." Sinan rubbed his hands clean on a patch of unburnt grass. "But the wise sorcerer in the Royal Court poet's story wanted to be able to frame both Jacques and Abarsam for their respective murders. I'm just not sure why."

26

GALLMAU

G allmau was relieved to get to the meandering river that came down from the bluffs to the north and fed into the lake near the chateau. Strewn with water-polished rocks and deep enough in the middle to make it difficult to cross, it had been a reliable marker on hunting trips with his father. If they were correct about their enemies' base in the caves, any riders coming after them from there would need to go far out of the way to get to their side of the water. That, combined with some cover from the vegetation on the banks, made the river the safest path to get them close to the bluffs—and Rixende, if she was still alive.

The four of them walked along the river's edge in near-complete silence—and not only to avoid tipping off their location. The tensions among them still ran high.

Sinan and Meri had reached a truce of sorts before

leaving the scene of Abarsam's murder. Sinan cautiously offered to say a funeral prayer over the Grand Vizier, and Meri accepted with a nod. She had placed coins on the faces of all three of the dead men while he spoke in Kushian, then removed the water-magic jacket from Baahir and gave it to Sinan without a word.

That was as close to an apology as Meri got.

He called for a break, and Sinan moved past him to go to the river and refill his water pouch. He was wearing Baahir's enchanted kaftan, as opposed to the light armor Gallmau had given him. The cloth took up the essence of the water as he drew closer, and ripples of light spread over the fabric as Sinan's sleeve dipped into the river. From Gallmau's angle, the cloth blended in perfectly, making Sinan's arm invisible. The necromancer cocked his head at the effect, then gave a small nod to himself.

Sinan did odd things. Like making his arm appear as if it had been cut off, or describing necromancer rituals for dismembering bodies to Meri when he should have kept his mouth shut. Gallmau took no pleasure in Meri transferring her fury from him to Sinan, but he understood the pain she felt. First Karabil and Tharin, and now her ex-lover Abarsam, cut down by their mysterious enemies who had access to horrible magic. Meanwhile, Sinan had yet to regain any semblance of his shadow powers—and that was Meri and Gallmau's fault as well.

"We're near the caves now." Gallmau felt he should say something to Sinan, since Meri had made it clear she wasn't interested in talking.

At least he knew why Meri was angry with him—questioning her ability to protect herself and blaming her for keeping secrets about Rerek had been stupid and thoughtless on his part. Why Sinan would focus on a poem, of all things, to be angry about was a complete mystery. "We're all that's left to save my sister. I'd like to go into this as comrades in arms, or at least not fighting with one another about made-up stories."

"The stories people tell matter." Sinan drank more water from his canteen and stood up. "Your courtier's poem lyrics in Soissons or Meri's coffee-house storytellers' tales in Abdju or even Valentina's stage performances in Amor—they all have their heroes and their villains."

"I don't have to be the hero in all of this." Gallmau waved his arm at the sky, the gurgling water, the familiar country-side he had come to love as a boy, now a confined death trap for so many who had entered through the Artifact. "All I want is my sister back alive."

"It's not only that people like you are always the heroes." Sinan sounded sincere but resigned, as if he wanted Gallmau to understand him but didn't think he could. "It's that people like me are always the villains. Poems, stories, plays—they make their own reality. So it becomes easy for the Noviodunam to sentence any of the Blessed they find to a horrible death. No one objected when they declared their intention to wipe out my entire city—your family supported them, in fact. No one cares when midwives are paid to make sure babies born with a Blessing don't take a second breath."

"I know you don't think I'm that smart." Gallmau tried and failed to make that statement less confrontational. There was some truth in it, anyway. He didn't focus on deep thinking that much, because he didn't enjoy tying his mind up in knots, and he was much better at action than contem-plation. "I'll admit I don't understand what stories about scary Bone Lords have to do with the four of us not dying in the next several hours."

"Ever since we walked through the Artifact you and I

have been in someone else's story, and so have they." Sinan gestured to Meri and Valentina, who had both taken a seat on a nearby log. "The brave Tomb Fighters, the medica risking her life for a friend, the water and fire mages—those are the heroes. I'm the villain, along with the beast master involved with Rixende's abduction. Whoever we're facing has set this up so all the heroes die, and the Blessed get blamed for it."

"Does it matter?" Meri spoke in a low, bitter tone. Abarsam's death had hit her so hard, and Gallmau didn't know what to say to make it less awful. "Whoever they are, why they're doing it—I don't care. Their flying beast came from the caves. Let's go there and kill everyone in them. That's my idea of a happy ending."

"We're dealing with sorcerers who've taken out one of Soissons's best incensors and the most powerful aquamage in Kush." Sinan shaded his eyes to look out at the horizon as he spoke. "A direct assault won't work. We need to tell our own story and make it believable enough that our enemies will fall for it."

Gallmau turned his attention to the sky as well, and spotted wings in the distance as Sinan raised his hand to point to the Azhdarchid bearing down on them. He hoisted his shield in one hand, and his short sword in the other.

"Everyone take cover. Now." Gallmau stood out on the exposed riverbank, as his companions dispersed into the trees lining the bank.

The Azhdarchid landed seconds later, its flight speed a hell of a lot faster than Gallmau had counted on. The monstrous Archaic stalked toward him, its legs alternating with its wing joints in rapid succession. It came within several feet of him and opened its wide beak to issue a challenging cry.

"Come and get it." Gallmau crouched, waiting for the bird-like creature to strike. "Let's see how you do without a sneak attack, you big feathered bastard."

The creature opened its beak again, making a series of odd cries which Gallmau could swear were a comeback to his insults. Pools of shadow spread out over the ground below the creature's feet, as if an ink pot had been tipped over.

Meri cried out a warning, and Gallmau spun, lifting his shield to block the blow from an entirely different beak. In another instant, he was facing two additional Azhdarchids, smaller than the first, but both possessing the toothed beaks and grasping wing hands the flying monsters were known for.

Gallmau cursed. The monster had called for reinforcements, and her two baby Azhdarchids had popped out of the shadows like little flying Bone Lords. Animals touched with necromancy were supposed to be sterile, like their human counterparts—except when they weren't, like Mother Naghwe.

Gallmau feinted toward one creature and slashed at the second, but the animals darted away from his strikes, moving together as if they were used to attacking prey as a team. He realized too late he wasn't the animals' target.

The mother Azhdarchid stalked toward the trees and his companions. He tried to follow, but the two smaller monsters alternated attacks on him. Even with the magically enhanced protection of his shield, the flurry of beaks slowed him down.

There was a shriek of triumph, and the Azhdarchid launched itself into the air, its feet clutching someone by the arms. Meri and Sinan burst out of the trees, both trying to slash at the creature as it rose into the air.

Valentina screamed, struggling in the Azhdarchid's grip.

The Archaic couldn't reach high altitudes with such heavy prey, but it coasted over the river, letting the medica thrash helplessly above the rushing water.

Gallmau tried to bash his shield against the smaller animals, his frustration and fear mounting. Sinan rushed in to help with a flurry of blows with his sword that drove the smaller creatures back for a moment.

They flapped upward, above his reach.

If Gallmau could only grasp Valentina's ankle, the Azhdarchid couldn't possibly handle his weight along with hers. There was still a chance he could save her.

He dashed into the water, but the mother Azhdarchid soared upward, and his hands missed Valentina's kicking feet. He stumbled further into the river until he was neck deep and unable to move with any speed. Gallmau could do little else but watch as the three monsters flew off in a low formation, the largest one holding tightly onto Valentina as they soared away.

Meri came in view downstream, kneeling on the river-bank clutching her head. Gallmau could tell she had tried to use her speed to save Valentina and paid the price the medica had predicted. He struggled to get out of the water to rush toward her, but Sinan was racing along the bank and was at Meri's side before Gallmau climbed out onto dry land, water streaming from his clothing and his stomach in knots.

Valentina was gone.

Meri was hurt.

And their enemies knew they were coming.

27

SINAN

Sinan trudged through a knee-deep section of the river, sending up a prayer to the Lady of Shadows for the souls of Abarsam and his son. Baahir's cloak was a marvel of aquamancy. He had needed to alternate walking through the shallows and swimming when the river grew deeper, but he appeared to be one with the water while wearing the garment. Its material had also kept Sinan warm during his scouting expedition, absorbing water from his clothing and leaving him relatively dry. Once, when he slipped and cut his hand on a river rock, the wound had sealed up as he pull the sleeve of the kaftan over it.

As the sun's last rays glinted off the stream's surface, he arrived at the bend of the river where he had left his companions and stepped out onto the bank. Gallmau leaned out from the underbrush, his face breaking into a relieved smile.

The Azhdarchid attack and Valentina's capture had ended their argument, at least. Sinan wasn't sure Meri would forgive him, but as long as she recovered from the awful effects of using her Gift to try and help the medica, she could yell at him all she wanted. He pushed his hood back and moved to join Gallmau.

"How is she?" Sinan knelt by the speed fighter, who was asleep, carefully positioned on a bedroll. After Valentina had been taken, he and Gallmau had carried Meri into the shelter of the trees and ignored her mumbled insistence, between bouts of retching, that they needed to leave her behind so they could rescue the medica. Instead, Sinan had left her cradled in Gallmau's arms, determined to follow the river to the caves they guessed their enemies were camped in.

"Better than a few hours ago." Gallmau searched Sinan's face as he smoothed his hand over Meri's forehead. "I could ask you the same question."

"Valentina's a prisoner, but she didn't appear to be hurt." Sinan hadn't wanted to give the two Tomb Fighters false hope, but the Archaic animals' behavior only made sense if the beast master controlling them wanted the medica alive. "The Azhdarchid and her two flaplings were guarding her in one of the caves, along with at least a dozen armed men. I saw her near the entrance once, with someone in a velvet cloak who was probably a woman."

Gallmau sucked in a breath. "Do you think it was Rixende?"

Sinan nodded. "It has to be her, although I couldn't see her face. She and Valentina were calm and talking to one another, but that's about all I could tell before they went back inside."

Sinan glanced down at Meri. The rest of his scouting

report wasn't good news at all, and they needed the Lioness of Abdju back in fighting form. He had no idea if he could use the healing sigils interwoven in the threads of Baahir's kaftan to help Meri—after all, he couldn't even summon shadow—but the power the sigils on the cloth had taken from hours in the river was incredible.

He lifted the cuff of his kaftan and rested it over an ugly scrape on Meri's arm. The fabric began to sweat out tiny beads of moisture which pooled on her skin. Then the water evaporated away, leaving a faint healed scar.

"You can use Baahir's coat to make yourself invisible *and* control its healing magic?" Gallmau beamed at him, drawing the wrong conclusion from this small display of power.

Sinan shook his head. "Like Meri's curved swords, its aquamancy is designed so anyone can use it."

Even one of the Blessed crippled by the effects of Amor Vitriol, he wanted to add. Instead, he pressed the sleeve of the blue garment against Meri's forehead, hoping to counter the effects of Meri using her speed too soon.

"Gallmau, I told you to wake me up earlier." Meri blinked her eyes open, her voice groggy, and then turned her head to focus on Sinan. He pulled his hand away from her as if burned, but she surprised him with a relieved half-smile. "I'm glad you're back. Now tell me everything."

After quickly recounting his sighting of Valentina and Rixende, Sinan summarized what he had learned. "I saw more than a dozen Shields—or armed soldiers who look like them." Sinan lifted his garment's sleeve off Meri's head and ran the fabric though his fingers, marveling at its craft-manship as he despaired over the loss of his necromancy. "I didn't see anyone who could be one of the Blessed, but the beast master has to be in one of the caves if the Azhdarchids are there."

"Rixende and Valentina are in the same location." Meri sat up, her voice now brisk and forceful. "If we create a diversion we can rescue both of them and get out. We don't need to take on the whole camp."

"There are the Azhdarchids to worry about." Gallmau fumbled for a water canteen and pushed it at Meri, nodding at her to drink. "Three, instead of one."

"They nest together after sundown, according to Valentina." Sinan picked up a few twigs and leaves, and began to set up a crude map, much as Gallmau had after they left the lodge. "There are several of the caves in use. One lower one is being used as a stable for the horses, with a guard posted in front. There's another next to it that's a barracks for the men. Above those is the cave where the Azhdarchids are guarding Valentina and Rixende. Then there's this opening in the cliff which is the highest in elevation"—he motioned to a rock he had placed on the ground—"and overlooks the river. I'm pretty sure that's where our mages are."

"We don't even know how many witches we're facing, much less what they can do." Meri's initial enthusiasm for battle settled into a clear-eyed analysis of the situation. "We're going to need one hell of a distraction."

"Cliona tried to kill me so I couldn't play a role in any attempt to rescue Rixende." Sinan ran his hand over his chin and the unfamiliar stubble that had grown in since he had lost his Blessing and his powers. He hated being so useless. "They might panic about the Prince of Shadows attacking them, but I can't help you with my necromancy. Even Gallmau has had more luck summoning a corpus animatum than I've had doing the simplest death magic."

Gallmau stared down at the crude map, and his somber expression broke into a broad grin.

"Speaking of your creepy magic, give me those eyeballs again. I've got an idea."

28

SINAN

A few hours later, Sinan stood chest-deep in the river across from the caves and prayed Gallmau's plan would work. The sun had long set, and scattered lanterns and a campfire lit up a small area outside the bluffs. More of the oversized soldiers he had spotted during his scouting trip were grouped around them.

The water he stood in was shrouded in darkness except for some starlight reflecting off the rippling surface. He would have been hard to spot even without the kaftan, but with it he was confident no one could see him until he left the water.

An unearthly howl resounded through the night, and the camp exploded into activity. Guards who had been idly chatting or playing dice rushed to grab their weapons—swords and bayonets, but not the muskets that would be useless against a magical attack—and then plunged prepared torches into the campfire. They scanned the darkness, holding in a tight formation outlined in the light of their flames.

Sinan had hoped he was assumed to be dead, but the guards were prepared for a necromancer to attack them and had their defenses ready. He felt his heartbeat quicken and sweat break out over his skin. Baashir's cloak absorbed that as well, drawing power from his fear and anticipation.

Another howl went up, and two ghost lanterns flickered on, their greenish light illuminating a hooded shape that floated over the surface of the river downstream from Sinan's position. The overall effect was ominous, and made more so by a pair of glowing blue eyes hovering near the spectral figure's shoulder.

Between the ghost lanterns and the undead rat, Gallmau did a damn solid impression of the Prince of Shadows. The prince had Cliona's relics, and right now the minor necromancy he could do with them was more than Sinan was capable of. The shroud cloak barely came down below Gallmau's knees, but standing in water up to the waist disguised the prince's tell-tale size.

The impersonation should be good enough to provoke a counterattack from at least one of the mages and tell them who they were dealing with. Whether their opponents were from the Order of Katil or not, they had to send out someone who could fight shadow powers.

A man strode out from the highest cave, his arms raised in the air.

Sinan couldn't make out the man's features in the limited light, but he didn't need to. The posture, the walk—he would never forget watching as the man on the ledge above him had taken the same steps and rained down death on so many people he knew and loved.

Odart of Dol was here. At least one member of the Noviodunam was involved in Rixende's abduction, and that revelation would rock the foundations of the alliance between the government of Soissons and the mages who wanted to destroy his city.

None of this would mean much if he, Meri, and Gallmau died at the hands of the former head of the benandanti. Odart would blame Sinan and Karakoncolos for the deaths of three Noviodunam mages and both children of King Syagrius. He would use that narrative as a cudgel to force Queen Xiaolian into another war with Karakoncolos and restore his position in both the court and the Noviodunam.

This explained so much and so little. Odart was a mirror mage and could do any magic except necromancy—but only when he took that power, by force or consent, from another living sorcerer. If fury at his political exile had led him to partner with assassins from the Order of Katil, he couldn't use them as a source.

Where would he get his magic now, when he faced a prince pretending to be one of the Blessed?

The answer came as the benandanti sorcerer sent a roaring ball of flame toward Gallmau. There was only one incensor who had entered Terra Amata—Jacques. Odart's son must still be alive and helping his father. Sinan hated Jacques, but even he wouldn't have thought the incensor would help in the abduction of Rixende, a woman he had wanted to marry, as well as the attempted murder of his former fiancée.

The blinding light from the fire blocked out any view of what had happened to Gallmau. Sinan could only hope the prince was safe as he dashed out of the water and ran toward the bluffs, keeping his profile low and hoping the guards' attention would be on the river and not him.

As he approached the base of the rocky elevation that housed the caves, the second distraction came, in the form of Meri and her double blades. Even without her speed, she was a frightening opponent to face in the darkness that lay beyond the circle of light from the campfire. Two of the guards lay bleeding on the ground before Sinan had advanced halfway up the narrow steps cut into the rock. The remaining guards milled in confusion, uncertain where the attack had come from. Meri melted back into the darkness, and a new threat came charging toward them. Gallmau barreled into the men, his shield held high.

Odart sent another blast of fire down, and Sinan cursed silently as he crept up the final steps to the cave entrance. He couldn't not look, even though he needed all the precious time Gallmau and Meri were trying to give him.

The fireball hung in the air, then exploded backward, setting two of the guards on fire.

Gallmau got in a few solid blows with his sword and shield, and chaos broke out among his opponents.

Sinan exhaled in relief and kept going. As bad as it was to face Odart again, it was excellent fortune it had been the mirror mage falling for Gallmau's ruse and not the other sorcerers they were facing. Odart had undergone the loyalty ceremony Jacques had avoided before the quest started. Gallmau's blood protected him from Odart's attacks, but it wouldn't help him against an assassin from the Order.

Sinan reached the final step and pressed himself against the rocky outcropping on the side of the cave's entrance.

A lacquered wooden screen comprised of multiple panels with mother-of-pearl and gold accents had been set up to cover the entrance, and it stood framed in electric light from within. An odd choice for a military encampment, even if it had been looted from the chateau. It featured a pastoral scene with elegantly dressed ladies in a garden reading scrolls alongside gamboling foxes.

At least there were no signs of the Azhdarchids.

"I'm going out there." It was a woman's voice, sounding young but quite self-assured. "If the Prince of Shadows and my brother want a fight, I'll give it to them."

Sinan leaned over to peer through the gap between the screen and the cave wall.

A woman stood with her back to him, short and slender and enveloped in a hooded cloak of green velvet. The interior of the cave had been transformed into a palatial space, with an enormous carpet covering the floor and ornate furniture pieces scattered around the room.

Fulgari lanterns provided light, and a brazier burned in one corner.

A cave fit for a princess. The woman in the velvet hood must be Rixende.

She didn't sound liked a cowed captive, and the luxurious surroundings were oddly considerate of her captors— unless she wasn't a prisoner at all, but part of this entire scheme.

Sinan shifted to get a better view of the room and was relieved to catch a glimpse of Valentina. The medica was seated on a chair with fanciful curved legs, a grim expression on her face.

"Gallmau came here to help you." Valentina's voice held a tired resignation, as if she had said the same thing many times and to no effect.

"You see, Mademoiselle la Reine, how your dear friend's mind is still afflicted by the wiles of the necromancer." This was a man's voice, and it came from a corner Sinan couldn't see from his position, until the speaker leaned forward. He was an older man with Qingian features, wearing robes

Sinan recognized as indicating the highest rank a mage could achieve in the Kingdom of Soissons.

Zhang Jue, the Sorcier du Roi, wasn't dead at all.

Sinan gritted his teeth. All this time, they had been battling the most renowned weather mage in either the Continent or Qing and an expert on Artifacts.

The royal sorcerer of Soissons continued, his voice smooth and persuasive. "That's why Gallmau has joined forces with the Prince of Shadows—to turn even your closest friends against you and steal your throne."

Sinan wondered who the headless body the Noviodunam had cremated and laid to rest with full honors had been. A trick like that would be child's play for any of his people to uncover, but since the Noviodunam didn't even allow their medici to study the anatomy of dead bodies, they had been taken in.

That knowledge now clicked.

Sinan shoved aside the wooden panel and stepped into the cave with his sword drawn. Zhang Jue's talents were vast but not suited for personal combat in a closed space. Most meteorological effects he could stir up in the cave would harm him as well.

The Sorcier du Roi let out a warning shout, and Rixende spun around to face him. Sinan had a moment of shock as he saw her face.

Then he was knocked backward into the hard stone of the cave wall and pinned there.

He flailed, unable to move his arms or legs, and realized he was being held fast by bones. They had flown from the back of the cave, arranging themselves into a glistening white cage of ribs and interlocked vertebrae, with a few femurs compressing his chest and legs.

An inhuman cry resounded through the room, and the

mother Azhdarchid came stomping up from the same direction as the bones. The Archaic opened her toothed beak and hissed in his direction.

A mirror mage, a weather mage—and a necromancer, working together.

The Order of Katil hadn't abducted Rixende after all.

The beast master was the princess.

29

SINAN

Sinan was still reeling from the revelation as Rixende came up to him, her hands raised in a threatening position. She'd had no proper training, of course, so she used hand gestures better suited for an incensor than one of the Blessed. Still, trapping him in a matrix of skeleton parts was awfully impressive for an untutored feral bone witch who could also control Touched animals.

He had a better look at her as she advanced toward him. A pair of tufted ears rose above her straight black hair, and fine lines of red fur outlined both her cheeks. A full tail, lush and soft, twitched underneath her velvet cape.

Rixende's Blessing was lovely.

A few years younger than Gallmau, her appearance must have recently altered to fox aspect—it wasn't uncommon for Blessed children to come into their Gifts and their transformed appearance as they transitioned to adulthood. Zhang Jue must have used some magic to disguise her new form before he lured her away from her mother and the court.

"Your Serene Highness." Zhang Jue added enough awe to his tone to emphasize his next words. "You've defeated the Prince of Shadows."

Saints, Sinan hated the son of a bitch. Everything made sense now.

The heir to the Throne of Soissons was one of the Blessed, and there was nothing Odart and Zhang Jue wouldn't do to stop her ascension to the throne.

Except kill Rixende themselves, which they couldn't do, because of the loyalty curse. It applied to the Shields of Thaschus as well, since they couldn't be ordered to kill Rixende by either mage.

Instead, Zhang Jue and Odart had convinced Rixende to travel with them to Terra Amata, then sent a taunting message to encourage rescuers to come and kill the mysterious Bone Lord who had abducted the princess. Like in Gallmau's poem, a hero would do what Odart and Zhang Jue couldn't—murder a necromancer who happened to be a seventeen-year-old girl.

"He's the Prince of Shadows?" Rixende cocked her ears forward as she regarded Sinan, giving her a quizzical air much like an actual fox. "He couldn't even stop me from using Plumette's bones against him."

"He came here with your traitor of a brother and the Lioness of Abdju to kill you." Zhang Jue came forward, his court robes swirling as he made an over-dramatic gesture at Sinan. "By the grace of Saint Elesbaan and your noble blood, he has been defeated. All you need to do now is cut off his head, and your curse will be lifted."

From her chair, Valentina let out a gasp of horror but didn't move.

Zhang Jue had convinced the princess she had been cursed by a necromancer, whose death at her hand would reverse her new shape and unsettling new abilities.

"You're not cursed." Sinan struggled again, but his bone shackles weren't going anywhere, regardless of who Plumette was. Rixende was one of his people, and if he couldn't convince her that he, Meri, and Gallmau were here to help her, Odart and Zhang Jue would find a way around the loyalty oath and kill her.

With his powers intact, he could have turned the bones into a hail of projectiles and riddled Zhang Jue's body like a pincushion. Unfortunately, that wasn't an option, and he couldn't expect any help from the Tomb Fighters. Their plan had been for Sinan to free Valentina and Rixende, then lead them to safety while they distracted their enemies.

Sinan had to reach her, to make her understand. "You're like me, one of the Blessed. Zhang Jue and Odart have lied to you. They don't want you to become Queen."

"It's a peculiar habit amongst the Bone Lords of Karakoncolos to consider themselves blessed by their twisted, horrible shapes." Zhang Jue continued lecturing the princess as if Sinan was an interesting zoological specimen, not someone he was standing next to. "It's part of their death cult, in which they worship the patron saint of fallen women and engage in vile practices of all types."

"My brother is the one who doesn't want me to become queen." Rixende, unlike Zhang Jue, did address Sinan directly and with a good deal of venom. "Gallmau wants the throne for himself, even though I'm the legitimate heir." She punctuated that last sentence by extending her forefinger at Sinan's chest. Bone chips flew into her hand,

and within seconds an ivory sword was leveled at his heart.

"Rixende, stop." Valentina squirmed in her seat, and Sinan belatedly realized she had remained unmoving only because she was shackled to her chair. "You can't do this. It won't change what's happened to you."

"Let me gag her." Zhang Jue removed a strip of silk from his pocket and moved toward the medica. "Her madness grows worse. It would be best if we let her rest in a different cave with the guards watching over her."

"No." Rixende whirled, sword in hand, and the mother Azhdarchid turned its wild eyes in the direction of the Sorcier du Roi. Her beak opened, then snapped shut in warning.

Zhang Jue froze.

The weather mage was afraid of Rixende for good reason. Even if he could attack her with his magic, she was already strong enough to threaten him. With training, Rixende would be an exceptionally powerful member of the Blessed. But no lie was more powerful than the one a person desperately wanted to believe.

"Valentina's not leaving my sight." Rixende lifted her weapon, gazing at the razor-sharp edge with fascination. She held the blade up toward Sinan's neck, as if judging what type of blow would best sever his head from his body. "She should be safe in Lutecia, not hexed by a necromancer my brother's joined forces with. I thank Saint Elesbaan I spotted Valentina's simar through Plumette's eyes and had her and the babies save her."

The Azhdarchid cocked her head at Rixende, as if recognizing her name. Well, that explained both who Plumette was and the source of the bones. The Azhdarchid's dining habits would produce an ample supply of animal skeletons

—and perhaps a few human ones. More ungainly shapes moved in from the gloom at the back of the cave, and Plumette's two flaplings stalked up to them. Each was the size of Gallmau, and they were threatening enough even without their mother.

"I understand your concerns." Zhang Jue raised both hands in a placating gesture, edging away from the Archaic animals. "We'll get Valentina the best medical help once we return to Lutecia. But we must rid you of your curse first. Take off his head, Mademoiselle la Reine. It's the only way."

"It won't because he isn't a necromancer." Valentina nodded her head in Sinan's direction. "He's only pretending to be one because Gallmau told him to."

Sinan gave her an incredulous look. Maybe Valentina was experiencing disorientation from everything she had been through, and Zhang Jue wasn't entirely wrong.

"He looks nothing like a Bone Lord," Valentina continued. "He can't be the Prince of Shadows."

Rixende dropped her sword back to rest on her shoulder and leaned in to examine Sinan more closely. "He's rather comely for a necromancer, I'll allow."

"His mother was a venefica." Zhang Jue gripped the silk tie in his hand tightly, as Sinan frowned in confusion at Valentina's words. "He's the murderous Bone Lord who slaughtered half of the benandanti in Zyx. You must end his reign of terror."

"He blundered into this cave waving a sword around and couldn't even come up with a simple spell to stop you from trapping him." Valentina kept her tone calm and conversational. "Sinan of Karakoncolos can split Artifacts in two with shadow and raise a cursed throne of bones from the floor of the Synod meeting room itself. This man is only a courtier your brother brought along—a wastrel poet of limited literary talents."

Now Sinan understood. Valentina wasn't losing her mind, she was doing her best to stop Rixende from killing him.

"You mustn't listen to her." Zhang Jue took a step closer to the bound medica, but Plumette gave another warning hiss and he stopped. "She's mad."

"Many strange things have happened to both of us." Valentina had the princess's full attention now. "If you're wrong, nothing will change, and you'll have murdered a helpless young man."

"He's an evil necromancer, not a person," Zhang Jue protested, but Valentina cut him off.

"I have a simple spell to help us." Valentina raised her hands off the chair's arms, ivory chains rustling as they stopped the movement. She was restrained by loops of inter-locked spinal vertebrae. "A temporary truth charm. Remember when you insisted I use it on the ladies of the Court during a party? I can cast one on this man and the honorable Zhang Jue, as long as they agree. Then you can ask both of them anything you want."

"I'll do it." Sinan wasn't sure where Valentina was going with this, but Rixende now seemed uncertain about beheading him, and that was progress.

"Your Serene Highness, as the Sorcier du Roi, I'm forbidden to submit to this type of magic." Zhang Jue's face darkened in anger as Rixende moved over to Valentina and waved her hands. The bone chains collapsed into a loose pile of skeletal parts, and the medica stood up. "Novio-dunam secrets could be revealed in front of this necromancer."

Rixende ignored him as she held on to Valentina's arm and pulled her toward Sinan. "Make him tell me the truth."

"Open your mouth and say 'ah'." Valentina reached out with her finger as Sinan complied and touched his tongue.

A vibration passed through him, sending his teeth chattering.

Medicus magic was horrifying.

"Excellent." Rixende nodded with approval, then leveled the tip of her sword at Sinan's throat again. "Did my brother tell you to come into this cave and bring me to him?"

"Yes." The word came out of its own volition. Sinan had no more control over his truthful answers now than he had over continuing to breathe. He could try and not speak, but the urge would eventually overwhelm him. Fine. He wanted Rixende to know the truth. "But Gallmau doesn't want to hurt you, he wants to rescue you."

Rixende waved that statement away with a flutter of her fingers, but Valentina gripped her arm. "Ask him if he can perform death magic for you, like calling up an undead spirit."

"No, I can't." Sinan was forced to choke out the words. "But I am one of the Blessed."

Rixende pressed her sword in until it stung, and a trickle of wet blood ran down Sinan's neck. "Only answer the question, nothing more."

"Ask him if he's Gallmau's lover." Valentina might be going a bit far with the game at this point. Hopefully Rixende would be too embarrassed to ask that question, because Sinan couldn't stop himself from answering it.

"Have you tumbled my brother?" Rixende didn't as much as blush.

"Yes." Sinan tried hard to bite that one back, because it

was none of her business, and why had Valentina picked this particular spell to try and help him?

"More than once?" Rixende prompted and pursed her lips when Sinan had to answer in the affirmative again. "I know Gallmau can't resist handsome men, but I find it hard to believe he'd seduce a Bone Lord. Still, why would he send his poet lover to lure me into a trap?"

"There's so much that's unclear." Valentina touched Rixende's arm again, and the princess turned to her. "Magic and curses, and too many men telling you what to think. Don't do anything rash. Talk to Gallmau and find out his side of the story. He's your brother."

"Ask this man to submit to a test of Amor Vitriol." Zhang Jue came up on the other side of the princess, a glass sphere in his hand.

There were a good deal fewer of the blue rocks inside than in the one Meri had thrown into the fireplace at the chateau, but it still would wipe away what little glints of magic Sinan had been able to regain. If he never heard of or saw the mineral again, it would be too soon.

"Submerge this into a bowl of water, and if he's unaffected, we'll know he's innocent of necromancy."

Sinan struggled again to break the bony cage pinning him to the wall. Zhang Jue wasn't trying to use the Amor Vitriol on him. The Sorcier du Roi had caught on that Sinan wasn't able to use his necromantic powers. Zhang Jue wanted to use the substance against Rixende. Maybe he had hoped to kill her with it, but he couldn't attack a descendent of the Grimoard line directly. What he could do was trick her into using it against herself.

"No." Sinan could still talk, as long as he spoke the truth. "Don't listen to him."

"It's a dangerous magical substance," Valentina added hastily. "It could make your curse even worse."

"Ask this *poet* if anyone in the room would be harmed by the Amor Vitriol if they weren't a necromancer." Zhang Jue's words were as soft and silky as the cloth tie in his hands. "He can't lie—Valentina did the charm correctly."

Sinan bit down so hard on his lip he drew blood, but when Rixende blurted out the question, he couldn't stop himself from answering. "No, it only harms the Blessed. That's why it'll hurt *you*."

"I'm not a Bone Lord." Rixende stomped one foot for emphasis, and all three Azhdarchids followed suit. "I've been cursed by the real Prince of Shadows—who's not some pretty-boy courtier my brother's bedding—and I'll prove it."

She snatched the sphere of Amor Vitriol from Zhang Jue's hand and walked over to a table holding a washing bowl and pitcher. Like everything else in the cave, the porcelain objects were exquisite, a translucent white with a blue underglaze detailing fish in a lotus pond.

Valentina shouted a final plea for her to stop.

But the princess tossed the glass object onto the water in the basin. Rixende watched with interest as it floated and bobbed on the surface.

Then the explosion came, a rush of blue fire throughout the room.

Sinan braced himself for more pain or perhaps even unconsciousness, but he felt nothing more than an unpleasant crawling sensation all over his skin.

The bone cage around him collapsed and Sinan lunged forward to attack Zhang Jue. He landed a punch to one side of the man's face, sending him reeling backward and hopefully disrupting whatever spell the weather mage might be about to use on him.

The Azhdarchids shrieked in fury as Sinan scrambled for his sword, which he leveled at Zhang Jue as he tried to see who the Archaics wanted to eat first. The beasts showed no sign of aggression. Instead, the three of them huddled together, their enormous eyes fixated on the floor as they made a low, keening sound of mourning.

Rixende Grimoard, the Dauphine of Soissons, lay crumpled on the carpet.

Valentina had gone to her side, laying her hand on her forehead as she used her healing powers. The princess's fox ears and tail remained—the physical Blessings of his people weren't affected by Amor Vitriol, and Sinan had no idea why his own internal Blessing had been taken away by the substance.

"If you weren't a traitor to your training at the Noviodunam you'd be using your Gift to end her life, not save it." Zhang Jue regarded both Valentina and the steel blade Sinan had poised at his neck with contempt, even though Sinan was close enough to be inside any magical armor the weather mage could summon. "And to think I protested when Odart insisted I send you an invitation."

Valentina hadn't been attacked merely because she was with Jacques. Odart had wanted the medica to die here so her death could be blamed on the Blessed as well.

"If you weren't a traitor to your Queen and your office, you'd be trying to help the heir to the throne." Valentina shot the words back at the Sorcier du Roi as she worked, her face tight with the strain.

Sinan shot another glance at the three Azhdarchids, who were rooted to the spot, watching as the medica tried to save their beast master. How they could tell Valentina wanted to help Rixende wasn't clear. Real intelligence lurked behind their enormous eyes. Maybe they could be of help, even if the princess wasn't able to control them directly.

"There's no cure for necromancy." Zhang Jue kept arguing with Valentina, but he didn't resist as Sinan bound his hands with the fabric the Sorcier du Roi had planned to use to gag the medica.

There was nothing Sinan would enjoy more right now than running Zhang Jue through with his sword. There were two problems with that. One, Valentina's powers would be diminished by the death, and she might not be able to save the princess. Two, if they succeeded in freeing Rixende and escaping, a living Zhang Jue would be a damning indictment of the treason of the benandanti.

"We have to get out of here." Sinan scanned the front of the cave. Gallmau and Meri's distraction wouldn't work for much longer.

"She's small enough that I can carry her down the steps." Valentina gave an offended glare at Sinan's expression of surprise. "I'm stronger than I look, and anyway, you're the one with the sword. I've stabilized her, but it would be better if I can keep physical contact to help with the healing."

"Fine." Sinan turned to the Azhdarchids.

Animal magic of any sort was notoriously difficult for anyone but beast masters to use, and he knew less about it than even his few ghost spells. But he didn't need to control the giant Archaics, only communicate with them.

"This man wants to hurt your master." Sinan gestured at Zhang Jue. "We want to help her."

Plumette cocked her massive head at that, then bent down to shriek in Zhang Jue's face. The Sorcier du Roi backed up against the wall, raising his bound hands over his face. Electricity crackled from his skin, a type of magical armor Sinan had seen used passively by the Shields of Thaschus. Zhang Jue's would be stronger, but it was a purely defensive magic. Once again, the weather mage was at a disadvantage.

The Archaics slammed their beaks into the crackling field of energy around the Sorcier du Roi, growing more enraged as their attacks failed to land. That should keep him busy for a while.

Sinan sheathed his sword and went back to Rixende's crumpled shape, preparing to lift her onto Valentina's shoulders. The medica gasped, and Sinan whirled toward the cave entrance.

Odart of Dol stood outlined in the entrance, two fireballs floating above each hand. Jacques stood beside his father, his face unreadable. Three Shields came up behind the mages, and the sight of the bound prisoner they herded in front of them sent a stab of fear through Sinan.

Meri.

That meant Gallmau was captured as well. They had taken their chance, and lost.

Odart gave Sinan a cold smile and raised his right arm to ready his fireball. "You're no prince, necromancer, and now you don't even have your shadows. Burn in Hell, death witch."

30

MERI

Meri took in the scene in front of her and jerked at the enchanted bindings on her wrists, knowing she couldn't break them. They also took away her ability to drop into her speed, not that she could try that without dying.

All she could do was watch as Odart killed everyone.

Valentina crouched over the unconscious body of the beast-master princess, her face pale with fear as she watched Jacques's stolen fireballs in Odart's hands. Sinan had moved to put his body in front of the two women, holding his sword with a grim but determined expression.

It was Meri's fault—she had taken away Sinan's powers with the Amor Vitriol after hiding her secret from him. Maybe if she had been honest from the start the three of them could have worked together to stop Odart and his goons.

"Now you're murdering women." Jacques succeeded in putting fiery disdain into every word he flung at his father, even though the fire mage wasn't in much of a better situation than Meri was, and Odart paused to glare at his son.

Odart's ability to mirror the magic of others siphoned off their power, and his theft of his son's fire magic had weakened Jacques and made him easier to keep captive. Odart had also clamped water-enhanced shackles around his son's wrists that left Jacques with no fire to fight back with.

The incensor still had his temper, though. "My own father, a traitor, a liar, and a thief—and now you want to use my Saints-given Gift to kill an unconscious girl and a medica devoted to the healing arts. I renounce you and everything you stand for, and I'll never help you put Gallmau on the throne as your puppet."

Their plan to distract Odart and the guards while Sinan freed Valentina and Rixende had failed to take into account that the loyalty curse gave Odart a link to the prince that allowed him to locate both Gallmau and Meri. The mirror mage couldn't harm the son of Syagrius Grimoard, but he could threaten to kill Meri in front of him, and that had been enough to force Gallmau to surrender. He had been left tied up and under guard, and Meri was grateful he wasn't here to watch this.

Odart kept the balls of flames above his hands spinning but made no move to throw them in Sinan's direction. Instead, he turned his attention to the other traitorous witch in the room.

"Use the fire to get these creatures of hers away from me." The older Qingian man, who must be Zhang Jue, Odart's partner in treason, sounded more irritable than nervous about the three Azhdarchids who had him pinned against a far wall.

Odart gave a grunt of assent and sent the fireballs spinning in the air toward the bird-like creatures. The flames hovered in the air, more like clouds than projectiles. The largest Azhdarchid shrieked, fanning out her wings to protect her offspring, and the animals scuttled away to the back of the cave.

The Qingian mage inclined his head a fraction—a movement so slight Meri all but missed it—and lightning lashed out from him toward Sinan. The Sorcier du Roi held up his bound hands, and crackling sparks dissolved the silk tie into ash.

Sinan fell to the ground, incapacitated but alive—she could hear him groaning. Valentina cried out and tried to scramble to his side to help him, but Zhang Jue came over to yank her up by the arm.

"Take her." The Sorcier du Roi gestured to one of the Shields—Captain Caron, that bastard—who stepped forward and grabbed Valentina roughly around the waist.

"Unhand her, you piece of filth." The words came out as a low growl from Jacques, and his lurch toward the guard was stopped only by another Shield jerking him back. Meri was beginning to like the incensor. He couldn't control his temper worth a damn, but he had courage.

"Perhaps if my only son wasn't a traitor to his kind, Dottoressa de Almania would be safely back at Court, no doubt criticizing the same benandanti who protect her and her guild." Odart held a particular grudge against anyone in the Noviodunam who expressed sympathy for necromancers, it seemed. "If I could have trusted you, Jacques, none of this would have happened. You would have ended Rixende's life and the threat she poses to the world itself in Lutecia. Quietly. Instead, I needed this charade to bring you here to do your duty—and then you dragged foreigners into it. Abarsam was a good man—for an infidel—and I had to kill him and his son."

You'll pay for that, I promise. The grief of seeing Abarsam's mutilated body on the ground welled up again, so strong she felt she would choke on it, but she kept her mouth shut and her attention focused.

Zhang Jue clucked his tongue and came forward. "Surely, Jacques, you can see your father has a point? The curse of necromancy can strike the noblest of families. Numerous times, I've had the sad duty of ending the lives of promising Noviodunam students when the darkness inside of them was revealed by the harsh but necessary methods of the benandanti. The kingdom of Soissons cannot be ruled by a necromancer—even if we could keep Mademoiselle la Reine believing her foul shape is a curse laid upon her by our enemies in Karakoncolos."

"The honorable Zhang Jue." Jacques spat the mage's title out like a foul-tasting liquid in his mouth. "You, sir, are even more of a scoundrel and a traitor than my father."

"Even the strongest tree has branches that need to be trimmed." Zhang Jue caught Meri's eye and came up closer to her. "Rot will spread if weak men allow it to. A strong woman such as yourself knows this. The princess was the one who attacked you and King Syagrius's son with her foul beast magic. Your job is to hunt down and kill necromancers. One lies helpless before you now. Assist us with this, and we will free and reward you."

Zhang Jue gestured toward the princess, lying on the floor like an overtired child taking a nap by the fire.

Meri wanted to slice open the Sorcier du Roi's neck as much as she wanted to plunge her blades into Odart's heart. She bit back any quick response, though. She wasn't Jacques and knew when to hold her tongue. "I'm not doing any work with no chance of payment."

"Enough of this." Odart pointed to the Shield holding Valentina. "Cut her throat."

Jacques roared in fury at that, and Meri strained against her bonds, again accomplishing nothing.

"Sinan must die first." Zhang Jue raised a hand as Captain Caron brought a sword up to Valentina's neck. "As much as I would prefer to harvest the most valuable body parts from the Prince of Shadows while he lives, I don't want any death that could give him power. How he came in without his cursed powers is still a mystery to me."

"Can you at least kill the Bone Lord who held you captive and murdered your men?" Odart shoved his finger into his son's chest.

"Swear to Saint Thaschus." Jacques's voice dropped to a whisper, and although his words were directed at Odart his eyes were locked on Sinan. The necromancer had recovered enough to raise his head to meet the incensor's gaze and to give his enemy a small nod. "Swear to our patron saint, Father, that you'll spare Valentina's life if I do this."

"I shouldn't have to promise anything for you to do your duty." Odart's face was red with fury, but Zhang Jue held up his hand again and smiled.

Odart's face darkened, but he muttered the oath to the saint of witches. Meri would have bet her blades the mirror mage wouldn't let religion get in the way of his plans for murder, but Jacques had done what he could to protect his former fiancée.

"Release Magus Jacques, please." Zhang Jue gave Meri a cold smile as Jacques rubbed his freed wrists and walked over to Sinan. The fire mage showed none of the enthusiasm Meri might have expected. "Our brave incensor has set his price for what we ask of him, and we will pay it. Perhaps a different contract with the Tomb Fighter would interest her."

Meri rearranged her features into a calculating smile. "I can't do anything with my hands tied. Or without my blades."

"We'll see about that." Zhang Jue's tone grew cold. "After the Prince of Shadows is dead."

A cold weight of despair settled over her, and Meri fought to keep her emotions from being revealed on her face. She couldn't stop Jacques from killing Sinan. That was a simple fact but a crushing one. The young necromancer she had wanted to murder a few days before now meant so much to her—and she couldn't save him.

Jacques lifted Sinan off the floor by the back of his shirt.

He said something in the necromancer's ear, and Sinan rose to his feet, staggering along with the incensor toward the opening of the cave. He was going to his death willingly, perhaps even eagerly, now there was no chance of escape.

The Shields backed away as the two men approached, clearly uneasy to be too close to the infamous Prince of Shadows. Jacques shoved Sinan against the side of the cave opening, and the necromancer stood propped against the rock.

The incensor backed away, gesturing for the Shields to move further back from him.

Jacques raised both of his hands into the air.

Sinan's head came up, and Meri prayed he would look at her one last time. She wanted to drink in the beauty of his dark eyes and share a final farewell. Maybe all of the religions were wrong, those of her people and Gallmau's, and Sinan's mother Naghwe was right. Sinan would go to

Paradise—or Heaven or whatever his people believed in—and one day she would see him there, along with Sanura.

Sinan turned his head toward Valentina instead, and he said a few short words to her.

They sounded like a prayer.

A roaring gust of hot wind knocked Sinan off his feet and out of the cave. His body was buffeted up by the force of the air Jacques had used his powers to generate. The blue kaftan that Abarsam had crafted with his aquamancy floated around Sinan, like the colorful wings of a bird. Then he fell, as the last leaf on a dying tree falls, and Jacques raised his arms again to send a swirling maelstrom of fire out of the cave and toward the ground where Sinan's body had landed.

Meri flinched back, the heat of the blaze burning her face and drawing the breath out of her lungs. She could only hope the fall had killed Sinan before Jacques's fire incinerated his flesh.

"Now." Zhang Jue came up to Meri, his gaze cold and penetrating. "I know you by reputation, Lioness of Abdju. Your hatred for the malandanti is well known, as is your skill in killing them. Rixende must die, and Odart's son is too weak to do it. Name your price, and we'll see if we can come to an arrangement."

Captain Caron jerked his head toward one of the Shields, who nodded and left the cave. That left two Shields and two mages.

Meri took in the room and calculated her chances.

No, not *her* chances. This would be for Gallmau, who would gladly die rather than see his sister killed. It would also be for Valentina, who might be a witch but had shown more bravery than most of the former soldiers Meri had worked with. Lastly, it would be for Sinan, who had died protecting people like Rixende. Maybe if the princess of Soissons survived, his city of monsters would be a little less frightening to the rest of the world and a little safer from it.

To save Rixende, she would need help from both Valentina and Jacques. The medica might follow her lead, but the incensor tended to act first and think much later.

It wasn't much of a plan, but it was all she had.

"First, untie me, and second, give me my blades." Meri rolled her shoulders, working out some kinks in her muscles. "Killing necromancers without properly taking off their heads is a good way to get cursed. And what do I want? To be the Queen of Soissons, of course."

Maybe that last was too audacious to be believable, but Jacques had been worried it was Meri's ambition all along, and he couldn't be alone in that thought.

"Then you'll help us keep Gallmau in line as well." Odart gave her a look that implied grudging admiration for both her amorality and bloodthirstiness. "Neither Zhang Jue nor I want the Grimoard line to end and have to endure another loyalty oath."

"I can handle the prince." Meri stood still as the odd material binding her hands was untied.

Captain Caron held out a familiar pair of curved swords to Odart. Abarsam's water-blessed blades—her weapons.

She ached to have them in her hands again and use them to stab both mages in the gut, so they would die slowly. "He thinks with his member, like most men. I'll convince him this was all for the best."

"Don't do it." Jacques's voice held despair, rather than his usual raging fury. "Rixende doesn't deserve to die this way."

Meri had hoped Jacques might pick up on what she was doing, but the incensor's opinion of her had been low from the start. At least it added realism to her performance. As for Valentina, she could only pray the medica was willing to break the rules of her guild again. She accepted her swords from Odart and walked over to the princess.

The girl's eyes were closed, her fine black hair fanned around the pointed fox ears on her head. She looked more like a lovely doll than a young woman and gave no sign she was conscious.

Meri touched her fingertip to Rixende's throat and felt the racing heartbeat of someone playing the same kind of game Meri was.

"I always say a brief prayer to the Prophets to guide my hands in righteousness and protect me from the curses of witches." Meri made that rather grand announcement as loud as she could, then dropped her voice to the barest whisper as her lips brushed against the downy softness of Rixende's animal ears. "I'll drop into my speed and take out the guards holding Jacques. Run for the river and then stick with him and Valentina. No matter what they offer Gallmau, he'll never betray you. He loves you."

There was the faintest twitch of the girl's lush red lips.

Meri raised both blades in the air and gave Valentina a look that said: *Now*.

An explosion rocked the room, and light flared inside the closed space. Meri had forgotten all about Sinan's flash-bang device, but Valentina hadn't.

Meri dug as deep as she could for her speed, throwing prayers up to the Prophets to give her one last burst, and they were answered. The world slowed, and she raced up to the guards near Jacques, smashing one in the nose with the hilt of one blade and slicing through the arm of another. Sloppy work.

Her speed faded too quickly, and a growing ache in her

head told her she would pay a huge price for trying to use her Gift too soon.

Maybe the final price, but that was what she had planned. She fell to the floor, time returning slowly enough that she could see Valentina reach out with her hands to use her powers against Captain Caron and Jacques pulling a sword off the waist of one of the guards she had taken down.

Good. If the incensor could use the weapon and his fire to hold off Odart and Zhang Jue long enough, Valentina could take Rixende with her to safety, and Jacques could catch up.

Then she saw an angry swirl of silks and red fur stalk up to Zhang Jue, a jeweled dagger better suited for opening wax seals on letters than doing any real damage in her small hand.

Meri's head exploded in pain, and a final thought crossed her mind.

Damn it to Hell, Rixende. I told you to run.

31

GALLMAU

Gallmau drew in another breath, the scents of manure and horse urine filling his nose, and tried again to break the ropes binding his hands. They were more insults than true bonds, knotted fiber he normally could have snapped apart with ease—if it wasn't for the candle.

It sat in front of him inside a tin holder, its only remarkable feature the gold flames that flowed down from the wick and pooled at the base—a miniature version of the fountain of fire in the Palais de Feu.

Saints damn witches and all their tricks.

The fire magic in front of him had drained away his strength, and even the two Shields left as guards weren't paying him much attention. They stood at the entrance of the cave, their backs to him as they waited to hear the ending to the story Odart and Zhang Jue wanted.

His sister, dead. Valentina too, if Jacques kept refusing to kill Rixende. And Sinan—Gallmau prayed he had somehow escaped, but he knew better. The Prince of Shadows wouldn't have left one of his people behind, and Gallmau now understood Rixende was one of the Blessed.

Odart only wanted Gallmau alive because he wanted to oust Queen Xiaolian and put someone he could control on the throne. If he refused, they would kill Meri.

Gallmau was about to get everything he never wanted, and there was nothing he could do about it.

Shouts rang out outside the cave, and Gallmau's two guards straightened and saluted as another Shield carrying a lantern stepped inside.

"The Prince of Shadows is dead." The man's face was twisted into a satisfied grin. "Odart's son finally did his job. The bitch should be next, then."

Gallmau swallowed, the impact of the news crushing, even though he had expected it. Images of Sinan's beautiful body, broken and burnt like Abarsam's, flooded his mind. He couldn't get past the rage and grief welling up inside him to think of any plan.

Worse yet, he didn't know which woman they planned on killing next.

Valentina, perhaps? He prayed Meri was safe, with her value as a hostage. His sister must be dead by now, deceived and lied to by men who had taken oaths to protect her. Hell, even Gallmau had trusted Zhang Jue. Now he wanted to kill him even more than he wanted to break Odart's neck with his bare hands.

All three men gathered outside the cave to point and talk amongst themselves. Gallmau could do nothing more but thrash around, trying to break the ropes. His agitation distracted him from the squeaking noise until it grew too loud to ignore.

A familiar pair of glowing blue lights hovered near the floor. The body of a rat formed around them, and the ghost animal began to sniff the air. Gallmau was still wearing Sinan's cloak, not that the enchanted object was of much use to him, and perhaps the animal wanted to be close to something that had belonged to his now-dead master.

"Sinan's gone." Speaking the words out loud made more raw grief well up inside him. "No cheese, either."

The animal straightened up at the mention of a snack, its whiskers quivering hopefully. Gallmau gave a half-sob, half-laugh.

Then he had a thought. "The ropes around my hands are made of cheese."

The rat cocked its head, a motion that mimicked Sinan perfectly.

The animal wasn't buying it. "All right, maybe not, but I need you to chew through them. Can you do that for me?"

The rat behaved in a most un-rodent-like fashion and scrambled behind Gallmau to do as it was told. His heart leaped, even as he had to bite his lip to not yelp in pain as the ghost animal chewed away enthusiastically at both the tough fibers of the ropes and the tender skin on Gallmau's fingers. In a few minutes his hands were free, and he could untie his legs.

Gallmau rose to his feet, cupping the rodent in his hand and letting it scramble up to his shoulders. He had to drag his weight along, and each step felt like it took an eternity.

As he moved away from the candle, his strength improved, bit by bit. His captors had left the Grimoard dynasty shield propped up against one wall, although they had taken his armor and swords elsewhere. Perhaps the

Shields had wanted to show the royal symbol some respect, or maybe they had merely been careless.

Only one of those guards now stood at the entrance, craning his neck to peer into the darkness outside. There were shouts and commotion, and the Shields acted uneasy —and focused on events outside the cave. Gallmau wasn't going to get another chance like this.

He could try to lift his shield and engage the guard in a fair fight—one he would likely lose, given the lingering effects of the fire magic. That would be the honorable thing to do.

Meri had told him his honor would get him killed one day. He could accept that.

What he couldn't accept was his honor getting Meri killed.

His eyes locked on the guard's back, Gallmau bent down and felt the inner lining of his boot with his fingers. The stiletto Meri had given him and insisted he always hide in his footwear slid out without a sound.

He came up behind the guard and slid the blade in between the ribs on the man's left side and thrust it high and up. His military training had not taught him this, but Meri had, and as the man collapsed to the floor, unable to even choke out a warning to his fellow Shields before dying, Gallmau grabbed the Shield of Soissons and ran out of the cave and toward the cover of the trees.

It was more of a stumbling, awkward jog, but no one tried to stop him. He heard more shouts of alarm and guessed something had happened to agitate his enemies.

Between that and the darkness, no one had noticed his escape.

The surge of relief he felt at that receded, replaced by hopelessness. Freedom didn't solve any of his problems. He couldn't take on Odart, Zhang Jue, and the remaining Shields by himself. Other than getting away from his captors, he had no plan. They still had Meri as a prisoner, and Jacques—who had proved to be loyal to his country and his Queen—was as helpless as Gallmau.

Then he made out a crumpled shape lying on the bank of the river.

Sinan.

If it was all over, if he would have to choose between serving as a puppet for his sister's murderer or watching Meri die, he wanted to pay his respects to the man they had both grown to care about, even if had been for such a brief time.

He held the rat out in his hand, using the unnatural light of its eyes to see. Sinan's body lay at the river's edge, his outflung right arm crooked at an impossible angle as the water lapped away at it. The magic coat Abarsam had created to protect Baahir flared around him, the material bobbing up and down with the ripples of water.

Gallmau placed the rat on Sinan's chest, surprised the body had no burn marks. His fingers fumbled to loosen the cloak around his neck, and he draped it over him, whispering a prayer to the Lady of Shadows, Sinan's patron Saint.

The river gurgled back to him, and his grief-stricken mind changed the musical sound into the young necromancer's voice.

"Jacques couldn't quite get me far enough. Close to the water, though. Enough that Abarsam's cloak worked. If I could only summon the corpus animatum, but it won't come to me."

Wait, he *was* hearing him.

Gallmau gasped in surprise and bent over Sinan's face.

The necromancer's long eyelashes fluttered, then cracked open.

"You're alive." Gallmau pressed his lips to Sinan's, stopping only when the necromancer groaned with pain. "Sorry!"

"I need the rat." Sinan got those words out with obvious effort.

"I've got the little guy right here." Excitement and triumph flooded through him.

Sinan was alive, and Gallmau was free, and that meant they could do something to save the others. What, he had no idea. He pushed the rodent toward Sinan's face. The animal gave a disinterested sniff and climbed back up Gallmau's arm.

Sinan opened his eyes wider, pain etched on his beautiful features. "My undead servant won't obey me. If the rat's here now in our realm, it could contact a corporeal spirit for us. It has no connection to my mother, but if Sanura hasn't passed over the Veil..."

His voice trailed off, and his eyelids closed.

"It listens to me when I tell it what to do." Gallmau picked the rat up again, his heart all but dancing in his chest. This had to work. "What do I say to it?"

"Complicated phasmancy." Sinan's eyes hadn't reopened, and his slurred words made little sense. "I'd have trouble with it even if I had my Gift back."

"Obey me." Gallmau held the undead rodent in his hands and tried to talk like a necromancer. It didn't sound believable, and he had no idea what phasmancy was, much less how to try it.

He did know Meri's little sister's name, though.

"Go fetch Sanura." Gallmau spoke in his friendly voice, the one he used with small children afraid of his size and hunting dogs when he scratched them behind the ears. "She's nice, and she'll pet you, and I promise I'll find some cheese."

"That's not how you issue commands to a corpus animatum." Sinan gave a weak cough.

The rat blinked its glowing eyes shut, and then it was gone. Gallmau's energy flagged, and he could do nothing more than hold Sinan's hand and beg him to hold on a little longer.

As he waited, a chill began to travel along his spine, creeping up his back like the tips of icy fingers. A glowing shape walked on top of the rushing waters of the stream, small but with a determined stride.

Gallmau reached out a hand, unable to stop himself. Even if she was a ghost, he wanted to be polite to Meri's little sister, who had come back from the grave again, this time to help them fight the man who had protected her killer.

Sanura accepted his hand, her glowing fingers solidifying in his grasp as she stepped onto the riverbank. She crouched next to Sinan, as the rat on her shoulder scuttled back up Gallmau's arm. "Meri sent me away, and I couldn't find my way back. She's in terrible danger."

"I need you to call up my mother." Sinan croaked out the words. "Bring Naghwe here, and I'll save Meri."

Sanura beamed, her face at once sweet and innocent and utterly terrifying. "I can do that."

A mass of shadows darker than the night around them undulated near the ghost girl, and Mother Naghwe formed from the twisting shapes. Her own smile was all fangs and glee, and it took everything Gallmau had not to run in the opposite direction.

"My son." Naghwe bent down and stroked Sinan's cheek.

"I waited for your soul, but it never came. I reached out with our bond, but I was blocked."

"Amor Vitriol," Sinan gasped. "My powers are gone, Mother. Along with my Blessing."

"No, they're not." Naghwe gave Sinan's head a fond pat. Then she plunged her hand into his chest.

Gallmau lurched backward, a choked scream of shock escaping from him, as Sinan convulsed, his arms and legs shaking.

The ground below him shook, and the cold dread he had felt in his spine spread throughout his body, making him shiver uncontrollably. Sloshing sounds reached his ears, and a wet, rotting smell filled his nostrils. He gagged and turned in horror to see dozens of bodies splashing through the water, a faint glow illuminating their misshapen heads, bloated bellies, and rotting limbs.

"Those are the hortdan." Sinan's voice sounded normal again. Well, not as normal as when he, Meri, and Gallmau had tumbled one another. More like the cool, menacing tones he had used when they first met. "Try not to get too close."

The necromancer stirred, lifting his broken right arm.

There was a crack and snapping of bone, and Sinan rose to his feet, the damage done by the fall healing at a rapid rate. He lifted his shroud cloak over his shoulders, and the entire garment glowed with the intensity of more symbols than Gallmau had ever seen on it. The cloth burned with death magic, and Sinan's eyes glittered dangerously in its unnatural light.

"You look scary as fuck." Gallmau didn't know if that was a wise thing to say to Sinan right now, but those were the only words that could make it past his lips.

Sinan turned toward him and smiled. "Thank you. I've

been thinking about what you said about stories, and I have a new one for you."

He strode forward, and Gallmau followed, eyeing the dripping monsters shambling around them with unease. Sanura clutched his hand again, her little fingers cold but comforting, and the ghost rat on his shoulder hissed at the undead protectively. Naghwe squeezed his biceps on the other side, which was—not so comforting.

"I hope it's a good story." Gallmau could see men and lanterns milling in front of the caves and wondered when Odart's men were going to realize the Prince of Shadows and a horde of monsters were bearing down on them. "They have Meri and I don't know if Valentina and Rixende are still alive."

"The story goes something like this." Sinan lifted his hood over his head, and the night itself swirled around him. "Raise the undead army, kill the Noviodunam mages, and save the necromancer princess."

"I know my sister's the beast master and tried to kill me." Gallmau corrected himself, since Rixende didn't give up that easily. "Twice."

Sinan cocked his head, that same familiar movement. Only now it held more challenge than confusion. "Still want to save your sister now you know she's one of the Blessed?"

"Hell, yes." Gallmau's strength flowed back to him, along with all of his fury at the Noviodunam witches who caused this mess. If Rixende was someone like Sinan, that was fine with him. His tolerance for creepy had gone way up since this whole thing had started, anyway. "That damn fire spell is gone, and I'm going to rip Odart's arms off for using it on me. Then I'm going to beat the shit out of Zhang Jue."

Sinan sent his shadow shields spinning around both of them. "Let's find out who gets to them first."

32

SINAN

Sinan strode out to the flat expanse of earth in front of the bluffs with an undead army of the hortdan behind him and the Prince of Soissons by his side.

Odart and Zhang Jue were waiting for him.

His enemies' strategy made sense. Odart knew Sinan could bring the entire mountain down on their heads if they stayed in the caves, and in the open Zhang Jue's weather powers would be the worst threat Sinan and Gallmau faced.

Of course, the hortdan would be the worst threat the Noviodunam's forces faced. Sinan couldn't have been more pleased to have Karakoncolos's deadly water soldiers with him for this fight. The hortdan were many things, but subtle wasn't one of them. Cursed to exist in their ever-rotting bodies for the crimes they had committed in life, the hortdan had two modes—lurking and the frenzied rending of living flesh.

He also couldn't be happier to have Gallmau walking next to him, still willing to do anything to save his beast-master sister. He'd be happy to have Gallmau beside him always, and Meri as well. But first they had to win this fight.

The remaining Shields were arranged in a defensive half-circle, and inside the mages held their captives. Meri was held up by the huge Shield who had engineered the attack against Sinan in the Lutecia tavern. Her head lolled to one side, and even though she couldn't possibly pose a threat to them in her condition, her arms and legs were trussed up.

The Princess of Soissons, on the other hand, was awake and furious, by the look of her. Zhang Jue had Rixende by the arm, and her fox ears were flattened against her head.

Naghwe had restored Sinan's necromantic powers, even enhanced them beyond what they had been before. He wasn't sure how much of that was his mother's strength or even an odd side effect of reversing the Amor Vitriol. Rixende, on the other hand, would no longer have her beast magic and bone witch powers.

Sinan felt confident he and the hortdan could kill Odart and Zhang Jue, along with the Shields. He was less confident he could do that and have Rixende and Meri alive at the end. There was no sign of Valentina or Jacques. He reached out with his senses, noting a freshly dead body in a cave near the hobbled horses, but he found no necromantic trace of the medica's or incensor's death. Hopefully Valentina was with Jacques, and he was keeping her safe.

"That's close enough." Odart gestured to the Shield holding Meri. "She can still live, Gallmau, if you'll listen to some sense."

"I've got some sense for you," Gallmau shot back. "I'm Syagrius Grimoard's son, and the brother of Rixende

Grimoard, Dauphine of Soissons, and my country's next Queen. All of you are guilty of the worst kind of treason and oathbreakers, to boot. I'm giving you one final chance to release the women you're holding unharmed and surrender. Otherwise, my Bone Lord friend here is going to kill all of you and let his undead army snack on your organs."

Saints, but Sinan loved Gallmau at that moment.

Not that the speech would change Odart's course of action. The mirror mage had gone too far to give up, as had Zhang Jue.

Still, the words caused an uneasy muttering among the ranks of Shields.

"Your father would have slit his daughter's throat himself, if he knew the monster she would become," Zhang Jue spoke up, the hatred in his voice all but palpable. "Then he would have done the same to you, his bastard, for your weakness in allowing the Grimoard line to be defiled by allowing a death witch to live."

Sinan wanted to slice Zhang Jue in half with shadow for daring to say that to the prince, but Gallmau didn't as much as blink.

"Maybe the King would've tried." Gallmau hefted the Shield of Soissons in one hand. "I'd have knocked him into next week if he laid a finger on my baby sister. Let her and Meri go. Now."

Odart ended the useless negotiations by sending a ball of fire toward Sinan. The mirror mage didn't have his son around to draw more power from, and Sinan's response, an arc of shadow, sliced through the flames and extinguished them.

The real attack wouldn't come from Odart.

Zhang Jue raised his hands to the sky—and this would

be one hell of a hit, if the Sorcier du Roi needed to use physical movement.

Sinan's hair stood on end as a metallic taste filled his mouth. "Gallmau, get Meri."

The prince had already taken off, charging forward with his shield raised as Sanura ran by his side. The bolt of lightning Zhang Jue summoned lashed out to the earth, directly where Sinan was standing. He pushed much of the necromantic power surging through him to expand his shadow armor into a dome over his head, and the strike broke against the barrier, weakening but not shattering it.

The hortdan surged forward and a few of the Shields ran, perhaps from a combination of the prince's words and the sight of cannibalistic undead monsters streaming toward them. It was chaos and confusion, and he couldn't see Gallmau.

He had no shortage of large and hulking targets, though.

Sinan sent a hail of shadow darts through the air, different than his usual precise sword strikes but a surprisingly easy magic to perform. The Shields' armor did nothing to stop the projectiles, and several of the men fell screaming to the ground. There was one death and another, and a rush of necromantic power surged through him.

There was no sign of Gallmau or Meri. Sinan prayed the prince had been able to get the Lioness to safety.

His attack did nothing against the two mages, though. They stood back-to-back with Rixende on the ground between them. Electricity crackled, shielding them from his shadow magic. Now Odart was using some of Zhang Jue's magic for defense.

Jacques was gone, and mirror mages could take any Gift but necromancy. The Sorcier du Roi was all the head of the benandanti had to pull power from.

Sinan would need to get inside the electrical shield protecting the two men, and the closer he got to them, the less likely it was that Zhang Jue would risk another lightning bolt.

He grabbed a short sword from the body of one of the Shields as he ran forward, the weapon too heavy for his taste but still a useful conduit for his magic. The entire facade of the small mountain in front of him could come tumbling down if he directed his shadow powers at it, but he needed precision, not power, to rescue Rixende and kill the two sorcerers.

Sinan was only a few feet away when the wind began.

It swirled out from Zhang Jue, the air buffeting Sinan and stopping him from getting any closer. His shadow armor blocked the worst of it, including rocks and branches ripped off the ground by the wind and turned into flying weapons. A Shield near Sinan took a fractured branch through the eye and went down screaming, drawing the attention of several of the undead, who swarmed him like ants fighting over a dropped glob of honey.

Sinan thrust his sword and sent a bolt of shadow through the twin spheres of electricity surrounding Zhang Jue and Odart. Rixende slipped out of the bonds holding her hands and used her small fists to hit the Sorcier du Roi. Zhang Jue held her with one arm and gestured with the other to create even more wind bursts.

Sinan couldn't bring his full powers down on the surging energy protecting the two mages without risking the princess. Even if his undead army took care of the remaining Shields, Odart and Zhang Jue had Rixende as a hostage they could use to negotiate their release. Gallmau would promise them freedom to save his sister, and Odart would craft a careful contract to ensure their safety.

Weather mages had few weaknesses, since the meteoro-logical phenomena they could control were so varied. Zhang Jue could—and had—used cold to weaken Sinan and had marshaled rain before attacking Jacques and likely a searing dry wind against Abarsam.

Zhang Jue's defensive armor, though, was all electric. His guild had been the fulgari before he had joined the benan-danti. That magic could best be countered by earth—and the dead things inside of it.

The two men were a formidable team, even against Sinan's enhanced powers and the hortdan.

Which meant he needed to split them up.

He turned his attention to the ground underneath the two men's feet.

Sinan concentrated on a half-remembered spell of enough complexity he wouldn't have dreamed of trying it before tonight, even in the Artifact-strengthened domain of Karakoncolos. Clods of dirt began to fly up from around Odart's feet, and grasping skeletal hands shot up through the earth.

The benandanti sorcerer sent circles of fire down around his body to burn away the necromantic magic, but they began to flicker and extinguish. He had used up his son's borrowed power—and that left only one source of magical energy that wasn't Sinan's necromancy.

More dirt boiled up around Odart, and his movements became frantic.

Now he sent down crackles of lightning from his finger-tips, but that was much less effective than the fire had been. He sank into the roiling earth up to his knees, and the winds around Sinan calmed.

Zhang Jue noticed too late what his partner was doing to him.

He screamed at Odart, the words lost in the din of battle around them, and the electric field around him and Rixende flickered and died.

Sinan lifted his sword to send a blade of shadow through the Sorcier du Roi's heart—just as Zhang Jue sent a bolt of electricity into Sinan.

Sinan flew backward, knocked off his feet and alive only because his shadow shields had absorbed most of the energy. He lay on the ground, gasping, as a familiar sensation of his hair standing on end came over him. His skin vibrated and tingled, and he wheezed in the sharp, clean scent of a lightning strike about to happen. Above him a storm swirled, flashes of light flickering in and out of bruise-colored clouds that blotted out the stars in the sky.

Sinan's body jolted, not with the power of an electric shock, but with the surge of power that came from a sudden death, nearby.

He crawled to his feet and saw Zhang Jue lying dead, a dark stain spreading on his royal sorcerer robes. Rixende stood over him, her bone sword dripping with the Sorcier du Roi's blood, and Sanura by her side.

"One traitor dead." The dissipating remnants of the storm overhead whipped at the princess's long, loose hair, and the fox tail at her feet twitched in fury. "One to go."

Thanks to Sanura, Rixende's necromancy was back, and with it, her vengeance.

It was Sinan's turn for revenge, and he had an excellent idea how to get it. He strode over to Odart, shadows crawling up the blade in his hand. He faced his worst enemy—the one who had haunted his nightmares since the final battle of the Witches' War.

The former head of the benandanti stood waist-deep in dirt.

Around him, the skeleton of an enormous snake slith-ered in and out of the ground, its bones gleaming in the moonlight that had broken through the wisps of the remaining thunderclouds. A snake skull rose in the air, fangs ready to strike at the mirror mage.

Sinan leveled his sword at Odart. "I know the benan-danti have living prisoners of the Blessed in your secret dungeons, as well as corporeal ghosts trapped in their bodily remains. Agree to a binding oath to release them, and I won't kill you."

"Such a generous offer, death witch." Odart showed no sign of fear or anger over his defeat. Only scorn. Sinan and his people weren't human in his eyes, or even animals worthy of mercy, and never would be. "I must unfortunately refuse."

Sinan had expected that, although he would have spared Odart for even one of the helpless Blessed the man had locked up, much less all of them.

It was his right to choose death, and Sinan would give it to him.

Sinan sent his shadow power into a clean strike at Odart's neck, but the action felt wrong and sluggish.

The blow never landed, and a sword made from shadow appeared in Odart's hand. One blow shattered the skeletal snake into shattered bone shards, and Sinan blocked the next only with a quick parry.

"Rixende, get out of here and find your brother."

His shadow armor had been blasted away by lightning, he was wielding an unfamiliar sword, and Odart had somehow stolen his magic.

He began to spar with Odart, the distance between them farther than most sword fights, with his own strikes deflecting off the shadow shields that now swirled around the sorcerer. Sinan was forced to parry and stay on the defensive.

This would be an excellent time for the hortdan to do something useful, but Odart would be only another necromancer as far as they were concerned. Not to mention they weren't of much help when a banquet of dead bodies was available.

The head of the benandanti pressed his advantage, hammering blows that Sinan had to block again and again. Sinan drew more power from the death around him, but it was like trying to close his fist around shifting particles of sand. As soon as he drew it to him, Odart siphoned it off.

One last hit knocked Sinan's sword from his nerveless fingers, and he was sprawled out on the ground again, this time with a shadow blade at his throat instead of a lightning cloud.

"I have no bargain I'm interested in making with you." Odart raised his sword. "I told you to die."

A flash of red hair and a circle of wood slammed into Odart, and the mirror mage was knocked to the ground. He staggered to his feet, his sword still in his hand, but he made no move to strike at his new attacker.

He couldn't.

Gallmau de Rohan, son of King Syagrius the 13th, was as untouchable by Odart as Rixende had been. He stood towering, his family's crest glowing with power on his enchanted shield. Next to him, Rixende had dropped into a sword stance, her bone blade out and ready to fight.

Four perfect circles of fire fell around Odart, stacking over him like the wooden rings of a child's toy over a peg, and wiping out every trace of his shadow power.

Sinan's Gift surged back as Jacques Collin de Plancy lowered his hands and faced his father.

"The Prince of Shadows made you an honorable offer." Jacques held his chin high as he addressed Odart. "An exchange of prisoners and an end to this madness. Take it, or I'll kill you myself."

Odart stared at his son, disbelief and fury on his face.

Then he pressed his palms together in a sign of submission—before stepping back into a void of black and disappearing.

For a moment, none of them moved.

Instead, they stared at the empty spot where the Noviodunam's chief killer of the Blessed had stood a second ago.

"I don't understand." Jacques had two fireballs hovering over his hands, as if calling up more flames might change what had happened. "My father was able to drain *your* powers—your necromancy."

"He could," Sinan agreed. "Until your fire circles stopped him. Then he had to use his own necromancy to shadow-walk out of here. Your father is a mirror mage—and one of the Blessed."

Jacques extinguished his flames and ran his hand over his hair, coated in dust and what looked like someone else's blood. He opened his mouth to ask another question, but Gallmau cut him off and grabbed Sinan by the arm.

"Valentina's with Meri, and you need to help her with your magic." His voice broke. "Otherwise, I don't think Meri's going to make it."

33

MERI

Meri inhaled, breathing in the scent of fresh fallen snow. She opened her eyes to see Sinan sitting cross-legged next to her, his eyes dark pools that drank in light and never left her face. The hint of warmth and realness had faded from his features, replaced by the ethereal beauty that had fascinated her from the beginning.

Sinan had not only survived, his Gift had returned to him.

Her head hurt like hell, and every part of her body ached. With a groan, she propped herself up and caught Gallmau's worried gaze. Thank the Prophets he was alive and well enough to hover over her.

Next to him, Valentina let out an exhausted sigh of relief. Sinan lifted a metal cup to Meri's lips, and she drank its contents down before noticing the skin on his forearm was blistered and deep red.

"You're hurt," she said.

Sinan shook his head and touched a sigil on his cloak. His skin began to heal before her eyes. "My Blessing's back, and I needed to touch Valentina to help her do her work."

Meri felt a lump at the back of her throat. Of course. Sinan could perform necromancy again, and along with that power came the inability to touch another living human being without terrible pain. She wondered how long he had needed to maintain contact, how much he had endured, all to allow Valentina to save Meri's life.

"The eyeballs helped." Valentina held up Cliona's relics to show Meri. The medica had overcome her squeamishness about quite a few things. "Sinan has experience with combining necromancy with medicus magic. A fascinating technique, but I won't be giving a public lecture about it any time soon. His support was the only reason I was able to get you back. No speed for a full month. Promise me."

"No speed for a while," Meri agreed, sitting up and wincing at the pain that caused.

Valentina opened her mouth to protest, then gave a weary shake of her head and stood up.

The sun had begun to rise in the east, and the area around the caves was bustling with activity—and necromancers.

There had to be dozens of Bone Lords strolling around, more than she ever would have imagined could be in one place. They wore white shroud cloaks, sigils blazing, much like Sinan. Meri climbed to her feet, ignoring Gallmau's protests, and stared. She spotted a small group of Shields, some obviously injured, seated on the ground and surrounded by more necromancers. A larger group of the oversized Noviodunam soldiers, even more obviously dead, had been piled nearby.

"Where are my blades?" Meri gave Gallmau, who had grabbed her by the waist to hold her up, an angry shove. "And what happened?"

"Gallmau and I thought it best you and your weapons remained apart until my fellow Blessed and I left." Sinan also rose to his feet. "As you can see, as soon as Zhang Jue's shadow wards collapsed, I called for help. Since you're not going to listen to Valentina and rest more, why don't you come with me to talk to Rixende? She's being...difficult."

"Get used to it." Gallmau grinned at Sinan and shifted his arm to Meri's shoulder and gave her a half-hug. "Let's go talk to my sister and not get into a fight with all of Sinan's creepy friends."

Meri hated not having her swords, but she had to admit there was little to be gained by arguing the point. Sinan wouldn't have spent hours of agony saving her life if he meant her any harm, and antagonizing this many necro-mancers when she needed help standing up didn't make much sense.

As they walked by various Bone Lords, each odder and more frightening than the last, Meri questioned Gallmau and Valentina about the events after she had collapsed. She continued to gape. Sinan had to be the closest thing to a normal human in Karakoncolos—at least as far as his appearance was concerned.

The giant Azhdarchid and her two flaplings that Rixende had sent to rescue Valentina stood near the river-bank, preening their wings in the morning sun. A hulking giant stood far closer to the flying beasts than seemed advis-able. He had a large vulture on one gloved arm, as a hunter would hold a hawk, and two Death Hounds lay at his feet, content as lap dogs. The man acknowledged Sinan with a scowl as they approached. Meri shuddered as she spotted the raised scars on the man's bald head and fierce face. Another assassin from the Order of Katil—hopefully one who was now on Sinan's side.

"The Azhdarchids have bonded to the new beast master." The assassin addressed Sinan with a snarl and gave a particular glower of hatred to the rest of them. Meri made a mental note to avoid this particular Bone Lord in the future. "That princess of yours needs to convince them not to eat anyone who tries to shadow-walk them and her back to Karakoncolos."

"Thank you." Sinan kept walking, shaking his head, and added in a lower voice, "I'll add that to the list."

"You're taking the princess to Karakoncolos?" Meri tried to imagine the conversation with Xiaolian during which they explained they had rescued Rixende, only to send her away to an entire city of necromancers. It wasn't something she looked forward to. "Gallmau and I promised the Queen we would take her back to Lutecia. *You* even promised that."

"I told you from the beginning if one of the Blessed was involved with Rixende's disappearance I would handle it my way. The Dauphine is one of ours, and we would like to offer her both asylum and education in our city."

"My sister has to choose what she wants to do." Gallmau gave a long sigh. "Trust me, she's good at getting her way."

They walked up to the princess, who was holding court, of a sort. Her curse—Blessing, Meri corrected herself—was more obvious in the morning light, with her hair parted around fox ears and a tail swishing under her long skirts. She had an all-white sword secured to her waist with a belt made of finger bones and was talking to two necromancers who listened to her with rapt attention.

No one could see her and not immediately know what she was.

Sinan had a point. Returning Rixende to Lutecia would involve taking on the entire Noviodunam, along with religious leaders and most of the city.

Unlike many of the Bone Lords Sinan had summoned from Karakoncolos, both men with Rixende were handsome and similar enough in appearance that they were likely brothers, with light brown skin that hinted at lineage from Meri's part of the world. The younger and shorter of the two had horns on his head and eyes that resembled those of a goat. His older brother looked normal enough, except for patterns that flickered across his face, as if an invisible pool of water was reflecting off his skin.

Jacques sat on the ground near the three of them, his head bowed. The incensor wasn't physically hurt, at least. He was guarded by a lean young man with more knives strapped to his body than even Meri had.

"The hortdan are all rounded up. Finally." The taller brother gave Sinan a genuine smile as they approached and spoke in the polished tones of a Soissons aristocrat.

"Mademoiselle Meritamun, I'm glad to see you're better due to Dottoressa de Almania's efforts." The shorter brother also had a courtier's manner as he greeted Meri and Valentina, but he held the medica's gaze a second longer than was strictly necessary.

Gallmau came closer, and both necromancers gave him a set of courtly bows. "Good morning to you, Your Highness."

"Don't call me that." Gallmau shifted his feet. "I'm not..."

"You're the Dauphin and you need to start acting like it." Rixende cut her brother's protests off with an imperial wave of her hand. "The future of our country is at stake."

"You should be the heir to the throne, not me." Beads of sweat broke out over Gallmau's forehead, and he was clearly more anxious about this conversation than many of the hellish situations they had gone through. "Maybe we could cover up your ears with a hat, or something. Not that they're not flattering on you. And the tail could be, I don't know, a new fashion in the capital."

"Your sister's right." Meri had to help Gallmau face the reality of the situation and do what was best for his sister and his country. "Rixende can't keep it secret she's a necromancer, and there'll be blood in the streets if a Bone Lord becomes Queen."

"You want me to lie?" Gallmau actually had to ask that question.

Both Meri and Rixende said yes at the same time.

"Not to my mother, though." Rixende's poise broke for a moment, and then she recovered her composure. "The Queen must know the truth. The official story will be that Odart and Zhang Jue plotted to betray the royal family despite their loyalty oaths, cursing me into the shape of a fox and planning to blame the Prince of Shadows for my death."

The best lies had an element of truth, and Rixende knew that. The princess of Soissons reminded Meri of the Sultana of Kush, but she kept that to herself. Rixende didn't need more compliments.

"What will we say happened?" Gallmau asked. "We've already had one fake funeral when they cremated the corpse that wasn't Zhang Jue."

"There'll be many stories about what happened in Terra Amata." Rixende gestured around them. "You and Meri will be in the best one. In it, the Lioness of Abdju and King Syagrius's only son had to join forces with the infamous

Prince of Shadows to battle treasonous witches from the Noviodunam. Together you fought monsters, overcame magical storms, and exposed the traitors. The grateful fox princess departed to a remote convent, where she will consult with mystics to learn how to reverse the curse."

"Your Blessing," Sinan corrected. "And speaking as your new mystic advisor, I still need a formal acceptance of my offer."

"Soon." Rixende waved that off, her focus on her brother. "The Queen will announce you're the heir to the throne in my absence, and every mage in the Noviodunam will be forced to repudiate Odart of Dol."

"Odart will still have witches loyal to him." Meri glanced over at Jacques, who kept his head down. The incensor had defied his father for Rixende's sake—and out of loyalty to the Grimoard line. Gallmau might not have liked Jacques much before this whole mess, but he would need an ally in the Noviodunam. "Even if we kill all the prisoners, rumors, gossip, and wild tales will spread like wildfire in Lutecia."

Gallmau gave Meri a shocked look in response to her comment about finishing off the rest of the Shields. She needed to give him another talk about being ruthless with his enemies.

"That's why Jacques will become the Sorcier du Roi after he takes the loyalty oath." Rixende's words made the incensor lift his head, his eyes bloodshot and ringed with dark circles. The princess nodded at the two necromancer brothers, whose approving expressions indicated they followed her political maneuvering better than Gallmau. "My mother will announce a non-aggression pact with Karakoncolos. That will lead to a re-establishment of trade with Iotape, which should regain our support from the merchant class."

"Speaking of Karakoncolos." Sinan put his own steel into his voice. "We need to take you there now, after you've had a talk with Plumette and her babies about your travel plans. The Artifact is no longer closing us off to the outside world, and a Soissons army regiment has already entered Terra Amata. They'll be here soon."

Rixende swallowed, and for a moment she was only a girl, facing a future where she never saw her family or home again. Then she schooled her features back to calm determination and gave the Prince of Shadows a nod.

"Rixende Grimoard." Sinan let the words ring out loud and clear, and all the necromancers nearby paused what they were doing to listen. "I will bear witness to the Councils of the Living and the Dead that you are one of the Blessed. We offer you asylum in Karakoncolos, with all of the rights and responsibilities that entails."

"I accept." Rixende stood up straighter, then pulled an envelope out and handed it to Gallmau before she wrapped her small frame around him in a tight hug. She embraced Valentina next, then turned to Meri and whispered, "I can't argue with your and Gallmau's taste. Sinan is awfully handsome."

"Allow us to escort you, Sister Rixende." The taller aristocratic necromancer extended his arm for the princess to take, and he and his goat-horned brother walked with the princess in the direction of the Azhdarchids.

"Get the word out that everyone but you and me should head back home." Sinan nodded at the knife-wielding necromancer. "We'll watch over the prisoners until the army comes and make sure whoever is leading the troops marching toward us is loyal to Gallmau before we leave."

"So we're letting Jacques live." Knife Boy sounded sulky as he gave the incensor a sour look. "Again."

He picked up a wrapped parcel from the ground and handed it to Sinan, giving Meri a challenging glance as he did. She responded with an amused smile, and he stalked off in a huff.

Jacques rose to his feet and stared at Gallmau, his expression one of utter despair. "I can't become your Sorcier du Roi. I've broken so many laws of the Noviodunam regarding working with necromancers that I should face execution. And my father is—also a necromancer. No one will believe that part."

Meri hadn't been surprised to hear Odart was one of the Blessed as well as a mirror mage. It explained why the head of the benandanti had covered up Rerek's crimes. The veneficus had used far less scandalous secrets to blackmail others.

"You haven't broken as many rules as I have." Valentina, for her part, sounded positively cheerful about it.

"If any of those Noviodunam witches come after you or Valentina, I'm going to order my undead servant rat to chew their faces off." Gallmau gave the incensor a slap on the back that all but sent him sprawling. Jacques was going to have to get used to Gallmau's idea of a friendly pat.

"I'd appreciate it if you'd escort me over to the prisoners." Valentina put her hand on Jacques's arm. She knew what to say to get her former fiancé to snap out of it. "Many of the Shields are injured, and if they'll accept my aid—I want to offer it."

Jacques gave Sinan a questioning look, as if unsure whether he was a prisoner himself, but the necromancer waved at him to leave.

That left the three of them alone, with the death and terror of last night burned away by the rising sun. Meri felt an aching pain in her chest that had nothing to do with the physical strain her body had been through. Part of her—a selfish desire—wanted to touch Sinan again, rub her skin against his, even though she knew how much pain it would cause him.

Sinan's Blessing wasn't even the main reason she and Gallmau could never be with him again. She and Gallmau were Tomb Fighters, no matter what fancy titles came their way, and Sinan was the Prince of Shadows, a defender of his people wherever he found them and whoever they were.

"I'd like to give you a hug." Gallmau sounded as forlorn when he spoke to Sinan as Meri felt. Not that she was going to show her raw emotions like that. "It wouldn't be a good idea, I guess."

Gallmau sharing Meri's sense of loss didn't make it any easier. Nothing good came of tumbling her fellow fighters, and this particular job had been an excellent example of why.

"No, it wouldn't." Sinan's tone was dry, but the corner of his mouth quirked up, and Gallmau beamed back. "Also, you somehow succeeded in binding a rodent corpus animatum in service to you, so unless you also figure out a complicated exorcism spell, my undead rat's all yours."

"I'll give him all the cheese he wants," Gallmau promised. "Even if he can't eat it."

"This is for you." Sinan handed Meri the parcel, wrapped in the spider silk material the Blessed used for their cloaks. "Your blades, as I promised. Also, I put the kaftan Abarsam created for Baahir inside. It saved my life, and I'd like to return it to his family. He was a brilliant and courageous man, and I know you cared about him."

Now Meri's eyes were burning with grief and gratitude, and she hated that. She unwrapped the package, its fabric smooth and cool to the touch, like the skin of the man handing it to her. A consolation, perhaps, for not being able to run her hands over him one last time. Her water swords were nestled in Baahir's blue garment, gleaming and polished.

"I dreamed of Sanura while Valentina healed me." Meri needed to share that news with Sinan and try to understand it better. "I know she's not in Paradise yet. Is there anything I can do to help her?"

"Let's ask." Sinan held out his hand, and shadows writhed in the air beside him.

A hand, wizened and bony, reached out to grasp his, and Naghwe materialized. Next to her, Sanura took shape as well, as solid in form as if she were still alive.

"Your sister fought death itself to save you." Naghwe gestured to Sanura. "Yet she is one of the very monsters you fear and attack."

Meri swallowed, knowing she needed to face another hard truth.

"You're one of the Blessed, aren't you?" The words spilled out to her little sister's ghost, and there was no taking them back. She knew the answer to her question and had known it for a while, but couldn't admit it to herself. "So were the little boys. Rerek preyed on his own kind."

It should have been unsettling, talking to a ghost, but the love that emanated from her sister wrapped Meri in a warm embrace of protection and power. Sanura had kept her soul on this plane for only one reason—to save and protect her older sister.

"They're at peace now, and so is he." Sanura's somber tone brightened. "But I want to stay here with you a little longer, Meri."

Sinan spoke up. "Sanura was able to become a corporeal

spirit with your help and can visit you any time she wishes. If that's distressing, you can ask her not to."

"I don't want her to leave me alone." Meri didn't even need to think about her answer. She turned to her sister. "Until you want your eternal peace, which you deserve as much as any of us do."

Naghwe nodded in satisfaction, and she and Sanura faded away into the motes of light from the early morning sun.

Sinan lifted his head to regard the sky above him, and Meri followed his gaze up to see a large vulture circling the area. Not surprising, considering the number of bodies piled up nearby. Then she remembered the bird on the arm of the necromancer assassin.

"The Gardes Soissons is close." Sinan stared down at a piece of dark paper that fluttered in his fingers like bat wings. His hand had been empty only a moment before. More shadow magic, and Meri realized the scavenger bird gliding in the sky above them must be able to share its detailed view of the landscape with Sinan's other beast master. "The force is being led by the captain who accompanied you before—Tumas. You should be in good hands when he arrives."

"Will we see you again?" Gallmau shifted his weight, his words thick with emotion. "As a friend, I mean. Not as someone we're fighting against."

Sinan paused, then answered with a catch in his own voice. "Let's hope we do meet again—and not as enemies."

Gallmau gave him a formal bow that would have made Queen Xiaolian proud, and Meri crossed her blades over her chest in an arena salute.

The Prince of Shadows gave them one last look, desire

mixed with regret, and walked off, his shroud cloak floating behind him.

34

MERI

M eri slowed Nada down to a stop as they approached the Witch Stone on the outskirts of Lutecia. The day was overcast and cool, and dried leaves rustled under her feet as she swung off the mare and stood in front of the ancient object.

There was no sign of the blood and gore from the violence of a few weeks ago, when Karabil and Tharin had died at this very spot, followed in death by the assassin who had killed them. Meri bowed forward, her hands pressed together, and recited a prayer for the souls of the two brothers.

It was hard to grasp that so much had happened in such a short period of time. She and Gallmau had returned to Lutecia and faced down a tumult of shock and uproar over the events in Terra Amata. The Queen had handled the truth about Rixende with poise and grace, but Meri had been with her when she unsealed the envelope that held a farewell letter from her only daughter and had seen the sheen of tears in her eyes.

Xiaolian had finished reading the missive, and her pronouncements afterward had left little doubt she had accepted both Rixende's decision and her advice on how to handle the aftermath, including naming Gallmau as heir.

Whether he liked it or not, her friend would be formally announced as the Dauphin soon, and he had asked Meri again to stay and join him in a marriage of convenience. To be more accurate, he had begged her to marry him. He didn't want to face the backbiting and intrigue of the Royal Court alone, much less be married off to a stranger for political calculus. And above all, he wanted Meri to be safe.

A life in the Royal Palace would be safe, not to mention filled with luxury and wealth. The wife of the heir to the Soissons throne would want for nothing. Meri would have the finest food, clothing, and entertainment.

The only thing she wouldn't have was her freedom.

Karabil and Tharin would have laughed out loud at Meri's hesitance over accepting Gallmau's offer. She wished she could talk to the twins about it. But her two friends were dead and gone, and there was only one other person she could turn to for help with this decision.

Of course, that person was dead as well.

After tying Nada to a nearby tree, she walked over to the Witch Stone. It smelled like the stale air of a long-closed tomb, and she hugged her arms close to her chest, a sudden chill coming over her as she drew closer to the structure. The movement reminded her of the subtle signs she had noted over the past few days. A faint soreness when she touched her breasts, a tingling in her chest. Her courses were late as well, but that wasn't unusual. Meri often missed a month or more with the demands of training and fighting —but she knew something had changed in her body.

She pulled out Cliona's relics and bowed her head again. The woman had come from the Order of Katil to kill Sinan and had murdered her friends. But if Meri was using parts of the assassin's body for her own purposes, she wanted to pay respects to Cliona's soul, wherever it might be.

Meri held up the eyeballs, the blood-drop irises a contrast to the ivory blankness of the Artifact in front of her, and whispered her long-dead sister's name.

The scent of the Witch Stone's magic sharpened as she breathed in and out, and then a pool of shadow spilled out onto the ground in front of her like a toppled ink pot. Meri took in a few breaths to calm her racing heart and knelt down to touch the unnatural shadow. Darkness crept up her arm, and then small fingers intertwined with hers. She stood up, and Sanura's body rose with her and became solid flesh.

"Hello, Meri." Sanura reached out to embrace her, and Meri tried not to cringe at the touch of her undead sister's cold skin. "I wasn't sure if you wanted to see me again."

"Is that why you didn't visit me in my dreams?" Meri pulled back and looked at Sanura, taking in her familiar wide smile and still-chubby cheeks. Her sister was frozen in time as the ten-year-old girl she had been before her murder.

"I thought you might need more time." Sanura clung to Meri's hands. "But I'm so happy you called me."

"I need your advice." Meri tried to organize her scattered thoughts and push away her fear. Her sister was an undead

Bone Lord who had returned from the grave, but she was family and Meri wanted to talk to someone who had known her before she became the Lioness of Abdju. "My body feels different, Gallmau wants me to marry him, and I'm not sure what to do."

Meri knew what she could do. She could take herbs to regulate her courses, for one thing. Then she could wish the new Dauphin of Soissons good luck and head out to hunt monsters again. A few weeks ago, it would have been an easy decision, even as fond as she was of her friend.

That had been when she had expected Rerek to kill her within weeks or even days. It had been before the horrors and triumph of Terra Amata.

It had been before she and Gallmau had met Sinan.

"I can see possible futures." Sanura gave her a wistful smile. "Not what will be, but what might be. But you know what's growing inside you. You don't need me to tell you that."

"You're telling me I got rid of one Bone Lord in my spine, and now I have another one growing in my belly?" Meri laughed at the absurdity of it all.

"Oh, but it's twins, dear sister." Sanura gave a giggle of delight. "One from shadow, and one from light. At least, that's a path that stretches out before you. I can only see so much, but there is heartbreak and danger with that choice, as there is with the others you might take. It's like—well, a tree that branches out to reach for the sun. It doesn't know which leaves will thrive or which will wither and die."

Meri considered that for a moment, then bent to kiss Sanura's forehead. "Thank you. I suppose in the end I should be happy I even have a choice to make."

Sanura nodded, then held out her hand. Something

black and fluttering descended down from the sky, and Meri jerked back before realizing it wasn't a bat. Her sister closed her hand around the absence of light, and a sealed envelope covered in loops of elegant writing appeared.

"This is from Sister Rixende, for her mother." Sanura handed the letter to Meri, and it appeared as ordinary as a royal missive sent through death magic could be. "She can be bossy, like you, but I like her."

She pressed her small hands together and unfolded them to reveal a single piece of paper, creased over and over into an intricate series of folds. "This is for you and Gallmau from Brother Sinan. He wasn't sure he wanted to send the letter at all, but in the end he told me that if you summoned me, I could give it to you."

"Please don't wait until I make a pilgrimage to an ancient gravestone set up by demons before you visit me again." Meri reached out to stroke her sister's cheek. "That annoying ghost rat of Gallmau's doesn't hesitate to pop into my rooms any time it wants, so I'm sure you won't have any trouble getting into the palace."

Sanura giggled again, the sound at once familiar and yet unexpected. She had been a happy child, and it shouldn't be a surprise that she had kept her good humor after becoming a ghost.

Her sister's shape shimmered, becoming less real. "I will, Meri. I promise. But for now I'll leave you with your decision and the letters. Whatever you choose, know that I love you and will watch over you."

She faded away then, and Meri was left alone with two scraps of paper and the memories of a life and family she had left behind in Abdju years ago.

Nada gave a soft snort as Meri walked over to untie her,

and she wasn't surprised to hear the sound of hoofbeats approaching.

Gallmau rode up on Argant, trying to look abashed that he hadn't been able to wait and allow Meri more time to meet with her sister alone. His undead rat clung onto one of his shoulders, the blue light of its eyes visible even in the sunlight.

"How did it go?" Gallmau glanced at the Witch Stone and then back at her. "My rat became excited all of a sudden, and I thought that meant Sanura had shown up."

"She did." Meri mounted Nada and nudged her horse closer to Gallmau. "Rixende is doing well. She gave Sanura a letter for me to give to her mother, so we should send word to the Queen as soon as we get back."

She looked down the road at the escort waiting for them. Gallmau had managed to convince his new royal guards, headed by his old friend Tumas, to keep a distance away and give them some privacy. The men were bunched up in a group on their horses, with a luxurious carriage in reserve, presumably in case Meri had a fainting spell, or some such nonsense.

"Sanura gave me another message, as well." Meri pulled the folded paper out to show to Gallmau and was only mildly surprised when it unfolded itself in an entirely unnatural way. She was even less surprised that the dark red letters on the page appeared to have been written out in dried blood.

To Her Serene Majesty, Queen Xiaolian, and Monsieur de Rohan, Dauphin of the Kingdom of Soissons:

The Councils of the Living and the Dead in Karakoncolos formally accept your government's offer of a non-aggression pact between your country and the City of the Blessed. We have communicated this agreement to the Governor of Iotape, as his city has security arrangements with Karakoncolos, and we withdraw any objections to their resumption of full diplomatic and trade relations with the Kingdom of Soissons. These agreements do not include the Noviodunam, and we continue to bar visitation of any of its members to Iotape without the Council's prior permission.

Below the flowing script, a bolder set of letters had been written out in ordinary black ink.

Dear Gallmau and Meri,

If you're receiving this shadow letter, I'll take it to mean that you both still agree to visitations by a corporeal spirit and a very disobedient corpus animatum. I therefore assume you will also accept a short note from me. I regret that our time together was brief and continue to hope that someday we will cross paths, and not swords, again.

Sinan

They both reached the end of the letter at the same time, and the look of longing on Gallmau's face was so intense Meri felt a pang of sympathy, whether for him or both of them, she couldn't tell.

"I didn't expect him to write." Gallmau accepted the note from Meri and tucked it into a pocket. She half-wanted to take it back and keep it herself.

The two of them set off down the road to the waiting guards and Gallmau blurted out, "Look, Meri, I know how difficult life in the Royal Court can be. If you want to get far, far away, I promise I'll help you slip out through the garden maze without anyone being the wiser."

Meri laughed. "Honestly, I'd make a run for it if I thought you would come with me. But we both have our obligations now."

Meri had always chosen her freedom over anything else. But that was in the past, and today she had made a decision about her future. She would stay in Soissons with Gallmau to take care of him and whoever else came along.

Her hand dropped to pat her abdomen and she watched as Gallmau's eyes widened. "Even Sanura can't tell me for sure what will happen, but I have a feeling it's going to get interesting."

AUTHOR'S NOTE

Thanks so much for reading *Prince of Shadows*, and I hope you enjoyed it. I love feedback from readers, so please consider leaving a review on Amazon or Goodreads.

FOLLOW M.A. GUGLIELMO

Linktree: https://linktr.ee/Aphemia66

BONUS MATERIAL

If you haven't read the Riftworld series yet, you can start with Remi's misadventures with Ceto, Sea Queen of the Deep. Download the free prequel short story, "Witch City Rift".

Sign up for M.A. Guglielmo's mailing list for sneak peeks at future book releases and special content only for subscribers.

ABOUT THE AUTHOR

M.A. Guglielmo is a neurosurgeon, mother of two awesome daughters, and a lifelong fan of speculative fiction. Her Italian grandmother may or may not have been able to cast the evil eye on difficult neighbors, and Maria loves telling a good story, especially if magical curses and witty villains are involved.

After having the wits scared out of her by ghost tales told to her over a campfire in the Moroccan Sahara, she's come up with a plan to travel to all the potential settings for her novels. Since those include the mountain-ringed home of the Jinn and a future dystopia complete with monster portals, some items on her bucket list might be harder to achieve than others.

Maria is always dreaming of the stories that will come out of her next travel destination.

ACKNOWLEDGMENTS

The novel is immeasurably better thanks to the developmental skills of Jeni Chappelle, and the stellar copy-editing by Janet Jones Bann. My thanks go out to Jo at Glass Slipper Webdesigns for the beautiful cover.

I'm grateful for help from the writing community, including my fellow authors in the Rhode Island Romance Writers group, as well as those in the Association of Rhode Island Authors.

A special shout out is needed for my Street Team members, who've provided beta reading feedback, left reviews, and shared their enthusiasm about my writing and my characters.

ALSO BY M.A. GUGLIELMO

The Riftworld series

Rifted Hearts

On A Rift's Edge

The From Smokeless Fire series

Summoned

Soul to Steal

Price to Pay